Praise for Speechless

'A splendid tour de force'
Le Monde

'The best Lanoye has ever written'
De Tijd

'Painful, gripping, and harrowing, full of verbal pyrotechnics'
Metro

'Heart-wrenching and hilarious'
De Morgen

'Lanoye breaks out the best of his narrative power and his stylistic brilliance'
Humo

'Lanoye leaves the reader speechless'
Elsevier

'A poignant and unforgettable book'
De Standaard

'Gorgeous, forceful, funny, and moving. Lanoye is a master at creating character, setting scenes, picking absolutely perfect evocative details, working with extended metaphors, and plunging you into drama whether of the intimate family kind or natural catastrophe'
LEV RAPHAEL, author of *Dancing On Tisha B'av*

TOM LANOYE is an award-winning, highly acclaimed Belgian novelist, poet, and playwright. Starting out as a poet and critic, he became famous for his prose and drama, as well as his politically and socially engaged columns and his unique cabaret-style performances. He is the author of more than 50 works of poetry, drama and fiction. His bestseller *Speechless*, voted one of the most popular 'new classics' in Belgian and Dutch literature, sold over 150,000 copies and was awarded several major awards. In 2017, *Speechless* was adapted into a film by Hilde Van Miegham. Lanoye has won many literary prizes, including the prestigious Constantijn Huygens Prize for his entire oeuvre. His work has been translated into fifteen languages. Tom Lanoye lives in Antwerp and Cape Town.

PAUL VINCENT (UK), Honorary Senior Lecturer in Dutch at UCL, has been one of the most renowned translators of Dutch literature for the past twenty years. He was awarded the first David Reid Poetry Translation Prize (2006) for his translation of 'Herinnering aan Holland' ('Memory of Holland') by Hendrik Marsman and the Vondel Translation Prize 2012 for *My Little War* by Louis Paul Boon. His recent translations include *The Hidden Force* by Louis Couperus, *While the Gods Were Sleeping* by Erwin Mortier, shortlisted for the Independent Foreign Fiction Prize, and (with John Irons) *100 Dutch-Language Poems: From the Medieval Period to the Present Day*, joint winner of the Oxford-Weidenfeld Prize 2016.

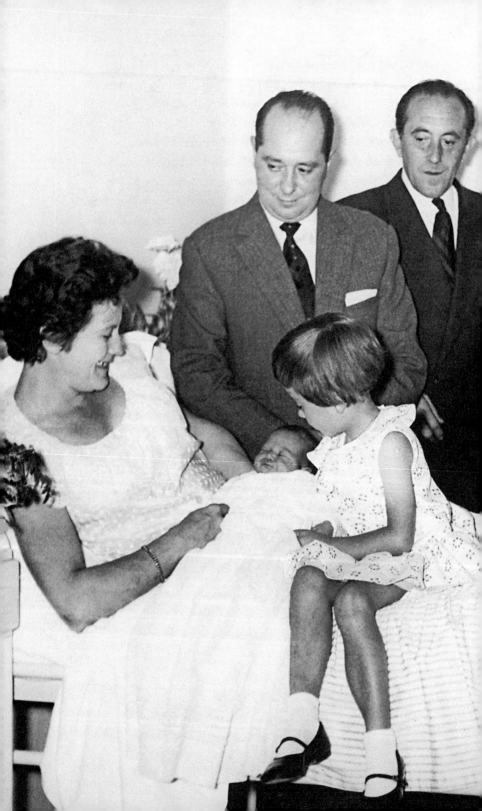

SPEECHLESS

TOM LANOYE
SPEECHLESS

Translated from the Dutch
by Paul Vincent

WORLD EDITIONS
New York, London, Amsterdam

Published in the USA in 2018 by World Editions LLC, New York
Published in the UK in 2016 by World Editions LTD, London

World Editions
New York/London/Amsterdam

Copyright © Tom Lanoye, 2009
English translation copyright © Paul Vincent, 2016
Images: all of the photographs in the book were taken from the family
archives, with the exception of the butcher's shop photo (taken by
Michiel Hendrycks)
Author's portrait © Tessa Posthuma de Boer

Printed by Sheridan, Chelsea, MI, USA

Library of Congress Cataloging in Publication Data is available

ISBN 978-1-64286-006-1

First published as *Sprakeloos* in the Netherlands in 2009 by Prometheus

This project has been funded with support from the European
Commission. This publication reflects the views only of the author,
and the Commission cannot be held responsible for any use which
may be made of the information contained herein.

 Co-funded by the
Creative Europe Program
of the European Union

The translation of this book is funded by the Flemish Literature Fund
(Vlaams Fonds voor de Letteren – www.flemishliterature.be)

Twitter: @WorldEdBooks
Facebook: WorldEditionsInternationalPublishing
www.worldeditions.org.

ni le bien qu'on m'a fait, ni le mal
tout ça m'est bien égal

EDITH PIAF
non, je ne regrette rien

◆

falling falling
down in silence to the ground

ANTONY AND THE JOHNSONS
rapture

he
17

she
77

I
337

AND THIS IS the story of a stroke, devastating as an internal lightning bolt, and of the agonizingly slow decline that over the next two years afflicted a five-fold mother and first-class amateur actress. Her life had always been dedicated to the spoken word, hard work, healthy food for all the family, economical indulgence and affordable hygiene from head to toe. And yet she of all people was repaid by life, which she had always honoured—employing limited means and unbridled ambition, proud stubbornness and stubborn pride—with ingratitude and blunt cruelty.

She lost first her speech, then her dignity, then her heartbeat.

Everyone who knew her had always expected that things would turn out differently. That her heart, fragile and wonky as she always called it herself, would not wait for two years. It would stop beating as soon as that mouth of hers could no longer speak, no longer scold, praise, taste, snigger and declaim—and I'm still omitting arguing and puffing frugally on her filter cigarettes, lighter and lighter as the years went on, and I'm still overlooking the contemptuous pursing of her thin lips when she didn't like something. I shan't even mention the mocking raising of one corner of her mouth and the opposite eyebrow when she wished to indicate that no one need try to tell her anything about her trade, her methods of upbringing, her cookery books, her view of excellent theatre or the rest of human existence.

And I'd like to warn you, reader. If you don't like works that are largely based on truth and simply supply the missing parts from imagination; if you're put off by a novel which according to many people cannot be called a novel, because it lacks a proper head, a beautiful curly tail and an orderly middle section, let alone contains a respectable coherent story by way of intestines; if texts that are at the same time a lament, a tribute and a re-sounding curse make you ill, because they are about life itself and at the same time present only one dear relation of the author—then the moment has already come for you to shut this book.

Replace it on the pile in the shop where you are standing, push it back among the other books on the shelf in your club, your rest home, your public library, your friends' drawing room or the property you have forced your way into.

Buy something else, borrow something else, steal something else.

And miss my mother's story.

he

(OR: THE STORY OF THE STORY)

TO EVERYONE ELSE: just take a look at that photo on the front cover. It's definitely her. Beauty is not necessarily passed down from mother to son.

Even in her own family, the Verbekes—an old dynasty of architects, builders and stonemasons, in which the men were mostly big but always bony, the women mostly tall but always with rather angular faces—even in her own family, then, it was not clear where so much beauty and elegance had sprung from. She was the youngest girl in a family of twelve. There should have been fourteen, but one brother died nameless at his birth, and another, having been properly baptized, died in his cot.

There were enough brothers left not really to feel the loss.

She, the smallest and daintiest of the dozen, was the only one allowed, at the tender age of sixteen, to study in French, in Dinant, for a whole school year, and afterwards even in English for a few months, in Northampton. Something to do with Domestic Science, Bookkeeping, Etiquette and Putting the Finishing Touch to All That. Something to do with strict regulations, exciting changes of scene and a few friendships made for life.

We are talking about just before the Second World War, the declining years of an unthreatened and seemingly endless interwar period, in which little Belgium, *la petite Belgique*, flourished as never before. For the first time since the ravages of the Great War, the worldwide conflagration of 1914–18, its franc was again called the European dollar, for the first time too its handguns and its regional beers became famous all over the planet. Its vast Congo—a world within a world, unfathomable in its customs and murderous in its climate—vomited an endless stream of colonial goods over the motherland, which with the aid of a ruler and a shoehorn would have fitted about eighty times into its colony. Out of that wild tropical empire everything continued to well up that could serve as a foundation and adornment of prosperity—from rubber to ivory, from copper to cobalt, a high plateau of zinc and tin, a cascade of diamonds, a sea of palm oil and cocoa, oceans of petrol, without forgetting the gold, and the uranium and the works of art in crude bronze and ebony. The little motherland capitalized on all this, handsomely in fact, thanks to its age-old trump card: its position at the core of Europe, right on the intersecting lines from London to Berlin and from Paris to Rotterdam.

You can't have a much better position in Europe, except when war breaks out.

But despite its nascent civil aviation industry—operating in white and blue, since its national colours were too similar to those of Germany—and despite its dense railway network with sturdy Belgian-made engines, and despite the breakthrough of a home-grown super-limousine, the Minerva, 'the Rolls Royce of the Continent', despite all that and much more, the interwar period in Belgium outside the capital—'*Bruxelles? Petit Paris!*'—and, come on, outside Antwerp and Liège of course, and on you go, outside Ghent and Mons too, and naturally also outside Charleroi—finally, to sum up: in the provinces and the depths of the countryside the interwar years in Belgium were somewhat reminiscent of the late nineteenth century. But without the carriages and the horse trams, and with more comfortable clothes in which, above the belt at least, a button might occasionally be left undone.

Also a woman who smoked in the street was still considered scandalous, also the dance halls that were popping up everywhere were intended for the working classes and the rabble; also the teacher-priests stood at the entrance of the increasingly popular cinemas, noting the names of pupils attending, who the following day inexorably became ex-pupils. And also it was not obvious that a well-brought-up young lady from Waasland should start travelling the world though she did not even want to become a missionary nun, but simply went on a course, to give it all the Finishing Touch at that, far across the Channel.

That could rightly be called curious, however bright the girl herself might be, however articulate, in three languages no less. But even the matter of those three languages? She had wanted that from an early age and had pleaded her case with everyone who needed to give their permission and with lots of others who had absolutely no say in the matter. As long as she could plead her case. 'Most of all,' she would say emphatically all her life, usually from behind her butcher's counter, and always with a tinge of regret, 'most of all I would like to have been a lawyer and gone to the Bar. But I wanted children. That came first. A person has to learn to make choices in their life.'

Well, who knows? Perhaps one day she had also chosen

of her own free will to become attractive and elegant? And it subsequently happened?

It wouldn't have surprised many people. 'When our Josée gets an idea in her head?' You could hear her eleven brothers and sisters bring it up on more than one occasion, frequently with a sigh, at New Year's parties and wedding receptions, just before or long after the eruption of yet another family quarrel that could drag on for years. Though it should be said that the Verbekes never showed themselves to be petty or small-minded at such striking family moments. They never failed to come back on parade, reluctantly or, on the contrary, in newly restored harmony, despite everything: here they sat again, reunited cheek by jowl, in their usual cacophony of harsh architects' voices, grating builders' jokes and foul-mouthed card-players' jargon. As the hours went by, singing actually rang out ('On the banks of the Scheldt now / Well hidden in the reeds ... '), interspersed with the loudly proclaimed opinions of the bourgeois who knows he has been a success in life.

And that's what they were. Successful and forthright. Yes, just look around, from one to the other: here they sit, the assembled Verbekes, glued to a festive table like bees to a honeycomb. Most are accompanied by their offspring. In their hands they hold a cigar or a glass of Elixir d'Anvers, one is sucking a Leonidas chocolate and the other is nibbling an almond biscuit from Jules Destrooper. But they all have faces that speak volumes, as only the faces of older relations can speak volumes the moment the conversation turns to one of the youngest and most turbulent fledglings of the collective nest.

'If our Josée gets something into her head?
Best keep out of the way.'

BUT DON'T BE fooled. I'm now talking again, jumping from one thing to another, sorry, about that photo on the front cover. It's not because that hat suits my mother —[she] 'All my life it's been like that, give me a hat and I look good in it, whether it's a flower pot or a flying saucer'—that in daily life she was often discovered wearing headgear. Certainly not such a striking specimen.

She preferred a simple hairband when she was sweaty and, well into old age, was unashamedly at work in a swimming costume in the vegetable garden of her allotment. Our summer house, which we had built ourselves, called 'the bungalow', or else 'our bungalow', was located a stone's throw from the centre of her and my birthplace, which was once promoted from an insignificant commune to a proper town by none other than Napoleon. He was already emperor at the time.

Since then Sint-Niklaas has acquired the greatest number of secondary schools in the whole area, the highest suicide rate in the country, and the largest market square—if you like, the largest empty space—in the whole of Europe.

In order to make up for everything, the emptiness as well as the suicidal thoughts, there rises once a year on that huge, empty market square, in commemoration of the Liberation—a term that awakens in the inhabitants increasingly new meanings and desires—a squadron of gaudy balloons, filled with helium or freshly baked hot air.

The latter, the modern hot-air balloons, are first rolled out on the ground by three or four balloonists at a time. An unrecognizable jumble that looks like a granny knot tied by giants is expertly disentangled and unfolded into a plastic puddle, capricious and crinkled, in which nevertheless the contours are discernible of the weird balloon shape that is about to astonish us. Or will it be another of those humdrum ones? One of those pears hanging upside down, as multicoloured as a beach ball with delusions of grandeur?

With lots of hissing and roaring a jet of flame shoots out of a burner which, together with a large fan, is incorporated in a frame that in turn is mounted on top of the balloon basket. For now that basket is lying pathetically on its side. The fan, sideways and rather lazily, directs the jet plus a first stream of hot air into the opening of the balloon. It has to be held open by the balloonist and his helpers. They stand on tiptoe, arms high above their heads, grabbing hold of the slippery edge of the opening with both hands and making sure that that they themselves don't get caught in the stream of hot air, on pain of having at least their eyelashes and eyebrows singed off, and usually also every hair on their head. One has to make sacrifices for one's hobby.

Behind their backs a colossus gradually takes shape, then stands up jerkily, as if after a barbaric open-air childbirth. It raises first its head, then its back, then its upper body. Slowly and majestically it seems to sprout from the ground itself, yes, it springs from our market square in slow motion, surrounded solely by brothers, as if it were one of the countless earth-born warriors which rose from the field that Jason had sown with dragon's teeth and which he would have to defeat in order to capture the Golden Fleece. In exactly the same way, overpowering and threatening, the modern supermen swell into view, ever fuller, ever higher, until they have clambered completely upright, pulling the basket straight beneath them, their first triumph. Their jets of flame sing louder and more love-struck the more powerful and mightier they become, and look, there they stand finally fully grown, waving the plumes of their helmets, in a neat row: our gentle mastodons, swaying in our inevitable autumn breeze, trembling with expectation as is appropriate after a birth, for the time being still restrained by cables like Gulliver by the Lilliputians, but ready to make an irresistible leap up to the heavens. A contemporary army consisting mainly of figs hanging upside down—they don't always have to be pears—in all the gaudiest colours of the rainbow. There are also some in the shape of a gingerbread house or a Smurf. There is even a crate of beer of a well-known brand which is also the sponsor of the feather-light monster, since someone has to pay the bills, even those for hot air.

A little later they climb into the sky magnificently and to loud applause. The scarce helium balloons, caught in fishnets with too large a mesh, just as a female buttock can be squeezed into a saucy stocking, quickly jettison some ballast—bags of river sand, bags of loam. That is: the contents of the bags are scattered to the four winds with exaggerated gestures, in a ritual reminiscent of the ancient sower who still adorns the cover of our school exercise books, although paradoxically no grain is sown, just sand. Sand on stone, sand on emptiness, sand on people, sand on sand.

It dissipates immediately, to the relief of the upward-looking spectators, since in extreme emergencies, for example to avoid a pylon, it is permitted to offload the sand with bag and all, at the risk of hitting a back-up car or an unsuspecting bovine or occasionally an unfortunate walker, and one disastrous year even, in order to avoid the sharp rake of a television aerial, a pram, thank God empty—the little passenger had just been taken out to peer, holding Daddy's hand, at the Smurf floating above them, and the next instant, right next to them: splat! A sandbag, slap in the middle of the pram, whose wheels flew off at the impact.

The hot-air balloons on the other hand, fizzing angrily, suck in an extra long burner flame through their clearly visible arseholes. A reverse fart that, even more in reverse, gives them an upward jerk, toward the wide firmament. In this way our helium globes and our hot-air giants rise in brotherly fashion above our two central church towers, one of which bears a gigantic gilded statue of the Virgin Mary instead of—as would be fitting, in accordance with our legendary Flemish national character, which bursts with modesty—a discreet weathervane or a sluggish dragon, one of those scaly monsters that enjoys being routed by the archangel Michael.

However, the people of Sint-Niklaas are not known for their discretion or modesty. As a result their Mary does not look as if she will ever permit herself to be routed, and certainly not with enjoyment, not even by an archangel. She is as high as two houses, our Mary, wears a crown on her head and carries a child on her arm. Our Holy Mary as a fertile empress armoured from head to toe in shiny gold leaf. Consequently she is popularly known as Gilt Mary. When there is sufficient mist, despite all the gold leaf, to remove her from sight, the popular sneer is that Gilt Mary is on her travels again, and that *she* can well afford it, with all that precious metal and all her spare time, because only one child? You can hardly call that a time-consuming task, hardly even a family. One is none.

Today there is no mist, far from it, there is a slight rain of fine sand, but apart from that it is a brilliant Sunday in September, and the colours are as unruly and shiny as in a Breughel painting, the ordinary people cheer and drink and eat hamburgers with fried onion rings and fresh tomato sauce, while—above the festive stalls and the chewing chops—a squadron of airships takes to the sky. They rise above our chimneys and slates, above our fashionable roof terraces and densely populated balconies packed with waving local celebrities. They brush past many gables belonging to cafés with names like De Graanmaat and Hemelrijck, or shops with names like Weduwe Goethals & Dochters, where they sell crystal glasses and cutlery boxes lined with blue silk, and of a chip shop called Putifar, after the circus donkey in a children's book.

They shoot upward, past the front of our relatively recent town hall, upward past the façade of our ancient jail—a former prison which in your childhood served as, what symbolism, a library, and which they shortly plan, what a sign of the times, to convert into lofts, just as they want to convert everything into lofts nowadays, even former libraries where you were once able to wreck your eyesight reading books, without a moment's regret, and where at a certain moment there wasn't one book left, according to your age category, for you to read, and where the librarian—may his memory be honoured, his name praised, his bloodline blessed—then gave you permission to start on the books of the next category, on condition that you talked to no one about it, and that was what happened.

They brush past that significant gable, failing by a whisker to pull off the gutter, plus some tiles from the year dot. Then they finally make for the open sky, the boundless heavens, majestic and silent, high above our roofs and courtyards and yet floating away precisely over the great access road on the ground floor, our Parklaan, which, surprise surprise, passes a park and is already jam-packed with hooting pursuit cars whose passengers wish to follow with their own eyes the Calvary of their favourite, secretly hoping for a cautious accident—the year before one landed in a castle moat, three got caught in barbed wire, and two crashed in the Westakkers military zone, almost resulting in an international emergency, since we are talking about the heyday of the Cold War.

At the end of this Parklaan, right above the busy junction with the secondary motorway from Antwerp to Ghent, the aerial flotilla seems becalmed for a moment. Just for a second the inverted pears and figs and plump women's buttocks just hang there hesitantly in the air, dangling like Christmas baubles without a tree. Then they resolutely choose a course. Not toward Ghent or Antwerp. Not to Hulst in Holland, but to Temse on the Scheldt. In so doing they first float past the local shopping mall, the Waasland Retail Centre, which when it was created seemed like a good idea with its ample parking facilities and covered shopping arcades, but which for years has been sucking the life out of the town centre like a tapeworm sucks the libido out of a prize pig that was nevertheless intended to provide semen for the whole region during its lifetime. And then at last, and with my apologies again for the long digression this time, but that's how I'm made, that's how people tell stories and commemorate in my area and in my family, that's what our language is like, what our flesh is like, expansive. We'll have to learn to live with it, you and I, at least for the duration of this saga, but so be it—after that Retail Centre, the balloons float above a section of green suburbia where, according to tradition and semantics, a patch of bog once lay that was noted for its population of frogs. It is still called the Puytvoet, but it must have been drained over the course of time, although the meadows and fields and football pitches of The White Boys FC are still convex in shape in order to facilitate the run-off of the generous precipitation for which our Low Countries are so renowned.

The streams of the Puytvoet are deeper and more numerous and every few metres boast a specimen of our beloved moisture absorber, our drainage soldier: the pollard willow, from which in earlier times we carved our clogs. The dirt paths too, the potholes and edges of which we have tried for years to repair with rubble and ashes from our stoves—a week later they have disappeared, like every kind of hard core, from half-sleepers to sections of wall, you name it, *everything* is swallowed up by our insatiable earth, which with its restless jaws can grind up a cosmos, from cat litters to skeletons, from coachwork to clapped-out pianos—those earth paths too then are lined, on both sides indeed, with water vacuum cleaners.

But these are slender sisters of the pollard willows which we call Canada willows and which, elegantly and supply and lithely rustling, wave their crowns and their silver leaves at the fleet of balloons high above them.

And there, finally, on the ground among the pollard willows and those Canada willows, in a plot carved out by streams and dirt paths, yes there, over there in her vegetable garden in her favourite swimsuit, black with a white pattern, looking up with one hand over her eyes, in her bare feet by a modest bonfire of dried potato tops—there she is. With that band in her hair.

She looks reflective or admiring, it is not clear which. Perhaps she is listening to the roaring song of the burners, a jubilant choir up above. Or perhaps she is just following the coiling veil of smoke twirling from her own fire to where it dissipates into nothing.

Or perhaps she is measuring one of the balloons with the naked eye, wondering how many evening dresses a skilful seamstress could conjure up out of it if there were yet another costume piece in the programme, *Le Malade imaginaire* or *L'Avare*—'there's always a demand for Molière, at the box office at least'.

A reflective woman in a vegetable garden, beneath a firmament of fabulous beasts, on a Sunday in September. A multicoloured and strangely soothing spectacle.

At least if there isn't a storm and it doesn't rain cats and dogs and the whole thing doesn't have to be postponed until next year's Liberation celebrations.

But a promise is a promise: this must not and will not be about balloons in the shape of figs or a crate of beer, but about my mother and her unacceptably cruel end. I have run away from this book for long enough, novel or no novel. It should have been written much earlier. Allow me a timeout to explain that to you. It will not, I promise you, be a delay. On the contrary, it forms part of the mourning process, at a time and in a community that has lost the ability to mourn. The lament no longer has a raison d'être. Sorrow must either be suppressed or lead to something productive.

And I am an obedient bastard of those two possibilities.

I have dragged my feet and bickered like never before, hiding out of cowardice from a pain that I had swallowed down without digesting it, but also without *wanting* to digest it. Because before I could abandon them to the great forgetting, my dismay and my pent-up concern, before I could submerge and dissolve in the Lethe of everyday life, I just had to do something with them. I had to convert them, with a click of the fingers pouring gold from lead, mindful of King Midas, because I can do that now, I told myself, 'make something out of nothing', capture something for ever, although only on patient paper. It's all I'm good for. From mud to marble in no time at all.

Yet I still couldn't start. A prey to continuing grief as if to a lung disease—I stood feeling dizzy in department stores and gyms, in bookshops and on literary platforms—I began to feel increasingly ashamed of my creative indecision, resulting in still more indecision. King Midas? Jonah, biting his nails in the innards of his whale. Job, idly fretting on his glorious rubbish dump. The urge to act paralysed by a thousand questions. I have to restrain myself, with the catalogue of Western art history in my hand, not also to resort to Hamlet, Prince of Denmark. That would be, apart from ridiculous, another flight, yet another postponement. Whoever hunts for comparisons is detaching themselves from reality, from the awareness of how overwhelmingly ordinary it is, but also how unknowable and devastatingly unique.

No greater swindle than the knowledge of art. Job and Jonah have no place here, let alone Hamlet and the rest of the sluttish international crew of the good ship Culture, that international floating escort bureau which provides a value-adding strumpet for every aspiration and every swoon. Stop the make-up and hair-curling, stop posing, as King Oedipus or the Good Soldier Schweik, Sancho Panza or his boss. It's about you and you alone. I mean: about me. That is precisely the point. Why should *I* suddenly have to write this book? There are enough people with deceased mothers, most of whom have had more spectacular careers than that of a butcher's wife from Waasland. No shortage of heavyweight women, with brilliant children and a life set in Mumbai or New York, Rome or Rio, instead of a Flemish hellhole. Let such fortunate orphans get to work. Let them grieve and honour and fête memories, in a geographical and historical framework that the reader does not first have to look up in the tiniest corner of his encyclopedia.

Let them glory. Not me.

The greatest pressure did not even come bubbling up from myself. From beyond the grave I could feel *her* pressure. Mothers never become human beings again, mothers remain mothers.

I saw the corner of her mouth and her eyebrow once more curling in disdain, her burning filter cigarette was again balancing between two fingers, and she herself was looking away—silent for a change, absolutely silent, ear-shatteringly silent, speechless with feigned indignation, as a grand *tragédienne* scarcely one metre sixty tall, acting her fathomless disappointment, displaying her displeasure at her youngest child every day that he did not write her story.

'If I feel contempt for any kind of person, it's those who speak ill of their parents.' How many times she said that to me! True, after she had come to terms with the fact that I was becoming a writer, counter to her express wish and preference. [she, the first time she heard of my plans] 'Writing is something for lazy people, drunkards and paupers.' A few years later she sat in the pitch darkness, glowing with pride that I turned out to be able to live from my pen, won a literary prize, and after all had no drink problem. 'I always knew. About those prizes. He's got more in him than he thinks.' She said that in my presence as if I were not there. Making no secret of the fact that she must have had a decisive part to play. 'Like mother, like son.' That is the essence of all text, certainly when spoken aloud: the most important thing is the subtext.

Sometimes, though, the text and the subtext simply merge. How often she longed quite openly, certainly after the appearance of my first collection of stories, with a photo of my father on the cover, for me to write more about her? But at the same time delicately warning me that it would be better if I produced a grand and positive story, a tome of fitting length, not a malicious memo. Noblesse oblige, after her double life motto, 'You must not spit in the spring from which you have drunk' and 'You've got more in you than you think.'

The latter should be taken literally. There is more in you. Yes, in you too. In all of us. Lots more. More and more. 'Of course you passed your exams with distinction! [she, rolling her eyes] That's only normal, isn't it? You could also have done it with the highest distinction. Oh God, a person can't have everything. See it from the positive side. Now you've got something else to look forward to. When are your next tests?' Does a human being ever become any more than that? The repetition of the same test, in ever-different forms, if need be that of a book. If need be this book. A classic biography which at the same time must have nothing classic about it, which on the contrary must produce something extraordinary. 'Oh yes! [she, with one hand held triumphantly above her head] Something original! Something spiritual! You have a completely free choice. As long as it's something that makes everyone say: it surprised us cruelly, but affected us deeply. We'd never thought Lanoye had it in him.'

While not writing I became aware of her ever-growing expectation that was not an expectation but a demand, a claim, a constitutional right, fed by her pretensions as an amateur actress, her lifelong dormant disillusion at being a butcher's wife against her will and her equally lifelong arsenal of the feminine tyrant, not used to not getting her way.

For oh my God in whom I don't believe—how perfectly she mastered the palette of domestic extortion! It usually won her respect, sometimes horror, and always obedience, regardless of her choice of weapon, always adapted to the terrain and the position of the family battle. Her armoury was full and the weapons adequately oiled. Little white lie alongside punitive threat. Offended silence alongside a furious torrent of words. Working in a whisper on private sentiment alongside pointing sarcastically at the approaching mockery of the whole neighbourhood and the whole school and the whole country. No role was beneath her, no retort too refined. 'There's only one kind of people who are more abominable than those who write bad things about their parents. They are the people who don't write about their parents. Though they *can* write.'

Admittedly she never made that last comment. But she could have. She would say it, without compunction, if she were reading over my shoulder now. Correction, she *is* reading over my shoulder. Has been the whole time. She is even losing patience because there's been more about balloons and myself than about her.

And, reading over my shoulder, she says in a throwaway tone but loud enough for me to hear—subtle acting it's called, her forte, both on the boards and in everyday life—although it must not go unrecorded that she excelled equally in 'giving people a piece of her mind'— so she says, reading over my shoulder, here and now: 'And meanwhile it's still all about you, you know. Anyway, lucky that you're not reading it aloud. Because dear, oh dear ... Where on earth do you still get that ugly "a" of yours from? In a small circle of friends I can understand it, people from Sint-Niklaas together. Or in the shop, when you're chatting with your customers. Good people, most of whom have never read a serious book, and have trouble with a paper. You have to talk to them in patois, or they'll think you're putting on airs, and they'll go to someone else for their meat. But someone like you? On the radio, on TV, on the platform ... Have you ever heard yourself? You didn't get it from me. Okay, if I have to play the maid in a country farce, then I sometimes use dialect. I like it. I can do it. Or for the old mother in *The Van Paemel Family*, poor dear. There dialect is moving and appropriate. But surely not with you? A writer, who is supposed to set a good example. How on earth did you ever stagger your way to your degree in Germanic philology? No one can understand. Sometimes I can't myself.'

Let her read over my shoulder as much as she likes, let her make comments into the bargain, even she will have to put up with my first writing a few pages about myself, because I haven't finished with that—on we go—paralysed nail-biting in my whale, that indecisive fretting on top of my mountain of compelling material. Its weight does not rest under my backside. It weighs on my chest, while I type this and this and this.

Why is it only my stories that will have to replace her, now she herself has gone? Why not those countless other stories of those who knew her? Daughter, sons, grandchildren, all those remaining relatives—an expanding list, an upside-down bread tree of bloodlines? Plus all her friends and protégés, because she had them, by the score—what would a diva of life be without an ample and loyal public in the only true arena, that of reality? What is a matriarch worth without some additional children outside her own family—orphans, rejected scions? Old friends, schoolmates even, for ever loyal, until death do you part?

Whatever I serve up here, in whatever order, or in whatever key, it will remain a noble lie, a splinter of the prism that was her life. Why should my one limited ray of light be worth more than the sum of all the others put together? My version of the fact of her life is perhaps doomed eventually to be the only one remaining, and hence will be all that is truly left of her. But at least, I hope, for a few years, a decade, perhaps two—what is the duration of a book in an age that seems to be turning away from books? But even then: for those few years, that decade, her voice will still sound, her star will shine, only through me. Why? Because I am the only one who spends my days weighing words and arranging sounds?

You can't call that awareness an injustice, but for a long time it had a dislocating effect. I felt sick with embarrassment and downright rage in advance at the pretension, the polite predation that dares to call itself 'literature'—that bloodsucking monster that vegetates on the lives of all those unfortunate enough to find themselves in the proximity of anyone who imagines he is a writer, himself included. Nothing is safe, everything is usable, the distortions in his memory, the fabrications from his neighbourhood, the gossip from his paper, and eventually everything seems only to have happened to provide him with excellent material, even the death of his own mother. Anyone who writes is a vulture.

I'm prepared to play the vulture as much as you want, but not here. This? This must not and will not become literature. Not here of all places, I beg you, I beg myself: no, not the same old boxes of tricks again, full of culturally correct curlicues and grace notes, full of approved writer's affectations alongside artistically justified metaphors. I have gone beyond literature with capital letters. And at the same time, believe me, there aren't enough capital letters and punctuation, there is a lack of hyperbole to sing the praise of the courage of an eighty-year-old woman who, when she realized what was happening to her, simply wanted to die and, when she no longer realized anything, went on living stubbornly, and went on breathing, to the bitter end. There are simply too few syllables to curse the shame of her decline, her unequal struggle. Her fate, and in her fate that of everyone.

That's why this must have nothing to do with literature, and at the same time it must be an improvement on the Bible, an immortal poem such as has never been composed. A militant ode, lofty and compelling and merciless, as if for the most fertile and toughest of all summers. And yet, at the same time, adamantly: a dry account, a list of scenes and tableaux, stripped of frippery and pretensions, quite simply 'life as it is', imperfect, fragmented and chaotic.

Nothing but capital letters and booming internal rhymes, and at the same time just naked facts. Nothing and everything at the same time, and preferably vomited up in one gush.
So get writing.
Or not.

First I compiled an anthology of my essays and reviews. Reworking them so thoroughly that I might as well have rewritten them entirely. Not a soul noticed the difference. Meanwhile I had anyway been nicely and meaningfully employed. I had gained six months, another half a year. Cowardice as easy-going self-deception.

I wrote two evening-filling plays, one of them actually in alexandrines from start to finish, to make it extra-entertaining, telling myself that I absolutely had to finish them both first and that in addition they made the perfect preparation for this book, this hard eulogy, that would be everything and nothing at the same time, written in a single gush, novel or not.
I was wrong.
High-minded cowardice.
Transparent deception.

I went to a stomach specialist and lay on my side in order, with the aid of a rubber intestine, to allow a sophisticated garden hose with a miniature lamp and a camera mounted on it to look deep into my innards via my oesophagus. Intestine to intestine, pipe to pipe. A person is only a machine with washers that wear out too quickly.

On my side and half fighting for breath in panic. Because if there is anything I have inherited from her, apart from minor everyday ailments, it is the self-inflicted lacerations of psychosomatic illness, multiplied by this certainty: with the same malady, only the more gruesome of two possible diagnoses can be the correct one.

In the inventory of her body, which shaped mine, there was a primacy of dry coughs and minor complaints. But in her legacy and hence in my thoughts there is only room for afflictions that can vie with those of Egypt. In addition: the work ethic as a caricature. Another neurosis that I hated in her and find in myself— I still don't know whether she and I possess it thanks to our blanket Judaeo-Christian culture of guilt, or else because of the specific hysteria of the shopkeeping classes. Perhaps this is a combination and there is a connection, not even that crazy, between a neighbourhood shop and a woodland chapel, a butcher's shop and a synagogue, a boutique and a cathedral. Anyway, every time I don't do what I think I should—correction: whenever I don't do something fast enough that I have undertaken to do, just like a computer that writes and loads and reloads its own programmes until it short-circuits— every time, then, that according to my subconscious I fall short of the image I want to project of myself, my right eyelid starts trembling (guaranteed: the final stage of a tumour), my wrists and my shoulders tighten up (guaranteed: multiple sclerosis), my fingertips seem to become lifeless, they tingle and flake (it won't be leprosy, but still something ghastly).

I get up with a headache and I go to bed with diarrhoea

and meanwhile my stomach produces enough sulphuric acid to scorch irreparable holes in its own wall, just as cigarettes smoked the wrong way round would hiss and make holes in a palate. At least that's what it felt like, the day I decided to call that specialist. That morning I had rolled out of bed and crawled to breakfast on my knees, reduced to the state of a reptile by abdominal pain. One mouthful of coffee and I turned into the foetus of a reptile, made up of contractions and cramps.

Over the telephone the specialist gave me a concise diagnosis that was intended to reassure me, but that in the few hours that separated our telephone conversation from his physical examination transformed into an imaginary life-and-death struggle.

I remembered the natural remedy with which she always combated *her* stomach acid. ('Acid? [she, with a dismissive gesture] I've got a gastric hernia, nothing can be done about that, it's to do with my weak spine and your difficult birth.') You peel a raw potato, chew each slice at length and keep swallowing the mash without drinking anything.

It has to be said: some relief could be detected. The reptile foetus unrolled, sat down on a chair at his laptop and typed in the word that the specialist had repeated five times. Reflux. Twelve million hits. One referring to a Scandinavian hard-rock band with undoubtedly appropriate music. All the others referred in every language on the planet to the symptoms of the phenomenon itself. Because the entrance to your stomach no longer shuts properly, your mouth feels stiff from morning till night, it is as resistant as dried-out leather because of the acid that creeps up during the day like vermin up a drainpipe and that at night laps against your tonsils thanks to the principle of communicating vessels—from stomach to mouth and back again.

And indeed, my tongue felt like the peeling tongue of an old shoe. My teeth, my pride—at almost every check-up my dentist sighs that my teeth will take me to 100—those once indestructible teeth suddenly felt brittle, vulnerable as china that has been washed too often, dry like after eating unripe cherries. Unless something were done quickly, my teeth, destined one day to crack walnuts and open bottles of beer for my 100-year-old companions, but now bathed daily in vitriol of my own making, would have only a few years to go before they split, crumbled, became inflamed, turned black, stank, fell out all by themselves, were pulverized and blown away. Apart from that—some sites predicted, as always mercilessly objective—the chance of throat cancer was scarcely a risk, it was a certainty, and that Adam's apple wouldn't last much longer either.

'You have some scar tissue at the top of your oesophagus and also at the mouth of your stomach,' mumbled the specialist, peering at his monitor, pushing the garden hose with the lamp and camera attached to it deeper and deeper inside me, as if it were an endless adder that would freely wind its way inside—I was sweating like a trapeze artist who, during a daring new act in the ridge of the tent, is clinging only to precisely that one mouthpiece, with precisely those teeth—'but apart from that I can't see much that is spectacular. Losing a few kilos wouldn't hurt you. I can prescribe you some stomach acid inhibitors, but more exercise and less wine will get you just as far.' At my insistence he took a few more samples from my stomach wall, to check whether I wasn't cultivating a handful of open sores, and actually mainly to confirm what I already strongly suspected. I had at least terminal stomach cancer.

The head of the endless adder turned out to contain, besides a lamp and a camera, a pair of forceps, three steel teeth that moved toward each other to grab and extract a piece of my stomach. I became aware of it. Something was gnawing at me, from inside. A death-watch beetle, a rotting space creature, a caterpillar leaving the cocoon, a just desert—something was nibbling at my guts. I had not felt the intestine itself, you have to drink an anaesthetic beforehand, probably distilled from the poison of a bird spider, which anaesthetizes your oesophagus so heavily that afterwards you mustn't eat or drink anything for an hour, or else everything will literally go down the wrong way, toward the lungs. Before you know it you'll be drowning in a cup of tea.

I didn't drown, I was simply hollowed out. I was still lying on my side, I was still biting desperately on the mouthpiece, as if I was hanging on to life itself, spinning through in the roof beams of our universe, sweating like a cheese round in the sunlight, with fanatically closed eyes—and yet I saw before me how, deep inside me, an endless mechanical snake, a monster with a Cyclops' eye and a miner's lamp on its head, started pinching bits of my stomach. I felt its clawing trident snipping around, at random, and I recognized it, dammit, I recognized the insatiable trident.

I recognized it twice.

We once had at home—how old was I? Five? Seven?—a pair of sugar tongs that I could not stop playing with. A silver-plated hollow stick with a button on one side, and when you pressed it on the other side exactly the same kind of primitive claw opened as the one now gnawing at my stomach, eating what was supposed to digest my food. Picking, nipping—a humming bird fighting a closed, carnivorous plant.

With the silver-plated tongs you picked up a cube and deposited it in a cup. I did it so often not because of the sugar but because of the playful delight of those perfect tongs, which were taken away from me every time, on her sighing orders of course, and I got a flea in my ear into the bargain because I wouldn't listen at once.

I couldn't locate those tongs after she found her way once and for all and inexorably into the closed institution where she would spend her last few months, among other human wrecks—carcasses with limited movement capable only of drooling and relieving themselves, most of them lopsided and tied, like her, to their beds, their armchairs, their wheelchairs. After that unwanted separation my father moved by himself into an old people's home four streets away from her. He left the flat where they had lived for almost two decades that was situated above the butcher's shop where they had done business for nearly forty years. Virtually none of their household effects could go with him.

For a week I was condemned to the role of arbitrator. I, the liquidator, handing down verdicts on every knickknack and every heirloom, both equally precious. The archive and register of two intimately interwoven lives, also the backdrop of my childhood, with all the props— it degenerated in my hands into a collection of anonymous things, whether or not usable elsewhere, sometimes with a market value, sometimes distributable, usually to be thrown away. Vanished, wiped out, passé. My father left the decision entirely up to his children, just as in the past he would have left it up to my mother.

Apart from photos of her, and his television set, there was nothing that he indicated was necessary for the rest of his existence.

However hard I looked for them, there was no sign of the three-fingered sugar tongs.

As a ten-year-old ringleader I used another claw foot, but larger and yellowy-white, and scaly, and with long horn-like nails, to terrify a girl who lived nearby and was two years older than me. A severed chicken's claw from our butcher's shop. I held it in my bunched-up sleeve and advanced on her with a contorted face, grunting, talking gibberish, drooling, swiping with my new limb at her freckle-covered arms and legs.

You could even fish out a tendon with a needle from where the leg had been hacked off and like a puppeteer pull the tendon taut with two fingers so that the chicken's claw opened and closed again. My little neighbour was already upset, but when she saw my new hand actually moving she started screaming.

A few years later she showed me, in our lock-up garage halfway down the street, where all the car owners in our neighbourhood rented garages, in a maze of gravel paths with rows and rows of long concrete compartments, all the same size, all with pink corrugated sheets and each with a rickety double gate—the complex itself was the limbo area outside a wood yard, which smelt eternally of diesel and pine woods—in the dim light of our lock-up garage, then, my easily frightened neighbour showed me, unsolicited, her pristine tits. Two swollen nipples actually, already deeply dark, that was true, silky and yet recalcitrantly stiff, the flesh around the areola lightly accentuated and as white as the cap of a freshly picked mushroom, but with freckles. 'They're going to be very big,' she whispered, 'later, like my sister's. Have a feel.'

And I felt, honoured and bewildered. I plucked and picked, not with the aid of a dead chicken's foot, but with three cautious fingers of my own, a mouth of fingertips, which sucked at her soft deep dark expectancy, first left then right, and the more I plucked and sucked, the more resistant her soft mushroom caps with their freckles became, the more she sighed in my face, closer and closer.

A smell I didn't yet know, something halfway between milk and almonds, dispelled the diesel and pine woods around me.

I LEFT THE stomach specialist determined not to wait for the result of the ulcer and cancer examination before finally getting down to writing. Anyway, the result would not reveal anything other than the palpable suggestion of the specialist: affectation.

The report proved him right. A month later, in which I had still not composed a note of what was to be a more exalted Song of Songs, a better Bible, a more beautiful Scripture, everything and nothing at once. In the hope that it would not, falling between two stools, simply become neither. For now it was even less than that. Eccentric escapism, respectable idling. For a year a mother was proved right with her prediction of the writer as a wastrel.

Twelve months, four seasons passed in a flash.

Because I also spent the previous European winter in the windy Cape high summer, in the Victorian house where I am typing this, on this laptop. This paragraph, this sentence, these three words, and these and these, at this very moment. I am writing them now instead of last year. Yet I was already here then. In my cramped study with its childlike office furniture and its wooden terrace at the foot of the almighty Table Mountain, in a neighbourhood called Oranjezicht, during my annual escape to this temporary paradise of isolation and sun and carefree writing and reading, without losing myself in the distractions that I can so seldom resist in my home country. Of course I am also a kind of actor, a failed one, a hopeless ham without inhibitions. Give me a stage and an audience, give me a microphone and a book of mine or one of my literary heroes, and I will read it aloud until the break of day. There is an element of, besides coquetry and greed, abject despair, I don't myself know about what, but I go on, and on. Another splendid battle won for the spoken word. Another illustrious day lost without having written.

I did do some writing here last year, albeit working on that play in alexandrines. Counting on my fingers for days like an ambitious toddler, always the same formula. The alexandrine consists of six iambic feet; explained for convenience that gives twelve syllables, linked two by two, alternately stressed and unstressed. 'Ta-tám, ta-tám, ta-tám. / Ta-tám, ta-tám, ta-tám.'

As far as content went I mixed Euripides with George W. Bush, Troy with Iraq, Manhattan with Troy, towers with towers, war with war. As far as form went I piled plosives on sibilants, internal rhymes on alliterations, as if I were a hip-hopper of ancient protest songs preparing for a poetry slam in the townships of Mitchell's Plain, on the other side of Devil's Peak, the brother of Table Mountain. Ta-tám, ta-tám, ta-tám! Turning my beloved native language, which is so much suppler and generous and colourful than most of its users are prepared to believe, into a beatbox.

I had six women—two elderly queens and four princesses—take the measure of one man, the Greek commander-in-chief Agamemnon. Seven lives, thousands of years ago, thousands of kilometres away, different continents, different centuries. While I should have been taking the measure of one woman in my own life. I fell short again, and I realized it. I began counting and running away even more angrily.

'O Muse, sing now for me. / Sing of my frenzied state.'

'At least be brave enough / to speak with your own blood.'

'Each second that ticks by, / once more she's here with me.'

My summer's writing was not as carefree as all that. Many a morning's sleep was wrecked by the whirring blades of helicopters flying low overhead. Everything in this country is massive and overwhelming, from poverty to economic growth, from language interaction to forest fires. In the case of the latter the helicopters sweep slowly and ear-piercingly over, like extras in a Vietnam film, to the reservoir round the corner, the size of two football pitches and as old as the district itself—the first foundations were laid by the Dutch and their slaves, in the service of the United East India Company.

Under each helicopter hangs a bright orange bag that can be closed at the bottom. However, it continues to leak and from the top too water sloshes out because of the movement and as a result of the whirring is immediately vaporized as if for a local shower of rain. On the return journey the bag, hanging open, still leaks profusely, so that at each pass my terrace gets soaking-wet, the corrugated sheets of the roof rattle like a washboard used for percussion, so that finally, distracted even here and tempted to enjoy myself, I just sit on that wooden terrace, with towel and binoculars at the ready, following the ballet of the fire-fighting helicopters.

Only when you can no longer hear them, they are so

far away by now, as small as flies against the monstrously high and steep wall of Holy Table Mountain—only then do they open their water bags, simultaneously and making a swerving manoeuvre, so that the water hits the seat of the blaze in an elegant fan shape, causing furious clouds of steam to rise from the side of the mountain, a filthy reddish billowing column, temporarily blotting out the sunlight, an orange ball behind a curtain of churning smoke.

Then the pounding mounts again and the iron dragonflies, quickly swelling in your binoculars, make straight for the reservoir, straight for you, with their dripping bags, their exotic rowanberry, bitten to pieces, emptied. Their rhythmical whirring mixes with the maniacal counting in your head. Wap-wáp, wap-wáp, wap-wáp.

Give me adversity. Cadence and poetry.

Misfortune has a right. To beat and poetry.

During one particular night, hours after the helicopter ballet had been discontinued because nocturnal sorties are too dangerous, even though the cargo consists of water and not of bombs—we are talking about the years of the Great Cape Fires, the year of my Elegant Flight Forward, also the years of the Wild Water Rumours: for the first time in living memory the bed of the reservoir was threatening to become exposed, baking in the fierce African sun, drying up in the hellish Cape Town wind, the feared 'South-Easterly', whipped up by the tropical summer heat and the two oceans that enclosed the city, one ice-cold, one lukewarm, the Atlantic and the Indian, making its good name of Cape Doctor a joke. It tortured the corrugated sheets and the swaying palms and made electric cables snap like the anchor lines of a tanker adrift, it screeched louder than the mistral and the sirocco combined and, no longer hindered by fire-fighting helicopters, it fanned fires on four mountains at once, Devil's Peak, Table Mountain, Lion's Head and Signal Hill, which together form a basin in which the old, vulnerable part of the city lies.

I was still sitting on my terrace, no longer with my feet on the balustrade, but staring around me in astonishment and fear in the red-glowing darkness, surrounded by more and more glowing scars, tangible heat, the angry, dense smell of scorching, the stink of sulphur, the demonic laughter of the South-Easterly, the snapping of distant blazing tree trunks. I was more and more hemmed in, like everyone else, like the city itself. Some way further up our street, twelve blocks up, there were fire engines with revolving lights. The inroads of the fire were being combatted there with traditional hoses and the struggle was gradually being lost. Still further up two houses were already ablaze; a little further down the residents were already carrying their furniture into the street and in the distance, across the whole side of Table Mountain, from top to bottom, ran an awful crack, hundreds of metres long, filled with blazing charcoal as if with lava. I couldn't stop looking; the obscenity of fire is inexorable, terrifying, fascinating.

It roared and hammered at the same time in my brain: didn't write, didn't write. Even here.

'The world is vast, it's true. / But everywhere the same.'

ON MY RETURN to the Worn-Out Continent, I finished the play in alexandrines, attended rehearsals and the first night, so, taking the most recent escape route to its end and completing it, I began after all on my song cursing her bitter lot. Indeed I got going industriously and built up a head of steam.

Then my father died.

And I faltered again.

Not because of death in itself. It was sad but also, I don't hesitate to say it, beautiful. After the horrors that had befallen her, during which he was condemned to be a helpless spectator—the star witness of her slow terror of being excluded for ever from a life that had formed the foundation of his—after that ordeal he was allowed to pass away as he would have wished. Not long after her, for a start.

And quickly. Two weeks or so, and he was gone.

And not in the aseptic, deadly hospital where he was supposed to die, but in his familiar room in the old people's home into which he had moved.

And without pain, high on morphine, sinking into ever-longer periods of sleep and finally coma, surrounded by his closest family, who took turns watching at his deathbed, staying awake as was proper: with a thermos flask of coffee on the table and a dish of filled rolls, as well as a bottle of Wortegem lemon gin, his favourite aperitif and favourite nightcap, and anyway a welcome reviver during the strange timeless nights, in which someone lies dying who saw you being born, and is now on the point of closing his eyes for ever. His television was on the whole time, from morning till night, as always, babbling more endlessly than an Old Testament woodland stream. The only concession was that the sound could be turned off at the last. In this way my father faded away, while football matches were silently lost and won, world crises were averted and revived in utter silence. They cast their flickering shadows pityingly on him.

And I was about to forget the most important thing: he was surrounded by all the photos of her that he had brought from their flat. One of them is that photo on the front cover. Just look at it. It won't be the last time. When I found it during the liquidation at which I acted as arbitrator, it was hidden among a mass of other photos—stuffed together in an old biscuit tin, so that the plain lid was pushed outward by them—and covered in scratches; it was not much bigger than a passport photo. Later, enlarged and framed, it took pride of place, often with a burning tea light in front of it, on his circular drawing-room table, the one with the glass top resting on a wicker base, one of the few items of furniture that had accompanied him from flat to room on his penultimate journey.

That room had gradually become less his living quarters than a shrine, a sanctuary where there was daily remembrance, and without prayers, prayers to a goddess of many manifestations. There was a photo of her on every cupboard and every side table. Three hung over his bed.

One of them was a grotesque print, at least for anyone who did not know the context. My mother, at the time long since retired, is depicted as Mae West. One of her favourite manifestations in this local church community consisting of a single worshipper, which compensated for the modesty of its numbers with the power of its devotion. Every morning and every evening he made his modest pilgrimage, shuffling in a circle round his dining table, from cupboard to drawing-room table to bed to cupboard, watching the treacherous wrinkles and flaps in the carpet, in order to wish each of the photographic manifestations an extensive good morning or good night, as the case might be. When he drank his aperitif he raised his glass now to one then to the other, taking care not to favour one of the figures over the others. He loved them all equally.

Yet he toasted most frequently that one secular saint's print above his bed, in which his idol wore a festive shiny ultramarine evening dress—Mae West at her finest, including black stiletto heels, a platinum-blonde wig, garish lipstick and false eyelashes the size of butterfly's wings. In a wheelchair but not yet secured, sitting in it entirely of her own will, actually wheeling around with bravura, from the look on her face not doubting for a moment the success of her statement. It is a souvenir of one of her most treasured roles, in a play about, of all things, old people with dementia. One of her few professional jobs, for the Royal Flemish Theatre, the Brussels municipal theatre that granted my mother a rebirth as one of the women whom she had so admired throughout her life. ('Just a shame she was so foulmouthed. [she, with an ugly frown] She went to jail because of it, "Mie Wust" or "My Sausage" as we called her in our young days. Thank God they never called me that. One's got to be able to laugh at oneself, but Mie Wust? I wouldn't call that much of a recommendation, not even in a butcher's shop.')

His wife, sparkling above his bed as a Dietrich-like Blue Angel in a continuous screening, flourishing as a well-preserved Hollywood icon, triumphant in a wheelchair, with too much make-up but as yet without a twinge of pain, with a piercing gaze in which there is not yet any bewilderment. On the contrary, she seems ready to burst into a faultless monologue and hold the audience in thrall. That was one of the last images which my father, taking shorter and shorter hazy glimpses of the world from which he was slipping away, absorbed, at each glance himself a little less lucid. A happy drowning man who still occasionally sticks his head up in the middle of a desolate sea, sees that it is good and lets himself slide back underwater, blissfully weakening, reassured, without complaint, satisfied, even smiling: look over there, there she hangs, my Josée. Does she look fantastic or doesn't she? Alert, protective, radiant.

Although when we squabbled she could stare at the same nail for a bloody long time. That's how she was. My Josée.

Come on now, Dad. Go ahead. We know what you want. Cast a final glance. Raise that tired head one last time. Lift it up one last time from that calm, flat sea of sheets. There's no need to be embarrassed. If there are people who when they read this want to feel vicarious shame for you, for me, for her—let them skip this page. Let them stop reading completely. They are in the wrong place here. They are not worthy of you.

Come on now. Just once. Look at that photo which, when you were awake and well, you sang the praises of so often, to nurses, the odd-job-man, the old pious, faithful nun on your floor—what's her name again?—to all visitors, everyone, more than once and again and again, just as in the shop you told the same joke a hundred times, the same bit of gossip to a different customer each time, and the next day the same. You said in your room, pointing to the place above your bed: 'Have you in all your life ever seen such beautiful legs? I agree they're on the short side. But apart from that? And she was already seventy-seven!'

One more time. Go on.
   Come on now.

I **HAVE NEVER** known anybody so ready for the final chapter as my father. Lucid, almost eager. A week before he died, with him and his GP, and in the presence of a son-in-law and the grandson who was his nurse, I went through the official list of questions which precedes the legitimate assisted dying which my country of origin insists on calling so euphemistically 'palliative care'. A state governed by the rule of law which has a large number of suicides wants to be sure that new individuals who are dying *really* want to die. They have to affirm that so often that some people who are dying start feeling guilty about their longing for death. Which is perhaps the intention of some survivors.

I am not going to get worked up over this again. I don't want to behave sarcastically or despairingly. Death is ultimately most difficult for the survivors. So don't let me start waffling here about the point or lack of point of such a compulsory questioning of people who are already half dead, inspired by bureaucratic distrust, imposed by religions that have gone to the dogs without a soul and without a future. I am not in a position to lecture anyone about neuroses and strange antics caused by someone else dying. Everyone has their own abnormality. Everyone has their own hereafter. And pity for everyone.

My father definitely did not feel guilty, face to face with his departure. He sounded relieved. Joking like the young rascal of fourteen that he remained all his life, comforting like the reconciler wise beyond his years that he also was, always placating in the background, a slaughterer who wanted to make life easier for everyone else, taking as many burdens as possible on himself, where and whenever he could—even now, dawdling on the threshold of death, his first concern was to avoid the raising of voices and sad scenes. Mad about teasing and being teased, a scallywag of eighty-eight—I really can't describe him any differently. An eternal rogue who was almost completely bald before he was forty and was constantly struggling with excess weight, since life consists, apart from working and producing children, of wholesome eating, and only fools refuse a good glass, be it beer, wine or old Dutch gin.

Not a father to fight with. Not a patriarch to murder, symbolically or with a real axe.

His mischievous round head of yore had become very emaciated in the space of a few months, and he had to keep tightening his belt, 'or else my trousers will fall off my bum.' His metastasized prostate cancer had become bone cancer, affecting and dissolving half his skeleton, spoiling his appetite and his blood with the calcium that was released. That does something to your stomach and to your intestines. Don't ask me what, I don't want to know. He was fed liquid and sugar through a drip, a kind of transparent plastic bag hanging on a mobile coat hook. Eating and drinking were no longer possible, almost overnight, whatever he ate or drank he instantly vomited up again into a cardboard vomiting dish—there are people who think up things like that, modern heroes, real heroes, an unbreakable vomiting dish made of calming rough grey cardboard, easy to hold to someone's mouth because of its shape: a hollow kidney, cut in half, and not cold and condemning like enamel or stainless steel, which would inevitably recall a poisoned chalice.

There were questions on the official list that my father did not answer directly, but rather with a smile and a digging motion of the hand: 'Dig a hole. Not too much trouble. No waste of money.' In answer to another question: 'Give me a jab. Nice and quick. No fuss.' With a broad grin and a wink.

When I took him cautiously to task and went on seriously asking for a real answer, he looked at me with feigned disappointment, chin on his chest, gazing up with great, bewildered eyes. He even started blinking with those real Bambi eyes of his, grimacing. 'You're not going to start messing about, are you? You know what I want. Write it down, lad. And no more messing *abart*. Or else go straight back to that *Antwarp* of yours.' Always those two words, 'messing abart' and 'Antwarp', spoken with an exaggerated Antwerp accent, with elongated syllables and in a high-pitched voice, almost feminine, or at least childlike.

They cut me to the quick. In a flash I realized the horror. He was actually playing the amateur actor in turn, right under my nose, just before his death. It's an infection, that acting, that manipulation, that flight. Not only within my family and my writing. In this old people's home too, with its understandable but strict rules, with its circuitous gossip among the staff, its tacit late-Catholic plot, through which everyone knows that an overdose of morphine is on its way to room 218, and everyone pretends courteously not to know—as if nothing is on its way except the usual procedure, with its poker face and, once more, its little white lies, its we-know-our-own-people, its mercy and its backstabbing, its silent cowardice and its silent compassion. Our massive impotence, face to face with the mystery of this life.

This whole country is acting, this shithole of Europe, and all the people who wallow about in it: it's a colony of play actors, it hams it up for all it's worth; not capable of real contact, it hides in the footlights of beautiful semblance and the expensive restaurant bill and the compulsive waffling about the bad weather and the tailbacks and the neighbour's dog turds, it suffers from overacting in politics and in cycling—but it hasn't been given a complete script for its true self, still not, neither have I; we are still yokels in overpriced suits with no other retorts than the boorish curse or the charged silence or the red face of shame. And if they are not enough, we quickly improvise a vulgar farce, an evasive dirty joke, a funny accent, a high-pitched voice. Still the inspirers of a medieval farce, *The Farce of Even Now*. Types, where you expect people.

For just a second—talking to my begetter about his approaching death—I felt irrationally and deeply sad and angry, at him, at everything he stood for, and because next week he would no longer be alive. I don't know if he noticed, but he gradually became his usual self again, and that was crazy enough. In reply to another serious question from his GP ('Do you want to be resuscitated, should you have a heart attack?'), he said, 'Doctor, I wouldn't bother any more in your place. You know what I am, don't you? No? I'm buggered.'

After which, disarmingly genuinely, simply the eternal adolescent as always, he started giggling. His shoulders, which had become so much narrower, laughed along with him, he shrugged them in time with his giggling, 'hu-hu-hu'. Literally, I'm sorry if it sounds daft or looks ugly on the page. 'Hu-hu-hu.' With one hand over his pinched pout, as if he had said something naughty that was *just* beyond a joke. 'Buggered. Hu, hu, hu.'

An altar boy who farts in the sacristy.

It was his last hit, his hasty prayer to conviviality, his charming, risqué term to reassure those saying farewell by eliciting a bittersweet smile. 'I'm buggered. Hu-hu-hu.'

To the manager of the home, to the physiotherapist, to the cleaner with a Moroccan name, to the good, pious, ancient nun whose name I have forgotten: 'I'm buggered. Hu-hu-hu!'

At first he looks at his granddaughter and her mother, who had come from Holland to pay their last respects, with a bunch of flowers in their hands, at a loss for words—he has just momentarily re-emerged from a sea of forgetfulness, and he does not recognize the two of them. He glances at the photo above his bed, at his triumphant Josée, and then back at them and suddenly, elderly charmer, the penny drops: 'Oh dear! You look good, the two of you. Very good. But you must take those flowers back with you, back home, they'll only stand here and fade, and who knows for how long it will be. No! You must take them with you. You must!'

And then, as he accepts their farewell kisses, his head raised half out of the surf, his lips pouting in thin air, his already chilled cheek against theirs, he says in a whisper, not unhappily: 'I'm buggered. Hu-hu-hu. But you look very good, both of you. I'm not. Completely buggered. Hu-hu-hu.'

A fourteen-year-old Buddhist butcher with the giggles and another 144 hours to go.

A YEAR BEFORE his death he found, in a corner of the paper that he read from cover to cover every day, with his magnifying glass at the ready—no one was able to persuade him to wear reading glasses, he had enough trouble with his hearing aid and his false teeth—but even while concentrating on reading his paper he still occasionally found time, if necessary at quarter to seven in the morning, to look up at his television screen for the repeat of a favourite soap, or for the fifth summary of a tennis match featuring Justine Henin, his little hero-ine—when Juju was yet again, after a bloodcurdlingly bad first set, on the point of winning the match after all, as he had thought and known from the start—to ring me up, at high noon or the middle of the night, whether I was in Cape Town, in Hong Kong or in Zwolle, he would call: 'Quick, quick! Turn your TV on! She's going to win! She's going to win!' After which he threw the phone down, so as not to miss any of the glories of his Petite Justine. The day that she announced she was leaving the professional tennis circuit was a black day; he rang me again, fighting back his tears now: 'She's packing it in, she can't take it any more, all that competition, that stress, just like Eddy Merckx back then, she's perfectly right, poor thing, but it's a shame anyway'—a year before his death then, he discovered in his paper the report that I wanted to keep hidden from him.

My mobile rang.

'What do I read? You're going to write a book about your mother?'

'Who says so?'

'It says so in my paper.'

'You mustn't believe everything that's in the newspapers.'

'If it's not going to happen, then why is it in my paper?'

'That's how these things work. It all has to be announced a long way in advance.'

'But that means it's true?'

'It's a plan, Dad. A plan can take years.'

'It doesn't say that, in my paper.'

'Who can tell? I've got to write it.'

'I think it will be very nice, a book about your mother.'

'How can you know that? I've still got to write it.'

'The very thought! A thick book about your mother.'

'I've still got to write it!'

'When will you finish it?'

From then on, and we are talking about long before the Hellish Season of the Great Cape Fires, his first sentence as soon as I entered his room in the old people's home, or in my cousin's bar-cum-restaurant where he was waiting for me—*everywhere* he caught sight of me: 'How's your book going?' It was also his first sentence on the telephone, whether I was I in Cape Town, in Hong Kong or in Zwolle.

The first time I was moved. The next five times I burst out laughing. After that I got more and more irritated, more and more desperate, more and more apprehensive about his question, which increasingly assumed the tone of an indictment. 'How's your book going?' The accusation gradually became a serial sentence. The charge was culpable dereliction, the judgment came in four words, fast-track justice: 'How's your book going?'

I knew in advance that sentence would be passed again, as inexorably as before, as soon as I was face to face with my mild, temporarily sad torturer, with whom I could not even get angry. Is there such a thing as stage fright in a family context? Before each visit, before each phone call, I was seized by family vertigo, provoked by the rift between his expectations and my nerves, both equally tautly strung. Again all kinds of gnawings began on the inside of my stomach. And when I managed to persuade him, after much begging and beseeching and promising, to stop beginning our conversations with 'How's the book going?', he began them with: 'I know I mustn't ask, lad, but how's the book going?' Not out of malice or to tease me, it was stronger than he was. And he suffered from it more than I did.

The expression, generally so crafty, with which he tried to assure the outside world that, all in all, things weren't too bad with him—'life goes on, you're confronted with it and you've got to get on with it'—and that wink, so confidential, with which he informed God and Everyman that, bearing in mind the sad circumstances, he could not be in a better place than here, in this home with the best reputation in town, with its generous car park, with its excellent nurses and young interns, 'and as regards food it's incredible here: if the mussel season begins we have mussels that week; if there are new herring, we eat new herring'—that waggish look, that reassuring wink, they disappeared as soon as he sensed I was there. The memory of a tiny article in a corner shot out unstoppably, an arrow through a tank, and the torturer looked at the accused painfully again, yearning, for a moment broken, with watery eyes even: 'I know I mustn't ask, lad, but how's that book of yours going?'

He was counting on me for nothing less than a minor reincarnation. The resurrection of Josée as she had been, through the years, on and off the boards. She had given birth to me? I must do the same for her. At least for him, and preferably for the whole world. Just as she had gradually broken down before his eyes, fragmented, unravelled, had little by little slid away, escaped him word by word—I had to rebuild her, sentence by sentence, page by page. Loss of language restored by language. That was all an undertone in his language, in his condemnation of just a few syllables, spoken with a look in which all the possible loss of the whole human species fleetingly gathered.

Immediately afterwards, in the twinkling of an eye, his face cleared up and there followed another stream of contented personal declarations. Cheerful, monomaniacal, passionate—as if he had to convince other people, but mainly himself. Mantra for a man alone: that he could 'really' not be anywhere better than here, in this oversized room 'actually meant for two people', with a view of greenery and even of a fountain, and with all those attractive staff around him, and nowadays he even had massages, for his sore back and painful hip, albeit from a male physiotherapist, 'a good lad who knows his job, and you can have the occasional laugh with him— but well, a woman's hand? That is and remains something completely different.'

After which he concluded with an iron train of thought of his own manufacture, butcher's logic which linked those therapist's hands with flesh and back massages and food: 'When the hunting season begins, we eat partridge or rabbit, accompanied by a baked apple full of blueberries, with a head of chicory, caramelized by the country butter, and with real potato croquettes.' He said that dreamily. Licking his chops. Already pouring himself a Wortegem gin, as his first aperitif of the day. Before drinking and clinking glasses in thin air, toasting one of the photos. 'Your health, my girl.' Without yet mentioning that book of mine.

Until his next greeting.

HE NEVER READ a word of what you are reading at this moment. He died and what I had written up to then I threw away, shortly after his cremation, shortly after his ashes were shaken out of the urn onto the same meadow, on more or less the same square metre, as her ashes, only a few years before.

United at last.

I erased what I had written radically and ritually, deleted it charitably, during a night that brought insight and austere melancholy, after I had stared for hours at the screen of my laptop as if into a mirror and could scarcely stand the sight any longer. Delete. Delete. Consign to the Lethe.

That same day I started again, on this, this novel that must not become a novel, not belles-lettres but not rubbish either, an improved Bible and an anti-book in one and the same cover. Starting again, in anger, looking straight into the digital mirror in which these words obediently appear as my fingers type them, and these too and these too. I type them manfully but am ashamed at so many lost hours, so much faint-heartedness. Embarrassed by my flight into other projects, to other places, into words other than the necessary ones. And look, even now, even after beginning again, I still had to go on for pages and pages—and hence still in flight—about so much other than the essence. So be it. It's as plain as the nose on your face. Even in the case of this renewed writing I first need flanking manoeuvres, epic feints to the square millimetre, encircling processions of monsters and trolls, from Gilt Mary to Napoleon, from hot-air balloons to Cape firefighting helicopters. A caravan of swaying anecdotes and barking woes. A parade of old acquaintances, veiled in *couleur locale* and perfumed with sweet memories. A force of manly facts and consoling market-stall holders rushing to my aid—Mie Wust, a pious nun, Justine Henin—in the hope that they will provide me, who have recently become a full orphan, with surrogate support, inspiration and help, I who never thought I would have to deal with inspiration and help, certainly not from outside, and certainly not here, at this loving liquidation, this intimate settling of accounts, a book which in my arrogance I had thought in anticipation would scarcely need a writer. It would compose itself, through the energy of its core.

It didn't. The cocoon did not allow itself to be cracked just like that. Diffidence is still there, in full force. And I am not going to apologize for that. Diffidence is part of the whole, perhaps even the central theme. Anyone who knows the answer can shout it out. I can only hope that the serried ranks of my demons and dwarves, my memories and my wounds, move in a centripetal vortex, and that that whole pathetic procession—why not here, within about three lines?—may finally be reduced to silence, at its own axis. In the frighteningly calm eye of the inwardly circulating whirlwind which it has itself produced.

And, well I never. The dust descends. Here it lies. The key, the quintessence, the spell. Staggering, simple and hard. This book is unavoidably also the story of this book, which refused to let itself be written while my father was still alive.

It has nothing to do with fear of failure with regard to him, the fear of not succeeding in his commission to raise her from the dead with my words. He of all people would never have disavowed my literary labour of Lazarus. He would have welcomed every attempt, however inadequate or mediocre, as a complete miracle, would have acclaimed it as a wonder of the world. Even more so than with my other titles, he would have stocked up on copies from the local bookseller, a few dozen in total ('I can't begrudge the man the money, can I, we're all shopkeepers together?'), gift-wrapped and all, in order to distribute them shamelessly and, despite my spluttering protests, to the whole staff, against all the house rules, in exchange for a kiss from the ladies and a shared drink with the men.

Fear of failure? The real reason is crueller. I type it with resentment, disgust even. Watch, as these cool words appear, just like that, on my screen and your page: his death was necessary, in reality and on paper, before I could really begin. Her life cannot be described without his, and vice-versa. That's what you get with those bloody eternal loves, those inseparable lives from an earlier period—they were proud of the fact that they had never exchanged a French kiss with anyone but each other, and I have never met anyone who contradicted that or even cast doubt on it.

For the book that he awaited so passionately to appear he had first to follow her. His end was one of the links in what he would have liked to read and distribute himself, with a kiss as thanks and drinks as his reward. 'Your health, my girl.'

There is a persistent and widespread misconception, among connoisseurs and laymen alike, that writing means 'preserving'. Establishing what existed, as it existed. Of course it is the other way round. Writing is destroying, in the absence of anything better. Only then and as a result does what you are writing about pass away. Literature is letting go. Writing is dispelling.

So come on then. Say farewell—you too. Draw a thick, bold cross over it, however gently. Over her, over him. Their neighbourhood, their period, their lives. The great scenes of a small neighbourhood and a family with lots of children, in a corner house without a garden, and a shop with a constantly jingling doorbell—I slept in the room right above it, and during many a morning nightmare I tried out our slicing machine on the fingers of our earliest customers, those unsuspecting anonymous sadists, those instigators of a daily terror, who harried and controlled from morning till night with their hellish jingling.

A cross over all customers, all meat hooks and that one slicing machine. Put the cleaver into this: the whole human zoology of my youth, in which the oddest beast bears my name, my glasses and my defects, my scars and my lisp. Only in that way will she, Josée, become what she always wanted to be. Bigger than herself, larger than life. Because just as one *cannot* talk about her without expanding on him, so I cannot write about the two of them without digressing on the whole damned world which I got to know, and over which she ruled, for years. And standing face to face with that realm of woman, I am bound one last time to incline toward sloth and doubt.

Why me?

Because, end of story. That's enough, now. Hack and pierce, fillet, expose every bone—begin. It doesn't matter where. But begin.

Describe for example with a grin your horror at this moment, your panic as a recognized customer-friendly purveyor of literature. Stick a skewer in the craftsman you so often maintain you are, and listen with pleasure to the sigh that escapes from the wound like a dirty, despairing fart: 'Dear me, dear God! I've started with the end! His death should have been at the end! For greater symmetry and melancholy pleasure!'

Laugh your head off at the palette and brushes of the professional painter of the senses you imagine you are, the cat's tail with which the literary whore whips himself into streamlined production: your bundle of themes. The key-word outline of a possible, hoped-for, future—who knows?—masterpiece. That must be the aim, always. We can't do it for less. [she, echoing] 'You've got more in you than you think.'

I have a printout next to me, of my themes. According to calculations from long ago I should by now, on page xx, have long since described our former landlady. Fat Liza was her name, miserliness and unpredictability her fame.

I should also have long ago depicted our Hardworking Hunchback. He lived round the corner from us. A tough, emaciated man who looked timidly around him, high on his back a shoebox of flesh and spinal cord. At the same time he was the proud father of a dozen offspring, which with the cruelty native to children we called 'the Humps'. Humps 1, Hump 2, Hump 3 ...

I should also long since have sketched Willy the Shoemaker in detail. He plied his trade half a street further on and was also endowed with a hump, which strengthened me from an early age in the suspicion that overground nuclear tests were once conducted in Waasland. The more so since he was the possessor of a hefty club foot, which he dragged behind him—he could patch up his shoe, which quickly wore out, himself, thus making a saving. Willy had the bushy eyebrows of a devil, the mouth of a monk, the brown eyes of a wounded deer and an echoing house without children which constantly smelt of glue and leather.

Tear them up. All of them. Joyfully. Your schedules, your memoranda, your reference stuff. Delete, delete. Consign to the Lethe. What matters is spinning around in your head ready to be remembered. From now on go only for the mercurial moment. The random clatter inside your skull. Reap the moment and pick the impromptu. We'll see where we get to, together.

For example, begin with what should have been the only true beginning. The starting gun of what is at once a domestic and a universal saga. The intervention of fate.

The scene takes place in the previously mentioned flat above our former butcher's shop. Where Fat Liza used to live, into which my parents moved on their retirement, and where later I would have to reach a verdict on each of their possessions. Because of that unity of place the decor actually looks rather familiar. Pieces of jigsaws from different periods that suddenly fit together unexpectedly and unpredictably. Playing jazz must be like this. Suddenly from the mess comes that one crashing chord, unrepeatable, and yet perfectly timed. Sent by favourable chance.

Gratefully received by the patient musician.

Or not. What if we no longer need to pay attention to planning or directness? After all, this is the end of the first section. An organ figure would not be out of place. A small tableau vivant, characteristic of the protagonist, while she is still hale and hearty and suspects nothing of the catastrophe that is about to engulf her.

We shall look for her where we left her. We shall zoom in on the plot among the pollard and the Canada willows, the streams and the earth paths. The balloon flotilla in the sky has gone, floated off to pastures new. The sky has been left empty, an immaculate blue. The canopy of a merciful summer.

She sits on the ground, in a bathing costume and with that simple band in her hair, rooting about in her vegetable garden on her knees, right next to her famous bungalow, which was built under her supervision and to her design from concrete foundations to corrugated roof by family and friends with too much free time and not enough resistance to her moral and friendly blackmail. ('You're coming to help, aren't you?' 'All the others are coming, you know.' 'Afterwards there's a barbecue with satay and scampi.' 'Oh no! The foundations have got to be deeper! Much deeper!' 'I should know, shouldn't I? Are you a builder's daughter, or am I?')

She is gardening intently as always, without looking right or left. Her Roger is taking a nap in the middle of the lawn in a deckchair under a large red plastic parasol. From the transistor on the table next to him pours bel canto song, alternating with match reports and weather forecasts for pigeon fanciers and canal shipping. He sleeps through everything.

It is a radiant Sunday in September, sometime in the second half of the twentieth century. She must be about sixty. It may be five years more or five years less. Doesn't matter. This is her. Made entirely of language and yet exactly as she was. She is digging up her harvest with her bare hands, from small earth banks, consisting of the sandy soil that makes our native region so suitable for growing asparagus and for not much else, unless it be floury potatoes.

She cuts the asparagus, thin and pale as the hands of a dead piano player, according to a fixed ritual, mercilessly tender, never rushing it. First she gropes around in the soil wrist-deep, where a crack or a small nipple that has already turned purple in the earth wall has betrayed the upward thrust of an asparagus shoot, sitting waiting milk-white in our dark earth. Her hand stirs about cautiously in the opening, while she herself closes her eyes, increasing the sensitivity of touch in her hand by excluding visual stimuli. At first she appears not to find what she is looking for. She stirs ever deeper. For a moment you are afraid that her arm will gradually disappear into the hole, up to her armpits, as if the earth is a pregnant cow and she a gentle-natured vet who has to arrange a number of organs, for order and neatness are important everywhere, definitely in the innards of a globe. But now she strikes with her kitchen knife—an heirloom with a bone handle and a blade that that has become wafer-thin with all the sharpening, the cutting edge has even worn into a half-moon shape. ([she, speaking with certainty] 'One fine day that knife will break in half, on a shoot no thicker than a child's little finger.')

By the time she is finished the sweat is running down from under her hairband. Standing up, she wipes it away with her wrist, dirtying her face as well with a shadow of poor earth and the sickly, slightly bitter smell of her harvest. It is displayed next to her on a piece of old newspaper. [she, just as certain] 'You're right, these are the first, still a bit skinny and stringy. It will be years before they can compete with the ones from Mechelen, which are the best in the world—don't let those Spaniards or Dutch fool you, they can have as much sandy soil as they like over there. But this here, look? Still enough for a pan of soup. With some chicken bouillon added, some fresh parsley, a dash of cream. There are restaurants where they can't put that on the menu. Unless from packets. [she, contemptuously] Nonsense, *that* may come out of packets. My soup? Never.'

Her eyes glitter combatively at the prospect of, by way of proof, preparing her fresh soup, this very night, for tomorrow afternoon. But each time she has stood up she groans, with one hand half on her hip, half on her back: 'Goodness me, I almost couldn't stand up. That back, that back, that back. I should have been in a wheelchair for twenty years. If it goes on like this it won't be much longer.' Unaware of the gross irony of that prediction.

This ailment is not in her imagination. Since her birth her spine, from coccyx to neck vertebrae, has exhibited an S-shape that is growing worse as the years go by. She is shrinking faster than other elderly people, and she is already so small. There are x-ray photos in which one loop of the S curls over one of her kidneys, while the other curls menacingly toward the opposite shoulder blade. 'If I ever fall off a step ladder, the whole lot will go splat.' [she, with strange pride]

In order to spare her constitution she should not lift anything and never work leaning forward. 'If I had listened to that, I should have lain in bed for years, paralysed from head to toe. Work and still more work, I say.

[she, cantankerous, rebellious] Only then will the muscles stay strong enough to support a ruin, however much they may creak.' Whereupon she sits down and pulls up weeds. Then, kneeling again, she trims all the rhododendrons, as intently as if praying.

Even on the lawn she kneels a little later, with a spoon and a jar of blue powder. The remedy given to her by the hunchbacked shoemaker—'push a bottle with the bottom knocked out into the molehills, neck upwards, so that the wind fills the underground passages with a terrifying whistling'—hasn't worked. The bloody creatures are once again ruining her lawn. She has to put an end to it.

Once and for all.

She scratches a molehill open and carefully spoons in her blue powder. A few metres away her Roger turns in his sleep again, smacking his lips with content, snoring in the shade of a plastic parasol. Sunday afternoon, his only moment of rest. The canopy remains unfathomably blue and bel canto and reports babble from the radio. Will Beveren be champions this year? Nothing and everything at the same time. Wap-wáp, wap-wáp, wap-wáp. In Saint Quentin thick fog expected, visibility less than twenty metres. I know I mustn't ask, but how is your book going? The minders wait before releasing the pigeons. No more running away. Buggered, hu-hu-hu. Delete, delete, the Leie. Sint-Baafs-Vijve: thirteen beam shots lowered. On the banks of the Scheldt. Well hidden in the reeds. Once more, come on. The canopy is blue. The world is vast. / Life too. / We're not.

That's enough.
Begin.

she

(OR: DUMBSTRUCK)

ON THE DAY that fate strikes they are eating pizza and watching the end of the evening news. She and he, Josée and Roger, side by side. Glass of red wine to go with it, and also a green salad with freshly chopped onion, slices of tomato and grated cucumber, all sprinkled with a simple vinaigrette and a garnish of ground parsley, 'since [she of course] just because you're eating a pizza, you mustn't lose sight of your vitamins, certainly not at our age, and especially not in the depths of autumn, and ... Roger! Can you turn that TV down a bit? A person can barely hear themselves speak. And anyway it's those football results again. Very soon you'll know them off by heart.'

Words to that effect.

The napkins are simple but indestructible damask, and from frequent washing have become as soft as a child's pyjamas. The cutlery, as old as their marriage, is silver-plated and has recently been given another polish. The handles, with their curlicued decoration, shine like they used to, 'because [she, militant] just because you're both in your eighties, there's no need to get sloppy. Style is a matter of will, and of continued will. People have only themselves to blame or to thank.'

True to that motto, every morning they complete the

crossword puzzle of their regular paper, *Het Laatste Nieuws*, together, to sharpen the memory and hone the mind. In case of disagreement a three-volume dictionary is consulted. With English supplements and French films she regularly consults her dictionaries, still in the old spelling. She has repaired the front and back covers, which had become detached, with black insulating tape, cadged from a theatre technician.

To strengthen the body too against wear and tear, after doing the crossword puzzle, on her initiative and against his wishes, they lie down together next to their table, on the Persian rug, for a series of cautious sit-ups.

'How many more to go?' [he, on the rare occasions when he grumbles]

[she, imperturbable] 'Be quiet and carry on.'

That's what their morning is like.

It's evening now and they are eating pizza. The crystal wine glasses have been produced, as they are every evening, from the china cabinet, in which the finest components of their finest service are displayed alongside their most precious ornaments, on glass shelves three or four storeys high. A school of motionless decorative fish in an aquarium brim-full of purple water, since the cabinet, narrow and high, has two doors and two sides with mauve leaded lights.

The pattern that the lead-lines follow is diamond-shaped. The glass is the same kind—with optical undulations and here and there a colourless pane—as that of the terrace door which, right opposite the cabinet, opens onto a balcony overlooking the street. Well, 'balcony'. A zinc base, two plant tubs, a wrought-iron balustrade in a black circle, that's it. The terrace door has exactly the same lead diamond shapes, in exactly the same dimensions, as the doors of the crockery cabinet. A mystery or a stupid coincidence, since it must have been put there before Fat Liza moved in, hence long before the cabinet was acquired to serve one floor below, where she and he lived for as long as they ran the butcher's shop. It's now twenty-five years since they packed it in. 'You can't believe [she, she, she] how fast the years fly by, though you've nothing to look after but yourself. How did we ever manage it back then? With the shop too? And five children? It was lucky that in those days I had no time to think about it. And that I had my theatre. And that bungalow. Otherwise I might have been tempted to give it all up and go and live as a tramp under a bridge in Paris, released from everything, from shitty nappies to customers. Believe me, I wouldn't have made a bad job of it as a tramp. If you do something, you must do it well. Even begging and roaming about.'

She isn't very interested in France as a whole, but Paris and its symbol, Édith Piaf, are in her top drawer. 'What a life that poor woman had to lead! But that voice, that voice! [she, between horror and rapture] She sang until she dropped. That's what I call great art.' There is one other French emblem that wins her favour. In the passage to their bedroom hangs a plaster replica of the death mask of the Happy Drowned Woman. An anonymous woman, fished out of the Seine fifty years ago, dead as a doornail but with a blissful smile like that of a teenager after her first orgasm. It is a popular image with her whole generation. Most of her sisters and cousins have one hanging on the wall too. A woman who died in complete intimacy, who defies death 10,000 times on many Flemish walls. Endlessly smiling, despite the colour of the wallpaper, let alone the flower pattern.

Back to the living room, where she and he are just putting a second piece of pizza onto their plates. Only the stained glass, in the cabinet *and* the terrace door, gives the decor of the room a certain coherence. This cannot be said of the rest of the effects, the furniture first of all. Eclecticism sets the tone, as everywhere in Belgium, from architecture to the constitution, from bourgeois interior to morality. One person calls it anarchy, another liberalism. A third bric-a-brac.

In the terrace door the mauve glass tempers the brightest sunlight. In the cabinet it quite simply tempers all light. Rumour has it that exposure to too much brightness is disastrous for ornaments in French biscuit— refined white earthenware very suitable for depicting longing faces, and hands with fingernails covered in jewels, down to the minutest folds in crinoline. But it is excessively brittle since it has only been fired once. 'Does that surprise you? [she, contemptuously] You know what the French are like? Great panache, but little aptitude for hard work and thoroughness. Even dusting they do half-heartedly over there. It's no accident that when we say "in the French way" we mean "carelessly".'

Anyone looking around doesn't get the impression that skimping jobs or dust will ever have a chance in this room. Although obviously not every biscuit ornament has a right to equal protection. On every cupboard corner, every windowsill and every table there is one simply gleaming in full light, usually surrounded by knick-knacks in terracotta, or dishes with or without fruit in them, or vases with or without flowers in them, or travel souvenirs in plastic and papier-mâché, or photos in frames of all sizes, or ashtrays in all shapes and colours, or plants and miniature cactuses in a wide variety of pot holders, from modern Delft blue to authentic

Cologne pots—one even in plasticized papyrus, a present from a thoughtful visitor to Egypt.

On the mantelpiece stands a three-part set with exuberant embellishments and gilt work, imitation-eighteenth-century, the centrepiece of which (a petrified whipped-cream cake) supports a round clock, a Cyclops eye wearing a monocle, which you can swing open to wind up the clock with a toy key. You can turn as hard as you like, the elegant hands won't budge: the internal spring snapped off decades ago. The outer elements of the trio—a female (left) and a male courtier (right), who each step forward out of a summer house—are actually two vases, which no one dares use because with flowers they would tip over off the mantelpiece, straight onto the gas radiator, which looks like a filled-in open hearth with a copper cover.

If you wanted to see Josée Verbeke politely irritated—although she knew well enough that you were just teasing her—you had to go into her living room, looking around with a sigh at the knick-knacks which she had accumulated over the years, and inquire: 'Where's the blunderbuss? This is just like a shooting gallery at the fair. And I don't think two hundred pellets will be enough.'

You could have said the same thing in her bedroom, if she let you in at least, which she was reluctant to do, because there must be etiquette, and etiquette likes privacy. [she, displeased] 'Not everything from before the occupation needs to be thrown overboard. The Germans destroyed much more than Zelzate and Zeebrugge, and later the Cinema Rex in Antwerp, with a flying bomb, the cowards. Manners were never the same again. And the royal family even more so.'

All her curios are on ornamental napkins or lace doilies, most of which are round and not much bigger than a beer mat. However, some jewels are assembled on a single oval napkin, itself ringed with a halo of fringes. The figurines are arranged on it as if for an extravagant group portrait. In it a porcelain ballerina from before the First World War can happily keep her crossed hands under her chin and raise her pointed foot up and to the side next to the obituary card of a former supplier of smoked ham and brawn, who a month ago had been run over on his bike by a municipal bus. 'The man had only just retired. [she, melancholy] Even his bike was brand new. The things that happen.'

Beside the deceased supplier of charcuterie there stands, cool as a cucumber, the wooden, slightly Cubist fisherman that she herself brought back from Japan— the furthest journey ever granted her by the theatrical bug and theatrical societies, thanks to an exchange project between the Flemish Association for Catholic Amateur Theatre and its naturally Shintoist counterpart in the Land of the Rising Sun.

The pièce de résistance of the collection is placed on her big cupboard, which is an angular and sparsely decorated affair, almost three metres long, with six square doors and whose main stylistic feature is robustness.

Her eldest brother, an architect, designed it himself and had it made just before their marriage, during the penultimate year of the war, when oak was prohibitively expensive and scarcely available. One of those six doors locks, and during my childhood *was* always locked. Behind the tough oak were the most expensive strong drinks and many of their little secrets.

(I knew where the key was, and on the few occasions

when they went out in style—to the Mayor's Ball, or the Annual Celebration of Christian Shopkeepers, and were suddenly out all night, 'because [she, worldly-wise, pig-headed] what if someone occasionally goes out? Then it's better if he does so properly. There's nothing better, after a night of dancing and pleasure, than a hearty break-fast: a pan of eggs and bacon, fresh brioches from the baker across the road and two pots of really strong cof-fee; then opening the butcher's shop with fresh heart and trying to keep your eyes open until the evening, when you can shut up shop again'—those few times, then, that they went out were sufficient for me, also staying up all night, and sometimes at intervals of six months, to read Jan Wolkers' *Turkish Delight* and Jef Geeraerts' first *Gangrene* novels, books I had heard so much about, although not from my parents, who never-theless simply had them in their mysterious cupboard.) (All other papers, including their marriage certificate, their passport and a handwritten accounts book with lots of deletions and addition sums, I left untouched. One should not try to know everything about one's par-ents.)

I still haven't said what that pièce de résistance is, on top of her long cupboard, in the centre in all its splendour. A sculpture, again in biscuit, but this time as big as a squatting cat. The Holy Family, painted in pastel shades. Mary, Joseph and the baby, with on its right shoulder a dove peeping round guiltily.

'Make sure [she, deadly serious] that no one tries to deny you that sculpture if anything happens to us. It's an heirloom from your grandmother. It survived the flight from West Flanders to here, during the last big gas offensive when your grandfather and her had to flee as fast as they could with the horse and cart, with the maid, a son and a daughter, and just a fraction of their belongings, including this sculpture. It's a miracle that it didn't get broken on the way in that wild torrent of refugees in which people and animals were trampled underfoot. It's older than your father, who was born here in the Vermorgenstraat. If you don't like it, you can get rid of it, I'm not crazy about it myself. But don't ever let anyone take it away from you. It's yours.'

The sculpture is on an oval wooden base and under a glass bell jar, to stop it getting dusty. Under that wooden base is also a napkin, of antique Bruges lace. When their house contents are sold off, in just over a year's time—he leaving alone for the oversized room in his old people's home, she for the institution for human jetsam—the lace napkin and the glass bell jar will fetch more than the Holy Family.

They have now almost finished their pizza and their salad, and are listening, chewing attentively, to the weather forecast, which this evening is being broadcast to them by their favourite weatherman, the one with the moustache. That gives us the chance, before the fatal moment arrives, to cast a quick glance over the rest of the setting. The decor is half the story.

The candelabra has three arms, each of which is gilded and elegantly curled and ends in a matt-glass rose, at the heart of which is a bulb. The arms are all attached to the outside of a ring, also gilded. On the inside hangs a graceful chalice of cut matt glass, hollow side upward. Underneath, at the centre of the chalice, a gilt protuberance hangs down, like the point of an inverted First World War German helmet, pointing to the round living-room table just below, the one with the glass top that rests on a wickerwork base. One of the few possessions that will survive the move to his oversized room in the old people's home.

Apart from a wall clock and a pair of bone-dry holy water fonts—a crumbling palm branch has been pushed behind each of them—only monumental items are displayed on the walls. Above the mantelpiece: a mirror with bevelled edges and a luxuriant frame, again gilt, almost as high and as wide as the chimney breast itself. On the wall opposite: a machine-woven tapestry, in which two late-medieval characters are riding through a wood on horseback with falcons on their fists, without noticing the many hinds and hares behind their backs, watching them go past in surprise. The tapestry is partly hidden by a two-person couch—an elegant, stylish piece of furniture with white wooden feet, curled arms and decorations in gold paint, covered in moss-green velvet, fastened with an endless row of brass drawing pins. The cushions are the same moss-green velvet and at the top, halfway along the back, where friends, family members and total strangers have to lay their heads, there is again a battery of napkins. 'To protect my cushions. [she, disgusted] You can't believe what people put on their hair nowadays. That's if they wash it at all.'

Above the cupboard designed by her brother stands a painting by her elder sister, Maria the Artistic, who for years lived a few streets away. 'You mustn't tell anyone, [she, slightly embarrassed] but I always thought your Aunt Maria was better than your uncle. Our Maria had a golden touch, everything she painted came to life, while he had to sweat and strain to achieve half what she achieved. He used to stand and curse over still lifes of hers, which were so striking, so natural. He had to become a house painter, and the rest didn't amount to much any more. But he saw to it that she stopped too. If only that woman had been able to go on painting! She didn't have an ounce of support, and in those days it wasn't usual, a woman making a career in art. Our Maria could have conquered the world. Now the poor thing is in an institution, she no longer knows what she said or ate yesterday, she has difficulty recognizing her children and can't remember her paintings at all. If I ever get like that, you must shoot me straight away. It's not compassion keeping someone like that alive. It's cowardice.'

The work by Maria the Artistic, above the long cupboard, is a copy of the *Negro Heads* by Rubens. Four times the same African with a fringe of beard, 'painted from life from different points of view', as art catalogues describe it. A black model, a lost soul from sixteen hundred and something, who can be found in many other paintings of the Flemish master as a Wise Man from the East or as a slave, and who thanks to Aunt Maria looked at me all through my childhood, indeed from different points of view. While I was reaching my verdicts, alone in the abandoned flat, I felt four pairs of eyes boring into my back. Each time a condemnation from the very same occasional judge from sixteen hundred and something.

(The junk dealer whistled in admiration. 'Not bad, for an amateur.' But he was buying it for the frame, he said. Sober, good craftsmanship, with a nice patina.)

Finally, just above the china cabinet there hangs, quite daringly in view of the colossal weight of the carved frame alone, the crown jewel of her pictures. An engraving of the old school, easily a metre square, probably printed at the beginning of the twentieth century, depicting Rubens' studio while he is painting and commenting, standing at his easel facing a white female model in a feathered hat. They are surrounded by visitors and walls covered in well-known masterpieces. 'They're going to be fighting over this! [she, proudly] It was almost included in an exhibition, here in the Municipal Museum, during the Rubens Year. But they didn't quite have enough space for it.'

(The Rubens House in Antwerp, when emailed with a photo of the etching attached, was to decline our generous offer with thanks. The junk dealer who took the Negro heads offered a ridiculously low price. The item remained in the family.)

Supper is over, and the plates are in a pile with the cutlery on top, ready to be taken into the open kitchen. Shielding her mouth with one hand, she digs at her dentures with a toothpick, mechanically, more from habit than necessity. 'Like a toothpick should be. [she, dogmatic down to the smallest details] Hollow with two sharp ends, in white paper packaging, and made of material resembling the shaft of chicken wings or hedgehog spines, which people once used to make their own toothpicks from.' On the TV an announcer lists the evening's programmes.

He has got up and opens the terrace door, giving in to one of his few vices. His curiosity. In the shop he had the nerve to interrogate everyone in a friendly manner, without distinction, from children to old bags, widows to the unemployed. He did not avoid any subject. Divorces, illnesses, rows, gossip. Until his Josée called him to order with a hiss, and also—invisibly, thanks to the counter—gave him a kick in the shins. 'What are you up to, Roger? [she, in a whisper, but meanwhile looking very affably at the same customer] You're giving that poor old dear the third degree. You're just like Sherlock Holmes, you are.'

He puts his head outside, full of curiosity. There's a wind blowing, it's drizzling, dusk is falling, not very inviting for a walk. The evening rush hour is almost over, except at and around this junction of which their property forms one of the corners and where, in spite of all the department stores in the town centre and all the shopping malls for miles around, a number of small shops still do good business, because together they form a mini shopping centre. A baker's next to a greengrocer's next to a newsagent's, a little further on a chemist's and a florist's, diagonally opposite a shop selling bird seed and bird cages and chewing rings for dogs, round the corner a supplier of cement and bricks, and over there a butcher's—it's true: no longer under their flat. Their previous tenant, without warning and just before his lease expired, opened a brand-new butcher's shop on the other side of the street, quite simply in a terraced house.

At first they were furious and desperate; now they are grateful to him. Their former business has become an added attraction, from which the whole neighbourhood benefits. Anyway it's a perfect location for a shop like that, on a corner and, mark you, on the oldest road to Antwerp. Actually it's something that was always lacking here. A chip shop.

'Roger, love? [she, annoyed] Do shut the door. There's a terrible draught.' That's the last thing she says in the language he is familiar with from her.

'They're queuing out in the street again,' he says, contentedly closing the terrace door and pushing the roll-shaped draught excluder firmly back against it. 'It's the same every evening at this time. One car after another parked or stopped in the middle of the road with all four indicators on. And to judge by the plastic bags, it's not only chips they're buying. One person takes away half a chicken, or curried sausages or hot dogs, or what do they call them nowadays? A chip shop like that sells everything, from cans of lager to soft drinks and cigarettes.' He turns round to her and has the fright of his life.

Her eyes are unrecognizable. Empty, deathly, icy. She seems to be staring at something behind him. Her lips purse, relax again, purse, relax. As if they were preparing to spew out something large. Saliva is leaking from her mouth. A first drop is already falling from her chin into her lap. Her napkin remains unused. Her hands are trembling on the tabletop.

'Josée?' he asks, at a loss what to do, then taking a step closer after all. 'Is something wrong?'

Finally she looks at him.

Her expression has not changed.

For a few seconds they gaze into each other's eyes. Then she flies at him. With a voice that is scarcely hers any more. And with a scream full of wordless revulsion and rage.

NO ONE, FAMILY member or neighbour, has ever known my parents fight, or even have a heated argument, as all of their children and grandchildren can do so well. She could do it too, with panache, with anyone if she had to, from policeman to director, fellow actress to offspring. Except with him. He offered no resistance, preferring to let everything wash over him, until the other person fell silent.

Anger did not suit him. He simply had no gift for it. Indignation, fury, disappointment, he bore them all equally passively, with a wounded dignity you would expect from old aristocrats, representatives of oppressed peoples. In addition there was something ordinary, even ingenuous about him. He just didn't like fuss, loud voices, aggression. There were moments when you worried that he did not belong in the world of carnivores. He could preach reconciliation with a look of gentle reproach, followed by a deep sigh and the shaking of his round head. Then he would turn away and go and fill sausages in his workshop, or scrub the floor, until people had come to themselves again and the storm had passed.

The real reconciliation, I suspect, took place in bed. Talking and otherwise. Passion—albeit behind the constantly closed doors of the parental bedroom—was obviously less alien to him than rage. Their eldest sons were born in the same year, the last year of a world war. The first came in January, the second in December. [he, with eyes sparkling] 'From sheer pleasure. What else do you do when you're young?' [she, shrugging her shoulders] 'We'd read somewhere that it couldn't do any harm, provided I breast-fed. After our second, though, we went about things more carefully.'

At the right moment she seized her chance of revenge, with identical weapons. They would be out, or playing cards with friends, or staying behind after a theatrical reception, anyway: he would have one too many and start playing the comedian. Telling bluer and bluer jokes, although always the same ones, and always to the same people—a caricature of his daily routine behind the counter. Except that here, after delivering the punchline, he was bold enough to wink broadly at the prettiest woman in the room, not counting my mother.

She would say increasingly insistently that it was time to go home. He would reply with mounting assertiveness that this was his very last pint. Finally she had to take the wheel of their car and when they got home shake him awake from his intoxication. And she did so only because she did not want neighbours or customers to see her other half in this obvious state. Otherwise she would gladly have left him sitting there in his Vauxhall Cresta, his head lolling back, snoring and smacking his lips with his mouth open.

He would spend the rest of the night downstairs, on the sofa. The next night the same. And the next night again. All that time she scarcely deigned to speak a word to him. It was not clear what stung her the most: that he had put on airs or that he had defied her, in the presence of everyone, I ask you. She let him work alone for hours 'in that shop of his'. When it really became too busy, with a surge at midday or toward dusk, caused by impatient housewives and irritable workers from the surrounding mills—the queue of waiting customers was starting to cough and shuffle like a theatre audience during an overlong scene change—he would come nervously and remorsefully into the living room to request her to come to his aid. 'The people don't understand what's happening. They're asking for you.'

Without answering she would go on ostentatiously filing her nails, plucking her eyebrows, hunting through the obituary notices in her paper for the tenth time. For a full quarter of an hour she let him and his customers stew in their own juice. Only then did she make her entrance behind the counter. With a frozen smile and a voice of stone.

After three days' penance she was finally prepared to listen to him. An audience was nothing compared to this. She: arms folded, thin-lipped, a look to kill, thawing out more slowly than a freezer cabinet. He: humbly begging, pleading, arguing for forgiveness, naturally promising that it wouldn't happen again, speaking more words than he usually did in a day. All in all a grotesque exhibition, no longer bearing any relationship to his misdemeanour, disproportionate revenge in the family arena.

And perhaps also a part of the foreplay. It was an early night that evening, and not only for the children.

Apart from this rare ritual—he getting merry too quickly, she having difficulty in forgiving him—and apart from their daily squabbling about trivialities, I never had to witness neurotic scenes from a marriage. Plates remained unbroken, glasses intact, voices spared. Coming to blows was completely out of the question. She wouldn't have tolerated it, and it would never have occurred to him. He made us laugh when occasionally, quite frequently at her instigation, he did dish out a pedagogical slap, which we deserved because we, as a family of seven packed into our far too small house, had again got up to monkey business. We saw *him* as the monkey.

In order to control his rage and still convert it into that one warning slap, he had to call on all his strength, running counter to his true nature, which was so strangely pacific. He could phlegmatically chop the heads off poultry, he casually broke the neck of a rabbit held upside down with the side of an extended hand, he skinned and quartered a dead hare while the customers waited, without interrupting his comments on the rather poor spring weather. In the abattoir too nothing upset him—the last squeals of pigs or the rattling of the chains with which a dying bull was hoisted aloft, ready to be ripped open from throat to crotch. But now he had to force himself. He had to assert his physical authority over a mischievous adolescent, one of his own children.

He raised his tightening shoulders until his neck threatened to disappear into them, held his trembling head half backward, opened his eyes wide, frowned and especially he pushed his tongue so hard against his bottom lip that the lip protruded forward, revealing his pink tongue behind the lower lip—all actions we performed when we wanted to imitate a monkey. Except that we also bent our knees and, scratching our armpits with our hands, wobbled and limped around producing jungle noises.

A chimpanzee. That's what our father reminded us of at the height of his anger. And his anger was already not very credible. The vicious smack that followed could never quite erase our hilarity.

On one occasion the hilarity turned into bewilderment and fear of injury. Guy, the middle child of the five, who was also the Brightest, Sportiest and especially the Most Awkward, the idol of every teenage girl in the neighbourhood and the whole of his football club Excelsior, and early fan of the Beatles and hair that was allowed to grow over the ears, had once again shown his most unmanageable side.

He did not need much to rebel against. Pocket money withheld after really bad school results. Refusing to admit that the packet of cigarettes in his satchel was his. Fibbing about his part in a fight after school or in teasing his younger sister—two of his favourite hobbies. Or flatly refusing, as everyone else did, to play a part in the many activities of the business. On the contrary, he demanded his right, commandeering the brand-new Schaub Lorenz transistor radio, to sit outside on the low windowsill of the bathroom, his royal box in the theatre of the street, from where he wanted to watch the tumultuous fall of a city evening, the newest makes of car and the little female beauty whom he whistled at together with the mill workers, some of whom were not much older than him.

My brother was not the only one who enjoyed witnessing the end of a working day in our neighbourhood. Lots of housewives placed a chair on the pavement with its back against the front of the house, and then, with their arms folded or looking around as they knitted with satisfaction, some of them already sipping a glass of Trappist beer, all chatted together imperturbably, if necessary from one side of the street to the other, with one hand to their mouth and raising their voices if a bus or a lorry passed by. Gossip was not whispered with us.

The mills meanwhile emptied out their workforce like a crude musical without a director. Exhausted and in blue overalls, workers, looking sullen or, conversely, mischievous, left their spinning mills, twineries, dye works, weaving shops—all sections of the local hosiery mill, the pride and wealth of a late-blossoming industrial town. The textile workers gave the blunt and frank impression that they were at least aware of this: that without them their bosses' prosperity would not be so opulent and that they needed very little provocation for a wildcat strike. The roughest section of our clientele.

They stationed themselves noisily at the bus stops, or they wobbled slowly away on old bikes with no lights, almost all smoking like Turks, almost all in the possession of a worn satchel containing an empty bread tin, an empty thermos flask and a couple of empty beer bottles. The office staff passed by without greeting, keeping up a brisk pace, lost in thought to the point of arrogance, the men in suits with hats and briefcases, the women—noses in the air—in two-pieces and medium-high heels. Very occasionally, when crossing a side street, balancing on the uneven cobbles, they lost their imperturbability together with their balance—much to the amusement of the housewives, and even more of the women among the workers, who earned their living in the spinning mills and weaving shops, where the work was more delicate and wages often higher than those of their husbands in other departments. Divorces were common, reinforcing the young town's reputation for godlessness. The women always walked about in a group in light-blue dustcoats and the loudest mules in the hosiery mill, as challenging as their male colleagues, giving as good as they got for every vulgar sneer—when they were not the first to shout and whistle at some hunk. Some of them popped quickly into our shop for a few last-minute purchases, steak for supper or filling for tomorrow's lunch box.

As they passed they all said hello to my brother. He knew most of them by name. They all knew him. One pinched his cheek, another offered him a cigarette. He refused her, blushing proudly, looking the woman who had offered it even more deeply in the eyes. A trainee Casanova.

His refusal to continue being a cog in the machinery of a family business—where there was always a mincer or a pile of bloody display plates to be washed up, where cheese, prawn and potato croquettes were rolled by hand and coated twice with breadcrumbs, where no more than 100 grams of ham on the bone or slightly salted horsemeat was sent for home delivery, by a son of the family on his bike, before he went to school, if necessary five districts away, because [she, waving her index finger] 'One must be happy with every new customer', 'no one is beneath us or too grand for us,' 'standing at the counter everyone is equal'—that refusal, that rupturing of the elementary harmony of the shopkeeping class, was what weighed heaviest in his reproach. The fact that in addition, with people outside, he was the most Popular One and in his intimate circle the most Unmanageable, did not plead in his favour. He was *asking* for a reprimand. An example must be made in order to avert a general family revolt.

She could confiscate the Schaub Lorenz for a while herself. But the smack. The mater familias judged that that was best dispensed by the pater familias.

All eyes were focused on him, a reluctant father in a butcher's apron, and him, a rebellious son, who since last month refused to wear short trousers, except on a football field. In the Waasland swimming club he is the hero, the great hope for medals. At competitions in the Municipal Swimming Pool, with its booming acoustic and its all-pervading smell of chlorine, the name 'Guy' is chanted even before the starting gun sounds, to intimidate his opponents and to urge him on.

'Tell your mother you're sorry,' says the father, more indignant than angry. 'I can't see why,' says the son, with *her* look, *her* stubbornness, *her* beauty. And with *her* eloquence he actually adds a plea, which is less a plea than an indictment against the manifest injustice that is being committed against him in this frustrating environment. That he hasn't enough time for his training sessions. That no one in his class has to do as much washing-up. That he is laughed at by his mates when he has to deliver half a pound of sausages just before school 'to some old woman' who also strokes his head when she pays. That in this house, in this system, he is abused, exploited, looked on as staff. That his pocket money must be increased, or else they should employ a real assistant. And that his mother herself cuts corners where she can, that she stays in bed a lot longer in the mornings than her own husband, and that she has a quite a leisurely breakfast before she is ready to help in the shop. And that she wastes more time with that stupid acting of hers than he is allowed to spend on his swimming club and his football.

That last remark is going too far. The indignation of the good-natured, taciturn butcher turns after all to anger. And sure enough, his eyes open wide again, and there goes his tongue—pressing against his lower lip, becoming visible, pink in his reddening, contorted face, an Oriental fighting mask, contrasting sharply with the white apron. The smack lands. Fiercer than ever.

For that very reason the butcher does not trust his trembling hands, with which he is so used to holding knives. He looks for a symbolic but innocent object, something that is designed to neutralize the violence with a certain slapstick component, and he finds a plate. Not even a big one. A dessert plate. From the everyday service. The kind you eat your rice pudding off. With ribbed edges. By the time he brings it down on the head of his son, he has regained enough control over his rage for it not to be more than an allegorical blow. A smack that must derive its humiliation from the everyday nature of the object with which it is dispensed, and not the strength of the blow.

Nevertheless the dessert plate breaks cleanly in two, to everyone's consternation. The broken-off half smashes on the stone floor of the workshop.

For a moment parent and child, equally flabbergasted, look at the remaining half-plate in the hand of the father-culprit. Only then does the son feel for his head with a loud cry, sink wailing to his knees, start rolling his eyes like a dying sheep and accuse his father, as pale as a ghost, of a crime.

And although it may become immediately clear that the unfortunate father picked up precisely the plate that shortly before had already been broken in two and that she, the thrifty homemaker, had tried to repair with glue that turned out not to be resistant to hot washing-up water—[she, indignantly] 'That stuff isn't the universal glue it's cracked up to be!'—and although as a result the rest of the family starts laughing at the crybaby, taking the side of their Dad and not the show-off, and although she finally draws a line under the incident by telling the son to stop whining and clear away the shards—he, the born rebel, goes on cursing and complaining about headache and domestic violence. He also shares some of her talent for acting.

After his stormy adolescence and far from smooth marriage, he, divorced and chastened, will make it up with her. A grown-up Italian rediscovering *la mamma*, suddenly discovering more similarities than differences. He will also, in the town where he lives, seventy kilometres away, tread the boards of the amateur stage, in substantial roles. Apart from that he remains what he always was since, on the windowsill of our bathroom, he let the world pass him by, with the Schaub Lorenz next to him and the music of the early 1960s in and around his head. Skirt chaser, life and soul of the party, hedonist, disc jockey to the day of his death. Fell asleep in the early morning at the wheel of his Honda Civic, left the road, hit a tree, neck broken, over and out.

Scarcely thirty-two.

Except for that dessert plate no household effects were ever broken in Mr and Mrs Lanoye's home in family skirmishes. Until that particular evening. They are both in their eighties and she flies at him after they have had a simple pizza. Without cause, foaming at the mouth, and with a cry in a non-existent language.

Now two plates and the same number of crystal wine glasses are broken. They fall off the table and are trodden underfoot in the tragic struggle of two eternal sweethearts.

IF HE COULD just make out what she is saying, he would be able to understand what has got into her. But she spews out an unstoppable flood of raw sounds, rough fragments of sound, stray plosives alongside long-drawn-out cries, snapping stammering, linguistic goo full of remnants of words and hissing, barbaric gibbering—a general slang whose vocabulary and grammar she invents on the spot, without realizing that no one else knows her diabolical tongue.

Her command is that of a demagogue at the height of his ranting. Her voice sounds shrill, terrifyingly forced, ready to break, her pale, waxy face is feverishly wet with sweat. It obviously pains her, yet she goes on stubbornly threatening. She waves an accusing index finger at her husband, as though he were committing a crime in front of her eyes. The less he understands her, the more furious she becomes. The more he begs and asks for an explanation, the less she seems to understand his language either.

It just makes her angrier.

She dives at him and grabs him by the neck, ranting on tirelessly at the top of her voice in her loud gibberish. He tries to squirm free without hurting her, but she clings to him indignantly, clasping his trunk with both arms, roaring all the louder the more he resists. There they hang, shackled together, inseparable, entwined in a suffocating, degrading tango. Two dogs after a failed mating—and one is trying to tear the other to pieces.

Riveted together in their gruesome embrace, they first lumber furiously against the corner of their china cabinet, their mauve aquarium full of fragile decorative fish. Inside all sorts of things break. Then they bump painfully hard into their table—also a robust design of her eldest brother, the architect. During the last year of the war they slept every night between the solid legs of this piece of furniture, with its reassuring double-thick top. Every day they made an emergency bed of pillows and rolled-up blankets, their temporary air-raid shelter of down, oak and wool, where she breast-fed her first-born and afterwards laid him to sleep between her and her young other half, who couldn't care less where he slept, on or under a table, provided it was close to her. Indeed, he found it rather playful and exciting, an improvised four-poster bed like that. Their second child may have been conceived there, under the table.

In the mornings she didn't like leaving the safe nest. 'And if I had listened to my instinct? [she, decades after the event, all the time] We would have stayed living under our table, long after the Liberation. [she, she, she in that splendid, never-faltering stream of words she used to produce, the mellifluous speech that for so many years she commanded so masterfully, her speech from before that disastrous evening, the language of her former self—*my* oldest source, my mother tongue, my verbal DNA: she, she, she] I would have liked to live under this tabletop until the Germans capitulated completely. I would have done the washing and gone to the toilet, cooked and eaten, I was so scared of the flying bombs. I had been able to see the devastation they caused with my own eyes. Wait for it, you could *hear* them coming. A long way off. A bubbling sound, like a moped in a deserted street. As long as that could be heard, everything was safe, but God help you if it stopped. First there was that silence that drove you crazy, and then—even worse—came that whistle, louder and louder, that sounded like destruction being delivered to your door, a cross falling over a school, a street, a neighbourhood, a town if need be. In the Gasometerstraat one fell in the middle of the night. All that was left of a dozen workmen's houses was a pile of rubble, full of groaning casualties and crushed bodies. On the pavement in front of me was an unshod woman's foot that had been torn off beside a man's hand with a wedding ring, waiting for the corresponding bodies, assuming they were ever retrieved from such havoc. I looked at it, that pink foot, that hairy hand with its wedding ring, and I thought to myself: what if a bomb like that were ever to fall on *our* place? Then there'll be no better spot to be than under our table. Solid Flemish oak! A double top! Even if five floors fall on our heads, we'll survive everything, we'll be safe for ever there.'

Now, grown old and joined in their heart-rending *danse macabre*, they hit it with full force. The table scarcely trembles. But the plates and wine glasses are swept off it in the struggle. They smash to pieces and crunch under the soles of their slippers as they stumble onward. A sound that goes right through you. A sound that has never before been heard here.

He beseeches his Josée to stop. He whines for explanations. Finally, caught in her arms, he does what she has hated all her life in a man. He cries. She pushes him away from her, strong as an ox, with the uninhibited force of the deranged, and she scolds him unabatedly in her infernal dialect of which he still doesn't understand a word, but in which the reprimand can be easily guessed. He is making a fool of her, he is torturing her, with his incomprehension, with his pestering, his existence.

Suddenly she calms down. As unexpectedly as she erupted. The silence is unnerving and ominous. She sits down, again staring straight in front of her, gasping as if in great pain, chewing on something imaginary, totally losing sight of the presence of her husband, not even paying attention to the broken plates and glasses, a sight which normally would have shocked her.

He takes advantage of the strange interlude to call his eldest son. Out of her field of vision. And in a whisper, so as not to reignite her wordless wrath.

IT IS NOT the first time that one of the two eldest sons is rung up to avert an acute domestic crisis. The most recent occasion concerned a more tragicomic scene that was played out in their narrow, far too small bathroom.

Everyone had warned them about it.

When the time came for them to retire and give up the butcher's shop—to the surprise of family, friends and acquaintances—they did not move into a convenient sheltered flat, or to more spacious accommodation with at least a lift and a garden. Everyone could go on imploring till they were blue in the face, everyone could point to Roger's dejected silence, whose protest as usual consisted of a sigh and a shrug of the shoulders accompanied by an 'Oh, what difference does it make', Josée stuck to her guns: there was nowhere better for them to spend their old age than in this familiar neighbourhood, on this familiar corner and in this flat, even though it was the former home of their ex-landlady, Fat Liza. The observation that she was now going to play the role of Fat Liza in turn—mistress of all those who carried on their business a floor below—made her angry. She had nothing to do with that woman. She would do things so much better, as a landlady.

Perhaps that was the motive of her stubbornness.

Revenge on a dead woman who had so often browbeaten her.

While she was alive Liza could be called quite simply an unpleasant and surly person. She was also grossly fat and lonely, although she did not even live alone. Her loneliness was in her head.

Her body reacted accordingly. It seemed to want to fill every gap, those in her mind and those in her surroundings. When Liza sat on a chair her shapeless bottom hung deep over the seat on all sides, occupying as much space as possible. The human body as an instrument of *horror vacui*. Her face also suffered from the need to fill up every available space, and gravity. Lips, corners of the mouth, cheeks, eyebrows, eyelids, eye sockets, earlobes, chins, everything about Liza was disproportionate and every hung down with complete conviction. Her bosom was no exception.

The word was that she came from a well-to-do Brussels family from whom she had become estranged through drink, a scandalous liaison in her youth, an addiction to gambling or a combination of all of that. The mildest and the melancholics were convinced it was an unhappy marriage beneath her station and nothing else. I never knew whether the mumbling ancient who wandered around in her rooms—in a sleeveless, dirty T-shirt and a pair of trousers the crotch of which was always swaying at knee-level—was her shameful lover from the past, her proletarian husband or a now demented chamberlain from a previous, richer life. He might also have been her brother. I never knew him say a word to her. Irreconcilability hung in the air, mixed with the odour of expensive cigars smoked long ago and stale piss.

In my memory Liza lives on as a shrew whom I scarcely dared peek up at, so much did I dread a witch of the sort found in my picture books and my nightmares. She looked the part, down to her hooked nose. Yet I went on boldly and nosily creeping behind my mother when she went to pay the month's rent, up the stairs to Liza's stuffy quarters. Our hell was on the first floor.

The stairs to it were narrow and steep with a sharp turn in the middle and at the top a door that could be locked. On the treads a worn carpet had been gathering dirt for years, and was scarcely kept in place by its brass rods, coming dangerously loose here and there and in one place even torn; I saw my mother looking at it and frowning while she knocked on the door, submerged in sombreness, louder and louder, until on the other side a bolt grated and a key was turned in the lock.

Liza, as always dressed in something wide and dark, did not say hello and shuffled back to her regular chair. She sank onto it with a sigh, at a table strewn with mending and papers, full ashtrays and half-empty glasses. 'What's wrong this time?' She knew well enough why we had come, but she couldn't help taunting my mother.

My mother sat down on the other side of the table, looking straight at Liza. She didn't send me away, back downstairs; on the contrary, she let me crawl onto her lap, of course in the hope that Liza would allow herself to be distracted by a curious, anxious child's face.

But Liza remained looking at her alone, through round, dirty, thick lenses, with tufts of unkempt grey hair sticking out a long way around her head, and with a voice full of shards: 'Right, what's the problem, Madame Lanoye? What do you need this time?' She stank of sweat and revelled in her power. She owned this property freehold, she granted a young butcher the privilege of renting, and hence she had his future and that of his family in the palm of her hand, and not a month went by without her threatening to clench that palm into a devastating fist, if necessary just for the pleasure of wrecking someone else's prosperity. She regularly announced the arrival of a mysterious relative who had supposedly passed an official slaughtering course and was just looking for a suitable location to start his own business. For the benefit of relatives one could throw tenants, who were complete strangers, out on the street, tenancy agreement or no tenancy agreement. That was the law and we would do well never to forget it. We needn't expect an accommodating attitude. Blood was blood. A butcher of all people should know that.

She refused to pay for urgent repairs, she tried to increase the rent as she saw fit and she pocketed deposits, complaining about non-existent water damage, or offensive smells caused by the waste from slaughtering, the twice-weekly collection of which she disputed, although she could have checked it with her own eyes if she had managed to drag herself to her balcony, into which her body just fitted—the few times that she stood there glaring, like an insect queen that had crawled out of its subterranean chamber, gasping for fresh air and blinking at the daylight. The wrought-iron, semicircular balustrade was like the skeleton of a hooped skirt, scarcely large enough to enclose her waist and thighs. It was a miracle that she was able to turn round and waddle back inside.

She pretended that she had heard rats running about in the false ceilings under her floor, and after one telephone call from her the health and safety services could come and seal everything, and that she would reclaim the lost income from us, if necessary with legal proceedings into the bargain. She invented purchasers who had offered fortunes for the whole corner property, to knock it all down within two months and replace it with an ultra-modern block of flats, with a hairdresser's on the ground floor and with herself, glorious Fat Liza, in an open-plan penthouse on the eighth floor, with a marble balcony overlooking the street and a spacious roof terrace full of plants and flowers—happy at last, fêted at last, finally truly appreciated, no longer with her prosperity frustrated by chronic debts and endless family quarrels and criminal offspring and ungrateful tenants, who refuse to see that their welfare was due to the benevolence of her and her alone, Fat Liza. She was just too good for this world. In proof of which she was prepared this month again to receive our far too paltry rent. Albeit with reluctance and in exchange for a handwritten receipt, with which she taunted my mother by making her wait while she entered the sum in her two cash books—one legal, one illegal, two different amounts.

Sitting on her lap, I felt my mother's body trembling. The trembling of someone who is trying to control themselves so as not to jump up, fly off the handle, run amok and take flight. I recognized the trembling of impotence. I also often found it difficult not to explode, in the playground, or on the way to school, goaded because of something trivial. A red veil of rage descended over your eyes, rage that almost automatically translated itself into actions, sometimes into stamping of the feet, but mostly into roaring, going wild, raging like the beasts. Short-fused and long-winded, a family affliction like any other. 'If they tease you, you must learn precisely not to do anything in reply. [she, on numerous occasions, with the air of one who knew from experience]

The best counter is to clench your teeth, however much effort it takes. By staying silent you can torment your greatest demons.'

I wanted to believe her, but it was just that I saw her put precious little of that advice into practice. She talked back to everyone. It came naturally to her, she did it well, and that made me proud of her. She used her violent tongue against everyone, wherever it may be, in the street, in her shop, and definitely on the boards of the municipal theatre. Few others had the gift of a quick tongue. That is why it shocked me that she simply sat there restrained and trembling, right opposite this bitch, this lumpy woman.

I looked up at her in disappointment. She? As silent as if she had been murdered.

She did not even look back. She kept her eyes focused on our landlady. Firm and confident of victory, defeating Liza's threats and body odours with the most deadly anti-aircraft weapon among women: openly displayed compassion. All the more humiliating the more one actually bites one's tongue, and cocks one's head properly, and carries an innocent child on one's lap that one can stroke on the head now and then, supposedly absent-mindedly, giving the impression that one is not going to let one's good humour and smile be soured by anything, by neither slander or insult.

Go on, goad us, just try to needle us, Liza. We'll give you a friendly nod, but we think you're pitiful.

Only when the door closed behind us again—she pulled me by the hand as if we actually had to flee a modest inferno—did she start to thaw out. Even on the dangerous stairs I heard her fuming furiously under her breath.

From front door to front door it was no more than thirty paces, by the time we were back in the workshop of the butcher's her capacity for bluster had completely revived. On the understanding that she raged in muted tones, since the floors and walls for which she had once again paid so much rent carried sound into the bargain. She refused to give Fat Liza the satisfaction of being able, possibly already lying flat in her kitchen with one ear to her filthy linoleum—to gloat over her tenant's vexation.

Instead of her landlady her husband got it in the neck. She: 'It's unbelievable the rubbish that lump of lard came out with.'

He: 'Don't worry about it. She's a sad old woman.'

She: 'She's a sadistic bitch who deserves her misfortune.'

He: 'It's over. You've done with her for another month.'

She: 'If you ask me, she washes her hair with lard.'

He: 'We weren't going to speak ill of people.'

She: 'Have you ever heard her when she gets going? While our youngest is sitting there.'

He: 'Leave him at home then, the next time.'

She: 'He has to get to know the world as it is. You take him to the abattoir too, don't you?'

He: [sighing] 'What has an abattoir got to do with Fat Liza?'

She: 'She wouldn't be out of place, upside down on a hook.'

He: 'We weren't going to speak ill of people.'

She: 'Why are you defending her again? It's always the same with you. When it comes down to it, you're always on the other side. Your own wife is the only one who gets everything wrong here. I always get it in the neck.'

He: [sighing] 'Shall I go and pay the rent next time?'

She: 'You? You couldn't cope with that cow, with her

blackmail and lamentations. You'd let her pull the wool over your eyes. Even if she doubled the rent, you'd be capable of thanking her on bended knees for what she was doing to us.'

She was about to add all kinds of other things, but he already turned round, shaking his head and sighing. Silent in his turn, the winner in his turn, although he saw it as anything but a triumph. He felt ashamed and unhappy rather than triumphant.

She did not apologize afterwards. She never did that. That must also be recorded, for the sake of honesty. Josée Verbeke? For all her gift of the gab, when it came to making excuses she relied again and again on the power of tactical silence. The pressure of work in the butcher's shop and the passage of time would excuse her automatically.

And indeed, her Roger allowed the wool to be pulled over his eyes. By his wife. He let himself, with satisfaction, be led into reconciliation without sound, forgiveness without confession. He knew, he *felt* that her regret was genuine. That was enough. For him there were already enough words in this world.

Equally, for the sake of honesty, it should be recorded that all who were in need, even Fat Liza, could call on Josée the Merciful. Anyone who appeared at the counter having gone all pale, or who was suffering from a stubborn cough was fobbed off, often unasked, with fresh chicken bouillon, or hotpot with sprouts and pieces of turnip and an ox tongue, or home-made herb tea in which a bitter taste was dominant, thanks to the dried and chopped dandelion roots that she had personally dug from the lawn of her bungalow, next to the molehills that just refused to disappear.

In the case of Liza the help was even more tangible. Twice a month a nurse from the White and Yellow Cross called on her, for a task with which a nurse could not cope on her own. The nurse parked her white and yellow 2CV outside our door, but did not come into the butcher's shop. With a sober cap on her head, and under her open blue anorak dressed all in white and grey, she stood at the largest of our two shop windows until she was noticed. She exchanged a discreet nod with my mother, who—seized by unusual anxiety—immediately untied her butcher's apron and crept out of the back door. This time I was not taken with her to the hell on the first floor.

And this time they scarcely spoke up there. The three people involved knew the routine and their part in it. Fat Liza was already sitting calmly, on her usual chair and with her upper body bare. She was washed in all those places that because of her size she could not reach for herself. My mother acted as assistant. Standing on a firm stool behind Fat Liza, she bent first over one then over the other monumental shoulder in order to lift first one then the other monstrous tit. Liza helped too, supporting her shapeless breasts as well as she could, in view of her breathlessness and lack of strength. Her hands and those of my mother touched during the process, which only increased Liza's surly embarrassment. But all she did was sigh and growl. The sneering was dropped.

My mother, bent over the nape of the giantess's neck, held her breath for as long as she could, then quickly breathed out deeply and in deeply. With her mouth open, not through her nose, so as not to start retching. Meanwhile the nurse went on imperturbably with her task, with a sober, neutral expression on her face, not condemning and not condoning. With her flannel she briskly rubbed Liza's oily white skin—smooth and blue-veined: soft marble. She regularly rinsed the flannel in the bowl that stood ready, wrung it out with both hands, lathered it with generous quantities of Sunlight soap and went back to work.

On days like this the rubbing of wet cotton on skin and the splashing of a little water in a zinc bowl were the only sounds in the modest inferno, besides the languid ticking of a clock. Apart from that there prevailed the intense silence of women together, women who know what can happen to a body—that it can love and expand in discontent or in peacefulness, that it can give birth in the most intense pains and spasms, and that it can become as cold and hard as pale basalt, when the time comes for its last wash.

When she reappeared in the shop, my mother looked a lot less belligerent than after paying the rent. First she went and washed her hands thoroughly, then she put on her apron again ceremoniously, then performed a few quite useless tasks—with both hands she moved a tenderloin steak from a bloody to a clean display plate, or she rearranged the bunches of parsley on and next to a dish of ribs on display—before we could hear her whisper to her Roger: 'Oh dear, that poor woman. She's not healthy. No one knows how much longer she'll last, herself least of all. She's afraid. She has worries. You can feel it. One day a moment will come when life is no longer worth living. For all of us.'

After which, anxious as she was, she fitted decorative sleeves made of festive white paper round the legs of the roast poultry.

ONE FINE DAY Fat Liza fell forward on the filthy balata flooring in her kitchen, flat on her face, felled by a heart attack and choked on her own vomit. Her husband, lover or lady's maid was by then already out of the picture—having moved house or died themselves.

There was no sign of relief or schadenfreude one floor below. All the more panic. Who would the rent have to be paid to now? After what threats and sneers? Liza's possession, formerly sole ownership, was to pass to just under a dozen heirs.

What were their plans? Did they have any?

One of the heirs was Lucienneke, called Our Mongol by every child in the neighbourhood, or else Mad Lucienneke, in both cases to her own great jollity, because she liked being popular with young folk.

She had her Aunt Liza's round head and broad shoulders, but she was only half as tall. A pristine twenty-year-old with Down's syndrome. If you asked her, she would pull her skirt over her head with a giggle and let you see her knickers, which were like a gymnast's shorts, except that they were grubby white and trimmed with a kind of coarse lace. Her pink thighs and knees were sturdier than those of a footballer. On her nose she wore a pair of glasses, the lenses of which made her eyes double in size. Playing around her mouth, from which her tongue was constantly flopping out, was a fixed smile which made you wonder whether, regardless of that syndrome of hers, she could possibly be related to Liza.

If you asked Lucienneke what she wanted to be later, she would reply: 'Canada.' If you asked her what work she wanted to do, she would reply: 'Canada.' What ice cream? What game? What sweetheart? 'Canada.' She had been left behind by Liza's niece, who with her two other children and her husband had emigrated to the promised land of that name, which offered a warm welcome to all hard workers and their children, provided they had no genetic defects.

Lucienneke had lived with her Aunt Liza for a while, helping in the house for a monthly allowance, transferred across the Atlantic to assuage guilt. You couldn't trust Lucienneke with much more than stuffing the wet washing into the spin dryer. And even then you had to keep an eye on her, or she would lift the lid before the spinning washing had come to a halt. Once she had almost lost an arm when she grabbed at a pair of her knickers before she had even switched off the machine.

On another occasion she made a mistake while washing up and put not detergent in the water but caustic soda, which Liza used to unblock drainpipes and toilets. By the time the mistake came to light, Lucienne's skin had been eaten away to above her elbows. Her hand looked like raw meat. Her huge, wide eyes were running, but her smile remained, even when she was given a ticking-off, which she answered faithfully and proudly with 'Canada'.

It wasn't to be Canada, it was a home. Cheap enough to have a little left over from the allowance from overseas. It gained Lucienneke a mention in Liza's will. That's how we translate feelings of guilt in Europe.

A more substantial heir, Liza's son, was nicknamed Elvis. He couldn't sing, but he had sideburns and a liking for Mustangs and old Mercedes. He couldn't afford them, but that didn't stop him buying them. He knew all the bailiffs by their first names. He was a head taller than the tallest of them and the head of the smallest fitted into his right fist. None of them dared to approach him without having two gendarmes with them. Sometimes they got hit anyway, all three of them.

His mother no longer opened any doors to him, neither the one downstairs nor the one at the top of the stairs. She recognized him from his way of ringing and the other tumult that he made, convinced as he was in advance that his mother would not lend him a cent again this time, 'the bitch'. In the middle of the night he pounded with his fist on the wooden shutters of her only window on the downstairs floor—the small washroom next to the stairs. Then he raised his fist, feet astride in the middle of the street, up to the first floor, where he knew that Fat Liza was listening to his cursing with her heart in her mouth. She gave no sign of life until her son roared off without accomplishing his mission in yet another Mustang, watched by half the neighbourhood, who were hanging drowsily out of their windows enjoying the fuss. Only Liza did not show herself.

Elvis had impregnated a sixteen-year-old child-woman on the back seat of a Mercedes convertible, and just before she gave birth had driven with her to their wedding in a Mercedes Pagode. There were ten guests at the celebration and still things ended in a fight. When his eldest daughter turned thirteen, he raped her in her own bed and started shagging her as often as he did her mother. The girl went to the police, and he went to prison. In view of his extensive criminal record, he was given three years. When he got out, he rushed in a taxi to his home and his many children, found his wife with a friend who was helping her in the house, forced the two women to go instantly to bed with him and afterwards beat them both black and blue 'from jealousy'. There was no new indictment. The eldest daughter had gone abroad. The younger ones cultivated eating disorders, in view of their approaching puberty.

Elvis dreamt of a career as a boxer or a dance-hall proprietor, but he worked alternately in construction and at the Antwerp docks. Nothing seemed to bother him or bring him down. Until one day he turns round in a wharf in bad weather and gets the hook of a crane full in the face. A deliberate attack could not have been better executed, and he has always remained convinced that it was a settling of scores.

The point of the crane hook bores into his mouth, knocking out all his front teeth. At the same time the hook begins rising at top speed. Normally it would have bored its way through Elvis's palate, penetrating his brain, perhaps even tearing his head open like a ripe fruit. But in a reflex both Elvis's hands first grab the hook. He pulls himself up on it as well as he can, so preventing his own weight from dragging him down to his death. But the hook is wedged immovably in his mouth.

Like a thrashing fish Elvis is lifted up, set down six storeys higher and freed with great difficulty. When he arrives at hospital he has lost two litres of blood and twenty teeth. He never fully recovered his self-confidence after that.

Mad Lucienneke was in her home, Elvis was at his last gasp in his hospital, so who would come and inspect the flat on behalf of the collective heirs? Liza's family from the Brussels area. In a shiny, one-year-old Jaguar.

It is a couple of fleshy giants that get out. The surly woman is, from hooked nose to bosom, a younger version of Liza. Her husband is a bookkeeping type, with braces, horn-rimmed glasses, a pinstripe suit and a nervous cough. They have money written all over them, and come striding into the butcher's shop at the busiest moment of the day, but they let everyone go ahead. The presence of two posh strangers who do not order anything deflates the usually jovial atmosphere. Suspicious silence predominates. Moreover, the pressure continues. Liza's sister, scarcely any thinner than the deceased, sits down with a sigh, peering sarcastically around her, on one of the two stools intended for elderly and pregnant customers.

Roger and Josée exchange a look of concern. Their stool, besides a seat in coloured Formica, has only three slender feet in chromed steel. An accident can easily happen, and an heir can be even more easily upset. Up there the woman, with a crocodile-leather handbag on her imposing lap, is leaning with her back against the most vulnerable rack. Preserved vegetables in glass jars, an expensive German make. If she slides backward the damage will be incalculable. Only last week Sidonie with the Hare Lip brushed it—she was drunk early in the day, as every customer had been able observe with his own eyes thanks to the shop window, in which Sidonie, well framed like on a cinema screen left the café across the road and zigzagged toward the butcher's, furiously raising her unopened umbrella at every car that tried to hoot her off the Antwerpse Steenweg—last week, then, Sidonie wobbled as she went out with her full shopping bag past that German rack. Four jars of mushrooms and two containing white beans in tomato sauce smashed dully on the floor, one after another, in a joyless delayed-action firework display. Sidonie refused to pay for them, and instead stood loudly protesting, pointing at her new shoes and worn-out bag that were covered in tomato sauce, to say nothing of the umbrella from which she was inseparable. One had to ask her, as always—and certainly now she was three sheets in the wind—a few times what she actually meant, before her hair-lip dialect could be deciphered: 'Pay for your jars yourself. You shouldn't pack your racks so full. That's the easy way to become stinking rich: take in a poor widow and put the screws on her over a few jars. You should be ashamed of yourselves.'

The next day Sidonie came to pay, accompanied by so many apologies that everyone gave up going on deciphering them. Eventually a butcher and his customers simply stood nodding their heads mechanically at a remorseful woman with a hare lip, who was justifying herself in roundabout riddles.

The stool with the chrome-plated legs holds up until all the customers have been served and have gone. Liza's sister gets up laboriously, puts her elbow on the counter and, flanked by her husband, begins a cross-examination of the two promptly paying tenants. My mother answers, coolly and calmly, flanked by *her* husband.

When did they last speak to Liza?

'When we paid the rent, ten days ago.'

Did they see or hear anything suspicious before the death?

'I wouldn't know what, madam.'

Did they hear the bump on the kitchen floor?

'You hear all kinds of things in this neighbourhood, madam.'

So *did* they hear the bump?

'We didn't hear anything for a week. That alarmed us more.'

Did they hear Liza calling or anything?

'No. Otherwise we would have gone and helped her, wouldn't we, madam?'

Did they see or hear anything suspicious afterwards?

'Like what, madam?'

Did they see anyone fiddle with the front door? See them slip inside? Did they hear footsteps? Banging, creaking, swearing?

'No, madam.'

Is she sure?

'As sure as eggs are eggs, madam.'

And what about the gentleman here?'

[He, surprised, caught out] 'Yes, yes. Of course. Certainly, madam.'

'Also as sure as eggs are eggs?'

'Excuse me, madam! [she, affronted, vehement, receiving a kick in the shins from her Roger in turn] If *I* say yes, then it's yes and not no. Okay? Did you require anything else?'

Moderately satisfied, Liza's sister pushed a visiting card across the counter, with the request to ring her immediately should anything else suspicious happen. Whereupon she left the butcher's without buying anything at all, followed by her pinstripe suit with braces, and started fiddling with Liza's front door herself with a pass key until the lock gave way.

Shortly afterwards increasingly loud creaking and banging forced its way through the thin walls. All the frames in the flat seemed to be suffering. The fact that the creaking suddenly became even louder proved that even the floorboards under the balata were not being spared. Now and then in the false ceiling the sound could be heard of a blindly rummaging hand, scratching like a roaming rat.

The demolition work lasted more than an hour and it was carried out with such intensity that you suspected that professional demolition men were behind it. Only then did the occasional demolition team come back outside, still panting from their efforts and adjusting their clothes, while Roger—in his capacity as occasional Sherlock Holmes—just happened to be sweeping the pavement at that very moment. He gave a friendly nod, but received neither a look nor a word in reply.

Just before Liza's sister pulled the door of the Jaguar shut, he heard her snap at her pinstripe: 'For Christ's sake, she blew the whole lot. On his Mustangs and his Mercedes.'

ONLY AT THE public sale, months later, does Roger see the two occasional demolishers again. They are sitting in the front row and once more do not waste looks or words on the butcher who for years has rented their inheritance at too high a price and today hopes to purchase it for a reasonable sum.

He is forced to sit next to them. There is no other chair free in the crowded back room of Café Hemelrijck on the Grote Markt. They even ignore his proffered hand. Deliberately, he suspects, to disturb his concentration and shake his resolution. He feels the storm approaching. This auction is going to be torture. The room is blue with smoke, the hubbub is mounting by the minute. An angrily buzzing wasps' nest, ready to explode in his face.

He is alone, in his Sunday best and ill at ease. Nevertheless this location is not unknown territory. As well as a venue for communion and wedding banquets, it also serves as a rehearsal room for their association, the Royal St Genesius Theatrical Circle. At least on evenings when it has not been commandeered by rival amateur companies, or diet gurus with constantly new followers, or travelling faith healers with their never-changing religious show.

He would rather be sitting here with Josée, just in

front of this familiar low platform, her favourite domain, on which a notary, an auctioneer and a clerk are now sitting at a quite ordinary café table discussing in what order the available properties will go under the hammer. He would also have preferred to leave the actual bidding to his wife. Josée the Versatile also has a better command of that side of life than he does: the vulgar but refined art form of the auction. Poker without cards. Bluffing without being paralysed by fear of loss of face, and damage to your wallet.

On Mondays, their quietest trading day of the week, she regularly goes with a friend or a sister-in-law to an auction room in Antwerp, where house contents are sold as a result of death or bankruptcy. The furniture and the largest items are auctioned off separately. The small items are sold by lot—collections of arbitrarily assembled objects, carelessly packed in old newspapers and stuffed into boxes, or umbrella stands or laundry baskets, which also form part of the lot.

Equally regularly she comes home with one of those surprise packages. Usually there are actually three. ('I scratch my nose, that auctioneer thinks I am making a bid and brings down his gavel. What can I say? I don't need it, I've already got two? That doesn't wash with those folk in Antwerp.') Only when you unpacked one of those umbrella stands at home did you know whether you had been cheated or made a coup. According to Josée the Versatile the coups predominated. Most of the figurines, vases and ashtrays in her living room and bedroom come from these bric-a-brac raffles. That is why they almost all have defects, a crack or a dent—scars of venerable utilitarian objects. Together they form inheritances briefly kept together. Little enclaves of past lives.

Collections once lovingly saved, now for a while spared from the diaspora of things thanks to a guardian angel who happened to drop by in Antwerp. In hanging on to things Josée can match the best of them. She refuses to master the art of throwing out. 'Does that surprise you? About me? [she, palms upward, shrugging her shoulders, eyes rolling] I've been through one war and heard my parents complaining about another. In a case like that you're reluctant to throw anything away. It's like with screws and drawing pins. They may be crooked or blunt, but you still keep them. They'll be of use one day, if only to repair a toy, or if need be some dentures.'

In each of her rooms there was an umbrella stand, filled with a bunch of walking sticks that no one ever used.

In that sort of room full of shouting, fighting verbally for a hat box full of knick-knacks, his Josée had nerves of steel. There bidding was exciting, a proof of boldness, a bravura act, the umpteenth role on the boards of reality.

In Café Hemelrijck it wasn't an umbrella stand that depended on the bidding, but the future of seven people, her family no less. Here of all places, in this room where she is used to trying out freely what occurs to her, to think up variations on the classics, with or without the permission of her director, in this room where she is not embarrassed to raise or distort her voice, always one of the first to be off the book, snapping her fingers imperiously at the prompter if her memory does occasionally falter after all, in of all places this royal domain of hers, between these four walls where she always seemed to have everything under control, she is absent. Her excuse: 'Someone has to keep the shop open.' The real reason: she can't always face reality. That is precisely the advantage of theatre. There you can pile adversity on misfortune, consider suicide *and* murder *and* adultery, genocide or genuflection, anything at all—but everyone at least knows their cues and their place, and the end is reassuringly fixed. Mostly there is actually a happy ending. ('And why not? People like it. A piece doesn't have to be a melodrama to go down well.')

An existence away from the boards is so much more treacherous. Certainly for mortals with a lively imagination and an oversize capacity for empathy. There is no shorter definition of an actress. Unless it is: 'Felled too quickly and passionately by empathy.' That deficiency caused her problems in many areas. She who so liked to appear strong.

She didn't care two hoots about football, but when she once went along to watch a game with her son playing centre forward—her Sportiest, her Brightest, her Most Awkward—during the first half at every pass she kicked excitedly at the backs and heads of those sitting in front of her. She felt a piercing pain in her own head whenever someone dared to clear a high ball with his head, she cried out herself when her flesh and blood was upended beyond the dead-ball line, she felt more than he did the shooting pain in the heart when he missed the target and was jeered and sworn at.

She followed the second half from the canteen. Without a view of the pitch, with her hands over her ears, with palpitations and nauseous with tension. 'Where were you then?' snapped her Most Awkward Son, scorer of the winning goal in the last minute, when the applause that had accompanied his entrance had died away. He asked loud enough for all the others to hear him. 'I don't understand a thing about that game,' she lied, 'but I am very happy for you and your team.' 'If you really are so happy, stay in the stand in future. I don't walk out of your plays when I can't make head or tail of them.'

After that she never went to another football match with him in it. 'My heart can't take it. And I don't think he likes it.'

When her eldest sons started to go out, and at night had still not shown up a quarter of an hour later than the agreed time, she was again seized by that nausea and those palpitations. No café brawl or concertina crash was big enough to equal her fantasy. Her sons had been mutilated, had gone missing, were ruined for ever. 'A mother knows, a mother feels.' Another quarter of an hour and she was half breathless with panic. She persuaded her Roger to call the police, the gendarmes, plus all the surrounding hospitals.

He had just got through to the second hospital when the prodigal sons came in cheerfully tipsy, immediately sobered up and put out by the sight of an extremely upset father with the telephone receiver in his hand, and a mother who, with a cold compress on her forehead, was lying full-length and delirious on her sofa, describing her terrors in half-sentences and explicit reproaches, and her feeling that she had actually been choking—and no one knew whether she was acting or speaking the truth. Or no: perhaps she had started acting so convincingly that she had broken through the reality barrier, like an aircraft breaks the sound barrier. Acting that she was seriously ill, she had *become* seriously ill.

But it struck everybody how quickly that compress no longer proved necessary. Even resurrection is a question of talent.

Liza's house is auctioned as the penultimate lot. The back room of Café Hemelrijck has already half emptied. From the café at the front comes the sound of lots of laughter and swearing, the popping of bottles of fizzy wine and the shouting of orders.

Finally the clerk reads out the summary description. 'Property for sale', 'business enterprise', 'favourable location', 'Antwerpse Steenweg', 'undivided estate'.

The notary starts the bidding low.

Although his Josée had so impressed on him not to do it, Roger is the first to raise his hand. Those who show their eagerness are in a weak position. But it is stronger than he is. He is eager. He is weak. He wishes it was over. With or without the house. What is he doing here? It is *his* heart that is now beating wildly. This will end in tears. You see it all the time.

But there is actually a silence after his bid. Most people know him and understand what he wants, respect his ambition, grant him his business. Or perhaps they are saving their fortune for the last lot, the pièce de resistance, an Art Deco villa on Waasmunster heath. Times are bad for property speculation. Interest rates are at a historically high level. One can't buy everything in times like these, and if one has to choose between a historic villa and a rickety corner house with a sitting commercial tenant?

The auctioneer points his gavel at him—'the bid is with the gentleman in the front row', his eyes scan the thinned-out rows while he continues to repeat the amount bid. Four times. Six times. Eight times—when will he knock it down? Surely it's obvious there is no interest? Ten times, twelve times. The auctioneer still points his gavel at the only bidder like a microphone at a minister at bay.

Don't move now. His Josée warned him. Never break the spell yourself. Don't cough, don't blink, don't fidget. Undergo the torture as if it was the accepted course of events. As it is.

The auctioneer keeps on repeating the amount. Fourteenth time. Fifteenth time. A note of irritation creeps into his practised voice. He casts a sideways glance at the notary. He gives a scarcely perceptible shake of the head, his eyes closed. The property is not withdrawn. The sale will continue.

Could it be that it is as simple as that? Raising your hand once, and securing your future for ever?

It is the woman next to him who with the voice of Fat Liza shatters his illusion. She does not even raise her hand. She barks a new amount that is ten per cent higher. All hell immediately lets loose. On the left, on the right, behind him, voices ring out, poking fingers and hands waving for attention are raised—people abandon their compassion, they smell an exceptional chance, why else would a stranger raise a bid by ten per cent just like that?

The auctioneer waves to each of the new bidders with his gavel as if blessing them with a sprinkler for their generosity, and at each blessing pushes up the price, rounding up the amounts, a neat piece of addition. He does not expect anyone to prompt him, he thinks for them and counts for himself. He only skips one of the bidders systematically—Elvis. He is standing at the back of the room, half his head hidden by a bandage. He is not capable of speaking, but raises his bear's claw all the more frequently, waving doggedly, in the hope of increasing his inheritance by pushing up the total amount, producing indecipherable sounds from behind his bandage.

The auctioneer does not bless him once, but all the more surely he ends up after each circuit with the butcher in the front row, who is ignoring his wife's advice and each time bows deeply again without fail, or raises his hand before it is necessary, and on one occasion, to his own shame, actually raises his right thumb, high above his head, thumbs up!, all okay!, fully visible to his opponents, in the hope of intimidating them with a show of self-confidence.

If they do become intimidated and fall silent, it is because of the price of the property. It has doubled in a few minutes. One of the best prices of the day. Only the man with the hammer seems unimpressed. He goes on imperturbably pointing the tool of his trade around, without blessings this time, till he arrives back at the butcher without having achieved his objective. 'The bid is still with this gentleman.' One final time his glance scours the rows. Even Elvis is no longer waving. 'No one else? Right then. Once ... '

Again a voice like Liza's rings out, from the front row. This time for a ridiculously small increase, instead of the ten per cent of just now. Such a move is unusual in the present state of affairs. There is furtive and disbelieving laughter on all sides. Even the clerk cannot suppress a head-shaking grin. The notary looks at his manicured hands. 'The bid is with this lady,' states the auctioneer, minutely repeating the new amount that he was not able to determine himself—with contempt, even he. 'No one else? No takers?'

He looks at my father paternally.

Josée has warned him even against this. There's no going back now. He should have passed a few times in the bidding frenzy. 'Let them think a few times that you're drawing in your claws. Give them plenty of chance to count their fingers and their cash. Make them doubt.' It's too late to sow confusion, and he knows it. He is paying more than he intended, more than he can afford, more than the property is worth. And over and above that extortion, which is his fault because of his inexperience, he now has to face the humiliation of trumping his neighbour's bid one last time, however pathetic that extra amount may be.

'Sir? Your last bid? The same huge increase?'

He doesn't give the auctioneer his assent immediately. He first bends over to Liza's sister and addresses her for the last time in his life: 'Madam, if Liza knew about this, she would turn in her grave.'

It is not the sister who answers him, but the pinstripe with the horn-rimmed glasses. 'I helped squeeze Liza into her coffin. It was hard getting a lid on. She won't ever be turning again.'

'Once, twice. Sold! To Mr Lanoye here in the front row.'

BEFORE SHE WOULD occupy the territory of her ex-landlady, Josée the Demanding ordered minor refurbishments and a thorough redecoration. 'There are just three things a house owner must pay attention to. [she, frisky, suddenly a tad parvenu] Maintenance, maintenance and maintenance. It starts with: your roof mustn't leak. Better a layer of roofing too many than a length of lead flashing too few. Apart from that an owner must rebuild and improve where he can. Every five-franc piece he spends will pay back handsomely later. Everything is an investment. *Everything*.' No one dared question her assertion.

Not openly at any rate. And not even face to face with her renewed stairwell.

Okay, the stair carpet had been exchanged for a cleaner and more sober one. The broken rods had been replaced, so that the twist in the narrow staircase no longer spelt danger for two recently retired people who would have to walk up and down it every day.

But all the mouldings, including the banisters, were painted a light green that would not have been out of place in an Italian dairy or on a Mexican roundabout. The wallpaper confirmed one doubt about investments that always paid off in full. Against a background of anthracite-black emptiness, luscious flowers opened wide with a cross-section of a metre, their petals and leaves executed in chalky white and shit-green, their calyxes in bright orange, their stamens in canary-yellow. They turned the narrow hall into a psychedelic jungle. Even the ceiling was papered. ('That's modern! It makes a change! [she, annoyed by the lack of enthusiasm for what she had done] One's got to keep up with the times.')

Anyone who liked a clash of styles could revel in a chest of drawers on the ground floor, panelled and French-polished, with inlaid brass ornaments, on her own testimony 'a late imitation Louis Quinze'. On the chest two candelabras recalled Prussian militarism. They were severe, clean-lined, sombre, heavy as bronze and four-armed. The arms fanned out from a single knob with a small eagle resplendent on it. You could lift up the creature by its wings, snuff out the burning candles with its hollow underside and then replace it on its eagle's nest. Except that no one ever lit candles here.

Among the candelabra stood a terracotta woman's bust with the nose broken off staring straight ahead with an offended look. On the floor in front of the wardrobe was a small Persian carpet. Above the wardrobe hung, surrounded by jungle flowers, the portrait of a completely unknown dignitary, full-length, wearing a pince-nez and with an atlas under his arm. She had picked up the painting cheap together with the candelabra, the chest, the bust and the carpet in her Antwerp auction rooms.

'On the very same day. [she, bragging] For a song.'

Anyone coming into this stairwell for the first time in his life wondered in desperation where he had wound up—the limbo of an independent freemasons' order or the vestibule of a rundown luxury brothel from the previous century. However, anyone who had known the stairwell under its previous owner showed understanding and even nodded approvingly. Josée the Much-Moved had wanted to make a radical break with the past. Her intervention was dramatic rather than aesthetic. She wanted to erase at all levels the memory of the horrid weight of her predecessor. For this, colours and motifs could not be daring enough. 'A first impression is the most important. That applies to applicants for a job, extras and interiors.'

Thank God not everyone lived according to her motto, otherwise most visitors would never have got further than her entrance hall. That would have been a shame. The rest of the accommodation had been adequately repaired and cosily fitted out after the demolition work of Liza's Brussels family, although admittedly a little excessively and seldom coherently, in accordance with the norms of our people. We sit together and feel—thank you very much—wonderful, from eating habits to narrative structure.

The only real problem had been the bathroom. The same one where so many years later their eldest son would come and rescue them from an awkward, then still tragicomic situation.

The second rescue would mark the beginning of the end game.

There had never been a bathroom on this floor before. No shower, no bathtub, nothing. In earlier years people washed daily at their bedroom washstands, standing on a towel, and weekly in the kitchen, standing in a half-full tub. As long as one could at least fill the tub and empty it again for oneself. That was the reason why Fat

Liza had sat waiting half naked on her chair until the nurse from the White and Yellow Cross came by to give her another wash, helped by Josée the Benevolent.

That doom—the memory of a surly, silent naked giantess in what was now *her* living room—had to be wiped away. Together with the spectre of ever being in the same situation: of having to wait helplessly until a total stranger was good enough to come by and wash you from head to toe, twice a month, no more. The fact that she had assisted at those sparse washes strengthened her in her fear. And she did not need much anyway to be horrified at the thought of defective hygiene. Her dislike of unwelcome body odours had a hint of obsession, her need for cleanliness bordered on a phobia of infectious diseases, and compulsive thoughts do not tend to cool off with the mounting of the years.

Her eye, trained from a young age by associating with masons and architects, fell upon the passageway that led from the living room to the bedroom. That was wide enough, she judged, to be divided in two with plasterboard and waterproof wallpaper. A second-hand internal door was easily found, and there would even be room for her heavy bathtub, which she wanted to move upstairs from downstairs, since the new tenant was only interested in their shop. ([she, uncomprehendingly, even rather insulted] 'He wants to live elsewhere. *I* could never have done that. The division of living and working? That's something for factory workers. A real shopkeeper knows better.')

The bathtub, made of solid old-fashioned enamel, could be placed lengthways against the existing wall. On the other side there would be just enough room, squeezed between the edge of the bath and the plaster wall, to shuffle to a simple washbasin, which neverthe-less would have to partly overhang the mixer tap of the bath to fit into the new room. 'Listen to me: if an oven, a fridge, and table, a shower, two beds and a wardrobe can be fitted into one of those caravans? Then this must be possible. Easily.' [she, quashing the last spluttering objections with a dismissive gesture]

Omer the Plumber, a friend of the family who had been engaged to do the job for a moderate price, had the cheek to contradict her, and in the presence of witnesses at that. 'I'm sorry, dear. That room is too narrow for your bath.'

She: 'You're wrong. I've measured it and done a draw-ing. Here.'

He: 'You're wrong. The bath is wider than in your drawing.'

She: 'You're wrong. You're counting the edge on one side.'

He: 'Suppose I have to saw it off? That will wreck your whole bath.'

She: 'You mustn't saw it off. You must make a groove.'

He: 'A groove?'

She: 'In the brick wall.'

He: 'A groove along the whole length of the wall?'

She: 'The same as for an electric cable, only wider.'

He: 'That's impossible. Your wall is too thin.'

She: 'I've measured it. It's just thick enough.'

He: 'Making a groove causes damp penetration. Always.'

She: 'Then you can slap some of that new product on.'

He: 'Silicon? That always comes loose.'

She: 'Then I'll put some more on myself.'

He: 'I don't like the idea.'

She: 'That's how I want it.'

He: 'It's DIY. It's nonsense.'

She: 'If you can't do it, then just give me that grinder.'

He: 'Out of the question. It's dangerous. Each to his own trade.'

She: 'Are you a builder's daughter, or am I?'

He: 'Are you the plumber, or am I?'

She: 'Are you the owner, or am I?'

The friendship was to suffer as a result, but Josée got her way. Against the conviction and the professional ethics of Omer the Plumber, who had been in the trade for over thirty years and had never before done anything against his own will. But who afterwards had to admit: 'You may be right after all, Josée.'

It was her all too triumphant laugh that damaged their friendship. Not the fact that she was right.

For fifteen years the bathroom with the caravan dimensions had served without a problem, leaving aside the sporadically bruised knee of anyone completing their toilet or shaving at the washbasin who turned round too abruptly and experienced at first hand how little leeway was left between edge and wall.

However, with the appearance of the infirmity with which age makes us pay for our past carefree behaviour, new rules were introduced in their smallest room but one. The treasured old bathtub, ponderous and deep, lost its attraction. It was *too* deep and its enamel too smooth. And because one of the edges was missing, having been ingeniously hidden, seamlessly slotted into the wall and finished with constantly new layers of silicon, their former handhold was missing on that side. For handles attached to the wall Josée the Mule was too stubborn. 'Handle? [she, not quite eighty] That's for old people and the handicapped. We're not either.'

Meanwhile, the last time she had indulged in a proper bath she had only been able to clamber out of the tub by first letting the water level rise to the overflow grille, and then sitting on her haunches facing the tiled wall, the way a frog half underwater prepares for a backward somersault, and then—helped from behind by her Roger, himself squeezed between the edge and the wall—had herself hoisted aloft until she could sit with her bottom on the remaining edge of the bath. Then she could carefully turn round, lifting first one then the other leg over the extremely slippery barrier, at the risk of sliding over during the latter manoeuvre and plunging backward into that bath, her two legs in the air, and with the risk of going underwater, perhaps even hitting the wall and breaking her neck, or at least her rickety spine, which needed only a caper like that to burst apart like a jigsaw puzzle on a trampoline ...

Well, a decision was taken—*she* decided—that bathing would henceforth be done as follows. First the bath would be filled. Then, half sitting, half standing, they would position themselves at one end of the bath. Not the end with the mixer tap, the plughole and the overflow grille, but the other end, where the edge is at its widest. First make sure that you are sitting firmly, then carefully turn ninety degrees, toward the bath of course, and again lift one of your legs, into the water this time, if necessary with the aid of both hands lifting up each leg below the knee. Held by the wrist by the other person, you can if you want stand in the bath, careful! careful! to wash or be washed, in fact the way people used to do it in earlier times: standing in a tub. But lying down was out of the question from then on.

'You can't have everything. We can cope.'

Her Roger misses the former comfort of lying, but he accepts the new regime. Prevention is better than an operation. One fine day he is actually sitting safely on that wider edge, with the length of the tub in front of him and with both legs soaking above the knee in a foam bath. But he can't reach his flannel.

She is not around, he doesn't want to call her, so he bends over, stretching for the wretched thing. He can't quite reach it. He bends a little deeper. He still can't reach it. He's a stupid centimetre away. He bends a little further forward. He gets hold of the flannel by the tips of his fingers. At the same time he feels himself slipping.

He tries to regain his balance, to grab hold of something, but his flailing hands find only enamel, smooth tiles, silicon, thin air. So he slides helplessly on his back: a fat child coming down the slide in a swimming pool—bent half back, legs up, bottom sticking out. His body makes a foaming wave that flows over the edges of the bath. He himself goes under.

That's how she finds him: on his backside in the bath, coughing, spluttering, rubbing his eyes, rising from a mountain of white foam as if from the gauze of a tutu that was too big for him. She has to laugh. Relieved that she is not angry, at the water on her wall-to-wall carpet, at the fact that he has tumbled into the bath again, he joins in the laughter.

The laughter subsides within five minutes. He can't manage to turn in order sit on his haunches for the frog position his wife has demonstrated to him. That one leg particularly refuses to follow suit. Last year he had an attack in it, some nerve or other packed up, and he had treatment, to no avail. He drags it behind him when he walks, nothing dreadful, but nor can it be hidden, everyone notices it. (To her annoyance. 'Look at the two of us.

Half a hunchback and a complete cripple. Soon we can go and live with Willy the Shoemaker, he's also got a hump and a club foot. But I was born like it, you weren't. You've just got to do your exercises, the ones the physiotherapist showed you. Well, do them then! Every day, it doesn't take more than five minutes!') (But he doesn't do his exercises, and he also refuses to wear his special support shoe, he chooses to combat the ailment by ignoring it, a butcher knows enough about flesh and bodies and tendons to realize that nothing can restore his leg to its previous state; 'my lazy foot' is the only concession he will make to reality, a pet name for an incurable ailment. He peers at himself in the street in shop windows, he sees himself hobbling past and shrugs his shoulders: 'A lazy foot—so what? There are worse things. As long as you're healthy.')

Now his lazy foot actually does trip him up. He can't get the damn leg either to turn or to lift. And she has too little strength in her old arms to lift him up, even though he is lying in willing water that can even float a steel boat. She simply can't get a grip on his naked skin, which is extra-slippery from the bath foam. It is not long before she is covered in it herself, in that snow-white foam smelling of pine woods that begins increasingly to get on her nerves. It is as if she has to pull a seal onto dry land and it slips out of her hands each time, back into its basin. She becomes desperate, he unhappy, together touchy.

[she, categorically] 'I'm going to call our eldest.'
'Wait! [he, unusually annoyed] But wait a bit. Josée? Let me try one more time!'
She has already left the bathroom behind his back. Leaving him alone. Sighing in his rapidly cooling bath water.

Half an hour later he allows himself to be hoisted out of the bath under her supervision by his eldest son. Naked, ashamed, reduced to a child by someone he had given the bottle to, whom he had put a clean nappy on with his own hands, under their oak tabletop, in their temporary four-poster bed, listening to the silence of the night, afraid of flying bombs. He lets himself be swathed in a big towel and rubbed dry, as he himself had done with each of his five children—when they were still small he threw them, still wrapped from head to toe in their towels, over his shoulder as if they were a newly delivered quarter of pork, and to their screaming horror he went into the shop with them, asking amused customers if they fancied a juicy cutlet—'You won't find fresher!'—after which he uncovered their bottoms and lovingly hit them till you could hear the slaps.

Silently he allows a dressing gown to be draped around him. So the three of them shuffle out of this far too narrow space, *her* domain, *her* brainchild, which—however narrow—has lots of cupboards and racks, full of powders and ointments and creams of hers, bottles of eau de cologne and samples of perfumes of hers, jars of pills for her heart and her liver, flacons of deodorant and nail polish, flat tins of eyeshadow and brushes, cylinders with lipstick and mascara, and cases with nail files and scissors and tweezers.

He doesn't pull anything of that over as he leaves, doesn't knock anything on the floor. But he refuses to join them in the living room, not even with the prospect of an aperitif.

He goes to the bedroom and does not show up for the rest of the evening.

IT IS THE same son whom a few years later he rings himself, at the end of his tether, because his Josée seems to have lost her mind after supper. He can scarcely believe what he has to whisper to his eldest son on their mobile, safely out of her field of vision—she is sitting on her chair chewing on something non-existent, as pale as a ghost, staring straight ahead glassy-eyed, sweat pouring from her temples.

He tells his son how she attacked him without provocation. How she tried to strangle him. How plates and glasses have been broken. How he doesn't dare leave her alone, but can't control her. How he doesn't fathom where she gets such force from. And: how he can't understand one jot of what she shouts at him.

The jingling of the doorbell and the entry of my brother jolt her out of her trance. She lashes out violently again, again at her husband, not once at her son. He has to interpose himself between his two parents to protect one from the other. She is not susceptible to reason or pleading.

At the end of his tether, the son in turn rings for an ambulance. She is far from pacified by the arrival of the ambulance crew. She fights them off. They are obliged to give her a tranquillizing injection and take her away.

Then the rest of the family is alerted.

Even in Cape Town the phone rings.
One day later I land at Brussels Airport.
An hour later I arrive in my home town.

She is in intensive care, eyes flashing lightning, after a night of enforced rest, again tirelessly foaming at the mouth in her unknown language, her brand-new devilish dialect. Wide straps tie her to the iron hospital bed. They are tightened across her ankles, her thighs, her pelvis, her shoulders. But even so she still tries to wriggle free. She bends and twists her small, bony body against the straps. She doesn't want any electrodes on her skin and even less needles and tubes in her arm. She has already pulled them out a couple of times. Therefore—'in order to protect her from herself'—both her arms have been tied, one on each side of the bed. At the wrist, elbow, upper arm. With thinner straps, which cut into her flesh. Her powdery, wrinkled old woman's flesh of soft silk, of splendid, tender parchment. You can see the marks and grazes where the restraints have squeezed her previously. A torture without the name of torture. The more movement, the more pain.

Nevertheless she tosses and twists her old body to and fro as much as she can, stubborn, recalcitrant, barking at everyone, doctor or nurse, whom she sees or senses around her, in her unending stream of garbled sounds in which there are even snatches of French and English, and one maniacally repeated invocation, one formula, one order, one complaint. 'A little.' Two of the few words that come normally out of her mouth, that she articulates as she used to, although sometimes unbearably loud and in different keys, one straight after the other, without transition. Insulted, pleading, sneering, painful, furious. 'A little.' Her whole register, tried out on a retort of just two words. All the more poignant because they recall the playfully rhyming refrain of the song of the same name with which Holland won the European Song Contest the year after she had given birth to me. 'A Little', sung beautifully by a truly professional singer whom she rates very highly, a slight winner that she always praised for its linguistic power. ('Why don't you ever write something like that? A witty piece to sing along to for the little man. Why not? Nothing is beneath the true artist. And you can earn a bomb into the bargain.') Teddy Scholten, 1959, Cannes, 'A Little'. In grainy black and white it sounded coquettish and whiny. In these harsh hospital colours, in this neon light, it is a litany of rebellion, incomprehension, rage, pain. 'A little!' Afterwards another stream of spastic stammering and growling as if from a wolf cub, foam on the lips.

Aphasia.

She hasn't noticed me yet, thank God. I lack the courage to look at her for longer than just a few seconds, I don't dare touch her yet, I have to recover first. From the shock and self-reproach.

I hadn't been able to make much sense of the panicky phone call from the home front. I was pretty sceptical. For the whole flight I sat and got annoyed in advance. ('That woman can't do anything normally. Time and time again it's opera, the biggest possible gesture, never-ending blackmail. Time and time again manipulations, force, manoeuvres on all fronts.') At the same time, whizzing through ethereal air, thousands of metres above ground level, I was dismayed at such suspicion in myself. Was I not in turn suffering from the tremolo of bad operas, with my premature condemnation? Surely this could not be another case of her classic self-dramatization? Even she would not dare to push things that far?

Not that this would be a first try-out. Josée Verbeke—that is how she was listed on every theatre poster: under her own name, not even on grounds of feminism, because she found that a term of abuse, she wasn't butch, she didn't need emancipation, 'liberation' was something for moaning Minnies and neurotic women—Josée Verbeke, for her part, never shrank from a challenge.

Each time I left for a longer period—definitely when my destination was Cape Town, where she imagined I was secretly completing the necessary formalities year after year in order one fine day, as a fait accompli, to announce that I had officially become a resident of another country, on a vast and bloodthirsty continent, as far as possible away from my native land—sorry: as far as possible away from *her*—each time then that I was on the point of leaving, she managed to do it yet again. She called me, preferably in the middle of the night, urgently. Papers had to be finalized relating to their will or my will—did I actually have one? No? Was that responsible? 'Is that how I brought you up?' Big fuss on the other end of the line which ended, despite our having said goodbye yesterday, in my having to drop round again to dot a few 'I's.

I didn't want to, but I went.

Another time I had to buy her bungalow there and then with all the accompanying land, as their pension was less generous than they had hoped, and I wasn't making a bad living, was I? And after all, in a little way, 'be honest', thanks to them, wasn't that true? My poor father on the other hand was one of the many small-scale self-employed with a pension, 'the new lepers of society,' and she with her official status as a helper of the self-employed person was treated even worse by the government, 'as a leper among lepers'. It was lucky that in her youth she had worked for a spell as office secretary in that jute factory near Lokeren, otherwise she would have had nothing but nougat balls for her pension. Damn, it was as if she didn't exist, 'as if I'd accomplished nothing at all in my life'. 'Forty years a butcher and a mother of five, I ask you, all of them went to college, sir, all of them got a diploma in one thing or another, and they all did well—thanks to whom?'

Apart from that they had had to buy that 'damned hole' of Fat Liza's much too late in their career, much too pricey, with far too high a mortgage. They weren't on the breadline, but you couldn't call it luxury. In short: wouldn't it be a good idea if, preferably before I left for Cape Town, I bought the bungalow in the Puytvoet from them? Not that she expected that I would crash in my Boeing—on the contrary, she mustn't think about it, or she would lie down in front of it on the runway—but when I got back I would finally have some greenery and pleasure to enjoy on *this* side of the planet. Anyway, that was really necessary, I wasn't looking very healthy recently, bags under the eyes, grey hairs on my temples ('Even our youngest is going grey!'), but well, that wasn't surprising, I didn't get out into the open air enough, that was the downside of my profession, that eternal sitting indoors, at my desk, or on the plush seats of an over-subsidized theatre auditorium, always on my backside, always fretting, and in addition to that: the quality of the oxygen in Antwerp—boy oh boy! It's terrible, it said so just last week in her paper, though it isn't even that far, that Antwerp of mine, on the other side of the Scheldt that's true, a river stops most of the filth, yes, yes high in the air too, that's general knowledge, water has upward forces, it forms a barrier, that's why you can discover an underground lake in a desert with a divining rod, didn't I know that? Did I actually read enough papers? But anyway, what if I took the road tunnel, under that Scheldt of mine, that is? In the future I could come and sunbathe on my very own lawn in a quarter of an hour, if it wasn't raining, I could come and use the motor mower on my very own grass and pick asparagus as I wanted, in the right season, and nowadays even her strawberries were doing nicely, as long as those wretched sparrows and magpies kept off them with their thieving beaks, and when it was summer I could go blackberrying for miles around until I was sick, and in spring I could cut willow catkins and yellow broom to put in a vase at home, that's very decorative, definitely in one of those Antwerp lofts, one of those shoeboxes with nothing but white walls. Well, what did I think? Wouldn't that be a brilliant idea? My buying that bungalow of hers, well! 'We won't take you to the cleaner's, mind, and *you'll* have nothing but advantages. You can come and visit your parents every Sunday, on a long weekend you can occasionally sleep over, and you can easily invite all your friends for a barbecue—if you want your father can source the meat from former suppliers at a special price, I'll make the salads and the rice pudding. Well, what do you think? Surely you're not going to say no? Come on, buy the bungalow! Make your mother a happy woman for a change, instead of just your public as always! Without me you wouldn't even have been there for them.'

Before each departure there was a loose end of this kind to deal with at the last moment, and it always came down to this. Don't have the cheek to leave us behind. Sorry: to leave me here. Not now, not ever. Stay.

(I didn't want to buy the bungalow. I bought it

anyway. On my father's advice I sold it again as soon as Josée had died. He did not want to go there any more. Not even just to look around. At the lawn with the knee-high grass, the overgrown rhododendrons, the vegetable garden overrun by thistles and dandelions, the open veranda with its rotting supporting beam. 'I can't cope with it. Not even the sight. Best sell it, lad. Then someone else can get pleasure from it. No better tribute to your mother.')

SHE OF ALL people, robbed of her speech? She of all people, violent with my father? This had to be a farce. More than once, as I soared high above Kinshasa and the Kalahari, befuddled by the wine that I, both concerned and recalcitrant, had imbibed in large quantities, that hope seized hold of me. Seamlessly linked, between nightmare and dream, with the bittersweet memories of her most daring scene. Wanted: actress/director expert in cunning family machinations. Overacting no obstacle.

I am about seven years old when late one evening I start awake in my bed from excited voices and screaming downstairs. Drowsy, yawning, with one eye closed, I stumble in my pyjamas a foot at a time down our stairs. A steep monster, like all the staircases in this house. But this one is also contained in a lopsided cylinder, with a wall without windows or banisters on the right or left.

The treads have dark-blue wall-to-wall carpet on them, on which you can see every piece of hair and fluff. Every week one of us, in turn, has to vacuum each of those treads clean from top to bottom, with the smallest brush on the hose. Knowing full well that half an hour later, as soon as anyone climbs the bloody staircase—however well he may have wiped his shoes or slippers on the coconut mat provided—it will look just like it did before. Again you can see bits of fluff, and hairs, and dust particles, and crumbs. The static electricity of the synthetic material attracts everything, in the summer even dandelion seed heads, miniature parachutes from some farmhouse or other.

Because the noise of voices increases as I descend the stairs, I hesitate and go in, with one eye sleepily closed, looking at the only thing to be seen here: myself in the full-length mirror. It hangs above the door that closes off the stairwell downstairs—open it, our stair door, and you look into our drawing room. If you stick your head right round the corner you see our cramped living room. There is our table again, our oak wartime shelter, now pushed with its narrow side against the only window, so that each of our meals takes place eye to eye with a slice of life from the traffic on the Antwerpse Steenweg. Only a single-glazed pane and a gauze curtain full of shot silk separate us from the cars, cyclists, lorries, buses whizzing past and passing walkers, whose conversation we can follow word for word, certainly when they flop onto our windowsill as they tuck into their beer and rolls, completely blocking our already limited view. The conversations we eavesdropped on made up for the loss.

But it is late in the evening now, the wooden shutter was lowered with a rattle hours ago, the blue carpet on the stairs tickles my bare feet and I am still looking at myself—in my pyjamas with their almost washed-out stripes, a hand-me-down from brother to brother to brother to sister. ('Pyjamas are pyjamas, lad. [she, testing the material between thumb and forefinger in the thinnest places] Once you've grown out of them, I'll make them into dusters.')

The din on the other side of the door subsides. I hear only a little groaning and faint lamenting. Disappearing a step at a time from the mirror in front of me, I creep down and push it cautiously open, our stair door. Through a chink a scene is revealed that could have been painted by Maria the Artistic. *Suffering Mother Surrounded by Almost All Her Family.*

She is lying back on her sofa again with a cold compress on her forehead, this time in a nightdress beneath a peignoir hanging open and with her eyes firmly shut. Her smacking lips hanging down at the corners gasp regularly for breath. She accompanies each gasp with a muted groan, and every few gasps throws her head from one side to the other on the pillow, as if trying to rid herself of an evil spirit that keeps coming to torment her. One hand grips the place where her heart is, the other— palm upwards—she proffers to no one in particular, it is a gesture of general helplessness: 'Another pill ... Quick! ... A Carter's pill ... My heart ... My poor heart ...!' Perfectly audible despite the sighing and the gasping and banging her head this way and that.

Around the sofa stand three sons, a daughter, a father. The youngest of them, my sister, is twelve. She is the only one who really seems on the point of tears. The predominant emotions in the others (her two eldest) head-shaking, impotence (her husband), and downright adolescent hatred (her Most Awkward One). He is the only one sitting on his knees, next to the sofa on her side. The tears he is fighting back are tears of rage. His sixteen-year-old fists are clenched. 'Come on, lad,' says the father, good-naturedly but forcefully. 'Say you're sorry. Ask your mother's forgiveness.' Literally. Ask your mother's forgiveness.

Their Most Awkward Child says nothing in reply. He shakes his head with *her* stubbornness, and with the scepticism of his two brothers in his eyes: how on earth is she going to manage this? Everyone in this room, including her, knows perfectly well that she is playing a game, that at all costs she is feeding him the forcemeat to show him who's boss, using the machinations she deploys best. Lived fiction. Pretending what could be true and hence, according to her private logic, ceases to be a lie.

'Come on, son. It's late. Ask her forgiveness.'

Again their Most Awkward Child shakes his head, but now just as stubbornly and emotionally as she does on her pillow. Imitation as an indictment. Her reply to this provocation is not long in coming. She lets out a scream that goes right through you, groping extra forcefully for her heart: 'Roger! Roger my love? Oh, Roger ...!'

'Is something wrong?' asks Roger, bending over her with a plastic cup of water in one hand and a Carter's pill in the other. The miracle cure with which she has already miraculously defeated more than one heart attack.

With an uncontrolled-looking but majestically executed arm movement she knocks both the cup of water and the pill out of his hands. The water fans out over her peignoir, the empty cup bounces onto the floor. 'Quick! Call Doctor Hellebaut! No! An ambulance! Before it's too late! Quick!' Followed by staccato moaning, accelerating in tempo, rising in tone.

No one can handle this. Even her Most Awkward Child concedes defeat. Crying now, in frustration at his defeat, he asks his mother's forgiveness. Literally.

And she manages to behave as if she has not heard him properly, so that he has to ask a second time.

(And yet. To be honest. She did have two heart attacks in her life. Both times after an operation, though.

'My first time? No one will believe it. None of the doctors in the Waasland hospitals had ever encountered it, they only knew it from their books, they said. [she, again with that strange pride, as if her ailments confirmed her status as a chosen one] Put vulgarly: my arse grew shut. I couldn't possibly relieve myself. They had to stretch me with a special apparatus. They call it a di-la-ta-tion and it hurts like hell. I've brought five children into the world. Well, let me tell you: giving birth is child's play compared with one of those dilatations. I woke up, on my tummy of course, and despite the anaesthetic I was immediately aware of that pain, there ... And wham! I felt my heart stop beating. I swear. It refused any further service. And I didn't care. I faded away with a smile. Thank you, Dear Lord, thank you! Anything is better than this pain in my sphincter. But well, what happens? They gave me electric shocks, and heart massage, almost broke my loose rib, the whole works. And they kept talking at me. About my children and about my Roger. And about the *Van Paemel Family*, which we were rehearsing and in which I was going to play the old farmer's wife, a very rewarding part. And I bit my teeth, as always. And I got through.')

(Nowhere can a true diva prove her excessiveness better than in her ailments. She has a piercing pain in her eye. For a week she put up with our taunts. 'Perhaps your eye will grow shut too after your bum?' 'Perhaps you have blisters in your eye, from winking at your public?' Until she came back, head high, from a visit to her ophthalmologist. 'The good fellow has never experienced or read anything like it, he says. [again that pride] Don't ask me how, a strawberry seed had lodged in the corner of my eye, where it's nice and warm and moist, and it has taken root. Efficiently! The shoots were on the point of penetrating my iris. Have you ever heard of such thing in all your life? Strawberries were growing in my eye. While in my vegetable garden they are better at rotting than ripening.')

(Allergy in her throat? There it wasn't a strawberry seed that was the problem, but a cat's hair. Though we didn't have a cat in the house. Or a dog. No pet at all. From when I was small I was familiar only with dead and butchered animals. Love of animals? We sold them, from sheep to horse, carefully wrapped and always fresh, by the 100 grams or more, to pay for our clothes and our studies, to say nothing of our daily bread. Remorse? On Fridays we gave double saving stamps from the Valois company, in the hope that the few remaining zealots would be persuaded not to buy dead fish on that day, but dead pig, or dead suckling lamb. Stone-dead guinea fowl, or whatever. A saddle of hare, a medallion of veal, sweetbreads. There's nothing better than the joys of the flesh.)

(I tell a lie, about those pets. I spent my nursery year with the black-skirted and black-hooded nuns of Our Lady of Presentation—Sister Tarcitia, Sister Geneviève, only their faces and their hands were uncovered. The Easter bells, they said, had brought chicks from Rome. Two for each child. Very much against my father's will I was allowed to keep the creatures, in a shoebox next to the coal stove in the living room. For the first few days they were two delightful little yellow balls of feathers, softly cackling, jumping comically up against the sides of their shoebox and falling backward with their orange feet in the air. Two weeks later they walked around, clucking, half naked and drab, pecking at imaginary worms in our Persian carpet, and there was absolutely no way to get them back into their stinking box. One of them even appeared from behind the counter, to its own complete astonishment, and to the hilarity of the customers. At each cautious step its head shot forward and back again in curiosity. It now even started snapping at worms on our stone floor, already with that touchingly empty, stupid look of an adult chicken. Until it winds up by my father's foot and looks up at a balding giant with a white apron over his paunch and a boning knife in his hand. The next day they had disappeared, and their shoebox too. In protest I didn't eat chicken soup for a month.) (Correction. A week. There's nothing as tasty as fresh chicken bouillon.)

(The second time, at an advanced age, her heart stood still after an exploratory operation on her knee. She had expressly demanded that she should not be given a general anaesthetic, since she now blamed that for her previous cardiac arrest. She thoroughly distrusted the young surgeon anyway, because he had refused to allow her to look at his monitor or her X-rays, which she still laid claim to, true to another of her many mottos: 'The master's eye makes the horse fat. It's my knee, not his.'

Before she realizes, she is after all given a general rather than a local anaesthetic. 'I wake up, on my back this time, and I realize I have been taken for a ride by that gangster with his stethoscope, and do I fly into a French fit? Wham! My heart stops. I swear. I simply can't stand injustice and fraud. They had to turn their whole clinic upside down, then had to take me to their intensive care, bed and all, two floors up, into the lift, out of the lift, more electroshocks, heart massage, talking at me for an hour, their whole day's schedule in confusion. That had never happened, they said afterwards, when I finally came round again: a cardiac arrest after an exploratory operation on a knee! I had warned you, though. Whereupon that gangster walks nonchalantly into my room, supposedly to apologize. I immediately started shouting. Get out of my room, my fine gentleman! Be glad that I haven't got enough money. I'd sue the shirt off your back.')

I STAND IN shame and helplessness by her bed in intensive care. Still in my travelling clothes and not yet recovered from the first shock, a shock I shall never recover from. I curse every fibre in my body, the body she made. Because I, even for a second, dared suspect that this was yet another of her tricks, a grotesque intrigue of our little tyrant.

That tyrant lies tied to the bed, looking at me with eyes full of despair and expectation. Her eyes dart imperiously to the straps restraining her, to the fetters cutting into her arms, the drip needle sticking out of the soft inside of her elbow. It isn't difficult to guess what she wants. But she can't say it. It's bad enough seeing her lying and suffering like this, but what comes rolling out of her mouth, now with the sound of anger, now with the timbre of a plea, is a crime. That she of all people should fall victim to this infirmity. That she of all people should be saddled with this blustering impotence. It is no accident that a fatherland is called fatherland, and no accident that a mother tongue is called mother tongue. One can move away from the former, if necessary to the other side of the world. The second one can never escape. I thought so at least. Until I saw my mother losing her tongue before my eyes, and mine along with it. Since that day I have been dumbstruck too, though I write what I want, as much as I want, where I want: how can I ever temper that furious slang of hers? What kind of word can I oppose to it, to cut it, scratch it out of my memory? How can I ever forget this chutzpah, the scandal that this was ever possible in what so many dare call 'creation' and attribute it to higher beings? She of all people. This of all things. I don't know what to say myself. I am only capable of sign language. Shattered, with a feeling of infinite cowardice, I lay my hand on her forehead and am alarmed by her cold sweat.

She is far from shattered or cowardly. Her body is restrained by straps, but that mouth of hers goes on moving, bravely spewing out its barbaric goo of language, with here a word of English and there a word of French, popping up from a mush of gibberish which she concludes every few seconds with: 'A little?' 'A little!' 'A little.' A record stuck in the groove. A foreigner asking the way with the only two words he has picked up in a no-man's-land full of deaf people. She tugs at her fetters again. I don't know what to do. My sign language is already exhausted. Hers is far from exhausted. Her eyes are her most important instrument. They speak volumes. They recall the promise I made by never contradicting her, each time she came back with her Roger from their weekly sick visit to her elder sister. Once Maria the Artistic, now Maria the Pitiful. Maria with Dementia. Maria Who Asks Every Time After Her Youngest.

Another scandal of what people dare to call creation.

Modest genesis. Maria the Artistic had four healthy children, two sons and two daughters, but a husband with thwarted artistic ambitions. Since the beginning of time such frustrations have been taken out on the children, preferably the youngest. In this case he is called Andreeke, also known as 'Our Youngest'. At the age of sixteen he is one metre ninety tall, the tallest of the bunch, but also the gloomiest, most tormented one. His first depression arrives. His name remains Our Youngest.

Since he was a child he was not bad at the cello, supporting his father's predictions that in him the artist would finally arise to which their bloodline had a right. But when the twelve-year-old scion took Holy Communion and was admitted to secondary school, the thwarted father changed his mind. It was not an illustrious musician who would arise in his son. It was a cardinal.

'After his first day in that college Our Youngest comes home,' the father brags to customers whose house fronts he is painting and who look at their watches while he tells his story, 'and all he does is laugh.' '"Is that Latin then, Dad? Rosa, rosam, rosas! Is that the famous secret language of the popes and scholars of the Middle Ages? Amo, amas, amat!" Child's play, that's what Our Youngest calls that Latin.' But at the end of the school year the future cardinal has failed across the board and has fallen out with his father for the rest of his life. He does not give up the cello.

He gets married, starts a family of three, becomes involved in voluntary work and seems happy, despite his tendency to melancholy. That tendency increases when his father loses his mind and dies, while his mother suffers from dementia. In the middle of a calm night, by now in his mid-forties, he writes a farewell letter to his family in which he incorporates a quote from *Oedipus Rex* by Sophocles. He leaves his bow to his second daughter, who shares his love of music. He goes to the front garden, pours petrol over himself and strikes a match. A grandiose gesture in a country where everything is small. He staggers around already ablaze and crying plaintively when he is noticed by a neighbour parking his car. By the time his family also notice him, looking down from the first-floor windows, he is already lying flat out on the lawn, surrounded by the last few flames. His youngest, his only son, runs out to help with a blanket. He is held back by the neighbours, to spare him the sight from close to. When the ambulance arrives, the wife is taken aside. Her husband is so badly burnt that he is actually suffocating. Only an overdose of morphine can bring relief. If she consents at least.

She nods without speaking. Not long after the funeral the orphaned family moves. To a house that no longer bears the scars of memory. That front garden. That front garden.

('People of Thebes, my countrymen, look on Oedipus. He solved the famous riddle with his brilliance, he rose to power, a man beyond all power. Who could behold his greatness without envy? Now what a black sea of terror has overwhelmed him. Now as we keep our watch and wait the final day, count no man happy till he dies, free of pain at last.')

'Where on earth has Our Youngest got to?' Maria the Demented asked my mother whenever she visited her. 'I haven't seen him for months. Come on, where's he got to?' She asked everyone in the institution. Everyone gave the same answer. 'What a shame, Maria love. He was here just this morning!' You've forgotten again! But do you see those flowers there? He brought them for you. He was chatting to you about the weather. He looked well!' Or: 'He just called you, but you were asleep. He sends you all his love. You're not out of his thoughts for a second, he said. Don't you remember?'

When my mother came back home after one of those visits to her sister, her voice had a strange undertone, something between rebellion and sadness. 'To have to lie like that to your own sister, about something fundamental. And the state that woman's in? It's life that isn't life.' After which she addressed everyone around her—her Roger, her daughter, her sons.

Me too. More than once: 'If ever anything happens to me like your Aunt Maria, and you don't shoot me? You don't strangle me, you don't poison me? Then I'll come and take revenge, in your dreams or something. Don't think I don't mean it. I *shall* be there. And I'll point out your duty to you.'

And now here I am in intensive care, next to her iron bed, with that cowardly hand of mine on her cold forehead. I don't strangle, I don't poison. I simply break my silence, superficially and briefly. I used the language I learnt from her and I use the oldest lies. 'It'll be all right, Mum. Shush now. It'll be all right.'

(I suddenly remember how that song went on, in Cannes. I don't want to think about that—no! Not now, not here, not that. But I can't help it: 'You felt regret, / But oh, my pet. / Sometimes you forget / a little soon yet / you swore to be true.')

Her body finally relaxes, but she turns her head away from me. She even stops talking, but just as I think she is getting ready to sleep, resign herself, accept, so that I receive my own absolution, she also loses, briefly and partially, her silence.

With her head still turned away she begins a faint lament, which again consists mainly of unintelligible mush. But still a few more words can be deciphered besides 'a little'. 'Let it go.' She says it with a sudden good-natured intonation. Once an actress, always an actress. 'Let the old woman go.' She says that, clearly, audibly, and: 'Can't do any harm.' She even tries to shrug her skinny shoulders.

'Can't do any harm.'
'Let her go.'

We didn't let her go until two years later.

HTTP://EN.WIKIPEDIA.org/wiki/human_brain. 'The human brain is the part of the central nervous system located in the skull. (Ancient Greek, "encephalon" in the head). It is the human organ of perception, direction, monitoring and data processing. Together with the spinal cord it constitutes the central nervous system (...) Our brain is constructed from many tens of billions of nerve cells (neurons), each of which is connected to a large number of nerve cells, sometimes many thousands. They direct and co-ordinate sensory systems, movement (both conscious and unconscious) and homeostatic bodily functions such as breathing, blood pressure and body temperature. They are also the source of language, cognition, logical thought, imagination, emotion and memory. Although it makes up only two per cent of the body's volume, it uses ten times as much oxygen compared with the rest of the body and consumes a quarter of the total energy. Twenty per cent of our blood also flows constantly to our brain.'

Forget the above definition. The brain itself dictates that it is deficient. Above all our grey matter is a kaleidoscopic power station, a blast furnace at body temperature which can make memory, perception and fantasy merge into mathematical propositions or experimental poetry, into persistent nightmares or a love letter, into nostalgia or desire, and everything in between. Our wet grey cauliflower welds the most diverse scenes seamlessly together. Unity of place, time or action is not required, any sequence can spill over into any tableau, assembled in shorter flashes than a worn-out bulb needs to go pop. Analysis alongside collage, Dada alongside dialectics—significant chaos, the pioneer's dream of all avant-gardists from the visual arts, film and the novel.

Take my brain, at this moment. Whisper a word to me, refer to a single object, and a French cancan of associations will explode in my head. Audi-visual timpani without a final chord, encephalographic free jazz, a modernistically fragmented cascade of chance and meaning, accompanied by the correct smells and an appropriate soundtrack. Ladies and gentlemen! Welcome to the Great Neuron Review! The Endless Daub!

Give me—I name something at random, since we are anyway in the twilight zone of symptom and medication—the sick-tray from my childhood. Our principal domestic tool in the ceremony of patient care. It doesn't even have to be called 'Rosebud', although it was slightly reminiscent of an antique child's sledge. Simply mention it.

And here we go, Johnny. Go, go, go.

It wasn't much more than a tray made of deal, varnished. It did, though, have underneath, on each of its short sides, a panel that you could fold out and fix at an angle of ninety degrees. *Et voilà!* The tray had become a table that you could put over the tummy of the person with flu, so that he did not have to leave his sickbed to eat and drink. He could even use the table to put the paper on if he wanted to do the crossword puzzle. Thanks to the raised edge he didn't have to fear that the pencil would roll off the tabletop if he nodded off to sleep.

Our table was folded up and stored away until someone had a high enough temperature not to have to go to school. So anyone crowned with the honour of being bedridden, with our mercury thermometer as their sceptre, was allowed to keep their pyjamas on, though after having first exchanged their cotton underwear for flannel or wool. Then they were personally installed by the earth mother on the sofa where she herself regularly lay back with that cold compress on her forehead.

First she combed your hair and then took your temperature, to officially exclude cheating. Then the spoiling started. You got the softest cushion for your back, the cosiest duvet over you, the magic table over your tummy and the newest strip cartoons within reach. ('Eek!—Aunt Sidonia sees a mouse.')

You were allowed to eat when you felt like it, but the fare was the fare of those who fell ill under the wing of Nurse Josée. Under no circumstances coffee, all the more so tea with honey and lemon. No rye bread, with chocolate spread from Adinkerke or fresh cheese from Hulst, but thin toast from Expobrood, with slightly salted horsemeat or filet de Saxe, cut wafer-thin, freshly supplied from their own shop. And, especially at the right moment, a Delacre biscuit or a Quality Street sweet. Those who are ill can use consolation, and consolation begins with sweet things.

On that sofa, half hidden under that table, I got to know the oldest lies when they were not yet lies: 'It'll all be all right, lad, don't you worry. It's normal for your muscles to hurt and for your forehead to be hot. The day after tomorrow that will all be over. Have another Véganine with a mouthful of water and sleep for a bit and in a while I'll bring you a praline. Or would you prefer a ball of minced veal from your father?' Being ill was playing despot over a concerned, loyal court which maintained its own very individual taste tradition. I still can't drink tea with honey and lemon without feeling pleasantly groggy.

But as soon as the temperature dropped? Table gone, cushions disappeared, privileges suspended. 'Have a bath and get ready for school. And don't leave too late, you've got to drop off half a pound of sausages at Mrs Sammels.'

Go, Johnny! Vrooom! (Sports car pulls away in *Michel Vaillant*.)

Bradaboom! (Professor Cumulus' lab blows up.)

The best thing was of course to avoid measles and snotty noses. The message was to be strong, and food remained the key. Man is what he eats.

So tinned food was something that you only sold to others and consumed as little as possible yourself, and the same went for frozen food. Fresh was the word, for vegetables and fruit, and apart from that resistance derived from meat, meat and meat. Morning, afternoon and evening, whether it was black pudding or pâté on bread, ham sausage or *Américain préparé*. If a topside of beef threatened not to sell, we fried steak in the afternoon *and* the evening. Always rare, since the real strength is in the blood—it's no accident that we call the liquid from meat 'youth'. ('But, my dear boy, you're leaving the best bit uneaten! [she, to an astonished friend of mine, son of the first vegetarians in our town] Take a double slice of bread and dunk it in your youth. You'll never eat anything as good as that in all your life!' [the lad didn't dare do anything but obey, but he hid from his parents the early discovery of this other youth])

Besides food the best protection was adequate clothing. 'Better a scarf too many than a cold.' Especially at an early age, unprotected necks and heads and ribcages and soles of feet were life-threatening, to say nothing of the bare lower back with its tender kidneys, which would catch cold in a trice. Go, Johnny. Go!

Despite all these precautions I had picked up whooping cough somewhere during my first year of life. The coughing fits and the production of phlegm were so stubborn that it was almost the end of me—head back, mouth wide open, no more air, no sign of life, face already gone purple, body in spasm from head to toe. Giving me a good shake was some help, holding me under the cold tap too. On one occasion I was saved by being passed from one family member to the other like a basketball, without dribbling of course. Another time my babysitting brother had to cope with it alone. 'I could scarcely throw you at the wall all by myself. Still, I saved your life. I sucked the snot out of your nose until you could breathe again.'

But I didn't get better. Finally the imposing Adhemar, the husband of my godmother Gerardine, assumed responsibility. As the head of Waeslandia, General Wares and Household Products, and as the fêted chairman of the local rally club, he called on his many connections and wound up with a bunch of amateur pilots and glider pilots, with a view to a treatment distrusted and even advised against by the medical world. I was smuggled into a propeller plane and with windows open flown hundreds of metres high, where the air is thin and purer, and still well supplied with oxygen.

'They can lie and curse as much as they like, the high

and mighty gentlemen of the Academic Hospital. [she, halfway between angry and grateful] That lad lay in that plane breathing for all he was worth, and since then he hasn't had a single coughing fit, scarcely even a snotty nose. The result is what counts, not a medical degree.'

Give it lots, Johnny: ROOOAAARRRR! (Buck Danny makes a dive in *The Japs Attack*.)
Takatakatakatak!

But the terror stayed. As a toddler I had looked death in the face and from now on deserved heightened attention. I myself can't remember anything about that whooping, it's an apocryphal family vehicle. What follows is one of my earliest memories.

I'm allowed to go for a walk holding my mother's hand, but outside there has been black ice, it has snowed, hailed, *n'importe*: it's freezing, so I'm wrapped up as if for a moon landing. Flannel vest, thermal underpants, Scotch woollen socks. My stretch bottoms with the *pied-de-poule* motif, my check lumberjack shirt, my smooth sweater with a polo neck, on top of that my double padded anorak, bought to allow for growth and zipped up to the chin. On my head a bright red hood, on my feet boots with a double sole, and on my hands leather mittens lined with sheepskin, the whole finished off with a colourful scarf that is wound three times round my neck and tied securely in case a hurricane suddenly erupts. With the same object the hood of my anorak, despite the hood I am already wearing, is pulled far down over my forehead, both strings are tied under my chin like with a woman's corset, with a double knot to ensure it doesn't come loose.

Because of all that clothing my arms are at an almost

horizontal angle to my body. I cannot move my chin and can scarcely move the rest of my squeezed-together face. If I want to take a step with my right foot, I first have to lean my body over to the left. Michelin man goes walking. If they run me over I will bounce from bumper to bumper to wall to gutter to sewer cover, and stand up again unscathed. The ultimate crash test dummy. Protected against everything.

Except for the sudden entry of Pit Germaine, my mother's eldest sister and inventor of *le racontage automatique*. She doesn't let the grass grow under her feet, does Pit Germaine. Setting down her shopping bag strategically and with elbows akimbo removing her plastic rainhood from her virtually concreted hairstyle, she blocks our way in the narrow passage leading from the workshop to the street. At the same time she starts holding forth to my mother, who nevertheless is in full walking regalia, but benevolently lends an ear to the detailed report of Pit Germaine's past week, which she, Pit Germaine that is, has once again passed with great pleasure in her work in the service and villa of the widow of the top boss of Europe's best manufacturer of flannels, towels, terry-towelling dressing gowns and indestructible bed linen. After the death of the beloved manager—'a heart attack while skiing, the man went up and down in his ski lift for half a day, they were able to put him in the mortuary without defrosting him'—the widow went on living in Wilrijk by herself, in a wonderful, beautiful villa with a thatched roof, an unused tennis court and an unusable swimming pool, from where she, again Pit Germaine, *la chroniqueuse magnifique*, has just come on the long-distance bus, which again had to make umpteen diversions because of a traffic jam in Zwijndrecht and a blood-pudding fair in Beveren, and so on and so forth.

By the time she has finally removed the hood from her hairdo, I can feel the first drop of sweat tickling its way from my spine to my coccyx. I can't scratch, with that double padded anorak and the rest. I simply cannot reach my anal cleft. Anyway, I'm now breaking out in sweat all over. It's high time I was out in the open air. But to my horror I see that my mother is adopting a relaxed stance, resting on one leg, completely forgetting me, even unbuttoning her own coat, making ample time for her sister who is like a mother to her since their mother died young, which led to Pit Germaine as the eldest taking responsibility for looking after the eleven other Verbekes, and later, when the last bird had flown the nest, not being able to find a husband, except when she was seventy, but that's a completely different story that thank goodness is not relevant here, and so on and so forth.

Meanwhile I am melting nicely, equipped for cold fronts and snowstorms, and still indoors, in our narrow passage, overlooked by everyone. Sweat is pouring from my crown, from under my cagoule and the hood of my anorak, into my polo neck, in the direction of my woollen vest. Drops are tickling my forehead, one runs into my eye, my hands in the mittens feel soaking-wet. I try to say something, but I can't move my chin. I produce an unintelligible mumbling that is lost in the wild narrative torrent of Pit Germaine, who has still only just begun on her experiences on Monday morning, though today is well and truly Saturday.

The upshot is that, feeling sick with the heat, I tumble over on my back, like a tortoise surrendering to the four elements or the fastest vulture. And to the court in panic: 'Put him on the sofa! Take off his clothes! Get the thermometer! And the sick table! Quick!'

Johnny, tu n'es pas un ange. (Go,go, go.)
   Mais entre nous: qu'est-ce que ça change?

'I make portraits of Flemish celebrities with the raw ingredients of their favourite dish, the more ordinary the
better,' says Isabel, the Catalan photographer who has
lived for twenty years in Amsterdam and has recently
moved to Antwerp. In reply to my sincere question
whether she put together such a book in the Netherlands, she bursts out laughing. 'Get real,' she says, shaking her head.

I: 'How do you mean?'

She: 'Name your favourite dish?'

I: [without thinking] 'Fried brains with sauce tartare.'

She: [squealing] *That's* what I mean.'

I: 'What do you mean?'

She: 'Over the border at Roosendaal South America
begins.'

I: 'South America?'

She: 'Naples at least. Barcelona, Santiago de Compos-
tela.'

I: 'In what respect?'

She: 'In what respect not?'

A few weeks later I am posing for her, in evening dress
and sitting in my most theatrical armchair, a curly
throne with white wood and a pink cushion. Like Hamlet during his most famous soliloquy; but I glance down
at my right hand, in which I hold not the empty, newly
excavated skull of Yorick but a handful of sheep's
brains, freshly bought from the Turkish butcher round
the corner.

I have looked up two things for her, I say, while she
studies me through her lens, assessing the angle of the
light, especially the reflection in my glasses. She doesn't

answer. Wouldn't it be cool to begin by printing the appropriate quote from *Hamlet* alongside the recipe?

'Alas, poor Yorick! Here hung those lips
That I have kissed I know not how oft.
Where be your gibes now? Your gambols?
Your songs? Your flashes of merriment?'

She nods, not really listening, still measuring me with her eyes as if I were just a statue. My second suggestion, I continue stubbornly, regards the recipe itself. Wouldn't it be nice to print it in facsimile as I retrieved it from my late mother's handwritten cookery books— simple, thick school exercise books with linen covers, lined paper and red-edged?

Without replying she finally starts photographing me. ('Can you look a little more haughtily at your right hand?') I start dishing up the recipe to her between shots. Initially mouth-watering. ('Poach in slightly salted water. Rinse and allow to cool. Peel carefully until there is no membrane or visible arteries. Bread with egg yolk and white breadcrumbs. Fry until crisp in real country butter, slightly salted. Serve with lemon, parsley, fresh toast and cold sauce tartare.')

But I falter halfway through. Moved, unwell, upset. The constant sight of that handful of brains in my hand turns my stomach. That sticky, formless, watery nothing—so vulnerable, so soft. They are close to being liquid, they almost drip through my fingers. I had especially forgotten how they smell. Earthy, fatty, helpless. ('It's the queen of organ meat! [she, pertinent as always, in her kitchen, waving a wooden spoon in her hand] Only sweetbreads are tastier and richer. And *rognons blancs* of course. But if you don't like kidneys, I'd forget about lamb's balls.')

'That's it!' cries Isabel. 'That look! Keep it like that!'

('Alas, poor Yorick! Here hung those lips
That I have kissed I know not how oft.
Where be your gibes now? Your gambols?
Your songs? Your flashes of merriment?')
'Yes! Keep it like that, keep it like that!'

Surabaya, Johnny.
Warum bin ich nicht froh?

Another old memory concerns not her, but my father. This time my hand was in his hand. Then death was still exciting and oh so beautiful. I can't have been older than three.

We were standing in our brand-new municipal abattoir, with white tiles everywhere. The cow was led to the slaughter room by four men in bloody smocks and wellingtons. One greeted my father by name, another made do with a gruff growl, the rest kept their attention on the cow. The creature was shivering all over, with shivers that I would later see again in police horses, which accompanied our annual flower parade. Their flanks and bellies, however, would tremble not with fear but with annoyance in order to chase off the fat, oily flies which had homed in on the smell of so many begonias and horse droppings.

The cow shakes its head slowly to and fro, and lifts now one, now the other back leg. With a sharp tap the hoof lands on the tiled floor again and slips a little. The men keeping the cow under control also slip now and then, despite their rubber boots. On the floor a trail of watery blood to the drainage grilles. The man who called my father by his name picks up a tool that is halfway between a drill and a pistol. He positions it on the animal's forehead and pulls the trigger. The cow sinks unresistingly onto its front legs. Its eyes scarcely change.

The quartet set to work. In no time the cow is hanging upside down on hooks and its innards come tumbling out of its belly which has been cut open, wrapped in a transparent membrane that breaks when it hits the tiles. The smell of blood mixes with something herby. Then the men start chopping. Before you know it four steaming quarters are hanging on as many hooks. One by one, thanks to the rails on which the hooks are attached, they glide elegantly out of the slaughter room, while someone already starts washing the floor with a garden hose. He repeatedly scrapes stubborn pieces with the side of his boot toward the drainage grilles.

In the evening I wait for an unguarded moment to climb on a chair and bend over the huge kettle in which my father prepares blood sausage. That's why we had gone to the abattoir just now: to get fresh pig's blood, in a churn in which farmers carry their fresh milk. I stick my arms past the elbows into the mush. Onion, bits of bacon, herbs, congealing blood, breadcrumbs. I start kneading in delight, intoxicated by the smell, fascinated by the composition of the mixture. 'I only wanted to help,' I reply, when shortly afterwards I am lifted off the chair and given a ticking-off. The browny-red is hard to get off my arms. 'It was almost ready,' I mumble, even prouder than I was just now. 'Almost black pudding.'

So it goes, Johnny. You've got more in you than you think! Delete, delete, wap-wap.

She again, with her infuriating lack of a sense of proportion. More! Always more! Witness her cold dishes. Witness her toasted canapés.

She: 'Toasted canapés, toasted canapés? Your mother

doesn't make toasted canapés. Your mother makes za-kuskis.'

Everyone: 'Za-what?'

She: 'Zakuskis! [one hand above her head, one hand on her side like a Russian dancer] Haute couture among cocktail snacks!'

No one could accuse her of finding a butcher's shop in a working-class district beneath her dignity, as a purpose in life and as a source of income. But in her day-to-day activity she missed the timelessness of art that she pursued passionately in her hobby. The opening of a showroom for imported American luxury cars gave her the chance for once to shine artistically in her professional life. The caterer who was to have provided the reception had gone bankrupt the day before the opening ceremony. In panic the car dealer had paid a visit to the nearest butcher's. 'Can you handle an order of this size, madam?'

She: 'That depends on the size, sir.'

The car dealer: 'Two thousand toasted canapés.'

She: 'I'm sorry. I don't make toasted canapés.'

The car dealer: 'I've been told that you do.'

She: 'I make zakuskis.'

The car dealer: 'Za-what?'

She: 'Zakuskis! Two thousand, tomorrow, six o'clock? It's a deal.'

All members of the family were mobilized, all leave was cancelled, all training sessions called off, all rehearsals postponed. Against his better judgement her husband ventured an appeal to common sense: 'There are two thousand, Josée. Can't we for once make do with something simple? A triangle of pâté with just a dash of mustard? A slice of smoked salmon with just a wafer-thin slice of lemon? It's only for eating. You must tell yourself. As long as it's tasty!'

She: [with barely concealed indignation] 'Everybody who's anybody in the town will be there, everyone of standing and class. Right, we're going to knock them off their feet!'

After a massive shopping spree and hours of arrangement, the actual production process follows, under the exclusive command of the earth mother and according to the principle of the conveyor belt. Every canapé has to do the rounds of the big worktable, at the end of which the aluminium serving trays stand waiting, for now covered only in pure white doilies, their edges perforated in lace motifs. On the corner of the table next to it, the first station, the canapés are taken in hand by the least artistic workers—two of the oldest sons. Still, this is an important step: ensuring that the canapés do not become sodden with their own toppings.

You are standing in front of a stone bowl in which a couple of kilos of butter are piled up and which have been taken out of the fridge for just long enough to guarantee optimum spreadability, and you butter one canapé with another. Don't use a knife! If you do you're bound to break half of the canapés through the force of the lever effect, which is difficult to control. Only when the canapés have been made moisture-resistant on one side can you put on the basic ingredients, selected for contrasting colours and ditto flavours. That is the second step, to be carried out by a battalion of moderate cultural barbarians: those with the biggest fingers and least patience—the father and one remaining adolescent son. The third, fourth, fifth and sometimes sixth stage is implemented by a third scattered unit, that of the tiny and refined—the artistic mother herself and her two youngest children, supplemented by Pit Germaine and by Wieske, the inseparable friend of the family, who during the day is a secretary in a nearby dye works, who goes to bed in her flat every night, but who morning and evening forms an additional member of the family, and as such is not averse to rolling up her sleeves, at least if a new film has not just come on at the Rex or the Palace or the Scala or one of our seven local cinemas. Everyone to their hobby. But this time she is loyally at her post.

The tiny and refined apply, again canapé by canapé, the various decorations. As far as the colour is concerned they may also strive for intense contrasts, but as far as the taste is concerned they must focus on harmony. For example, for a canapé with black caviar—note: the affordable, extra-salty kind, made of lumpfish roe—the four sides are first garnished with parsley. Then the glistening black gold on top is finished with a square piece of peeled tomato, a triangle of peeled lemon, and a knife-tip of crumbled white of boiled eggs. Careful! The ornaments must be the same size on every canapé and put in the same place everywhere.

The slice of boiled egg is a different kettle of fish. To begin with, it must be just slightly bigger than the canapé itself—the two ends of the egg, consisting mainly of white, can be crumbled with a fork and be used elsewhere as a decoration. In the middle of the bright yellow yolk you put, as if it were an iris in a Pop Art eye pupil, a rolled-up anchovy with, in turn, a caper in its heart. Then you squirt a dab of ketchup on the left, a dab of tuna mayonnaise on the right.

The pink of a piece of smoked salmon you first garnish on four sides with finely sliced shallots. On top you place a pinch of chopped chives, right next to it a triangle of a slice of ordinary peeled lemon, and next to it a knife-tip of crumbled egg yolk.

Gouda cheese, partridge pâté, camembert, Parma ham,

prawn salad, crab salad, sour herring and so on and so forth. All equally richly and symmetrically decorated. On the dishes too the canapés lie in perfect symmetry, row on row on row. But on one dish the rows are ordered in a draughtboard motif, on the other in a goose board motif, on yet another in straight or oblique stripes. No two dishes must be the same; on the contrary, they must each form a work of art that demonstrates even more appetizingly the essence of the zakuski.

The only fuss during the production process was the fault of the Most Awkward One, who had profited from an unguarded moment to form a swastika flag out of white, black and red canapés—camembert, lumpfish roe and marinated pepper. Apart from that the stressful chore proceeded in a strictly ordered and well-oiled fashion, as if everyone understood fully what was at stake. A financial breakthrough, and above all the honour of the family and its strange productivity. The six o'clock deadline was met by the skin of our teeth, in an atmosphere of euphoria. Everyone, even the youngest, was allowed a mouthful of sparkling wine, albeit sweet plonk from the Grand Bazar, six bottles for the price of three; 'You can't argue with that.'

'Put your dishes down somewhere here,' says the maître d' of the reception, a chap from Brussels in a dinner jacket with a napkin over his right arm. The brand-new showroom, brightly lit and shining with American chrome, is deserted, except for the dealer and his wife and a handful of silent employees plus a few neighbours in their Sunday best. One would have sworn that it is a funeral and not a launch.

'If you should feel peckish yourself,' grins the Brussels maître d', 'don't hold back. There'll be more than enough.'

My mother, who has done her toilet in haste—'so as to look respectable, alongside all those chic people'—has to stand by while a Brussels maître d' in the back room of a car showroom stuffs a handful of her zakuskis into his mouth, thereby completely ruining the motif of a whole dish.

She: 'Did they order any other snacks perhaps?'

He: [laughing with his mouth full] 'I hope not for their sakes.'

She: 'Are their guests late?'

He: 'Guests? The dopes forgot to send out the invitations.'

She again. (Go.) Baroque down to her canapés, she could not make even a cold dish without nurturing higher aspirations, on a bed of cabbage lettuce and watercress she arranged garnishes of rolls of ham, braised endive, chicken legs, slices of salami and tomatoes filled with prawn salad, as if for a still life seeking a place in a national museum instead of on a meal table for strangers.

She could endlessly twist slices of veal roulade, honey ham and jambon d'Ardennes into more and more daring shapes, putting her failures aside with displeasure for later, as toppings for her own family, setting the seal on her triumphs on the other hand with a satisfied nod of the head. From smoked ham particularly, with its Bordeaux-red marble shades and its decorative edge of fat, she could twist an unforgettable rose of flesh which cried out to be used as an example in professional magazines. Not that she was sitting waiting for photographers of expensive cookery books. Her greatest reward was the ecstatic smile of her regular customers, who thanked her in advance for a successful reception of friends from Kortrijk or Ghent who were difficult to impress.

Her greatest irritation was the cautious question from her husband and any one of her family: why did she charge so little? Why did she never ask a little extra for her and our time? She only charged for 'les matières premières', as she preferred to call her ingredients. Probably because of the rhyme, and quite simply the richer sound. She shrugged off all questions. The answer was surely as clear as crystal? Art came first, always, and assumed greater importance, if one committed to it free of charge.

Bohemia in the family.

She again. She irons the wash standing and I sit, as soon as I can read properly, on the other side of the table on a chair with her script in my hands. Her speeches are underlined, while I read in all the other parts. A tableau of maternal multitasking *avant la lettre*. The ironing? Done. The part? Learnt. The youngest? Under her care and with his language improved yet again.

And for the rest of his life infected with dramatic literature. Like others with football or polio.

She once more. Have another look at the photo on the front cover. Taken by a local photographer, not a Catalan as far as I remember, in the former foyer of our Municipal Theatre, after one of her brilliant parts in a costume drama, I forget which, I forget when, all I know is this. That she was wearing a tight-fitting top, almost a corset, and under it a wide skirt with lots of silk and tulle, and that she and her fellow actors had come straight to the foyer for the reception instead of first changing and taking off their make-up. That several photos were taken of her, because her costume was so successful; 'You're madam Baroness to the life, you are.' And that I was also in one of those photos, dressed for the occasion as an underage gentleman—knickerbockers with drawstrings, white shirt with stand-up collar, wine-red bow tie with long ends.

I lay back on her cascading lap and stared candidly into the lens. While she herself looked around her, ignoring the photographer, chatting with a fellow actor, her fine chin raised, in one hand a glass of cider, in the other a filter cigarette. Superiorly nonchalant. But she had succeeded in finding a seat with me on the only chaise longue that stood right underneath the only crystal chandelier, a monumental affair that dominated the room. People could see us from afar. They couldn't avoid us. People did not come and talk to us, they had an audience. I felt like a prince.

(The photo on the front cover was processed by the photographer when he printed it to make it look older. A so-called half-blurred edge, *flou artistique*. A few scratches, coincidentally right next to her face. False wear and tear: a costume drama squared. I couldn't find in the old biscuit tin the photo in which I am lying full-length on her lap, among the masses of other photos, in dividing up and selling off the effects in their flat. Perhaps it never existed, except in the power station in my head).

She for ever. In the 1970s avant-garde theatre made its modest entry into the amateur stage, at least for the duration of one play, written by a local journalist, the son of a not very active member of the circle. In the spirit of the times it was a savage social indictment, entitled *The Sentence*. I liked it, and was more or less the only person who did.

She played the judiciary all by herself and was dressed

in a jute sack with a cockade in the Belgian national colours on her right shoulder. The age lines in her face were exaggerated, her cheeks made up to look hollow, her eyes blacked up all around like early Punk, and her hair particularly was a hit. Temporarily dyed grey, it stuck out, combed into stiff peaks all over her head. An unintentional parody of the late Fat Liza.

All through the performance she banged on the table from behind which she passed judgment with a judge's gavel, shouting retorts and sentences at everyone who appeared on the stage, which on her own testimony she only half understood. ('And I'm not really a lover of all that symbolism, all that complicated stuff. [she, at our ironing board, during rehearsals for 'the most difficult part in my life'] At a certain moment I shout at one of the accused: "Take your blindfold off, Sir." But he simply keeps it on! "Can you see the truth now?" "Yes, your honour," he cries. With the blindfold still on! [sighs]. And then they're shocked when the houses empty.')

And the play was *not* a success. But a photographer—another one, more interested in authentic expressionism than in false wear and tear—had taken a photo of her during rehearsals. From a worm's eye view so that her expression and hairdo seemed extra-macabre. Printed in harsh tones so that the expression of her made-up face was further accentuated. He won a prize with it and hung the enlarged photo in his studio window. ([she, with her nose in the air] 'I'm glad people don't recognize me. I'm astonished that that shop hasn't gone bust. If you put something like that in the window? No one is going to go in and order wedding or christening photos.')

She again. Until late at night, with reading glasses on, swearing under her breath, bent over her accounts, which she filled in herself before they were taken to the bookkeeper for checking. 'Whatever you can do yourself, you should do.' And she had indeed studied the Principles of Bookkeeping, to put the finishing touch to them no less, as far afield as Dinant and Northampton. She still drew lines as she had done at school. And she began a new page if even one line in her view was at too much of an angle.

Her handwriting was like that in her cookery books. That of a solicitor's clerk. Steadfastly regular and with old-fashioned panache. 'You can tell a stubborn cuss by his handwriting.'

She and us. In the locked section of her robust cupboard, where she kept the most expensive strong drink and the *Gangrene* novels of Jef Geeraerts, lay five envelopes, each with the name of one of her five children on it. Next to their names in ink was the pencilled sum that she calculated was necessary for school fees, clothing, enrolments, pocket money, extras. Sometimes, when a supplier insisted on immediate payment for a delivery, you could see her open that locked cupboard door with a worried expression in the presence of everyone—an unusual and disturbing fact. For a while, with her back to everyone, she was busy with rustling banknotes and papers and her pencil. Finally she locked the cupboard again and you could hear her say to the supplier in the shop: 'You can have it next week, sir.'

She and I. We appear together once on stage. In our Municipal Theatre, In *All My Sons* by Arthur Miller. I am ten and have one speech. She has a leading role.

We rehearse for all we are worth by the ironing board, but in the rehearsal room I must listen to the director, she says. And at the curtain call I mustn't come to her and take her hand. I must stay on the other side and take the hand of the man who was my father in the play. A good play continues for a little while, when the applause rings out and the actors bow together. You mustn't confront the audience too quickly with reality. The show must go on, for as long as possible.

('Not bad,' she says, coming straight up to me as soon as the curtain has finally fallen and the applause has died away. Kneeling down to me, she surveys me, smiling from head to toe, as if to check that I am still the same person. Arranging my hair unnecessarily with one hand, wiping away an imaginary mark on my cheekbone with her thumb and some spittle, and afterwards giving me a mild tap on the cheek. 'But you really must learn to articulate better, or nothing will become of you.')

She ad infinitum. Already retired and yet, suddenly: the crown on her career. That particular role on the professional circuit. The Brussels Municipal Theatre is doing *King Kong's Daughters* by Theresia Walser. The play is set in a home for old people with dementia. Out of a strange sense of philanthropy, or discontent with the hopeless care of human flotsam, three nurses decide to kill their patients one after the other, after dolling him or her up as a Hollywood icon. She is allowed to die as Mae West. A privilege, she thinks. But she also thinks that she doesn't have enough lines. Her part requires her no longer to be able to speak.

That does not stop her from investing heavily in metalanguage at the première. She has one scene in which she stands alone on stage. Correction. Sits. In a wheel-chair. She wheels herself to a side table, puts a tape in a ghetto-blaster that is standing ready, presses the start button and looks into the audience. The eyes of the character could be called dreamy. But the eyes of the actress are well aimed. She looks straight at her son, a well-known novelist and playwright, very exceptionally present this evening, just before leaving for abroad again. He is her youngest, but already forty-two. He is hiding in the middle of the audience, because he knows her tricks. In vain. She keeps looking straight at him, so that the rest of the audience turn their heads toward him, nudging each other with their elbows. 'Isn't that ...? But yes! That's him! And why is that woman looking at him like that?' On the tape in the recorder her theatrical son, in a voice that could be a parody of mine: 'Hallo, Mum. It's me here. Sorry I wasn't able to come by again. But well, you know how it is. Work, work, work. I'll try to come next week. Or the week after or something. Okay? Right. Bye, Mum. See you soon. By-e!'

She goes on looking at the middle of the auditorium. Even long after she has pressed the stop button.

She, on a Sunday during a rare high summer. The streams that border her plot have dried up. They are fringed with dry grass and brambles that don't even have any more berries. She can't stand the sight. Grumbling, fretting, moaning. 'If that catches fire? Because some stupid walker throws his cigarette end away in it? The whole lot will go up in smoke, my bungalow included. It can't go on like this.' So she sets light to the grass herself.

She is in a bathing costume and looks on watchfully, resting her elbow on the handle of her hoe, with a bucket of water at her feet, just in case the fire should dare to defy her will. With an audible sigh of rage and the speed of a heath fire, half her stream is suddenly ablaze.

She calls for help, swiping wildly with her hoe at the highest flames, and in her panic knocks over her bucket, not even sending it into the seat of the fire. Friends and relations, who were just playing cards and chatting, rush to her aid, armed with spades and blankets, and tubs and vases full of water. They cannot get the fire under control. She gets more and more into a panic. 'My bungalow! My bungalow!' They literally have to hold her back to stop her running into the crackling sea of flames to put them out with her bare feet. She wants to make up for her stupidity by risking her own life—she who once carried a burning chip pan out of her house, resulting in second- and third-degree burns on her arms and face, and was only a whisker away from losing the sight in both eyes. ('I'd do the same again. I saved my house with my own hands. Who can say that, in his lifetime?')

'Let the middle section go on burning,' says a gardener who is present, Gust, a distant cousin of hers, 'we must first check it elsewhere.' He shows us how: at either end of the stream loosen and turn sods of earth, piling the earth up, and working inward toward the course of the fire. Flames and embers can best be put out with large, leafy branches—he cuts a few off with his pocket knife—after which a helper can pour another bucket of water over, brought by the human chain, because that of course remains necessary. Come on! Action! Action!

After an hour the fire is put out. Three streams, ten bushes and twenty trees are left charred, but the weekend cottage is saved. The guests are exhausted. She however is tireless, ebullient even. She pours beer and Portuguese rosé for everyone and opens all the packets of crisps and salted nuts she can find in her store cupboard.

'You can see that I was perfectly right! A stream full of dry grass like that? It's a danger to life and limb.'

She finds it strange that most of her guests leave soon after.

She, she, she. A French cancan of associations, a welter of scenes and images. They well up by themselves, but I can also summon them at will. All thanks to that source of energy of billions of neurons, the millions of synapses in my head.

I can not only recall such events, I can also describe them. I can serve them up at a banquet. I can type them out in words like these, and these too. And you, reader, can read them. Just as they once appeared on my screen, here and now, so you are reading them on this page, at this moment, your 'now'. Yet there is only one blood clot required, smaller than a louse, that shoots via your arteries to your brain and there blocks and atrophies your speech centre—a few minutes are enough—and you will have lost the plot for ever. One minute clot, and these words will change before your eyes into insulting cuneiform script, a battlefield of indecipherable scratches. And one clot in me and I no longer know the purpose of the piano resting beneath my fingers. That screen there? I would stare at it and wonder who wrote the text and wonder why it absolutely had to be in Cyrillic-like scratches.

Chicken scratches. Runic carvings.

One clot each and we are alienated for good.

Shut off from everything connected with language.

AT FIRST RECOVERY seems possible. The medical team persuades us of that hope on the basis of lots of statistics and one scan of her brain.

'Strokes like this, resulting in aphasia, are more common than you think and more treatable than you fear. Your mother would have been worse off with apoplexy —cerebral haemorrhaging, due to a burst artery. With thrombosis, due to a *blocked* artery, the capacity for speech returns more easily, sometimes up to its previous level. Her thrombosis, thank God, is not the more severe category. There has been no one-sided paralysis of the body, or even partial facial paralysis. The sporadic aggression, quite frequently directed at the most familiar people, will reduce, perhaps even disappear, as the shock is absorbed. Meanwhile the seriousness of the situation must not be overestimated. Her whole nervous system has been disrupted, at least temporarily, and one can never tell to what extent brain damage will be permanent. You could compare it to a worm virus on the hard disk of your computer. You never know what documents and programmes it has eaten its way through. These things have to emerge over time. It's best if the patient is transferred to a specialized facility, where other elderly people with this affliction are housed. A shared lot alleviates the desperation and encourages recovery. Tailor-made medication, intensive therapy and lots of relaxation do the rest.'

The facility is in Beveren.

Twenty minutes' drive from the parental home.

The hope awakened seems justified. Her lifelong dislike of hospitals and the elderly, 'all those old people', is strangely tempered—or blunted? Perhaps she is mainly relieved that she is no longer tied down.

She submits to the fussiness of some nurses without responding ('How are we feeling today then? Are we going to eat up our soup or do we only feel like our biscuit?') She is soon tired and sleeps a lot, but when she is awake she co-operates remarkably smoothly with all the therapies. From boredom? Or because she really hopes to get better soon—you've got more in you than you think, even here? She tries, stubbornly but without result, to form words with enlarged scrabble letters, until she is forced by migraine to lie down on her bed again. She fills a whole exercise book with writing, and she works on it long and seriously, again with plenty of attacks of migraine. It produces no more than scribbling. An illiterate child pretending to write a treatise. It goes no further than that one exercise book.

We bring daily papers and magazines for her—she, who never let a morning go by without at least the leader, the crossword puzzle and the horoscope of *Het Laatste Nieuws*. After leafing through them for a bit she puts the pile to one side, disheartened, and after a week she no longer looks for any new copies. Watching television isn't much of a success either. She stares at it like someone who has stumbled by accident on a Chinese channel, where familiar faces continue stories from the past without subtitles. After a while the remote remains untouched, the TV off. Or it stays on endlessly without her looking at it. If you turn it off yourself, she glances around in alarm, fruitlessly searching, uncomprehending, surly. If you turn it on again she is completely furious, grabs the remote out of your hand and turns the TV off herself.

She still seems to recognize everyone who comes to visit her. Her face brightens and she conducts you to her table, to a dish containing her virtually untouched breakfast. She opens a sandwich and shows you the filling, while she taps her forehead with a forefinger. 'A little!' Before you can agree with her, she drags you by the arm to her washbasin and points burbling to the soap that is nearly finished or to the towel which she gestures needs replacing. When you show her for the third time in a week where the clean ones are kept—on a shelf in her little built-in cupboard—she looks at you in astonishment, hands on hips as if you had performed a conjuring trick. She is very pleased, though. She immediately replaces the towel and pushes the used one into your hands. 'A little?'

At each visit she lets herself be persuaded to come and sit next to you and go through the specially compiled photo album together. It contains snaps of all her loved ones, from husband to great-grandchildren. The idea is that you point to them and give their name and last name. She nods and nods and nods at each name. Now and then she points to someone herself and looks again, deadly serious, certain. She doesn't repeat the names. She doesn't even make an attempt. There is no indication that she is aware of any connection between the list. The only photo that is missing is that of her Most Awkward Child, who died twenty years ago. We wanted to spare her that never-healed source of sorrow.

There is no indication that she knows he is missing from the list.

Strangely enough her pride and joy are the movement therapies. Dressed in her dark-blue tracksuit and her white gym sneakers, she does what I have never seen her do before. Grinding out tens of kilometres on a home trainer, slowly and at the lowest setting, moving purely for the sake of moving. She even takes part in what she used to say she hated. Group gymnastics. The exercises of the young instructors are manfully imitated but irrevocably distorted by the elderly pupils, as if to prove the whole gamut of what age can do in the way of creeping damage. One cannot raise his arm higher than his shoulders, the other can no longer bend his knees, a third cannot get up again after floor exercises without help. There are few who complain. If they do complain, you can't understand what they're saying.

True to the way she has lived up to now, she chooses her enemies here too for herself and exuberantly makes friendships for the rest of her life. Among that latter category, the friends, there are no fellow stroke-sufferers. Those she avoids or ignores. She identifies only with what is vital and at least half a century younger. In this way the nursing staff fall into two groups. Those she walks gruffly past, and those whose arms she falls into, with whom she plays around, by whom she lets herself be teased and helped, who she doesn't mind turning up unexpectedly in her room, whom she tolerates trying to point her the way in her lost speech, once her pride and joy. In the presence of this favourite circle she assumes a girlish, tempestuous quality, as if her stay here were just a new finishing course given in a strict boarding school, surrounded by like-minded girlfriends. The long vacation will soon be here! Hearing her giggling and seeing so much female camaraderie—with one therapist she only walks arm in arm down the corridor—I can finally reconcile myself to some extent with the fact that we did not listen to her lament in intensive care. ('Let the old woman go. Can't do any harm.')

Toward the other nursing staff, her enemies, chosen for inexplicable reasons, she shows that undisguised expression of contempt in her face, that implacability à tout prix, which could always make her look so ugly, and sometimes downright hateful. (Her eldest brother was on his deathbed, the architect who had designed her robust cupboard and her oak table bunker and had them made in the last year of the war. She refused to pay him a last visit. They had fallen out years ago, he had hurt her feelings, said something wrong about her sons, exactly what had long since ceased to matter, he had *said* it, that was enough. 'Because someone is dying you don't have to eat humble pie at their bedside. The truth is what it is, to the death.')

While she can scarcely write, her speech actually does make some progress. Separate words come back, though an undiminished number of English and French ones crop up. (The therapist: 'The cells in which her knowledge of foreign languages is stored may have been less badly hit. Anyway, our brain stimulates all its unaffected cells to take over as many tasks as possible. Neuron switches try out every possible alternative route.') The language mush coming out of her mouth becomes more melodious and inventive, but without any gain in meaning.

Still, communication becomes easier and easier for

her. There are three other languages of which she has not lost her mastery: gesture, intonation and imitation. Often she needs nothing else to counter her absurd private slang. ('A real actor? [she, in the past, rather blasé] If necessary he can play the telephone directory. I'm sorry! A real actor can shock and move *without* a text.')

She gains the reputation of being a bit of a humourist. She waits for you in her room with the door wide open and gestures for you to hurry up. Before she shuts the door she casts a quick phoney glance behind your back at the corridor where three men with dementia sit all day long on a bench next to her doorway. She turns to you and starts imitating all three of them. She exaggerates their crooked faces, their dead haddock eyes, the tics they have been left with after *their* strokes. She depicts them as the three monkeys in 'Hear no evil, see no evil, speak no evil.' She imitates their stumbling walk in *commedia dell'arte* style. With one hand at the level of her right temple she makes grabbing gestures in thin air, to indicate that the three, unlike her, are gaga. (She can even say it: 'gaga!') The apotheosis relates to her greatest point of dislike. Blowing on the back of her hand she produces three imitation farts, from high to low, one for each monkey, then squeezes her nose and eyes closed in disgust, while waving the imaginary stink away with her free hand. Whereupon she herself bursts out laughing, to indicate that the show is over.

It turns out to be a regular turn. She does it again next time. And the time after that.

She starts imitating everyone, from maintenance staff to the director, although she has a preference for fellow patients whom she dislikes. She amuses many people, to her visible pleasure, and she annoys some, with whom she doesn't bother. The therapist does not check her. 'The main thing is that she communicates. The rest will follow, in time.' He has already been proved right in this: her attacks of aggression occur only exceptionally.

Not that she suddenly shows herself perfectly accommodating with her Roger. He remains afraid of her, she can feel it and it makes her furious and suspicious. The harsh looks she sometimes gives him go right through you. The next moment she is as sweet as can be and tenderly strokes his bald head. Her embraces, however, remain wooden and scarce, with everyone. It is a sign that she just can't place, and a hiatus in the vocabulary of her body language. The embrace: what does it express? Her arms hang so vaguely and awkwardly round your body when you say goodbye, her eyes are so fretful.

When she makes fun of my father, which happens regularly, a poisonous laugh is never far away. She points at him and makes cheerful dance movements, as in the expression 'When the cat's away, the mice will play.' 'Oh yes,' she adds, with a meaningful wink at everyone sitting next to him. She points to him again. 'Oh yes!' Now she dances around like someone at the carnival and with her right hand makes tipping movements in front of her mouth as if she were downing twenty pints one after the other. 'Oh yes!'

But she only gets really angry again, foaming at the mouth even, when on my advice he turns up in sports gear to take part in their collective movement therapy, so that he also finally gets some exercise. ('Not bad for your lazy foot, Dad.') She drags him off the home trainer, again exercising demonic strength, again letting rip with her most barbaric infernal speech. The staff have to restrain her or she will attack, even if he is lying on the ground.

Only when he has disappeared from sight does she calm down.

He quickly gets changed in her room, shaken to the core, frightened that she will come back and erupt again. She does come in, but she is pleasantly surprised to see him, as if it has been a week since the last time. They look at the photo book, side by side, on the bed. He points to the photos and lists the names of the people who have populated their lives. She nods and nods and nods, until it is time for him to go home. He gives her a kiss and hugs her. She hangs her arms ponderously about him, again with that empty look. Standing pensively in her doorway, she watches him go.

Outside, on the ground floor, he does not immediately open the door of his car. He has to be careful of the traffic rushing past, this is the ever-busy road to Antwerp, close to Beveren's Grote Markt. He looks up at the window of her room. This time she is standing there. And she's waving. She doesn't always. Why this time and last time not? He must learn not to worry his head about that, everyone says. He waves back, leaves, but on the roundabout at Kasteel Ter Veste he turns back and as he drives past looks up at her window again.

She is still standing there, but there is no indication that she notices him this time. Of course she isn't waving any more.

After a few months the therapists say the time is ripe for a first excursion. For some time she has pointed every morning at her dentures and then at her mouth, with a grimace expressing a great deal of pain, after which she points to the dentures again. She wants to go to her dentist, that is clear enough.

It will be her first time outside the walls of the institution. Also the first time she will see the neighbourhood again where she lived and worked for so long.

And I am the one who will take her and bring her back.

COME ON, JOHNNY. Come and dig in my memory. Grab the wheel of my sports car and lead me, accompany me on that wintry drive back then. Sketch how I sat next to the speechless woman who gave birth to me and brought me up, who gave me her language and her ailments, who taught me to love endives, mussels and Hugo Claus. ('That is: his early plays, if they don't have too much nudity in them, because he knows a thing or two about that, our so-called genius.' [she, at times too prudish for words])

My passenger looks vulnerable, smaller than ever, anxious in bursts, and yet proud. She is finally dressed up again, as far as possible. Not made up but in one of her favourite coats, a short number with a fox-fur collar. On her head is a coquettish but not extravagant hat, to hide how uncoloured and unkempt her hairdo is. In her hands, without rings or watch, she carries her flat leather handbag, an eccentric affair that in the past she only ever used for special occasions as an artistic accessory, but which she now clasps like a piece of flotsam in an ocean of hectic images and loud sound. Her eyes flash from the charging oncoming traffic on the left to cyclists we are overtaking on the right. From the park on this side to the railway on the other side. Her hands play restlessly with her handbag. Click, open. Click, shut. But thank God she is silent. I don't have to listen to her hellish speech. There is even a touch of normality.

Come on, Johnny. Take us to that dentist's. The route will take us through our former neighbourhood. Show her and me the reservation. Make us think of what it used to be like, in that closed village in the lap of a much bigger town. In that sovereign hamlet of five streets, where every year at the first ray of sun the housewives sit on a chair on their pavement, relishing the prospect of a new spring and tired gossip. The neighbourhood where once a butcher's shop and family of seven was supported by working folk from the hosiery mill and by a collection of neighbours you couldn't make up. ('There's no such thing as small parts! [she, every time she missed a lead] The small characterizes the big, more than the big by itself, and that small suits us fine. One has to be what one is, on pain of being nothing at all.')

No one sits in front of their door any more. The hosiery mill has moved or collapsed, and the same goes for the neighbours of the past. Perhaps the sight of our streets, familiar but desolate, will give my passenger something new to hang on to. Perhaps the roof tiles and house fronts will also appeal to her memory. Perhaps in that way she will recover a few syllables, gain another two words, through what she sees and remembers through that seeing.

Come on, Johnny.

Go.

There was, besides Our Hardworking Hunchback and his fellow sufferer Willy the Shoemaker, besides Fat Liza and her niece Mad Lucienneke, also Parchment Nieke. ('Call me Nieke. Nicole is for arseholes.') Unmarried, she lived obliquely opposite us and swore by Groene Michel cigarettes, without filters if you please.

The parchment referred to her face and hands, and the deep wrinkles and liver spots displayed by both. You never got to see the rest of Nieke, otherwise known as Nieke Spiderhead. In her doorway she kept her light-blue peignoir buttoned up to the chin, to hide her old body and especially her tortoise neck. With a Groene Michel screwed into one corner of her mouth she still managed to call out orders to the milkman out of the other. Or the eelmonger, or the knife grinder, or the soup seller or the ice-cream man. People always rang her bell, invariably men of a certain age, most of them melancholy. They didn't stay long.

Her bare calves did stick out from under her peignoir. Blue-veined, unhealthily swollen, always with a bandage round a calf or an ankle, but she always squeezed her feet into high-heeled crocodile-leather shoes. 'In moccasins I don't feel like a woman any more.'

Her voice was hoarse, her laugh creaky, her motto famous. 'In my life I've given a lot of men a lot of pleasure.' People still spoke with awe about her unequalled beauty. When she was found she had been watching the same TV channel for three weeks. Attacked by her own starving cat. But still with those shoes on.

Go, Johnny.

Go.

There was also our baker, unless I'm wrong: Etienne. He lived and worked on the corner opposite ours. He already had asthma when he developed an allergy to flour. 'Of all the things for me to get. If it were to strawberries, or to salted nuts. But no. To flour. And I really enjoy being a baker. Is there anything more beautiful on earth than a good roll? Or a butter biscuit with raisins, baked properly? A marzipan cake with crème fraiche instead of butter cream? My great-grandfather was a baker and I've never learnt anything else in my life, or wanted anything else. And now they take it away from me.'

He tried to hold on for a few more months, but in the early morning had such a rasping rattling and cough that his customers began to suspect that he had caught not an allergy but consumption. That didn't help sales. When he signed the transfer papers he cried like a little child. He made his successor promise that he would never reduce the range. 'From rolls to frangipani!'

He never came by to check on the promise.

There was Philomèneke Van De Prior. A short, globular body and on top of it, without a neck as a transition, a round, forever smiling face. Her red cheeks glowed like two apples, her eyes shone with joie de vivre and the urge to tease. Her husband, a huge, lively chap, sacrificed his vocation as a long-distance seaman when they got married. For two whole years he worked for Niko, a manufacturer of switches and plugs. Then he said: 'I've seen enough plugs. I've got sea legs. If you miss my company, you must buy a dog while I'm away.' To tease him Philomèneke bought a Chihuahua. 'A Chihuahua!' he cried. 'Is that the dog you identify me with?' 'Of course not,' she laughed, 'but there's nothing even smaller, darling.' Her darling's ship went down with all hands off the coast of Senegal. She mourned for a year, renamed her Chihuahua after him and got on with her life.

Under her wide nylon housecoat she wore dresses with colourful, tiny flower motifs. She worked in textiles, but after the death of her darling she earned her living by selling football forecasts. On the front of her workman's cottage hung a neon sign: 'Prior Prognostics!' On and off, day and night. Always someone home.

'This week you're going to win,' she said every week with a smile to each of her customers, 'I feel it. But you've got to take chances. If you don't play, you always lose!' No one in the area ever won more than 100 times their stake, and no one ever bet more than 100 francs. People played to please a widow, not to win. She herself didn't bet. 'If you play, you always lose!' she once confessed, drunkenly bragging. When she drank, her smile disappeared and her urge to tease became arrogant and rancorous. 'In all those years I earned more from my commission than all of you together with your badly filled-in coupons. Dumb idiots! Suckers!' For the first time she lost herself: half her customers. She shrugged her broad, round shoulders, went on smiling and a month later was again selling as many forecasts as before. All she did was to have a glass less in the café.

She got diabetes, lost her sight, her dog and three of her limbs before she died. The neon sign stayed up there for years. Without going on and off.

There was our hairdresser, a vain sod who smelt more penetratingly of aftershave than his female customers did of perfume. He won the Best Hairdresser in Belgium prize, regularly had his photo in the paper, but to his despair fathered three children who were covered from head to foot in eczema. The children of Our Hardworking Hunchback (Hump 1, Hump 2, Hump 3 ...) seized their chance of finally making fun of someone else. They waited until the hairdresser's three children were once again covered in scabs and then advised them, one after the other: 'Perhaps you should ask your father for an anti-dandruff shampoo.'

There was Eddy the Paper Man. Six times a week he got up at five o'clock, loaded up his delivery bike with papers and magazines and started out, whatever the weather, on a round that would take him as far as Kallo and wouldn't bring him home before about noon. On Sundays he also got up at five o'clock, but to go fishing in Overmere-Donk on his delivery bike. Usually he didn't catch anything, but still his papers smelt of fish.

Except on fishing Sundays, his wife got up with him, but she only did her shopping just before he got back home. A *filet pur* for her poodle and half a kilo of pork sausages for him. 'I wouldn't mind doing it the other way round, but then they'll both be unhappy. If my poodle eats sausages, it starts vomiting, and my husband's stomach can't take *filet pur*. To each his own.' Her own was Parma ham and vol au vent. If there was any left, the poodle started being sick on that too.

She and Eddy had a daughter together whose beauty left everyone dumbstruck. ('She hasn't got an ounce of her mother in her and she hasn't anything of her father in her.') When that beautiful girl breaks up with her first boyfriend after five years at the age of twenty-five, he comes calling at nightfall. Father and mother are already in bed, because tomorrow it's the round again. The beautiful girl opens the door herself. Her rejected boyfriend, crying, shoots her in the face with a double-barrelled shotgun. He then tries to commit suicide, but in his emotional state he has already fired both cartridges.

The affair is front-page news for days on end, in every publication. For that period Eddy doesn't do his paper round. Then he resumes his fixed pattern. 'What else can a man do?'

He never says much more than that again.

There was, I mustn't forget, Sidonie with the Hare Lip. The story of how she shuffled off this mortal coil has not been preserved. In contrast to the story of her inseparable umbrella and the account of her rain dance.

First the umbrella. One fine afternoon Sidonie comes running into our shop and launches, with her arms above her head, into a litany which has the tone of a curse. Her language, a prefiguration of my mother's barbaric stammering, makes her difficult to understand. 'Where's your umbrella?' asks my father after a while, just for something to say. That's just the point, Sidonie is able to indicate, and she launches into her tirade of curses for a second time. Little by little, as if in a charade, the butcher and his customers guess at her words and so work out what has actually happened.

That Sidonie is walking unsuspecting along the pavement and that a friendly total stranger stops next to her in a red Chevrolet. That the man winds his window down and asks the way to the station. That Sidonie is afraid he won't understand all of her hare-lip words and in consequence wants to have her hands free to lend force to her driving instructions with gestures. That, as a result, in a reflex she hangs the handle of her umbrella on the door handle of his Chevrolet, and begins in her pathetic gibberish: 'You take the first street on the right [sticks up one finger and points to the right], the third left [sticks up three fingers and points to the left], two hundred metres straight ahead [chops the air with the side of her hand] and you're there, sir!' Whereupon the man, who has listened to her open-mouthed, says: 'I'll find it for myself, madam.' Sidonie: 'And the bastard drives off! With my umbrella still on his door handle!'

Second, her rain dance. That was how she celebrated a stroke of financial fortune in one of our nine neighbourhood cafés. Today there's only one left. Café Den Toerist, on the bend toward the Raapstraat. At that time all nine were flourishing, even the smallest, Wivina's, a dark-brown dive with panelling on the wall, a stove in the middle of the bar and a drainpipe above the heads of the customers which described a couple of bends and finally found its way to a flue high in a corner. In the winter a kettle of water stood bubbling on the stove or chestnuts were roasted on it.

Wivina, a decrepit widow, ran the café capriciously by herself. ('*Garçon* is another word for thief.') Her soup and her meat-salad sandwiches were famed far and wide, but her alcohol? She refused to serve beer from well-known but expensive brewers and refused to pay duty on spirits—Dutch gin, cognac, gooseberry or quince liqueur. She sourced everything from clandestine distillers, and hid her bottles of Dutch gin and liqueur quite openly in a wicker shopping basket hanging on the hat stand by the front door. If the Excise inspectors ever raided her, she bragged, she would act innocent. 'Spirits? In a basket? Someone left it hanging here, sir, I wouldn't know who.'

In order to intimidate her, her few regular customers staged a raid themselves, with a few mates from Hamme in borrowed uniforms. The four of them charge in, snapping, and make straight for the shopping basket. They take out three bottles of contraband, just opened. 'What's that here, madam? Evading the law? That's going to cost you a pretty penny.' Knees trembling, Wivina comes out with her retort. 'Someone left that basket hanging here, sir. I wouldn't know who.' Whereupon the instigator, Jef the Undertaker, says: 'Come off it, Wivina! That's my basket. You know that, don't you?' Whereupon he rushes out with basket and all, leaving Wivina in a swoon with four phoney Customs men.

She remained inconsolable, shaken to the core, long after the culprits had explained to her, increasingly guiltily, that it was a practical joke. They got up a generous collection, enough for six of her bottles. Wivina wouldn't take their money. She shut her door and a month later her café.

But anyway, we were talking about Sidonie. She was in The Glass Roof Café dancing like an Indian around a campfire on the wooden panel that was put over the billiard table in the evening to protect it. With her handbag in one hand and her umbrella in the other, lifting up one knee after the other rather inelegantly, letting out cries of triumph. She had won with her Prior forecast. 'Bloody stroke of luck!' she shouted now and then, already nicely drunk. She knew nothing about football, and had let Philomèneke help her and she had advised not to be frightened of a few exaggerated results. And blow me down: the long shots paid off. There was a small fortune waiting for her. Finally Sidonie had some luck in her life. 'Bloody stroke of luck!'

'What does she keep yelling the whole time?' asked a newcomer of a regular. They were sitting together at the bar watching her Red Indian dance. 'Bloody stroke of luck,' translated the regular, who had known Sidonie and her gibberish for quite a while.

A little later Sidonie dances past them on the ground floor, leading a polonaise, as she has paid for another round for everyone and has told the son of the landlord to feed the jukebox enough coins for an hour's party music. She leads the human chain like a majorette, waving her umbrella and swinging her handbag. Happiness goes to the head. 'I'm so hot, who wants to fuck me?' 'And now? What's she saying now?' asks the newcomer. 'God knows,' lies the regular.

But Sidonie, pausing at the bar to drink a mouthful of her Rodenbach with grenadine, now says it directly to them. Right in their faces, with sweet and sour breath: 'I'm so hot! I'm so hot! Who wants to fuck me?' 'Sorry Sidonie,' says the regular. 'I really don't know what you're saying, lass. Say it again?'

Sidonie says it about five more times. The man stands firm: 'Sorry lass, it's my fault. This is my twelfth pint.' She shrugs her shoulders, turns round and goes on celebrating. 'A shame, though,' says the newcomer, watching Sidonie go with pity. 'Absolutely,' says the regular. 'If she were a bit younger and not so drunk? It seems it's fantastic for giving head, a hare lip like that.'

The next day Sidonie couldn't find her coupon. She had to save for months to settle her tab at The Glass Roof.

There were also The Mother and The Daughter. The former getting on for eighty, the latter approaching fifty, together a new dimension in the phenomenon of neighbours' gossip. They had little except two vocal cords and an elementary vocabulary, but it was enough for them to give voluptuous voice to their mutual hatred. Two vixens without a husband, son or father, without a soul except for themselves, two self-styled exiles from the centre of town, two shrews who didn't show their faces in any local shop or café and lived next to us in a terraced house, where no one ever cleaned the windows and where no one ever called, except the occasional bailiff or an optimistic encyclopedia salesman—they didn't open the door to either of them. Their net curtains were grey with dirt and never a month went by without my praying at least once that those dusty curtains would soak up their blood, the Rorschach stains of my joy, since they had clearly killed each other, as far as I was concerned, preferably with a blunt axe and a blunt chainsaw.

Their most epic quarrel lasted two full days and nights, toilet breaks and meals included, they simply went on, they screamed at each other from the loft to the cellar, from their wc to their yard, and you could trace the route of each of them going by the wandering sound of their voices. Not for a moment did those two bitches' mouths stop, not one quarter of an hour went by without stamping or throwing of plates and glasses, except when they themselves chose to shift their register from roaring to hissing like Biblical serpents, till they finally dozed off from exhaustion, and even then their drunken snoring, obscene grunting as of pigs ready for slaughter, kept us awake—me especially, as my bedroom was next to the Daughter's, where most of the shouting matches took place, in so far as one can speak of shouting matches. They were oral trials of strength, invocatory alternating songs of endlessly repeating insults and curses, occasionally punctuated by a hollow laugh, the imitation of a madwoman by another madwoman, all in all a wild polyphony of two troubled souls who could easily tear out each other's throats, which they regularly promised each other but declined to do because they did not know what they would do with their time without each other.

For example, The Mother would shout: 'Knock it off then. Knock it off then. Knock it off then.' Thousands of times, for hours, in impeccable rhythm, in every conceivable key. The Daughter replied, equally often and with equal virtuosity, from high to low, from dry to almost yodelling: 'Shut your trap. Shut your trap. Shut your trap.' The Mother: 'Who have you crawled on top of this time?' The Daughter: 'Clark Gable. Clark Gable. Clark

Gable.' Or: 'The first one who comes along. The first one who comes along. The first one who comes along.' The Mother: 'Where's my pension? Where's my pension? Where's my pension?' The Daughter: 'In my arse. In my arse. In my arse.' The Mother: 'Just kick your mother downstairs. Just kick your mother downstairs. Just kick your mother downstairs. Just kick your mother downstairs.' The Daughter: 'Get cancer and free me. Get cancer and free me. Get cancer and set me free.' Meanwhile I lay in my bed with my fingers in my ears: 'Tomorrow a Latin exam. Tomorrow a Latin exam. Tomorrow a Latin exam.'

We tried to get our revenge, at first at night, while their tirades were going on. Shouting back all kinds of things, and all banging on the partition wall until our fists stung. No effect. Then we went into the street and stood shouting under their windows, gradually banging again, now on their front door, or the shutters that had meanwhile been rolled down. First with our fists again, then with our slippers, then with our climbing boots which we had retrieved from the attic. Banging and drumming and shrieking until the neighbours came out and after some explanation joined in enthusiastically, banging and drumming and shrieking for all they were worth. No progress. The two bitches went on arguing imperturbably until we slunk off, shivering with cold, doubly frustrated by our defeat.

During the day, when we suspected they were lying dozing, recuperating for their next long day's journey into night, we turned our transistor radio on full, our TV and cabinet gramophone to maximum volume, the speakers directed at the partition wall or placed right next to it, so that even the neighbours from the other side came to complain, to us this time, because of the cacophony and our preference for Édith Piaf and The Beatles.

Finally we rang the police. At first only the local patrolman came by, a good-hearted chap. He found the nocturnal scene of a whole family, sulking in pyjamas and peignoirs, so moving, and the language used by two indomitable sirens so amusing, that he brought more and more colleagues with him to our night-time parlour. After a year every member of the local police force had been to see us, and we knew most of them by name. They now began just dropping in, of their own accord, toward midnight, gossiping neighbours or not, because they could also get a glass of spirits and sandwich of mince and onions in exchange for their sincere sympathy. They couldn't alleviate our misery—going by the decibel meters the din could not be classed as nocturnal noise, and when they rang at the bitches' door, they simply turned off the bell.

Nothing helped. As a child I crawled into bed with an imitation German tank helmet which I had won myself at the fair, in the hope that my ears would finally be shielded enough under the liftable flaps, intended for ancient headphones, and now equipped with a scrunched-up sports sock. I put up with the stink.

My parents were alarmed by a rhythmic, hollow pounding that they had never heard before and that seemed to come from The Daughter's room. Heading for the din, however, they found me, in my own bedroom, sitting in my bed like someone with autism, swinging his upper body from front to back, though constantly banging the back of my helmeted head against the partition wall, to the cadence of my own share in their primitive polyphony: 'Shut your face [bang], bloody cows [bang]. Shut your face [bang], bloody cows [bang].' My mother was strengthened in her conviction that the recurring nightly pandemonium was not having an edifying effect on my intellectual development.

She became fully convinced when one night completely different sounds rose from the adjacent bedroom of The Daughter. The two voices were the same, but now they were singing an endless sound that was halfway between grunting, giggling and panting. Their panting rose to a crescendo and faded away again, and shortly afterwards mounted again more intensely, rising in tone in a lunatic fashion. It was still shouting, but sounded more plaintive, pleading, and the most commonly repeated word had become 'yes'. First The Daughter: 'Yes! Yes! Yes! Yes!' A little later The Mother: 'Yes! Yes! Yes! Yes! Yes!' Now and then one of the two also cried: 'Clark Gable! Clark Gable! Clarke Gable!'

I was led away from my bedroom by parents looking at each other in disbelief. A bed was made up for me with pillows and old blankets in the heavy bathtub in the bathroom—the room that was furthest away from all party walls. The duty policeman, who had seen a light still on and came to conclude his evening beat with a drink and a sandwich, was invited to take a seat in our one-man armchair, as if for a rare recital. 'Well I never,' I heard him say in astonishment, 'a mother with a daughter!' In the background the two voices were still singing their endless series of yeses. 'I'll have that drink,' he concluded, probably to my mother, 'but that sandwich with meat salad you'll have to eat yourself. My stomach couldn't take it.'

(I saw him again recently. Ten years retired, still a slim bear of a man, his beard and his hair turned white, his face a little more wrinkled but apart from that the same as before. He raised the subject himself. 'I saw a lot in my career, but those two crazy women next door to your parents?'

The matter had so intrigued him and his men that they had shadowed The Daughter out of hours, during the few excursions she made. She drove at night in her clapped-out Volkswagen Beetle to Antwerp, to cocktail bars in the Schipperstraat that were frequented by Asian seamen and downmarket whore-chasers. 'We couldn't even pick her up, she worked without a pimp and didn't charge anything. She seemed to be pleased if someone wanted her. She had obviously never been a beauty and at fifty she couldn't be called appetizing at all. Sometimes she simply went and stood waiting under a plane tree till a trucker stopped and took her with him, God knows where. One time I approached her myself in one of those bars. I said she should behave herself, she and her mother. That it was no fun and no life for her neighbours and their children. Do you know what she did? She sat astride her bar stool. She had nothing on underneath, I swear. Take a good look, she said. Take a good look and we won't say any more about it.')

There were the rats as well. At set times they came crawling out of our worn- out, too-narrow drains. Grotesque dark-brown gnawing monsters, twice as big as the hamsters that our local animal lover sold in his specialist shop for pets 'from ponies to parrots'.

It happened at every summer cloudburst. In a few minutes our streets were underwater. Raindrops and hailstones lashed our steaming cars, whipped our canvas awnings, and flayed the arched backs of surprised walkers. The latter were even more frightened when from sewer grilles and loosened sewer lids one rat after another shot out in front of their feet, zig-zagging over the submerged asphalt, tripping over the surface of the water like persecuted saviours, surrounded by splashing raindrops like impacting bullets, and leaving behind then an elegant wake, drawn by their bald tails. They sought asylum behind car tyres and rubbish bins, but were chased by all the ringleaders and dogs in the neighbourhood, who were soon accompanied by the bravest and drunkest café drinkers, who didn't mind getting soaked as long as they could cool their vague fury at their cushy existence on such a permitted enemy, such a shitty rat, such a monster, such a bringer of disease and doom, which in mid-chase could turn round and leap hissing for your throat or crotch. That threat, always repeated, never proven, sealed their previously signed death warrants.

Beneath flashes of lightning and thunderclaps, to the cheering of bystanders and supporters, and while the municipal buses kept tearing past and with their wide tyres threw up sheets of dirty water and more and more rat blood, a cull was carried out with billiard cues and broom handles, in some cases with the heel of a shoe, and very occasionally—to the horror of the landlord of The Glass Roof—with billiard balls, of which afterwards only five of the sixteen were found.

'My Chihuahua, my Chihuahua!' Philomèneke Van De Prior walks down our street soaking-wet, looking around. Her eyes are no longer shining, they are burning. 'Those filthy rats are much too big for him! Has anyone seen my Chihuahua?'

Two customers of The Glass Roof look at each other. 'That's what I thought,' whispers one, cleaning his billiard cue guiltily with his handkerchief. 'How funny the rats look this year, with that short tail and those weird crooked feet.'

There was also the squeal of brakes, the screech of tyres, the dull thuds. Our junction, the corners of which were occupied by an asthmatic baker, a café called Wivina's, a specialist pet shop and a butcher who was known for his cold cuts and cheese croquettes—that junction was considered one of the most dangerous in town. Although still well within the built-up area, the Antwerpse Steenweg invited drivers to put their foot down. Straight, wide, well asphalted; a racetrack at least 1,500 metres long with only one treacherous cross street, the Lindenstraat, which by the way had flagrantly appropriated its name under false pretences: like the Acacialaan, the Berkenstraat and the Beukensteeg, it did not have a single tree.

It's probably the fault of our house fronts, which did not excel in colour or inventiveness, so that as in a trompe-l'oeil the perspective appeared uninterrupted and the Lindenstraat did not seem to exist: anyway, several times a day drivers had to slam on the brakes to avoid an accident with a crossing vehicle and at least once a week there was a splendid direct hit, from superficial bodywork damage to total write-off. Our four corners would have been better occupied by a towing service, a bodywork specialist, an A&E department, and a plastic surgeon.

In those days safety belts were expensive gimmicks that no one used. Numerous passengers were catapulted through their front windscreen, in the best-case scenario no further than their bonnet. The unlucky ones flew over it and a metre lower came to a juddering halt, scraping the rough asphalt with their hands, their face, their whole front. Or worse: they slammed, head first, into the side of the lorry they rammed. And even then they were luckier than their driver, who smashed right onto his own steering wheel. Either with his face (losing his teeth, upper or lower, or both) or else with his ribcage (ribs broken, peritoneum perforated).

Once a Fiat drove into our baker's. Shop window smashed to smithereens, the nose brought to a halt within a whisker of the counter, the only customer unhurt but covered in fragments of glass and two days in shock. Another time a Citroën DS, screeching alarmingly, slid toward the front of Wivina's Café. Miraculously it stopped with its right-hand front corner precisely in the gaping doorway, where Wivina was standing with the doorknob in her hand, ready to go to the early-morning market. It was ten minutes before they had released her hand from the doorknob and half an hour before she could say anything coherent. ('Give me a double cognac. On the driver of that wreck.')

Before the police and ambulance arrived the casualties were taken to our shop. Automatically, no one thought twice about it. 'Casualties? Take them to the butcher's!' There they were advised to have a seat on one of our slender stools, with their heads back and pushing a clean tea towel that had for years been used to absorb blood against their runny noses and split lips and grazed foreheads. The butcher gave them a glass of tap water, a careful pat on the least damaged shoulder and the assurance that 'it wasn't too bad, considering the bang'. The butcher's wife recommended that they eat mainly oxtail soup in the weeks ahead. 'That strengthens both the body and the nerves.' [she, dabbing the wounds of everyone in need, irrespective of his background or injury]

One Christmas Eve in the 1960s three of them crashed through their front windscreens in quick succession. 'On a holiday people can always take a few more risks,' commented our by now hardened customers, viewing the spectacle increasingly laconically through our shop window. One of the unfortunate ones, a respectable lady in a BMW, was clutching an ice-cream gâteau from Crèmerie François in her hands as she sailed through the air, an airbag *avant la lettre*. Her face was full of slivers, but afterwards she only sat wailing about her ice-cream gâteau, which she had squashed against the asphalt with her bosom. 'What are we supposed to have for dessert tonight? What a sad Christmas it's going to be.' Until she catches a glimpse of her face looking back at her in the showcase mirror, just above our dish with entrecote on it. She slides off her stool and lies flat on our floor, out cold. Right in front of our counter, on one of the busiest days in the year. It is obviously super-busy for the paramedics too. The woman lies there for over half an hour, eventually with an inflatable cushion and with a constant supply of new tea towels on her face. She has long since come round, but everyone advises her not to move. 'Stay where you are, dear. You've fallen enough for today.' Around her, without interruption or fuss, the annual ritual takes place: customers collect their Christmas orders en masse. Cold cuts, prawn croquettes, veau Orloff, turkey with vegetable wreath, *tomates farcies*. Life goes on.

(After the woman is finally taken away, everyone has been served and the shop door has been closed, the great manoeuvres finally get under way: our own Christmas celebration. For a second the family factory seemed close to exhaustion, after the preparation and wrapping of hundreds of croquettes, a dozen turkeys, ten chateaubriands with vegetable wreaths, prepared quail with poached pears, Breydel starters with instructions, ossobuco with potatoes au gratin, ox tongue with purée and Madeira sauce ... But as the work table is cleared and relaid for our own festive meal, with our best service and our crystal glasses, courage mounts and with it the mood and the appetite. Five courses for twelve diners is a minimum. Prawn cocktail, lobster soup, baked appetizers with sweetbreads and Paris champignons, and as the pièce de résistance stuffed piglet with sauce Brabançonne, ice-cream gâteau and sweets. All with appropriate wines, corny jokes and unwrapped presents.) (A week later, on New Year's Eve, after another day's labour, again the same bacchanalia. With as many participants, a different menu, no presents and the same jokes.) (The day after. New Year's Day, another monster dinner.) (After her recovery the lady with the ice-cream gâteau brought a bouquet that she could scarcely hold, it was so big. 'I didn't recognize you at first, with all those scars,' said my father truthfully. She didn't become a regular customer.)

One calm summer night it finally happens. Screech of rubber on asphalt, screams, a deafening bang, followed by a silence that sucks in everything, leaving only the sound of a lonely hub cap tumbling over and spinning to a halt. We call the police and go straight into the street. The two passenger cars have been slung twenty metres apart. One is lying on its side, with its door open upward. With the other, a Beetle, the two doors are open, as is the badly hit bonnet—two wings of death and a smashed carapace. There is smoke coming from the engine and it is unusually quiet. [she, pointing] 'A shoe! I can see a shoe lying there. [to me] Inside. At once! [to Etienne the baker, who has also come out, coughing, rattling, suffering] An odd shoe predicts a body. A stretcher bearer told me that during the war. For every shoe, a body.' In all she identifies three. She is proved right. Less than a month later our junction is finally supplied with orange flashing lights. The number of collisions is reduced by half.

Of course there was my father too. Always at work, from six-thirty in the morning to late in the evening. Even Sunday, his day of rest, he was busy cleaning or filleting. A nap after lunch, a doze after supper, and back to work. Eternally cutting, eternally scrubbing. Eternally fiddling with his mincing machine. Except in the abattoir to inspect the livestock and reserve quantities of meat, he spent scarcely an hour outside his business. And except for when he went to Café Hemelriijck, in order finally to buy the property where he did business, he never took a day off. He never shut up shop, except on Sundays and holidays or for a wedding or a funeral of relatives as far as the second degree, no further. Attacks of flu, runny noses, eye inflammations, a cold on the chest, arm bruised, neck pulled: he ignored everything. The show must go on. Driven by character, out of habit, with a little support. During the coldest winter days that meant a stiff shot of cognac in his thermos flask, before he filled it with pitch-black coffee—a full litre, which just about got him through the day. During the dog days he went for a few minutes every hour to cool off in his cold room, where it was tolerably fresh, pleasantly quiet, and a good place to be among the sides of beef with their white-veined flesh and the beheaded maize-fed chickens with their naked and butter-coloured bobbly flesh. Among well-stacked kettles of bouillon and ready-made soup, which he prayed would not go sour and start foaming. (It seemed that you could hear it, *le moment minable*, the fraction of a second in which soup irrevocably curdles. 'Ting!' There went your investment. It was one of the few times he was glad he was half deaf on one side and hard of hearing on the other. Nothing so sad as soured velouté of asparagus or champignons.)

The prospect of a holiday made him nervous. What must his customers think of him? That he no longer needed to work? An insulted customer could switch to other butchers overnight, who he judged could use his money better than a wealthy wastrel who shut up shop just to go and amuse himself on some sunny beach or other. Jealousy was soon created and there were enough competitors in the neighbourhood.

Until late in his career his only holiday consisted in him closing on Saturday afternoons, on the dot of twelve, on the first three weekends in July. In the following hour a lot of surprised regular customers rang at the back door. He served them without complaining, indeed with polite excuses. The holiday excursions were identical every year. Everyone was crammed into the Vauxhall Cresta, Pit Germaine and Wieske included, for an afternoon's shopping. The first week in Antwerp (the Meir), then in Brussels (the Nieuwstraat), then in Hulst (the Hema and Wilkins department store). The trip to Hulst was his favourite, because then the children could swim afterwards in the big open-air swimming pool in Axel, while he himself could doze off on the lawn beside the pool on a picnic blanket, and afterwards down mussels to his heart's content in Philippine, 'Mussel Town Number 1'; and with all those noisy Dutch people, Zeeland Flanders gave you a little bit of a feeling that you were many days' journey from home. ('You don't need much to make you feel you're abroad. Sweet mayonnaise and weak beer are enough. [she, with her knowledge of finishing courses and theatrical exchanges] And on the way back we can smuggle a couple of kilos of butter, at half the price. How do those cheese heads manage it?

They milk each other, I think.')

He also refused to close at lunchtimes. The customer was king and a king deserved to be waited on hand and foot. However, the capricious king took the form of a retired stay-at-home who could just as well have done her shopping at ten in the morning or three in the afternoon, but who chose to try his shopkeeper's patience at precisely twelve-thirty. Was he finally sitting quietly eating his midday soup? That rotten doorbell would go again, summoning him to his counter as if to a scaffold. He got up sighing, slid the curtain of the half-glass dividing door, recognized his tormentor through the net curtains—'Bugger me, it's that bloody woman from the undertaker's again'—before making his entry into his own shop, beaming all over his face: 'Aha! Madame Marquise of the Great Happiness! What'll it be, my lamb? What can I do for you, apart from a million and a twenty-year-old body?' He spoke to men with the same broad smile. 'Aha! The Minister of Internal Outer Tubes! What can I do for you, apart from a new car and a twenty-year-old wife?' By the time he reappeared at table, his soup was cold and his mood ruined. For no longer than five minutes, though. One doesn't protest against a lot one has chosen for oneself.

He never wanted to introduce lunchtime closing, not even a quarter of an hour. He found it as inappropriate and vulgar as 'price-cutting' or, still worse, giving away something for free. Three chicken legs for the price of two? A hundred grams extra when buying half a kilo of crab salad? That was beneath him. On Fridays and Saturdays we gave double Valois saving stamps on cash purchases. That was enough of a concession to the popular will. 'Quality doesn't need any stunts. It undermines your reputation.'

Meanwhile the whole family combed through the advertising magazines, in order to buy our coffee beans or our washing-up liquid in this Sarma or that Priba—if necessary in the Co-op, from the forever-undercutting socialist business wreckers, just because it worked out at three francs cheaper per item than from Marcel and Marcella, our very own man-and-wife grocery team. We had to unload those kinds of clandestine groceries at lightning speed from the boot, and smuggle them in via the back door, in unmarked cardboard boxes, to make the contents unrecognizable to the all-seeing prying eyes in the neighbourhood.

Sometimes the children themselves were promoted to spies, the youngest first, as innocence is the best disguise, and according to my brothers and sister no one could look as innocent as I. My father also preferred to send me as a secret informant to his competitors. The nearest one lived next to the Humps. The idea was that I should make friends with one of those Humps, so that *en passant* I could have a glance in the window of his neighbour, in order to find out how much the bastard dared charge for a kilo of veal sausages or horse fillet. The most humiliating moment came when that strange butcher—an unseemly imitation of my father, in the same kind of apron and with the same kind of hands covered in scars, but with a ridiculous cap on his head, a white cotton beret, lopsided—when that fraud recognized me and started holding up his price tickets, one after the other. Pointing first at the price with thick sausage-like fingers, their nails cut back to the quick, then at the respective product on his counter.

When *she* sent me out to spy the humiliation was no less. She targeted shoe and clothes shops and waited on the corner, while I had to go in and ask the manageress whether madam gave double savings stamps from the Association of Large and Young Families. Whereupon the woman in question, this time like a caricature of my mother, looked at me tenderly, but all the same said to me in a voice full of ammoniac: 'Your mother had your little sister ask that last year. We haven't changed our minds since. But you can go ahead and tell her that we shall expect your whole family again at this season's sale. Traditions should be honoured.'

What more could I do except nod and leave her domain in silence? Tail between my legs, two eyes boring a hole in my back?

There was, of course, me too, Johnny. Besides my father and Wivina, rats and accidents: me from nought to twenty. What shall I bring up about 'I', from this sea of vicissitudes that washed over our junction and contributed to my upbringing?

During the school year I got up half an hour later than my father, at about seven, that is, to get breakfast ready. He had already set out plates and cutlery the night before, cups upside down, butter dish still covered. My work did not consist of much more than pouring water on the coffee, boiling eggs and putting out the paper ready for my mother. I was the only one still at home at the time, the rest had flown the nest—married, gone to college, moved.

During the half-hour before I got up, he had received all the handwritten orders in his shop from the factory workers, whose numbers had dropped off sharply; the crisis in the textile industry was raging with full force, bankruptcies were ten a penny, factories moved to industrial estates on the outskirts of town or suddenly to some distant foreign place. The remaining workers would as before come and collect sandwich fillings in the afternoon and in the evenings beefsteak—the most tangible and perhaps the only form of socialism in our rich region. But now, still at seven, I saw my father sitting on his knees in our living room, in front of a stove that we call 'our continuous stove', because the intention was that it would stay lit continuously, from early autumn to late spring, a perpetuum mobile of fire. Next year we were to switch to natural gas, but for now our iron god of flame had to be raked and anthracite had to be thrown into its open maw, underneath its ash tray had to be cleaned and emptied into an iron rubbish bin—if it caught fire it couldn't do any harm, as long as the lid was kept on.

The dexterity with which my father got the fire going again every morning with only a single small poker and two handles that were linked to horizontally moving grilles in the innards of his continuous stove, that knowledge of controlled heat, that science of repeatedly reawakened warmth—all seemed to me directly linked to the oldest customs of mankind. The daily covering and scratching-open of a campfire, the tending of an eternal flame, the endless rise of the phoenix from its ashes ... He poked here, he rattled there, he blew over there, and all his movements together—refilling from the top, taking out from the bottom, in the middle shaking and prodding and rattling and sifting and blowing—formed a wordless morning prayer, a percussive Singsong For The Almighty Coal Stove, with which the new day was declared opened. The prayer was not concluded with 'amen' but with a door that was closed with a cautious squeak, like an altar-tabernacle. Afterwards the anthracite glowed again, deep red with black edges, behind the mica windows the incomparable comfort of the stove's heat began to spread through our living room. To the greater honour and glory of our silent breakfast.

One morning I come down and no one is sitting in front of the continuous stove. The mica windows are still deathly and dark. I cast a glance into the shop through the net curtain of the inner door: no one. I go and look in the workshop: no one. I pull the back door open: no father to be seen in the street either. The usual Aubade of The Piercing Doorbell has nevertheless already sounded in all its annoying lustre, the workers have come to drop off their orders as always. Where is he then? Yesterday he and his Josée went to play cards with François With the Glass Eye and his Jeanneke from the Post Office, who easily put away a pack of Mort Subite Gueuze Lambic in an evening. He probably drank his share, but he didn't misbehave by the look of it: the sofa wasn't slept on last night. And half an hour ago I heard his alarm go off in their bedroom. Then I heard him stumble downstairs, that staircase in the narrow cylinder. Not without a din, despite the treads with their muffling carpet, so he won't have sobered up completely. But where is he then? In his cold room? As a remedy against a hangover this time?

I find him in the shop after all. Stinking of beer, true, but with the most blissful grin on his face, because he has finally, after all those years, found the solution for reconciling his duty as a loyal shopkeeper with his thirst for a few extra minutes' sleep. He has crawled onto his big, whitewood chopping block and lies there sleeping it off, on display to every passer-by, as if he himself were a prize animal after slaughter. He doesn't need an inflatable pillow to get comfortable. He is lying on his side, his face turned toward possible customers, and he supports his cheek with hands laid on top of each other, as a plump shepherd would do at night, in a painting by Jacob Jordaens.

Every day he scrapes this chopping block with a wire brush, he sweeps the soft sawdust up with a dustpan that has become greasy. Where the blood has penetrated the greedy wood furthest, he scrapes hardest. In this way over the years two faint dips have appeared in the surface. The curves of his body fit perfectly into them. He is almost as comfortable as on our sofa. Peaceful, smacking his chops, content. If he had been lying on his back it would have been a complete prefiguration of his deathbed so many years later. ('I'm buggered, lad. Hu, hu, hu.')

This chopping block is the jewel in our crown. Two metres wide, one metre deep. With, at the back, along its whole length, a groove from which the handles of his knives stick up like a row of black stalks robbed of their calyxes. Just behind it is a triangular decorative panel, in the same white wood as the whole block. The panel edges are decorated with curlicues, the centres with a pig's head in bas-relief. All the other decorations of the block, such as the fittings at the corners, the convex, shield-shaped ornaments and the large rings with which the two drawers are opened, are copper. Apart from the weekly dusting of our hundreds of tins of preserves, and besides the daily washing-up of scores of meat dishes and decorative plates, my traditional task in the family factory is the polishing of these rings, these fittings, these shields, with a steel-wool sponge until they sparkle and I can see myself reflected in them with a distorted head, bulging frog's eyes and puffed-up cheeks.

When I was still too small to help with anything, and could still only just see over the top of the block, I often stood there peering in admiration, on tiptoe, at the ease with which my father first cut the meat of a veal cutlet with one of his smallest but sharpest knives and then lifted his chopper from the groove and with two simple, calm blows chopped through the bone. I loved that sound. I loved the panache with which, with the flat of the chopper, he also flattened the cutlet—it was more a caress than a blow. I wanted nothing better than to be able to cut into such pink meat. To be able to conjure up slices of ham out of nowhere with our electric slicer, to be able to arrange them one after another in a fan shape on special two-sided wrapping paper and then to throw it from a distance onto the scales and cajole: 'Do you mind if it's a little over, madam?' The oblong money drawer with its separate compartments—on the left one for quarters and half-francs, next to them the francs, next to them coins of five francs and above, and finally the notes, arranged from large to small—had a magical attraction. Not least because of its dull, incomparable amalgam of smells. The inside-pocket smell, the sweat smell, the wallet smell, the grabbing smell, the unwashed hands smell, the café smell, the body odour of quite simply hundreds of customers who had got their money from hundreds of others in turn. Why: money doesn't stink, does it?

'Stop rummaging in those dirty quarters,' warned my father, wiping my hand clean with a clammy towel, 'I've got something else for you, come on.' He led me to his chopping block and with one of his widest knives cut off a wafer-thin piece of tenderloin. For a moment it lay there, half on, half over the top of the block. Then he let his knife tip over. The wafer-thin piece allowed itself to be spread out on a corner of our magnificent block. With two lightning movements—one at right angles to the other—he chopped up the piece and scooped up the mini-portion of *biftec haché* with his knife. Then he took my grabbing hand in his free hand, with both our palms upward. Slowly and carefully he wiped that wide knife clean on my hand taking care that the blade did not touch me.

I felt the cold steel stroking the side of my hand, in which layer after layer of freshly chopped tenderloin was piling up. A well-filled child's mitt. 'Have a taste. Nice, isn't it?'

She the word? He was the meat.

(When he retired the only item of furniture that fetched a respectable price was the chopping block. A few years later when I call the antique dealer to ask if I can buy it back, he laughs at me. 'A month later it was on the boat on its way to America. It's now the pièce de résistance in the foyer of a restaurant.' He refuses to tell me where. When I ask him how much he sold the block on for, he hangs up.)

There were finally, don't worry Johnny, the fairs, the *braderies*, the sausage stalls, the Sunday markets. The Antwerpse Steenweg was not always a stretch of race-track. It could be cordoned off on both sides with red and white crowd barriers fencing a traffic light and two orange flashing lights.

On one side of the temporary promenade a covered stage could be erected, on which a dance orchestra murdered hits old and new on Saturday evenings. One-day fans danced their hearts out on a wooden dance floor in front of the stage. The floor itself was ringed with tar-coated posts between which dangled the leads of coloured lights. A little touch by the Alderman for Festivities, who hoped for re-election.

The following afternoon the floor was strewn with folding tables and chairs—wooden top or seat, an iron frame. Proud grandparents sat listening with emotion to a talent competition of the kind they had once experienced themselves, in their day. Now their grandchildren were announced on stage with a blare of noise by a lively editor from *Het Vrije Waasland*, got up for the occasion in a dinner jacket with a white begonia in the buttonhole of his lapel. The youngsters sang on tiptoe and at the top of their voices. Preferably tearjerkers, in the hope of moving the jury to give higher marks and the grandparents more pocket money. One of them, standing at the microphone with clenched fists and bewildered, questioning eyes, turned out to have forgotten his words, purely from the effort of not forgetting them. Before he could burst into tears publicly, the master of ceremonies asked him if he knew another song. The freckled face of the little boy brightened: 'The Belgian national anthem!' [the master of ceremonies, hunting in his memory in amazement, doubting whether he as political editor actually knew all the words himself] 'The Belgian national anthem?' The little chap, nodding vigorously, plunged straight in: 'Oh Precious Belgium, the donkey cannot dump now, / Because his poo / Is all sealed up with glue.' He received the biggest ovation of the day, but finished in last place. The jury also got something for its pains. Boos and empty cardboard cups, thrown at them by elderly hooligans who had had one over the eight.

On the other side of the promenade a mirror tent arose which used to appear at fairs but was now sponsored by our last local brewery—the others had been swallowed up by a beer giant from the Leuven area. In this mirror tent, during a family matinee, the Grand Christmas Raffle took place, with prizes in kind, provided 'in sympathy' by local shopkeepers, one more generous than the next. ('Traffic-free, traffic-free,' grumbled the supplier of cement and girders, 'my customers don't come on foot, you know.' He hadn't donated a single prize. 'Who wants to win a roof tile?')

On the last day of the neighbourhood party a race was nevertheless run along the Antwerpse Steenweg. On soapboxes. Then everything was dismantled and a few hours later the first long-distance buses were tearing by again. Only squashed cups in the gutters and the last lorry loaded with tables recalled the frivolity of a summer that was now over.

You had to wait for spring, Johnny, the beginning of May, before signs of a new vitality manifested themselves. The brass band of the socialists paraded, and not long after the band of the Catholics. Each preceded by their respective gymnastic clubs, veterans at the front, then the young girls, then the boys, and each followed by their respective parliamentarians, town council members, representatives of their medical boards, as well as a few loyal party invalids from two world wars. The whole pack was pursued, hopping along, by everyone younger than twelve who had not made up their mind ideologically.

The liberals didn't have a brass band. They had a Sunday criterium cycle race. To prove that they—although it was only for one Sunday, and only from eleven to four—could declare more streets traffic-free than just the Steenweg. It was short on atmosphere, but one of those pelotons was still an experience. It was as if a compact body whooshed past you, a displacement of air on fragile wheels. A massive cloud of men's bodies and sinewy heads welded together, diffuse jersey colours, black shorts, sparkling spokes and rims. Flashing past in a sigh, it left behind only jerky fragments of images on your retina, full of gleaming, balloon-like calves and broad backsides and self-confident numbers on backs, 21 7 17 49 83. Especially the sound, frighteningly thin for so much clenched power, was impressive. The greased turning of scores of chains rose to a single great hymn to propulsion, a giant swarm of happy insects, with as a *basso continuo* the scores of tubes that seem to be passionately sucking at the asphalt and letting go of it again with a single lingering kiss. Little rose above that heavenly hymn except sporadic swearing and constant rattling, together with the blowing of noses out of one nostril while pushing the other closed with two fingers. Occasionally the swarm threw an object out of its deepest core. On contact with our pavements, the elegant arc that it followed changed into a wild, hollow-sounding bouncing motion. An empty drinking bottle. We took them home but we didn't dare use them. You heard enough stories about the eating habits of racing cyclists.

As the number of shopkeepers decreased on our once so well-appointed access route the number of *braderies* also fell. The last two attempts were rained off. The brass band paraded less and less. Despite its name the harmony band had a bust-up, the mirror tent was sold abroad, the soapbox race disappeared and even the criterium race went downhill. First because the racers refused any longer to change in the banqueting room of an establishment that had been called simply Café Commerce, but had now been redubbed Café of the Velvet Hole. They had already been laughed at for less. Lastly, because the course marshals could no longer manage to post competent safety stewards on every corner and at every junction. Finally even Mad Lucienneke had had a tricolour armband pinned around her biceps. She stood waving her board at everything and everyone—round and red and on a stick, with a flat white strip on both sides. Afterwards she refused to give it back, for once not smiling, but on the contrary crying inconsolably: 'My ping-pong bat! Got it as a present!'

Right, Johnny. Let this be enough. That is more or less the whole fresco. More or less the peacock's tail of official facts and private tradition, together the former arena of at least two lives, mine and that of my speechless passenger. I am taking her to the dentist in my Italian hot rod and I hope fervently that, face to face with her former surroundings, she may regain some of the formulations with which she always sang the praises of that micro-environment in such flowery terms. I'm not asking a lot. I'm content with the above anecdotes, raked up by her in a handful of keywords. A fragmented sentence of twenty syllables, when we pass a spot that reminds her of a striking adventure. Three separate words will be enough. Two even. I would settle for one trophy.

Grant her, grant me, at least that.

From 't Zonneken onward, and certainly in the Bellenstraat, which will shortly continue as the Antwerpse Steenweg, she becomes restless. Her eyes dart back and forth more and more timidly. The nature of her restlessness is difficult to guess. Fear? Apprehension? Regret? Or despite everything: the urge to talk?

We drive under the railway and cross the Singel, as our small ring road is called. Now we are driving along the Raapstraat. We still have one bend to negotiate before we reach that straight stretch of asphalt 500 metres long with which the Lindenstraat still forms a junction.

The junction. Today with that chip shop, still a baker's, and that specialist pet shop. On that last bend is Café Den Toerist. Next door lived the Humps, next to them our competitor, that unseemly imitation of my father. Both properties have been demolished, in exchange for a modest apartment block under construction. We take the bend at a leisurely pace.

Finally the Antwerpse Steenweg stretches ahead of us. Here I once finished in a shameful last place on a soapbox: tears by the bucketful, laughed at by everyone. Now I'm driving here in a real car, but almost as slowly and with my mother on my right-hand side. What is she thinking? What does this length of street remind her of? What does she want to tell me? What story don't I know yet, or have I clean forgotten?

I don't hear anything. I glance to the side.

You can't even tell if she is moving her lips. She is holding her flat handbag in front of her face with both hands, like a suspect in a murder case when he has to face the paparazzi. Few of her former neighbours are still alive and she knows only a few of the people who live here now by name.

Still she doesn't want anyone to look at her. She is ashamed. Of who she is, of who she has become. She of all people is hiding. She of all people tries to efface herself. She would like not to be here. She would like not to *be* any more, quite simply not to exist. Or is it the other way round? Perhaps she wants to spare herself the sight. Perhaps she wants to be excused having to see the pain of what she has lost and can never regain.

The facts remain the same. We drive through the street where for forty years she worked and lived and she holds her handbag in front of her face. From shame or self-protection, what is the difference? She does not want to look around and wants to remain unrecognizable in the neighbourhood where she brought me up. My mother hides her face like a criminal.

Her teeth were fine.
     On the way back I chose a different route.

A MONTH LATER the therapist decides that for the benefit of her recovery she should go home for one day during the weekend. Just she and her husband, together in the flat like before. A familiar environment and automatic domestic behaviour may help accelerate the healing process. It's a test. If this first stay goes satisfactorily, more will follow. They can be extended to a whole weekend, then three days, four, five. Finally back home permanently.

The optimism is well grounded. She has made progress, just not greatly in her speech. But she no longer needs any help with getting dressed and undressed, with eating or exercise therapies. Tidying her room has actually become an obsession. She would gladly tear the vacuum cleaner and floorcloths out of the hands of the cleaners to make herself useful—or to do the work properly, because behind the backs of the often foreign women she plays the clown. She squeezes her nose shut, points first to the cleaner and then to her own armpit. She runs a fingertip along the windowsill and sticks it pontifically in the air, full of horror, retching as if her fingers were not only covered in dust, but also filth. All this accompanied by her nonsensical abracadabra with odd snatches of English and French, her refrain of 'a little', and only a few new sounds and words.

'We mustn't give up hope,' says the therapist. 'I've known cases which made slower progress and which still achieved a complete recovery. And even then. Even without language life can be worth living.'

She gets out of the car at the door of the flat as if there is no problem, as if she has been away from home for only a few days, a day, a few hours. Her months in Beveren were the excursion, not the coming twenty-four hours in this familiar property.

On the way she did not shut up for a moment, excited as if on a school trip. Again it was not possible to make head or tail of her chattering, but this time at least she did not look shyly around. She did not seem to be frightened of anything and not once did she hold her handbag in front of her face. On the contrary, she looked around freely and openly and sometimes waved to complete strangers at the side of the road. They usually waved back in despair, frightened of disappointing a friend or acquaintance in that car flashing past. Every wave returned made her giggle.

Her mood is jolly without reserve. It must have got through to her that a barrier has been surmounted, that she can at last go home again. But does she also understand that it is only temporary? And that tomorrow she will have to go back to the institution? How do we deal with it, if she doesn't realize?

The front door is scarcely open when she charges up the stairs, leaving my father and me behind in the entrance hall with its frenzied jungle flowers on the walls and the ceiling. He and I lug her suitcase and bags upstairs and find her in her kitchenette, where, grumbling happily in her best slang, she is already checking the fridge. She

takes out everything that does not strike her as sufficiently fresh or that she just doesn't like, a plate of leftovers after a Tupperware container with leavings in.
Constantly grumbling but with a smile round her
mouth, she puts all those portions and leftovers together
on a dish, places the empty plates and containers in one
of the two washing-up bowls and takes the brim-full
bowl to the toilet. We follow her, looking at each other,
not really knowing what to do: should we intervene or
let things run their course?

She tips the collected leftovers into the toilet bowl and
flushes. She pushes the empty bowl into the hands of
her flabbergasted Roger. He actually gets a wink into the
bargain, as if she wanted to impress on him sweetly:
'What is a man like you supposed to do without a woman
like me?' He immediately passes the bowl on to me, as
she is already making energetically for her next target:
their bedroom. For a moment I hesitate: should I follow
them, or first return the bowl to the kitchen? I finally
follow them anyway with bowl and all.

She is standing in front of her opened linen chest and is
pulling a pile of clean bedding onto the ground. He tries
to stop her, but in surprise she knocks away his calming
hand and then goes over to their bed. She strips it, stuffs
the stripped linen into a ball and pushes it into his arms.

She takes the dirty bowl out of my hands with a mocking laugh, puts it on one side, bends down, stuffs the
clean bedding on the floor into a bundle and pushes it
into my arms. She herself takes a pack of clean towels,
neatly piled, out of her cupboard and grasps them
between her left and right palm, the way she used to
serve up a half-metre of her freshly baked waffles.
('Crunchy and light as a feather! [she, giving away her

secret every time with the same satisfaction] You wait until your waffle iron is red-hot, and only then, just before you start to bake that is, you mix half a bottle of sparkling water with your dough, You can give it a good shake beforehand, the important thing is the fizz in that water.')

'Come,' she says now. Brightly and clearly. But that one word, at the right moment, on a correct occasion, because she wants us to follow her: 'Come!' And the three of us walk, goose-stepping, each with a load of linen, down those stairs again, to the washroom on the ground floor. There she stuffs her towels in the machine and orders us, with gestures and confused exclamations, to deposit our load of sheets and pillowcases in the empty laundry basket, yes that one there! That one!

We obey, but look at each other behind her back. She's going to do the washing? She certainly is. Her automatic domestic behaviour has remained intact. She still knows where the packet of washing powder is—in the cupboard under her old-fashioned washbasin. She finds the sliding soap drawer without hesitation. She pours in the necessary quantity of powder without spilling any. She closes the round window as is required. She turns the knob to the right setting. And she ratifies every action as she used to. With a smug nod of her head.

The machine hums, and the drum starts to spin. She looks at the two of us with a chuckle, than at the round window behind which the washing is tumbling, becoming ever wetter, less and less playful. The three of us stand watching for a while as if at the joyful birth of a litter of stray cats, touchingly blind in their cardboard box full of rags. 'Come!' she suddenly says again, gesturing for us to follow her. On the way to what is undoubtedly the next chore with which she wants to celebrate her homecoming, with which she wants to demarcate her lost territory. Again she leads us upstairs, again we follow slavishly.

It happens of all places in the kink in their stairs. She turns round without any pretext and walks quite hard into her Roger, resulting in my bumping into him. All three of us come to a halt, in the middle of that dangerous staircase. We are bewildered. She is alarmed and actually frightened. She seems to think that we are trying to bar her way, that we want to banish her upstairs, that now she won't be able to come and go as she pleases even at home.

From one moment to the next she panics. Her eyes again spew fire, her mouth belches the most resounding curses in her sardonic dialect, and before we can explain or do anything she throws herself from the higher step. With the unbridled, reckless strength of the mentally ill. In less than three seconds she has again reverted to her behaviour of months ago.

Her Roger can't do much more than protect himself from her swipes. He holds an arm over his head and with the other arm grabs her waist. To reassure her, or to make hitting more difficult by keeping her as close as possible by him, as an experienced boxer would do. Or perhaps it is above all a reflex of affection. The tragic translation of incomprehension.

His hold makes her even more angry than she already is. She tugs her body back and forth, as if to free herself. He keeps hugging her. They lose their balance together and fall intertwined, embracing, onto an even lower step. Full-tilt into me. I have to brace myself with both legs to prevent the three of us from tumbling downstairs. With one hand I grasp the banister, keeping my other hand pressed against the wall.

So there we stand, pushing and tugging at each other, half fighting, half fending off. A balancing trio on a narrow staircase. We screech and beg without listening to each other. Once more a polyphony, this time of rage and helplessness. In a hall that is papered from floor to ceiling with monstrous flowers, scornfully gaping giant beaks against a background of anthracite.

IT IS NOT the first time in her life that she has lost her language, but on the previous occasion she suddenly also lost her voice. Just before the war broke out—she isn't yet twenty—she is sitting in the train to her work in the jute factory in Lokeren, where she is being trained as a management PA, when the Luftwaffe has Lokeren in its sights.

The railway line, the industry, a bridge over the Durme. She sees it all happen through her window.

'You never forget something like that as long as you live. First one of those Stukas that drops through the firmament like a goose that has been shot, and which gives you the shivers just with its howling, and which pulls out only at the very last instant—just as you're thinking: it's going to smash to pieces on our beet fields—releases its bomb on a hangar, turns away again, and shortly afterwards comes falling out of the sky a second time, again howling, but this time firing machine guns at everything that moves, human, animal, freighter, bus, you name it, with extra attention, the bastard, for everyone who comes running out of the burning hangar, or dares to start extinguishing it. [she, telling the story in a kind of ecstasy, each time with more or less the same formulations and gestures, only touching up her little epic in bits and pieces, in search of just a little more effect without losing the glow of the previous time, as a narrator from vanished civilisations would do.]

'That hellish whine of those Stukas! And at the same time, the beauty of that fall. Simply perfect. You can say what you like about the Germans, but they're a race apart. Their other bombers, the Heinkels, were less elegant, but they also had a dreadful beauty about them. First they hang lazily swerving and shining above the useless little thudding clouds of our anti-aircraft batteries, but suddenly they release a large black pack up there. Something square. Something that starts to descend at lightning speed and suddenly falls apart. First you think: but it's a Bible! It's a missal falling to pieces, into a hundred fine sheets! And only now do you see it, as the roaring becomes audible, the many-voiced whistling. Each of those sheets is a bomb.

'As you realize that, the first ones are already exploding. And you see it happen, over there in the distance, in the town where you hope to build your future. They explode with a force that hurls bits of buildings and plots of land into the air. A primeval force that makes our train rock on its rails, that makes our windows shake in their frames. But it doesn't slow down, our train, let alone stop. It is taking us straight to where the sheets of a murderous missal are whistling down, sowing blood and fire, pain and rubble everywhere. No one has the idea of pulling the communication cord, everyone is far too busy screaming and pointing and crying and pleading. Everyone, except me. I open my mouth as wide as the rest, I want to shout as loud as I can, but nothing comes out of my throat. My vocal chords seize up from the power of the shock. It was two days before I spoke my first word again.'

She remains working in Lokeren during the war years, in the factory which is meanwhile under German control and incorporated in their war industry. She is now a management PA, even authorized to handle cash. She is at the beginning of a career open to few women of her generation, and she is still only in her early twenties.

'But, well, how do these things go? First we marry, still in wartime. The family on your father's side is given permission to come all the way from Torhout and Middelkerke to the Waasland, which was unique in those days. At home your father's father and your uncle Gaston, also a butcher, had good contacts in the food industry, thank God. Everyone saved or put things aside instead for the wedding party of Roger, the youngest. Everyone felt sorry for us, a young couple doomed to get married in the shadow of a world conflagration. A few eggs came from here, a leg of ham from there, a tub of mushrooms from elsewhere, from a farmer who was indebted to them. At the slaughterhouse the cows standing ready were milked a last time, under the noses of the collaborators on guard who knew absolutely nothing about animals, so that we would have enough milk and cream for our wedding cake. Just imagine! While food was on ration and people queued up outside half-empty shops, we were able to serve fifty guests four courses, with even a few glasses of wine and a piece of white bread for each, a mug of real coffee and even a glass of cognac, which someone or other had managed to scrounge from his great-aunt, a holier-than-thou pro-Belgian who had wanted to save her two bottles of Courvoisier Napoléon for the Liberation, but who thought that that young couple should not go short through the fault of the Germans. We even went on honeymoon, with the water-polo club your father belonged to then.

In the early evening they played a game, at night we were given a separate room. Love moved around with us. To Tournai, which was half bombed-out. That doesn't seem much of a destination now, but for us that ruin was paradise.

'After that reality kicked in. I went on working in Lokeren for a good year, and they offered me a considerable rise if I would stay on; in time I would be in charge of the whole office, they assured me. But, well. How do those things go? When you get pregnant, and you have to take the train every day to your work, through wind and weather, or in the heat of an old-fashioned summer? It's an easy calculation to make. All the more so because we were paying a fortune for assistants in the shop. Shortly before my first was born I cut the Gordian knot. Roger, I said, hold on to the mast head. I'm stopping working in Lokeren and I'll come and help you in the shop. I didn't dare ask you, he said. I know, I said. But I have two conditions. That doesn't frighten me, he said. That you let me do the bookkeeping and fire those girls. And that you never take my theatre away, I need something to express myself in. I know, he said, and I wouldn't want it any different. I'll give up my water polo. And so the bargain was struck.'

What she didn't say is that a portion of her family and friends turned their noses up at her choice. Well, perhaps they did, and she simply harboured the suspicion—or was it the fear?—that people declared her mad for letting herself be downgraded from top assistant to butcher's wife, in not that big a business. Perhaps she never came completely to terms with it and that was why she got so irritable if you dared ask—casually, purely for information, with no other intention but to satisfy your curiosity—whether she, looking back on it, when it came down to it, wouldn't she at the time have preferred to stay on at the jute factory, with the prospect of the top job. 'You don't ask that kind of thing,' was the answer with which she closed the matter before it was even opened.

But sometimes, very occasionally, revealing that she did still worry her head about it, she replied: 'I would have been in a fine state. The whole sector moved away. What would I have had to do? Move too? Leaving everyone behind? To a country full of half-Chinese who now manufacture what we used to make, only ten times cheaper? As it is I stopped on my own initiative, otherwise they would have had to fire me. I was spared that disgrace. I have never had to thank or reproach anyone for the course I've taken. Never!'

She doesn't lack enthusiasm for her new vocation. Butcher? You can learn everything. And you get used to everything. Even washed pig intestines, which arrive packed in coarse salt and are used, filled with mince, to become sausages. But she never goes to the abattoir with him. In that respect she prefers the denying silence of all those who love animals but also like fur coats and beefsteak.

What she did occasionally sketch, very vividly, and always with a lasting note of astonishment, was the new family in which she found herself. That trade? All well and good. But that patriarch?

'I still remember it well, I went to see them for the first time, in the Vermorgenstraat, where your grandfather still ran his butcher's shop, a big business with lots of regular customers. He's sitting in the back, they said, he's having his tea. I think, oh dear I'm going to disturb the man over his bread pudding or his plate of strawberries. Forget it! He's sitting at table reading his paper *L'Écho de la Bourse*, checking the state of his shares, he's holding the paper in his left hand and with his right he is putting roast lamb cutlets in his mouth. One after the other. He bites off the meat with one snap and puts the bone aside without stopping reading. Four lamb chops in all. I counted them. I saw it all with my own eyes. He went on reading and eating as if I wasn't there. That was his idea of tea. For breakfast he had six eggs with bacon, in the winter twelve. Then a sandwich with lard, and in the winter a couple of slices of fried udder. You have to ask yourself what he could have put away when he really started to stuff.

'I simply stood there, rooted to the spot, counting cutlets, surprised that my sweetheart's father could find his mouth so easily, his jowls were so big, his chins were so numerous, his bacon neck was so broad. When he died, your father inherited his wedding ring. When you laid that ring in the palm of your hand? You won't believe it. You'd think: that isn't a wedding ring, that is a ring that has been in the nose of a prize bull when they had to pull it on a rope to the livestock inspector. It was so big, that ring, so heavy with gold. And don't forget: your grandfather wore it on his little finger, because his other fingers had grown too thick for it.

'He has finally finished his tea, our colossus, with *L'Écho de la Bourse* in his mitts, he wipes that small mouth amid his great cheeks with a napkin and he looks up. At me. I jolly well had the feeling that I myself was being inspected like a piece of meat, and what's more was to his taste. He said something that resembled a greeting, an approval, or something in between. I couldn't understand a blessed word. He never spoke anything but West Flemish. Except at the bank, in bureaux de change or at the horse races in Ostend. There he spoke French. I returned his greeting in a friendly way and left him alone. With only one thought in my mind. If my man ever develops cheeks like that? I'll put him on a diet of water and dry bread.'

That patriarch of ours was called Noë. That is Noah spelt the French way. Besides his name and his inseparable cap he had all the other qualifications for being a patriarch. Obesity, contempt for his fellow man, a permanently foul humour and a mistress, a sturdy figure of a woman who served at the same time as a live-in maid in the house he shared with his wife, my grandmother —herself a thoroughly good and fragile woman, who didn't seem to suffer too much from being able to leave love and all it entailed to her cleaning woman, together with the rest of the household chores.

Neither of the two women got to see their lord and master very much, for, as became the captain of an ark, he was also a pigeon fancier. Every week he spent more time in the forever cooing pigeon palace that he had had built in his garden from Congolese hardwood, knocked together with rusty nails, than indoors checking whether his bills were correct, or what his bonds would fetch if he cashed them in in advance.

He spent the rest of his time inspecting livestock for slaughter and arguing with pig breeders and gentlemen farmers, either about their poor tactics in playing whist, or over the dead-end complexity of Belgian politics. In discussing the latter he played even dirtier than at cards. If he read in the morning in *La Libre Belgique* an article about a bill that would obviously affect his café acquaintances, he would cut it out, slip it into his wallet folded up and during a game of whist would bring the conversation supposedly by chance round to the subject in question. Only when the discussion had flared up sufficiently and was almost losing focus did he produce his cutting. 'Here, look! It was in the paper, idiot! You must know what you're talking about before you start laying down the law to someone like me!' It was his size that saved him from a thrashing. That and his antique, mysterious language of invocation full of sing-song gutturals and brutish snarling, West Flemish, which he boasted was older and better and more beautiful than any kind of Dutch. He showed off with it like some military men do with a medal or a scar on their face. 'It's the language of the genius Guido Gezelle,' he was wont to say proudly. Although, as a loyal West Fleming, he pronounced it as the 'henius Huido Hezelle,' so we could scarcely contain our laughter. The 'henius Huido Hezelle! The henius Huido Hezelle!' we shouted at each other behind his back. He was even more hard of hearing than his youngest son.

Just before the last gas offensive of the First World War, late in 1917, he had been given the urgent advice to leave everything behind, his pub-cum-inn, smithy, butcher's shop, accommodation—and take flight with the human stream to Antwerp. With horse and cart and the bare necessities, from wife to maid. He who hated the masses became the equal of thousands of other refugees, most of them without two pennies to rub together, scum that he would have enjoyed chasing off his property, that he would have shown the door of his inn the moment they showed their unwashed mugs, and whom he now had to beg for a mouthful of water, and from whom he had to manage to scrounge bread in exchange for a mother-of-pearl earring of his wife's. He had intended to emigrate at once, to Chicago, via

Antwerp. He stopped en route, in Sint-Niklaas.

When, a year later, after the Armistice of 11 November, he wanted to visit his business near Ypres again, a surveyor he was friendly with had to show him the way through the ravaged areas. 'Somewhere here must have been your stables and here your bar.' The whole plot, the soil itself and everything that was on it has been so ravaged, seared, ploughed up, soaked with blood and filth and mustard gas. He sells his drenched land and returns embittered to the town where he has washed up as a refugee, and where in a short space of time he will again make his fortune by selling fresh heifer meat, with, as his speciality, boiled udder. His nickname remains however The Refugee, and as he grows older the fortune which he maintained he lost in West Flanders increases, and in comparison with it his present prosperity increasingly pales. 'Without the Great War I would have been a multimillionaire. A man whose word was law for miles around, in the place where he was born. And what am I now? A homeless man. A town dweller. A strange bird. For ever and always a refugee.'

He has two sons. The elder takes over his business, and he helps the younger find a new one. The start-up money that he lends the younger for the purpose gives him the right to come and meddle, even long after everything has been paid back. At least once a week our arkfather drops by on his virtually solid cast-iron bike, with tyres almost as thick as those of a wheelbarrow, to spew his negative comments on everything his butcher's eye spots. The mince has been ground too fine, the sausage filled too thick, the veal is too watery, the poultry has been supplied by a poison-mixing poulterer, the smoked ham by a fraud, and the ink paper by a band of gangsters from Brussels, who anyway are on the verge of bankruptcy, if you are to believe *L'Écho de la Bourse*—and if there is anything you should believe, it is *L'Écho de la Bourse*, and not God and His priests. Nothing is any good in his eyes. The conversations between him and my mother don't go very smoothly. For convenience they both blame it on his West Flemish.

Meanwhile he definitely does lend a hand. That cannot be denied. No one is handier with the meat needle. The soup meat that he sews into a roll never comes loose during cooking. Even La Josée has to admit that his rolls of *bouilli*, laid on a porcelain dish and decorated with celery leaves, have artistic qualities as a visually attractive object, and they sell noticeably well. When she pays him a compliment on it, in a wave of conciliation, he looks at her as if she is insulting him. 'What do you know about a butcher's business, you poor sheep?' He doesn't waste another word on it, but shuffles silently to the shop door and goes out as he came in. Tantalizingly slowly, carefully turning round the door and on his own axis, and shouting 'Me' loudly as every member of family is supposed to when they arrive or leave, so that people know in the workshop and living room that a familiar person has made the shop bell ring and it is therefore not necessary to appear behind the counter. With him that 'Me' sounds like 'Meeeeeeeee' because he is doomed to slowness by his size and age. In this too we often mimic my grandfather, without his noticing, since his hands move fast, and not only to sew soup meat. 'Meeeeeee!' we shout, walking just as slowly in and out, for fun. 'Meeeeeeeeeee!' Remarkably, to the annoyance of his daughter-in-law. She doesn't tolerate any mockery of him. 'Laughing at old people is easy. Wait till you're worn out yourselves.'

It is the only time she says anything like that. Otherwise

she is the first to make fun of old people who nestle in the privileges of old age. We suspect that she thoroughly enjoys poking fun at her father-in-law, but that she disguises the urge by severely rejecting our mockery.

For the same reason, we suspect, she won't tolerate us making fun of our ark-father's maid. Yet we have been able to catch her grinning, our mother, when we confessed our nickname for the woman. Flor with the Moustache. It's true too. Flor is a candid, always noisy and always radiantly happy woman from the coast, with greasy hair twisted into an eternal bun on the back of her head, and with always laughing slit eyes which remind us of the Artis / Historia print of Ghenghis Khan. That same Flor has stubble under her nose and on her chin, as bad as a man who has not shaved for a day. She loves us all to death, purring at us every time we visit. While we actually only love our silent little grandmother, who sits on a chair and watches as Flor receives us exuberantly, bellowing each of our names through the house as if she has to announce us in the attic, and after this announcement grabbing us one by one in a bear hug and, oh horror, giving us a kiss that lands just next to our mouths. You can feel her stubble scraping, your skin is grazed afterwards. I, being as the youngest the most cuddly, start crying at the prospect—which she finds especially touching and which gets me a couple of extra smacking kisses. I am her big favourite, she says, pinching my cheek. 'Here he is, look! Here he is! My little favourite! My favourite child!' Which makes me start whining again, even after she has explained to me that favourite means darling, in her dialect, which she learnt a long way from here, around the Zwin—don't I know where that is then? The Zwin? On the sea! Close to Knokke. The Zwin. The Zwin! The Zwin!

All that time Flor goes on indestructibly radiating happiness and hospitality. Only when we crawl onto the lap of our silent grandmother, would you swear that a touch of sadness crept into her eyes and in the gestures with which she aimlessly wipes her hands on her flowered apron. The next moment she is bellowing again. We can come to table, she chimes, we don't need to wait for our ark-father. 'I shall go and call him!' she warns, all happiness. 'He's with his pigeons again, the old idiot!'

After the death of our ark-father we never saw her again. It was whispered that she gave up the ghost shortly after him. From grief and aimlessness.

The ark-father himself died in his sleep, in the middle of the night, weighing 150 kilos, as always with a nightcap on his head and sitting upright with five pillows at his back. Under his bed was a worn-out case full of shares. Most of them were from Union Minière, Katanga, Congo. There were even some from pre-revolutionary Russia which had survived the flight from West Flanders. But whether they came from Russia or Congo, they were equally worthless. *L'Écho de la Bourse* had after all been proved wrong. All the failed investments of a refugee, collected in a suitcase under his deathbed. They were sold to a collector of securities which had become worthless.

His two sons and two of his grandsons were recruited to get the dead ark-father to the ground floor and then to the hearse, down the narrow stairs and through the equally narrow passage. It was difficult for them to lift him, even with four of them. To make the transport detail less morbid a sheet was laid over his body. As they take the bend in the stairs—the sons support their father by the head and shoulders, the grandsons support their grandfather by the feet—the body of the ark-father bends. Immediately a roar is heard from beneath the sheet, in the well-known bass voice that always cried 'Meeeeeeeeee!' The sons and grandsons are scared out of their wits, the weight of the body escapes them, and the ark-father crashes down the rest of the staircase, between and over his two grandsons, bobbing wildly, feet first, hitting his head hard on each successive step. He comes to a halt in the passage. Without a sheet.

'It's a normal phenomenon,' explains the undertaker, 'the air in the lungs is compressed and expelled and the vocal chords do their work, that's why they're vocal chords, we encounter that quite often.' 'But suppose he *wasn't* dead? Seemingly dead, or what do they call it?' asks one of the sons, still pale as a ghost.' 'He'd be dead by now,' concludes the undertaker. 'Even a neck of that size can be broken.'

WE DO NOT fall on our stairs, many years later. My mother, my father and I. Under our canopy of monstrous jungle flowers. Shouting and screaming and fighting and balancing.

As unexpectedly as our tussle began, it is over. She has stopped shouting in her devilish dialect and has calmly slipped past us. Without falling, without injury, without problems. And we follow her yet again, back downstairs, back to that washroom. Condemned to walk-on parts on this first day of judgement, her first excursion to her former home, in the hope that many more may follow.

The sight of what she gets up to in the washroom knocks the bottom out of our hope. She tugs like a woman possessed at the round window of the washing machine which she turned on not long ago. She turns the knob fanatically, she bangs the machine with the flat of her hand, as you had to do with one of our earliest TV sets, because it would only produce sound after a couple of bangs. She even kicks the corner of the machine and hurts her ankle—for a moment she hops around furiously like a figure in a cartoon film, bent over with her hands on the injured ankle.

My father and I try to protect her from falling over,

both equally sad, equally ashamed, equally concerned. She doesn't notice any of that in her Homeric anger. And that language is back. That mark of shame, that doom, that scratching on my eardrum and on my soul. Nothing language, garbled language, phoney language, no-language, nix-language, non-language, a-language, mis-language, nil-language, not-language, anti-language, contra-language, un-language, bloody language. I can't bear to listen to it any more.

And I can't bear to look at it any more. At how she finally manages to shake up the machine and open it. At how she pulls out half the washing and carries it in her arms, still dripping, to the spin dryer. She herself gets soaking-wet, while behind her a couple of litres of washing water has just gushed out of the machine onto the floor. At how she, with those soaking-wet hands, grabs the plug of the spin dryer and tries to stick it in the dodgy point that she never wanted to have repaired. (I'm not Mad Lucienneke, I watch what I do.) And at how here too after two minutes she tries to take the wash out of the still-whirling spin dryer, without first taking the plug out of the point again. And at how she protests when her Roger prevents her from doing that and pulls out the plug for her—the thing falls in a puddle on the ground. And at how she flies at him again. That language, that language.

It's unacceptable decay.

('And he suddenly asks me: would you like to come to the cinema with me? [she, in the past, again reciting one of her little epics] I scarcely knew him, he was on his bike and it was a splendid summer's day. To the cinema, I say. How dare you ask, you snotty-nosed kid? Why, he says, I'm seventeen, how old are you? Seventeen too, I say. A little white lie, because I was only fifteen. [laughs] I was two years younger than him, but I called him a snotty-nosed kid. Aren't you ashamed, I shouted at him, go to your cinema by yourself, and take a dog with you!

'But he kept insisting. He was there again every day on his bike. Will you go to the cinema with me? Will you go to the cinema with me? Later it was: Can I give you a kiss? Can I give you a kiss? He wasn't the most handsome man, but he had a wonderful head of curls in those days, and such a lovely, sensual mouth. Every day I melted a little more. I felt as if I had a fan club. I've never kissed another man in my life.')

My father manoeuvres me with friendly insistence out of the washroom and even out of the front door. 'I'll sort this out, lad. I'll take her back to Beveren myself tomorrow. Don't you worry. It'll be all right. Within a few weeks she'll be properly back home, as she used to be, as always.'

After which he shuts the door gently but decisively.

Shutting me off from the pandemonium behind his back.

WHAT'S THE difference between being gay and black? It's a joke I picked up in Cape Town, where both types of human being are very much in evidence. It's best if you ask the question twice, to let it penetrate in all its shattering simplicity. 'What's the difference between being gay and black?'

You leave a nice pause, and only then do you provide the answer. 'If you're black, you don't need to tell your parents.'

On the other hand, if you're a gay man or woman, you know that one day the moment will come when you will have to have one of the mutually most uncomfortable conversations a person can have in their life with their parents. Being yourself a product of sex between the two of them, you will have to talk to them in all seriousness about sex. An experience no child is keen to embark on. You will have to witness unfiltered bewilderment or despair on their faces, since they are totally unprepared for your revelation, since you are the one who can choose the place and time of the disclosure—your own home-ground advantage, unless you are stupid enough to allow yourself to be caught by them with your trousers round your ankles with the boy next door.

You will have to test the balance between their love

for you and their expectations of you, between their prejudices and their trust. Between the increasingly free attitudes with which you have been able to grow up and the petrified period in which they came to maturity, with all the morals and ideas it entails. They may appear complete old-hat by now, but *they* were shaped by them, and that foundation, that youth, that frame of reference, they can never change.

You know from an early age that such a conversation is coming, as you are also aware that, without that conversation, you won't be a worthy child of parents who have always impressed on you that you must be above all honest, and brave, and never ashamed of who or what you are. While you realize just as well that those same parents during that conversation will be beating themselves over the head for not having made more of the advantages of charming hypocrisy and sexual discretion.

You know them well enough to know that you will hurt them, just as you also know damn well that it is not you but their own views and their past that cause the hurt. It doesn't matter, that hurt will come and *you* will strike the blow, against two people who are very close to you. What difference does it make that they are only illusions that you are smashing to pieces? You have borne them and tolerated them up to that moment. The fact that you have never asked about their illusions doesn't matter. Since the onset of puberty you have maintained them and hence magnified them.

The wound of disappointment can be all the deeper. 'Can,' because the upshot is uncertain. You risk a life-long falling-out, but at least as bad is the risk of being treated to a casual shrug of the shoulders, followed by sighs like 'Is that all?' and 'We've known that for a long time.' As a result of which your years of prevarication and strategic planning will seem shamefully clumsy, your courage shamefully meagre, your faith in them shamefully inadequate. So whatever is about to happen, you can never get it right. That's why, before the moment comes, you want to be strong enough to weather the storm, however fierce or stupid it may turn out to be, without capsizing, and with as little damage to all concerned. Pain, happiness, acceptance, relief, concern, hysteria, indifference—you don't want to be knocked for six by anything. Certainly not when you have a mother who, in more than one way, has the reputation of being a *tragédienne pure et dure*.

I was extremely late in being ready for the step. Already twenty-one, a student in Ghent. December 1980 had just begun. Before New Year I was determined to break the spell, still just in the last month of that brandnew decade. Eighty would be great. Then our Most Awkward One drove into a tree in his Honda and broke his neck. It didn't strike me as the right moment for a conversation with my parents about sex. I could just as well wait a bit longer.

That 'longer' turned into a few years. But indirectly the death of our Most Awkward One provided me with the tactical crowbar to prise the door of a suffocating closet off its hinges.

Christmas 1980 meanwhile was a dark and hopeless event. The birth of the Saviour was celebrated a few days after we had been through the funeral of a son, a brother, a young father. The days preceding the funeral he was laid out for a last farewell in the funeral parlour of Jef the Undertaker round the corner, who had also made the coffin, because he was in the first place our local joiner. The Most Awkward One was laid out there so that everyone who had lost sight of him would have a last chance to see him again before he disappeared for ever in our familiar sandy soil. After all, he had resided for years in a strange town, where he had lived as he lived among us. He had tasted life to the full without all that much planning.

Although it should be recorded that in later life he had after all started seriously studying, and had even made it to a qualified audiologist. 'A profession that doesn't even exist in our backward Belgium,' he bragged, to counter the charge that he worked in the Netherlands, in a hospital just over the border. He of all people, the disc jockey, had to measure the amount of hearing loss patients had suffered. Unmasking social hearing fraud was also part of his work. As a jovial bon vivant he was very good at this, it is said.

('They pretend they've gone stone-deaf, for example through working with an electric drill. Some are very cunning at it. You can hit a gong with a hammer behind their backs, but they don't look up from their paper. What you must do is overwhelm them and only then catch them out, in an unguarded, as stupid a moment as possible. For example you receive them very courteously, you give them a tour of the complex, you speak clearly and exaggeratedly loudly and well-articulated, with lots of gestures, you show them all the supersonic equipment you have available. The sound-proof booth. The hundreds of knobs which all produce a different sound, from ultra-sonic to a deep hum. The needles which will register all those sounds on an endless roll of squared paper, together with their reactions, as with a lie detector. The guided tour can easily take an hour. Only when they are nervous enough do you leave them alone in a booth with a set of headphones on their head. They brace themselves. They are fixated on the needles of the lie detector. They expect a cannonade of sounds and sonar bleeps and whistles. All you say is: "Testing, testing. Are you ready?" At that moment ninety-nine per cent of the frauds helpfully say "Yes." End of examination.')

I refused to go and see him in his open coffin. They didn't dare suggest it to La Josée. She did not even attend the ceremony at our parish church, the Friars' Church of the Sacred Heart. A modern building in wine-red brick, with a cupola above the altar, on the inside of which is depicted the Saviour showing us His radiant heart, on a background of gold paint and at the age that was to take Him to the Cross. Coincidentally the age that Our Most Awkward One had reached when he dozed off in his Honda.

The father sat in the front row, punch-drunk, more taciturn than usual. Afterwards, surrounded by his remaining children, he shook hands with everyone who left the church and thanked them for coming, which was 'a great support'. The mother stayed at home, in her bed above a closed butcher's shop, heavily drugged by her GP and to be on the safe side with a bottle of spirits within reach. She did not wish for one grain of consciousness during the hours that a son of hers was covered in incense and buried.

She kept the tranquillizers and the drink within reach during the succeeding days too. In the shop all new Christmas orders were refused, from turkey to croquettes, and of those already placed half were cancelled. The same went for the New Year's orders. The customers showed understanding and bought their dishes elsewhere.

Twice in as many weeks not much came of our own exuberant festive meals, previously set up after the last *veau Orloff* and cold cuts were dispatched off the premises. They were replaced by a scanty meal with few people in a hushed atmosphere, which broke up before it was even midnight.

She did not appear behind the counter any more. She only got up toward midday and after just an hour was groggy or drunk or both. She did not read her paper any more. Days of anaesthesia became weeks of the same. I tried to feel sorry for her, but what I felt, as a young man in his twenties, was not even lack of understanding. It was something approaching hatred. I saw someone who was so caught up in her desire to give form to her grief that grief itself lost out. She simply couldn't find a suitable role model to translate her suffering. Hedda Gabler was too bourgeois. Mother Van Paemel too meek, Martha from *Who's Afraid of Virginia Woolf?* too vulgar. What was left was a cocktail of her own invention, a grotesque swansong of self-pity and pretension. Lots of pills, lots of drink, but seldom tears and no consideration at all for her husband.

Again he put up with everything from her. He wore himself out looking after the housekeeping and at the same time keeping the shop open. She walked past him in a daze as if he didn't exist. As if her pain was his fault. If he hadn't given her those children, she wouldn't have been able to lose any. She slept alone in the marital bed. He downstairs on the sofa, night after night after night.

She did show bursts of energy, it must be said. For a day she acted out her previous life, washing windows and net curtains and serving customers with frightening zeal and a terrifying energy, which toward evening made her sink down exhausted and disheartened, and reach for the bottle and the pills again, ready for another week of anaesthesia.

It was during one of those days of rare resurrection when I observed her by chance, full of horrifying new joie de vivre, clearing out a suitcase in which it turned out there were unwashed clothes of her Most Awkward One. I also immediately recognized them, also with a jolt. Nothing could have characterized him better in just two objects. His colourful, slightly older playboy's polo shirt and his faded, eternal football fanatic's sports shirt. The number on the back was 13, the same one with which Gerd 'The Bomber' Müller became world champion with *Die Mannschaft* in 1974. He sometimes even let a moustache and a five o'clock shadow grow to look even more like that German, because he had the same constitution—thick-set, explosive—and had always been a goal-stealer in his glory days with Excelsior Sint-Niklaas.

She sinks to her knees, her lower jaw trembling, kneading the two items of clothing with trembling hands as if she wants to wash them centimetre by centimetre, here, now, on the spot, without water. She examines them from all sides, still not uttering a word, not making any other sound but her asthmatic panting and the scarcely audible rustling of the material between her kneading fingers. She finally brings them to her face, the two shirts. And she smells them. She snuffles at them as an animal would do, still on her knees. Only now that her face is covered, submerged in a remnant of his smell, does a cry come.

My hatred melted away and again became a simple lack of comprehension.

(I never told her that I saw her crying on her knees, as she sniffed clothes that would smell less and less of the Most Awkward One the longer he lay in the ground. The incident was too intimate for that. But we did once, briefly, talk about parents who have to bury a child.

She: 'I shall never be able accept that fact. It's unnatural.'

I: 'Everything is possible in nature, that's precisely the cruel thing. Cats and crocodiles can eat their own children, and at the same time there are she-wolves who bring up a young puppy, or a human child.'

She: [resolutely shaking her head] 'With the jungle as your example you can prove everything. I'm talking about the normal course of events. I liked being a mother very much, but if I had known in advance that I would have to lose one of the five? I would have said no thanks. Losing a child is hard. In my next life I don't want any.')

1981 arrives and spring comes. I don't have any conversations about sex with my parents. I have mainly no conversations with them. Mourning pushes you apart. And creates embarrassment.

The grave was closed months ago, but her theatrical grieving for her Most Awkward One continues, with days of resurrection and fortnights of medication and drunkenness. The customers who found another butcher for Christmas and New Year have not all returned to the once warm, now chilly stable. Others who do come back, so as not to break the link with their familiar circle of friends, their shopkeeping family, find a lonely butcher who keeps going with the courage of despair but who no longer has any time or enthusiasm for chat and gossip, let alone the patience to listen to the claptrap and worries that he used to be so curious about.

The business goes downhill, the butcher wilts, his wife is seldom to be seen these days.

One Saturday lunchtime, previously one of the busiest times, their eldest son enters an empty shop. 'Me!' There is no reply. He goes into the living room and the drawing room: no one. He opens the door of the steep stairwell: the door upstairs, to their parents' bedroom, is still closed, so their mother is still in bed, drugged or drunk. In the kitchenette and the bathroom: no one. In the workshop: no one. Finally he pulls open the heavy door of the cold room. There he stands, their father. In the consoling cold, among his quarters of beef and his pots of bouillon, with a handkerchief to his nose. Unusually for him he immediately pours his heart out. 'I can't take it any more.' 'Something's got to happen.' 'Like this it will finish both of us.' 'And the business too.'

Religion doesn't rate too highly in the slaughtering business. But the previous week the priest of the Sacred Heart church offered to pay a parochial house visit with his curate, because they were both very concerned since certain rumours about the mother of the deceased mentioned—how shall he put it?—a high degree of disorientation, which was unfortunately apparent at the sacrament of the funeral, the strengthening power of which she was unfortunately forced to miss. In brief: they offer to come round to raise madam's Christian morale, in the name of the Lord, *per secula seculorum*.

On the advice of his eldest but one he calls the priest back, arranges the home visit for two days later and that evening manages to get her to agree. She says that she attaches a warning to her agreement—'I'm doing it for you, and for no one and nothing else'—but this does not alarm him. He is happy enough that she actually answers a plea of his.

And what about that parochial visit?

Doesn't do any good, or any harm either.

She has made herself up soberly, dressed in black from head to toe, and has stayed sober since the day before. She did not even want to take pills. At first that makes him happy, but as soon as the priests of the Sacred Heart make their entrance into the living room, he realizes that she simply wants to be lucid out of belligerence. There is a score to be settled with some agency, the higher the better. This becomes her *moment de vérité*, her outside chance of a confrontation, which she prefers to the soft, sweet lies and promises of a funeral mass.

She allows the priest and his right-hand man to sit down awkwardly on her sofa. She sits, suffering and acting suffering, in an armchair. She allows the two gentlemen, in response to the question of her Roger, to opt for a glass of sherry, in order to break the ice and loosen the tongue. She herself refuses such a glass, to improve her reputation with the priests and to keep her head clear. However, she does not omit to thank her husband expressly, because—regardless of the gossip and her misbehaviour of the last few weeks—he still offered her a glass. That gesture of his moves her. His loyalty. His naturalness. *His* pain.

But she fights back her feelings. Her attention must and shall be centred on the representatives of the Almighty. They are sipping their glasses and praise the dryness of their drink, which has to be called the best conceivable aperitif in this spring weather, much less syrupy than for example port, which also goes to the head much faster and hence is jolly treacherous, especially if you've come in a car. They first each take a nut and a slice of dry sausage and finally get started, scarcely addressing themselves to the lady of the house, under whose silence and stern gaze they have, however, become slightly nervous.

They first both once again express their deep condolences, and assure her that it was a beautiful and well-attended funeral, 'the most beautiful we have experienced in months in our church,' and that there were splendid speeches, by among others her son's boss; 'we have to concede that to the Dutch, they can speak in public, on each occasion they find the appropriate tone and the correct formulations,' and so on and so forth. They complement each other with details and figures. 'We have seldom moved so many hosts.'

Finally only the priest himself speaks. He has been at most a quarter of an hour in this room, together with her, face to face with her. He coughs and says: 'Madam, there is one thing that you will have to try to understand. No, you will have to learn to accept it. It concerns a central passage from the Bible.' He leaves a pause and then says it after all: "The Lord tries first those whom he loves most."'

Whereupon my mother rises from her armchair, throws the door of her living room wide open and asks both men in black to leave her house instantly. 'What kind of God is that that hurts him or her most who loves him most dearly? I think that is ungrateful and cowardly, sir. I would never do such a thing, and do not wish to be under one roof with people who approve of it and propagate it. Goodbye to you! And I hope never to see you here again.'

By the time the two clerics, alarmed and shocked, have left by the back door and he comes back into the living room saddened and discouraged, she has disappeared again. Upstairs.

Taking the bottle of sherry with her.

(For the rest of her life, at set times, she was to take flowers herself or have them delivered to the brick Church of the Sacred Heart, where her son's coffin had last stood before he disappeared into our ground. Sometimes she cut off all the flowers from her rhododendrons next to her bungalow and laid them, wrapped in old newspapers, on the step of the vicarage, as if she were leaving a foundling. The priests knew who the flowers came from and gave them a place of honour, in front of the statue of St Anthony, or the image of Christ with the bleeding side and the crown of thorns.

She gave them her flowers in abundance. She never offered her apologies.)

TWENTY YEARS LATER she brought the first excursion to her own home to a successful conclusion. At least if we can believe her advocate and guardian angel on the telephone: 'I took her back to Beveren without any problems, there she immediately put on her tracksuit in order to cycle on the home trainer again, she even waved to me when I left ... What? Oh yes, that fuss in the washroom. That was not a very edifying moment. That sort of thing couldn't be avoided. But she helped me to clear everything up and that was that.'

He maintains that after that they actually had an enjoyable evening. 'We ate together, watched TV, didn't go to bed too late, everything went as always. It was a pleasure not to be by myself in that apartment for once. And as far as I'm concerned she can come again in a few days' time. The only thing we didn't do was complete the crossword puzzle in her paper. It's still a bit too early for that, I fear.'

His wish is granted. There are further excursions. They come faster and faster. And they pass without too many problems, he stresses each time, afterwards. Although every entry into her former crown domain continues to go equally turbulently. The first half-hour is the most difficult.

As soon as the front door is opened she charges in, goes upstairs and starts on a major housekeeping task with a fury that cannot be tempered. But whether it is a matter of unhooking the curtains and net curtains, which she makes clear by babbling and gestures urgently need to go to the cleaners, or of moving her heaviest items of furniture so that she can scrub or polish or vacuum underneath, she always interrupts those actions before they are properly executed. The curtains and net curtains, just unhooked and put to one side, have to be hooked up again at once, unwashed. Returning from the toilet she regards the furniture that has been moved at first with amazement and then, stamping her foot, demands that it should be put back in its original place, without the areas that had been uncovered being first scrubbed, polished or even vacuumed. Then she calms down as if the chore has been finished and is finally over with.

The impulse, no: the packaging of some actions has become more important to her than the content. Not the washing of bedding so that it is clean is what counts. Washing as an obligation all the more so. As a vague memory, as a duty without meaning. Washing as a record of loss.

But the progress that she is still making is unmistakable. The therapists even feel that the moment has come for a first appearance in public, on condition that it is an easily recognized occasion in which she has participated before, preferably in familiar surroundings in a small circle of intimates. No strangers, no surprises, no long journeys.

My father's heart leaps up. The traditional birthday dinner of his ninety-year-old sister is approaching. That meal never has more than ten guests, including me and my sister—the favourite godchild of the birthday girl, who herself is childless. The location has been the same for twelve years. A rustic café-restaurant that was once started up by my eldest brother and is situated in a leafy suburb between Beveren and Sint-Niklaas. It was named Malpertuis after the home of Reynard the Fox, butaccording to time-honoured Flemish custom serves mainly classics of French cuisine.

He asks me to make it clear to my mother what is about to happen. And to help her with her toilet. He himself, he admits, would get too nervous from all that fussing about, and anyway she didn't like him looking over her shoulder when she was dressing up. He is frightened to death that he would, now of all times, drive her to a new attack of aggression, though such attacks have come increasingly to belong to the past.

I say with pride and enthusiasm that I will assist her in his place.

It was to be the last time that she showed herself to the outside world in her full regalia. And the time and language-area in which you and I are forced to live, reader, demand I that I should here and now report to you on that last make-up session and that last appearance in the most sober terms, according to the slogan 'Less is more' which in recent decades has become so popular that one can easily speak of a pathology called literary anorexia nervosa.

I'm very sorry, but I say no to impeccably spare writings. Not even by vocation or on a doctrinaire impulse. I say no because anorexia in writing would mean a betrayal of my subjects and their surroundings. In this matter I also have myself against me, my temperament that I owe to no one else. I see no virtue in forced silence as a representation of a storm or a symphony, I am not crazy about spareness as a translation of luxury, I despise pastel tints and fragile aestheticism as a depiction of flesh and blood. Everyone must do and not do as he wants, certainly anyone who in these days wants to venture into the noble art of writing—but if there are ten terms for one and the same phenomenon, why should someone like me of all people use only one instead of all ten? Why shouldn't I try to think up a couple of new ones? Isn't a vocabulary like a treasure chest?

Spare us the war cry of the school pedant, that hackneyed 'Not a word too many'. An adage that you should obviously also pronounce with a face as if you had just drunk a chamber pot full of vinegar. Not a word too many? In the instructions for iPod earphones and electric toothbrushes, there shouldn't be a word too many. The directions for everything that a person has to stick in his ear or in his mouth and by extension in all his bodily orifices—the explanation of those, okay, must be succinct and dry. But where literature is concerned, which in the first place is not after beauty, but truthfulness, even if it has to burst its joints in the process and creak and lash out and shriek? So for the love of God don't keep coming up every time and with every theme with that damn shitty phrase 'Less is more,' which with a few masters, I openly admit, has produced brilliant books, timeless texts, humbling masterpieces, but which apart from that is mainly abused by the impotent and untalented to hide their deficient grasp of both their material and their equipment.

Less, fucking more? I'm sorry I've come back to food again—although that is of course no coincidence, we are quite simply what we eat and what we read, the only difference being one of calories—but why was nouvelle cuisine ultimately never an overwhelming success, and not at all in Belgian establishments? Because the portions were too small, the vegetables half cooked and the portions of fish systematically provided with too little sauce. Although invented in France, nouvelle cuisine was made to measure for the stomachs of crypto-Calvinists and other Scandinavians. *Les peoples du Nord n'ont pas de cuisine, ils n'ont que de la nourriture.* This was what Léon Daudet said, who is famous for little else except this pronouncement, unless it is his reputation as a diehard anti-Dreyfusard and French monarchist, the latter costing him a two-year stay as a political exile in the Brussels of Marx and Multatuli.

Translated freely, Daudet deduced the following: those who let Calvin call the tune know only nutrition and not gastronomic culture. They learn from the kindergarten to old age to mash their food so as not to be sure what it consists of. They eat veal croquettes from an automat and hotdogs which a vegetarian can become addicted to, because they are guaranteed not to contain a shred of meat, but are all the more cardboard-flavoured with the chemical components of brown gravy.

(She tried it once, Josée The Suspicious, elderly but still fully her vital self, at dusk, in the centre of Amsterdam, in one of those automats in the Leidsestraat: a veal croquette, because the rest looked even more pathetic behind their greasy windows. She bit off the top of that veal croquette, chewed on it once in bewilderment and, retching, spat it out into the rubbish bin hanging there. She threw the rest of her croquette after it and forbade the homeless guy who wanted to fish it straight out to do so, even wagging her moralizing finger. Instead she pushed five guilders into the 'lad's' hands with the instruction to go and buy something suitable and on the way go to 'the barber's', yes 'the barber's,' because she knew very well that he would interpret 'coiffeur' wrongly and would take her five guilders to another dealer, so that an hour later he would be lying with a needle in his arm [she] 'lazing about in that Vondelpark', when 'at the same moment he could have been looking for a respectable job, even if it was only sweeping the streets in the centre of town, which between us wouldn't be luxury in some part of that so-called fantastic Amsterdam. But well, that's because of all those croquettes, isn't it. Too few minerals, zero vitamins. Boy oh boy. Do you know what it tastes of? Their so-called veal cutlet? Among the Eskimos, in a pathetic igloo, sits an old woman, she opens a packet of Royco 1-Minute Soup, mushroom-flavoured, brings up a nice lot of phlegm into it, that toothless old woman, stirs it with her forefinger that hasn't been washed for twenty years, and that sticky mush? She covers it with breadcrumbs and fries it. That's what it tastes like.')

Sometimes less is just what it is. Less. And even if I of all people am spat and shat on, and irrevocably predestined, inevitably mutilated by a culture of 'Do you mind if it's a little over, madam.' Even apart from that, in all honesty: 'less' is a lie. 'Less' is weak construction, facile fraud, minimalist kitsch. Life is not a gallery painted from top to bottom in sterile white, with just one Cubist winter landscape on the wall, or with one piece of excrement hanging twirling from the ceiling on a single thread, or with one aquarium in which a poor creature is floating in formaldehyde, having been neatly cut in two, or whatever else is put forward as 'the art of the modern memento mori'—try working in an abattoir, you pathetic suckers, and see if you last a week, for a measly wage instead of ten million per creature.

Life is much more what a few other visual artists certainly do dare to show. Chaos as chaos. A shooting gallery with a chaotic mass of plaster figures. Not a cornucopia but a magic dustcart emptying its lopsided container above a bottomless abyss, and the stream of waste is also endless. Yet you not only see the stream in its entirety. Just before the figures disappear again out of your field of vision, you see here an Oriental chandelier popping up from the fermenting rubbish and there a dog's corpse, over there an intact sidecar of a scooter and a little further a stuffed bird of paradise, next to a jukebox with neon lights and an afterbirth in a bread bag. And the essence is that the context of all this does not fade away. They are contained in each other. Without context art loses its balls and becomes a cold diminutive of itself. A responsibly constituted healthy lolly where you expect raw and still-warm organ meat, or a honey cake with slivers of glass, or a chocolate marshmallow with barbs, or something that you cannot immediately place because there are precisely no instructions for use attached. Something you're frightened may infect you and may even kill you, but which you hope just as well can protect you, even if it was only for five seconds, from all the ills you think are dormant inside of you. And if it brings no cure for ailments—which you don't really expect anyway—let it at least splint the memories that ooze pus and creak in your head, that burn with gangrene, but which you would not have amputated or lobotomized for all the money in the world. Because despite all the pus they are too dear to you to let them continue existing as artistically justified phantom pain.

Less *is* less. And that's that.

She sits blissfully grinning at her table with its double oak top, with her beauty case open in front of her. She has not selected her most extravagant evening dress, but neither can we call the item she is wearing self-effacing, with its gold embroidery and its motifs in silver leaves on a background of black silk, combined with a shawl of coarse beige silk. At first she wanted to wear her boa of white ostrich feathers, but I was able to dissuade her.

Her hair has been permed by her granddaughter who helped me with the selection of the dress, and, women together, also helped with the choice and putting-on of her underwear. Her granddaughter also helped select shoes and a matching handbag from the abundant choice, the result of decades of saving and shopping in the sales. The shoes they chose together are black with ankle straps and low heels. The handbag is modest in size and beige like her shawl.

She stood hesitating for a long time in front of her opened hat cupboard. This is also well furnished, especially with items that recall parts she once played. She bought them at a discount afterwards or simply scrounged them off the wardrobe mistress. Here an Oriental-looking hat that dates from *The Chinese Country House*, her first success. Over there a flying saucer that she wore as an American millionaire's widow in a play by Agatha Christie. There the beret of the eccentric artist in *Eva's Apples*, her anniversary performance, in which she played seven parts, a triumph. For a laugh she wrapped the black headscarf that she wore in *The House of Bernarda Alba* not around herself but around me. And finally concluded, inspecting herself in the mirror of her dressing table, that she did not need any headgear today. Finally her hair had been properly done. She didn't want to ruin it.

The last stage of her toilet—painting her nails, make-up, choosing jewels—is completed not at the dressing table in the bedroom but, true to tradition, in the living room, at the table where she may have spent the larger part of her life, the table on which she ironed and filled in the cash books, the table at which, on the waxed cloth with an old paper on top, she cleaned her vegetables, chopped her onions, peeled her potatoes.

There is no paper now and on top of the waxed cloth is her pride and joy, her lace tablecloth. On it, as always, on the window side a few succulents in Delft-blue pots, in the centre a filled tin fruit dish, and apart from that, spread over the tabletop, a few ashtrays, her patched-up dictionaries, her old-fashioned-looking alarm clock that she bought in the Hema in Hulst, and finally, as was said, her open, brim-full beauty case. On the inside of the lid is a mirror in which she looks at herself close-up.

She has already painted her nails, in Bordeaux red. That fiddly job went remarkably well. Again she turned it into a show, well aware of her public—I, who had to see her, worried, first setting to work with the nail file, and then, still worse, opening the bottle of nail varnish. I wasn't allowed to help her, she rapped me on the fingers and laughed at me sarcastically. Thank God not for a moment spiteful or resentful—on the contrary she seemed to be having a great time.

Was I imagining it or did she exaggerate the elegance with which she gripped the bottle cap between thumb and forefinger, with the little finger raised? Did she exaggerate the controlled panache with which she kept aiming the brush precisely in the minuscule neck of the bottle, and then withdrew it, half pressed against the neck, and then with a steady hand painted one nail after another with the thick varnish? From the quick to the edge of the nail, never the other way round, in nice straight stripes. It was amazing how efficiently she managed this task, and how she enjoyed my restrained anxiety. There was only one nail where she gestured to me, fishing a ball of cotton wool and bottle of solvent from her bag: I had to take the varnish off again. The stripe was not straight enough compared with the other nine. Perfection remains her favourite hobby.

Now, peering in that mirror, she starts on even more fiddly jobs. Powdering herself is effortless. She acts like a Madame de Pompadour from the time of wigs, so absurdly playful is her handling of the powder brush, as if she were dusting herself with a miniature *plumeau* full of flour. She even imitates a coughing fit and waves the cloud of powder away with a flutter of the hand, more mime than theatre. Then she gets out her lipstick and her eye pencil. She feels my alarm growing at her side, but it doesn't make her angry or nervous, rather even more cheerful.

She turns the lipstick resolutely up, sticks out her chin, tensing her lower lip too. She starts in one corner of her mouth and draws the lipstick with a slow but determined stroke toward the other corner. Perfect. Now the top. Voilà. Just as smooth. She rubs her lips together, pouts at her reflection, turns that pout toward me, kisses thin air and is already putting her lipstick away. Scarcely two minutes have gone by. But now comes that eye pencil.

She holds her face close to the mirror. She wants to draw a line on the lower lid of each eye, on the inside, just below the eyelashes. To do that she pulls down the skin under one eyelid, so that her eye with its blue-grey iris and its small veins is alarmingly exposed, together with the deep-pink inside of the eyelid and the delicate light-pink membrane between the eye and the lid. I have never realized until now, but there is so much in an eye that can be injured. A fingernail can be enough to damage everything. Just before she starts on the inner corner of her eye with her pencil, I see that she has forgotten to remove the pointed metal protective cap.

In a reflex my hand reaches for her wrist, though I only realize then how dangerous that is. At any moment she will start and through my fault will stick that cap in her eye. She notices my curtailed movement and is alarmed enough to interrupt her own movement in turn. Again without a trace of anger. She now notices the cap herself and removes it, rolling her eyes at herself and her forgetfulness.

Again she pulls down her eyelid with that one fingertip, again her iris is alarmingly exposed. Her hand, I see now, has lost some of its steadiness since she painted her nails. She is trembling, more and more intensely. The point of the pencil, black as charcoal and sharp enough to wound, trembles along vaguely, waiting to be able to alight somewhere, find a foothold. So her pencil point dances uncertainly toward one corner of her eye, while her gleaming iris looks on from close by.

I decide not to intervene. This is a day for peacefulness and risks. This is not just a line that she has to apply. It is a signature under her certificate of provisional recovery, a stroke of the pen under a period of doom and impotence. She must write that signature herself, draw that line herself. That is precisely the point.

She doesn't make a bad job of it. With the other eye her hand slips for a moment, thank God downward, away from the pupil. She puts her pencil away and again looks at her reflection. The imperfection of the line on that second eye troubles her, as was to be expected and foreseen.

She pulls a kittenish face of regret, with an accompanying cry of disappointment—'Ooohh ... '—whereupon she retrieves a gossamer-thin handkerchief from her handbag, moistens a corner with spittle and hands it to me. Pointing to that eye. I can do the retouching. It feels like a privilege. Certainly when she then rummages deep in her beauty case, fishes out a gold-coloured pair of tweezers, thrusts them into my hands too and points to an insignificant hair that has refused to follow the line of her plucked eyebrows. I can pull it out. It feels like an honour I do not deserve.

I have to pluck three times before I get hold of that damned hair. She checks the result in the mirror and applauds with soft claps and an exaggerated grimace of admiration for my achievement. Then she retrieves her jewellery box from its secret place—a small hollow space under the tabletop, somewhere in the mechanism with which both leaves can be slid apart, each to one side. She discovered the hollow there when she was sheltering from flying bombs and has always been convinced that no burglar would find it.

We choose together which of her three delicate watches she will wear, what earrings, what bracelets, what brooch (she opts for her favourite, a two-coloured cameo) and finally what rings. In recent years they have all become too loose on her, but she refuses to spend money on adjustments. On the underside of each ring, invisible to anyone looking, she has stuck a piece of flesh-coloured plaster, enough to stop the jewel slipping round her finger and, who knows, falling off without her realizing. She has one with a sapphire and one with diamonds. She decides to wear them both.

She dabs a drop of perfume behind each ear and looks at herself in the mirror again, now from different angles, a few times even with her flapping hands in view. She concludes the presentation with her traditional nod of the head. She is ready. And she has stood the test brilliantly. I sit and look at her. If she can do all this. If she needs so little help. The therapists are right. The door to complete recovery is ajar. She can become her old self. She will become her old self.

But, looking at herself a very last time, she suddenly grabs, unthinkingly, as if it is the ultimate finishing touch, her alarm clock from the Hema. It is a rotund aluminium affair on feet, with big hands and clear numbers that light up in the dark. At the top of the round body of the clock are two bells, with between them a hammer that moves to and fro when the alarm goes off. Still looking in her mirror, an eighty-year-old almost in love in full regalia is combing her hair with her alarm clock. Thank God with the smooth front, the round glass over the clock face.

Her perm stays intact. My hope of a recovery goes up in flames. My mother is combing her hair with her alarm clock.

The meal at the Malpertuis restaurant takes places in a slightly euphoric atmosphere. She parades into the dining room as she used to: predictably the centre of attention. She greets and kisses the managers as if they are intimate friends she has not seen for decades. She is the first to clink her glass of champagne. At a given moment she smokes her cigarette with panache. She eats little of the sumptuous meal, as has been her custom in recent years. ('Because of that damned stomach hernia I eat less than a sparrow. A waste of all that lovely money, to say nothing of the food.') According to her equally recent habit she produces from her bag the deep-freeze bags without which she no longer goes to a restaurant, and in which, looking ostentatiously around her, and to the amusement of her fellow guests and the watching waiters, she wraps and saves the tastiest leftovers, next to her paper handkerchiefs and her purse, as well as the separately wrapped sugar cubes and cakes which she scrounges from everyone who has coffee with their dessert in her presence.

Although almost no one understands what she is talking about, she holds forth with panache, from *amuse-gueule* to dessert. Again she greets lots of strangers from afar, and giggles when they wave back. She lures me into teasing her and is attentive to my father, sweet to the point of condescension. A week later she has her second stroke.

The beginning of a whole series.

BACK TO TWENTY years earlier. After she had shown the priests of the Sacred Heart the door, things went from bad to worse with the wife of the butcher on the corner. She didn't get out of bed any more except to drink and she didn't leave the house except to buy tranquillizers from an increasingly reluctant pharmacist. When he advised her to seek professional help, she went to another pharmacist.

The butcher still slept alone night after night, downstairs on the sofa where each of his children had so often been honoured as lord and master of children's illnesses and on which his wife had feigned a couple of heart attacks in order force those same children into submission. He was silent as he had so often been silent and went on working as he had always worked. Until one day he did the unthinkable.

He left his shop door shut.

She comes downstairs after lunch, dishevelled. Unwashed, with a stink of alcohol on her breath that would reach from here to Tokyo, and she sees him sitting at her table, in her place, reading her paper. Only then does she realize. This morning, in the hours between sleeping and waking and tossing and turning, she hasn't once heard the doorbell go. 'What's wrong?' is all she can think of to say.

He surprises himself with his eloquence, which is increased by the fact that she is too drowsy and full of drugs to say much back. He must have sat here for hours rehearsing to himself what he wants to rub into her pale face. He lays down the law to her calmly but sternly. It is the world turned upside down. He talks, he sighs— although he doesn't need to rant to add force to his words. It is his mildness that upsets and scourges her, the softness of his voice, and the quantity of minutes that he is suddenly able to fill one after another. His indictment boils down to the fact that he will only reopen the butcher's shop if she gets a grip on herself. One without the other is no longer tolerable. He doesn't want to underestimate or belittle her pain, he couldn't do that, he feels the same pain. But something must happen and he even has a proposal. He would like her to listen to it first, to the proposal as a whole, before she says yes or no.

The wife of Omer the Plumber has rung and told him about a cousin who has also lost a child. Much younger than the Most Awkward One, but also through a stupid accident, something to do with an unattended swimming pool, in which the little one tragically drowned. His mother was just as helpless, just as much on her way to suicide in instalments. But through people she knew that woman got into contact with a spiritualist medium and she has helped her pull through marvellously. That same medium is giving a séance tonight in the back room of Café De Graanmaat on the marketplace. The plumber's wife and her cousin are going, and he would like her to go too. Without him. And sober. And properly dressed. And not hostile in advance, like the last time, with the priests of the Sacred Heart.

There is a pause, during which she simply stands

nodding her head, looking at her carpet, unsteady on her feet, shivering in her peignoir, ready to fly at him or ready to collapse. She does neither. She raises her head to him, looks him in the eyes and nods, goes to the bathroom and begins on her toilet for the first time in ages. She has accepted his proposal and the admonishment. But to affirm that in so many words? A nod and the deed must suffice.

He is content with that. He had not expected anything else. He opens his shop and works through to evening, alone. He doesn't want her to help him. It's up to her how she spends her time. Toward eight she drops by, dressed up but with a severe, sad expression, to announce she is leaving. Now it is his turn to nod without words. Standing in the back doorway he watches her go, without waving. It's the first time in months that she has driven. Thank God there's little traffic about at this time of day.

He stays watching until she has disappeared round the corner. Then he goes inside and gets out a cassette tape that he cannot listen to when she is around or even threatening to come in. It is a recording of the address that the Dutch director of the audiological centre gave at the funeral. There is a terrible amount of echo, but if you listen closely, and you know the words more or less, you hear what the man and after him the priest have to say. He listens to it regularly by himself. He can even mouth the words of the speech here and there. Every creature prays in its own way.

At about ten o'clock his wife comes back home. Lively, combative and strengthened—a new woman. She almost radiates light. She says, no she sings: 'I got a message. From him. He's happy and he's doing well over there. We mustn't worry any more, he says. All he asked was that you should come too next time.'

She does not reach for pills or drink.

For that reason alone he is happy to go along next time.

For a woman who tirelessly appealed to common sense, fanaticism was not alien to her and she had an unbridled longing for a higher realm. She turned her sober GPs into demigods. She attributed the value of wonder medicines to their often simple prescriptions, even if it was only a matter of a capsule of Véganine ('the only thing that helps with snot discharges') or a tube of Inotiol ointment ('against burns, spots, hangnails, insect stings, nappy rash', actually against everything, a true wonder ointment). Despite that unshakeable belief in doctors of her own choice she has always been susceptible to palmists and card fortune tellers to supplement the blessings of modern medicine. The way she could never fix a plank to the wall without a few nails extra. The longest and the thickest first. 'Better safe than sorry.'

Among her dictionaries, hanging out of its binding, was a well-thumbed lexicon of the plant kingdom, phrased in an accessible idiom. The life's work of Wardje The Herb Doctor, a Waasland phenomenon who also enjoyed celebrity as a diviner. Walking over arid fallow land with his divining rod, Wardje was able to indicate the best place to bore for a well. With his pendulum—a chain with a ball on it as large as our most expensive marble, but in silver—he visited not dry fields but women on their sickbeds. He let his pendulum swing above their uncovered bellies and could tell from the swings of his silver marble whether they were developing an extra-uterine fibroid or a child with hands and eyes and a palate. If his marble spun to the left it would be a girl, to the right a boy. If the pendulum did not spin, he predicted a breech delivery.

She sometimes had the predictive gift as regards re-production herself, thanks to her somewhat clairvoyant dreams. Sometimes she was plain wrong—she once congratulated a woman neighbour, in the presence of a full shop, on her pregnancy, whereupon the woman, deathly pale and affronted, came out and revealed to the remaining customers that she had been involved in a divorce for months and since then had become addicted to chocolate and whipped-cream cakes, which perhaps represented a more correct explanation for her weight increase. Such errors were easily forgotten, since they did not outweigh the times when she was spot on. In ad-dition, two years later the chocolate woman turned out to be pregnant after all, by her secret lover. The predic-tion had not been totally wrong.

Every morning, while she was reading her favourite paper, she gave an account of the most bizarre dreams by which she had been visited the night before, plus her interpretation of them. Such an explanation could take half an hour. She seemed to remember more and more of the double life that her brain staged for her at night. 'Do you know who I saw again? Ginger Stremans. He comes toward me in his underpants and says: I'm looking for Joske Zurenbal! I'm looking for Joske Zurenbal!'

Laughing, we shook our heads in disbelief. But blow me down: the same day we receive the news, by oral cus-tomer post, that Joske Zurenbal has died and that it is his card pal and bosom friend, Ginger Stremens, who found him; the poor devil had drowned in his own bath. It should be observed that for two weeks the parliament in front of our counter had been wondering where on earth Joske Zurenbal was hanging out, since he seemed to have disappeared off the face of the earth, and even his best mate, Ginger Stremens, had no idea.

'Do you know who suddenly came by last night? Dressed as a harlequin, dancing like a Cossack, drumming on his biscuit tin, as he did in *The Servant of Two Masters*? Willy Verbreyt. How would he be getting on? Haven't seen him for *months*.' 'And what do you know: who stops outside our door this afternoon in his sports car? Come on, guess! Skirt chaser going downhill? Made his pile in textiles, but started living off the interest in good time? Always well-tanned and halfshaved and with a white scarf round his neck, though his shirt is open beyond his breastbone? To be sure! Willy Verbreyt.' Though it must be admitted that Willy paid a visit *every* spring, when he had rolled open the hood of his convertible and didn't immediately know where to drive to display his availability to the ladies.

It's the same as with her daily horoscope in *Het Laatste Nieuws* and her quick prayers to St Anthony. ('If you can't find something right away, you must pray to Anthony. Then you'll find it. If not today, then tomorrow.') No one can deny, she thinks, that in those simple remedies there is often a staggering basis of truth and effectiveness. 'If you just read the characteristics of the sign of Virgo? They're not very far wrong, if I'm honest with myself.' And it's not because people will soon be able to play football on the moon that henceforward all mysteries will be banished from the world. That applies even to the Catholic Church. That pope, with all his gold and all his possessions and jewels? She doesn't want to know about him. 'Those men of the Holy See have each stolen millions, to start with in missionary work, and earlier in our poor Flanders too, with the sale of their indulgences and reliquaries and scapulars and their other con tricks.'

But there have been real saints in the Catholic Church who had nothing to do with the Pharisees of Vatican City. Besides the plant lexicon of Wardje The Herb Doctor, she treasures two other books. The biography of Brother Isidoor De Loor, a passionist from Vrasene, and that of Thérèse of Lisieux. Nor does one make fun in her presence of Brother Damiaan, the hero of Molokai, apostle of the lepers. And when they bought their first car, just to be on the safe side they drove for the first ten years to the new Church of Don Bosco, where the priest gave up a whole Sunday afternoon of his spring blessing one motor vehicle after another with his aspergillum in the name of St Christopher, patron saint of carpenters, painters, pilgrims, fruit dealers, bookbinders and motorists. After this conveyor-belt blessing of the cars, you could also buy a blessed palm branch to fix to the rearview mirror on your front windscreen, then you were completely assured of a year of safe driving.

They bought two each time, in case the first got lost. 'You never know where it might come in handy.'

She had gone to the séance in the back room of De Graanmaat with the same attitude. There were about twenty or thirty people spread over the chairs. You could easily tell who was here for the first time and who wasn't. The newcomers looked as sombre and washed-out as she did. The old hands sat happily and expectantly.

The admission price was low. That reassured her, you read enough horror stories of swindlers who earned a fortune from other people's misery. And the medium did everything herself, from selling tickets to closing the doors at the beginning of the séance. She liked that too. That practical attitude from someone you would be more inclined to credit with absent-mindedness and a high-flown manner.

What she liked less about the medium were the dishevelled hairdo, the exaggerated eyeliner, the abundant necklaces in organic materials and the exuberantly jingling bracelets of the superannuated hippy. Her dress was in keeping: flapping cotton in drab tints, too loose and smelling of patchouli. Still, the balance was positive, because of the frank look in the blue eyes, the wide, open smile and the no-nonsense tone. Her name was Ludwina, she laughed. But Winnie was okay too, and she even preferred it. Winnie, from Winnie the Pooh or Winnie Mandela, it was all the same to her. That was how her séance began. With a warm welcome to her audience, the declaration of her familiar name and the dimming of the lights in the room, after which she sat down at her table on the small stage.

Before actually starting Winnie warned everyone, particularly the newcomers, against over-high expectations and against sensationalism. 'I can't promise anything. I am only an intermediary. I have no control let alone power over entities.' That's what she called them: entities. Spirits, she said, appeared only in comic strips and cartoon films, never with her. 'My role as a medium is simply to give the entities a chance to manifest themselves by me. If they want and when they want. No one can force them. We can ask them nicely, though. They actually like that.'

In order to invite the immaterial entities to manifest themselves in De Graanmaat Winnie needed tangible objects. She passed around a wicker basket in which everyone could deposit an object that had belonged to a dear departed one. A ring, a pair of glasses, a watch. Photos were also acceptable.

The earth mother is prepared for this. The plumber's wife has impressed it on her on the telephone. 'Bring something with you, it doesn't matter what.' She passed away the hours between her toilet and her departure largely in agonizing about what to give. Just imagine if something goes wrong with that object? She has already lost enough of him. His wedding ring and wristwatch are too precious to her. His photos too. With an anxious pain in the heart she put into the basket Her Most Awkward One's bunch of keys, which has become useless. Even his car keys were still on it.

That bunch of keys is the first thing that Winnie retrieves. From a tangle of rings and hangers and holiday snaps showing laughing total strangers in better times.

'You should have been there,' she says, radiant as a convert, later in the evening, in her again acceptable living room, to her again lovable butcher. 'That Winnie mentioned things about his work and about his children that no one can know except us and him. Then she passed on a message to me. I sat there as if struck by God's hand. I didn't dare to believe it was true. That Winnie sees that and she comes over to me, to say that she has only rarely received such a clear and powerful message. And she asks if she can see a photograph of him. Luckily I had one with me. I show it to her, and she goes as white as a sheet. Madam, she says, I must be honest with you, there is some mistake. The entity I saw has a beard, and your son has only a moustache. So it can't have been true, forget what I said to you, I'm truly sorry. She wants to give me the photo back, but I can't even take it. I'm sitting in my chair jerking and laughing and crying at the same time. Everything fell away from me. My doubts, my suspicion, my grief. My shame at the last few months. Dear Winnie, I say, as soon as I can speak again, that photo is from last year. He really did die with a beard. And while I'm still saying that, I feel myself filling with pure happiness. It almost hurt, the cuttingly hard way I became filled with joy, a bit like it is described in the Books of the Apostles, who on Whit Sunday could preach in all the languages of the world. I'm still dreadfully sorry that he is no longer here. But I am overjoyed that he died with that ugly half-beard. It *was* him who spoke.'

The butcher also becomes a convert. From the first time onward he shares his wife's enthusiasm. Together they allow themselves to be conducted into a brand-new universe of consolation.

Besides the object séance there are also séances with the round table. Each session a dozen followers sit with their ten fingertips on the tabletop. The messages now come through letter by letter, directly from the entities themselves. Winnie intones the alphabet, and each time she says a correct letter the table jumps a little diagonally and bangs down on the floor again with its legs. Halfway through the whole word can be guessed, by Winnie or the addressee of the message. If the right word is given, the table hangs lopsided again, followed by that confirming bang.

There are also flower séances. Everyone brings a flower along; these are collected at the front in a vase and in the course of the evening a procession of invisible departed comes past in order via Winnie, with extra-encouraging words, to give a flower brought by one person to another, so that finally everyone can go home with a flower. A flower which in addition seems to bloom for longer than usual. When asked about this Winnie smiles modestly. She cannot confirm or deny anything, she says. This is simply not part of her domain.

There are also séances that fail. Not a single entity visits, which makes Winnie more gloomy and discouraged than her supporters. Or some joker comes along who hands in his own ring, or the wallet of his mate who stands unsuspectingly downing beers at the bar of the café. Winnie deals with these comedians quickly and severely. They go deathly pale after a message from their own departed, or after the revelation of a faux pas that they have never confessed and which is now communicated openly for all to see, through their own fault. Winnie omits the most embarrassing details, because she has already had a visitor who threatened her with death. She calmed him down by looking straight at him and laughing: 'You think I'm frightened of death, sir? Do what you have to do. But I would be careful of overexertion. Here next to me is a relative of yours who died in a fit of anger, of a triple heart attack.'

Sometimes there is a journalist in the audience, planning to unmask her. She unmasks him. 'You there, sir? Yes you. With your notebook. There is an entity next to me who maintains that you write for a newspaper.' She doesn't avoid his interview, on the contrary she fills half her séance with it. She isn't a clairvoyant, is her friendly reply to his irritating goading. 'I have only two aims, sir. To free spiritualism of its bad reputation. And to prove that there is life after death.'

With the butcher and his wife the months of grieving turn into a cross between euphoria and an urge to convert. That applies especially to the butcher's wife. He is perfectly pleased to have his wife back as she was, and that from now on he has more options for remembering his son that just that one cassette tape which is wearing out. She, however, will not rest until she has won over humanity to her new faith. She has even stopped smoking, for the tenth time. But this time, she says, it is for keeps. She does not want any other stain on her clean slate.

That Winnie was not exaggerating when she mentioned to the journalist a taboo that was on spiritualism, they now experience for themselves. Conversations dry up, with friends, at the theatre club, in the shop, when they—mainly she—sing the praises of Winnie, and certainly when they repeat literally and in exalted tones the messages that they have only recently received from their Most Awkward One and that invariably boil down to the fact that he is doing well over there, that his parents need no longer grieve, and that the hereafter is absolutely not miserable or dark, on the contrary it is pleasant and peaceful dwelling there.

There are a few desperate souls, bound up in their grief as they used to be, to whom they can show the way to the handy redemption of séances—although a few of those souls return more deeply depressed than when they left home, because they do not prove receptive to this light. The rest, however, from friends, customers and business contacts to colleagues in amateur theatre, give them in answer to their paeans of praise either the silence of friendship or the silence of embarrassment. While they conversely had expected ecstatic congratulations and sincere expressions of support. Neither are the quite cheap membership cards of Winnie's association easy to sell, however much Josée Verbeke tries to breathe new life into her lost dream of being an advocate.

Finally this message also gets through to them, for once not deriving from a dead entity. On the contrary, it is a piece of current popular wisdom, which for centuries has helped ensure that in these parts life, even among the living, is not so bad: 'To each his own convictions. And apart from that let's not waste any more words about it.'

We take the indifference also expressed in this along with the rest.

Their urge to convert focuses all the more powerfully on their core family, the remaining children first and foremost. To begin with Winnie is invited increasingly often outside the back room of De Graanmaat. She pops up at family meals, she pops up at barbecues, she pops up at the premieres of plays. She is accorded by the grateful butcher and his wife the blind trust they used to reserve for their GP.

In addition my mother develops with Ludwina the same close, friendly woman's relationship that she will later, having been struck dumb by her first stroke, also build up with a couple of her nurses at Beveren. It helps that Winnie does not show herself at any moment keen on money or material advantages—two sister souls full of creative bohemian spirit. And to make the bond complete, all things considered a spiritualist also stands on a stage, face to face with a kind of audience. That artistic aspect of the séance sets the seal on their pact of friendship. Winnie is at the same time her pal, confidante, guide, colleague, anchor and saviour.

Precisely because of that, she argues, it hurts her 'as the mother of a deceased son' that her other children want no part in Winnie's séances, not even in the least astonishing, that with the flowers. She launches a verbal persuasion offensive against each member of her remaining family, using her whole arsenal of female tyrant. According to her we are abandoning our brother. We are gagging him by staying away. We are undermining her and her regained hope and energy. Through our fault she risks going under again, and our father with her. Is that what we want? Is that to be her reward? Is that the encouragement that we have to offer her after a catastrophe of that magnitude? 'Going along just once to a séance, is that asking too much? Sacrificing one stupid evening. At least do it for your mother, if you don't want to do it for yourself and your brother.'

It was Winnie who put an end to this blackmail. By chance. She was visiting the bungalow, she heard my mother hissing with rage at me, and she did something that up to then I had never seen anyone do. She came into that kitchen uninvited and called my mother to order. And my mother accepted it. Just like that. Albeit sulkingly. So Winnie the Saviour did even more. She reminded my mother that she also had children who were still alive. Not only the dead are worth a two-weekly trip, she said. There was more in prospect for mothers than a life of just commemorating and looking back.

As a proof she used me.

I am still in my early twenties when a spiritualist medium and friend of the family grabs me by the head in my mother's presence. Unexpectedly but softly she lays her hands on my crew-cut crown. I do not dare move. I don't know why, but I let her do it. In the distance I hear dogs barking. A nearby finch calls 'Tweet! Tweet!'

She shakes that head of mine gently to and fro, with a spinning motion, as if my head were a bowl of waste water, a sawn-open coconut full of milk that has to be churned. Her bracelets jingle modestly. 'Ohlala,' she says. With eyes closed. Her eyelids are made up in garish purple and green. On one cheek she has a beauty spot. 'The things this lad has to offer. He may yet need you, as a support. My hands are almost catching fire from the inner pressure. He's clearly his parent's child!' Her eyes are still closed. 'You're going to be surprised by him, very much and very soon. Ohlala!' My mother allows herself to be slowly calmed down. Her recalcitrance turns into the beginnings of pride.

Too slowly, to Winnie's mind. She lets go of my head and grasps my mother's chin with one hand, in a gesture of tender reproach. I have never seen anyone do that before either. She speaks firmly but not didactically. 'What did you ask of him just now? No one must demand something like that. Of anyone. Not everyone is ready for it. Not everyone needs it. If there's anything you should have learnt from me, it's that. Let him loose, let go. Let everyone go their own way. Things are as they are.'

I never went to a séance. But since that day in that kitchen I knew one thing. I had found my instrument to force my coming-out. She had a beauty spot and she smelt of patchouli and eternally fresh flowers.

'Tweet! Tweet!'

THE LAST TIME my mother visited her own flat, I had her taken away by two paramedics. I rang them myself while she sat unsuspecting in the living room coming round from a new attack of rage full of foaming at the lips and ranting. She had pulled over chairs and smashed a plate on the laid table. The slivers, including those of a glass, had scattered in all directions. She could have been hurt. It was impossible to calm her down and she was on the point of smashing still more to smithereens. China figures. The television. The china cabinet with the mauve leaded lights. The glass over the painting of the Negro heads by Maria the Artistic. There was so much that could be smashed in their flat.

I closed the door of the living room behind me and rang the ambulance service from the bedroom, where I had sought cover with my father.

Her second stroke, weeks before, had wiped out all the progress she had made and all hope of recovery. She had been found by the night nurse, by her bed on the ground, virtually unconscious. After recovering from her night-time fall and the shock of the stroke itself—the consultant compared it to an epileptic fit, and perhaps it had been one partly—she had difficulty walking, for the first time in her life. She hung heavily on the arm of her young women nurse friends, whom she scarcely recognized for the first few days. Her glassy look became somewhat clearer after a week, and even then it wasn't certain if she recognized you. One hand shook, the other was sometimes frozen in a claw, even when she reached for a glass with it, or for your hand. The dose of the medicines she was already receiving daily was increased.

After a while the trembling stopped on the left side, the claw on the right relaxed and she could walk again without accompaniment, although she never regained the carefree gait she once had. The new words that she had acquired recently with so much effort had all deserted her again. For good, as was to become clear. The relatives in the snaps on her photo album had again become strangers. She looked at them with detachment, however much you pointed and repeated the accompanying names. The doctor warned us. He suspected that from now on more and more clots would bore their way into her brain, destroying more and more cells and functions. In my mind I saw a plain on which a rain of meteors descends, sowing destruction, leaving behind a pockmarked desert.

In the course of the last month that she spent at the facility in Beveren—before she began her Odyssey to institutions for ever severer cases—she would have flickers of recovery as she had had them long ago, during her months of drunkenness and narcosis, her unreasoning period of mourning for Her Most Awkward One. On one of those mornings of renewed hope and energy I left her behind in her room with a kiss on the forehead. She was in remarkably good humour, she had performed her classic show in which she imitated the three old men on the bench outside her door, blowing raspberries on the back of her hand. She waved at me in the doorway with a smile and she also waved a little later at me at her window on the first floor, while I waved back on the ground floor and got into my car.

That same afternoon I get a phone call. Can I please come immediately to Beveren. She had attacked a cleaner, she had drawn the curtains of her room and would not let herself be approached by anyone, not even by her friends among the nurses.

I enter her half-darkened room, prepared for the worst. All the same I am alarmed by the picture and the sound. She is sitting at the head end of the bed, with her back almost against the headboard and with a pillow on her lap that she is clinging to. She is rocking her body maniacally but softly backward and forward. It is her face that is most frightening. It is like a Greek mask, that of despair. She opens her mouth wide as can be and makes a quiet whining sound without crying and looks straight ahead, bewildered. With those deep furrows in her face, reinforced by the shadow of the curtains, and with her bulging eyes, her hollow cheeks and dishevelled hair she is reminiscent of a photo from the past: she as a judge, in that avant-garde play *The Sentence*. But here there is no more acting involved. What she is embodying here, without trying to show or interpret, is the rock bottom of an existence, the end of the line. Perhaps she only now realizes what has befallen her. I don't know what she is looking at or what she is thinking about. She radiates impregnability. The sight is unbearable but I don't dare move. My petrification lasts ten, fifteen minutes. Finally I simply go toward her and put my arms around her. She does not recognize the gesture, or it doesn't affect her. She changes absolutely nothing in her position or her movement. Her mouth remains wide open like that of a mask and produces a quiet whining sound. I might just as well not have been there.

She never returned to her own home after I had had her taken away. Not that she did not make attempts. Her brave stubbornness seemed to grow as she went downhill.

Once panic broke out among the staff at Beveren. She was nowhere to be found. Not in her room, not in the gym, not in the chapel where she sometimes went and stared straight ahead. Until someone sees a window open on the second floor that gives onto a flat roof. And sure enough, there she is, unhindered by vertigo or the raw weather. She is walking along the edges of the flat roof, peering down unafraid, effectively making as if to crawl down via a gutter. They are just able to prevent this in time and take her back inside. She does not protest. She allows herself to be tucked up in bed and eats her soup as if nothing has happened.

Another time, just as it is getting dark there is a ring at the door of the flat in Sint-Niklaas. My father, sitting by himself eating a takeaway meal from the new Chinese restaurant on the corner, looks at his watch in amazement, opens the terrace door that gives onto the balcony on the street side and gets the fright of his life. There she stands, looking up with her dead eyes, next to two policemen and their idling combi van. In Beveren, wearing her coat with the fox-fur collar and her simple hat, she succeeded in slipping past the security entrance. No one knows how long she has been wandering about. It is a fact that on the marketplace, more than half a kilometre away, she buttonholed passers-by fruitlessly in her devilish dialect and when it didn't work she sat down in the middle of the square, flat on her backside, on the cold stones, looking around her yawning, a lost soul in the evening bustle, her reflex of revolt foundered on a square full of strangers. A worried passer-by notifies the police, and one of the policemen called out finds her wallet in her handbag, with the official address in it.

My father calls me, at his wits' end, full of guilt, afraid. I advise him to explain the situation to the policemen and ask them to take her back to the facility. There is no point in her staying with him, as he suggests, as she can easily fly into a rage again, he cannot control her alone, and apart from that she needs her medication. If she really wants to come home another time, we'll organize that later, I say, not now. Later! Even as we hang up, we both know that 'later' will never come.

Five minutes later he calls me again, crying. To reassure me, he says. She has let herself be taken back without a fuss into the combi van, in which she will be returned. One policeman came hurrying up the stairs to hand over the money to him that was in her wallet. 'Not very safe, sir, for your wife to be walking about the streets again, in her condition.'

The day that I had her taken away from the flat had not actually begun badly. A poor copy of her first outing, but in any case a copy. Except that when she came in she did not charge upstairs, but climbed up laboriously, a step at a time, with me supporting her back and my father pulling her up by hand.

Once upstairs she throws herself like a fury into a household job. She casts a weary—or is it an already mildly disturbed?—look around her. The superficial happiness I thought I noticed during the drive here has gone. She takes off her coat with a disgruntled gesture, drops it on the ground and goes after all to the kitchen.

There she begins emptying the fridge, while my father puts her coat away on a hanger.

Everything that she finds in the fridge she puts on the worktop. Then she looks around meditatively, opens a cupboard and unerringly fishes out the bread basket with a half-empty bag of bread inside. She looks in it, takes out a crust of bread, tastes it and pulls a face. With an accusatory gesture she shows my father the opened bread bag, the *corpus delicti* of his neglect, and launches a first salvo in her demonic gibberish, from which we conclude that she thinks the bread is stale.

Even so she takes the bread to the table, shaking her head, walking with difficulty. Then she starts laying the table, though all three of us have only just eaten, my father and I before we left here, she before she left Beveren. We let her have her way. Even when she gets three crystal glasses from the china cabinet. Even when she then brings everything she previously took out of the fridge to the table. That takes many laborious trips, but she won't tolerate our help—when my father and I make as if to help her, she fires a second salvo in her non-language, louder and sharper than just now. She barks orders for us to take our places at table, where we are obviously supposed to wait until she has lugged in all the available food and drink. That takes a while. We let her have her way.

Finally she is ready, and the table is packed. She places the last jar of jam next to the bread basket, surveys the battlefield and picks up that last jar of jam again. She unscrews the lid and places it next to the jar on the table-top. Then she does the same with the jar of chocolate spread. Then the jar of instant coffee. And so on and so forth, until all the jars and bags and coffee jars and tins and cardboard containers and wrapping papers and bottles and the milk cartons have been opened. We let her get on with it. It is a wild and overloaded still life that is growing on our table. Here and there among the foodstuffs and the bottles there are still some of her plants and figurines.

Then comes the moment when the compulsive opening behaviour is finally finished. A silence falls. She is still standing, we are sitting. My father and I look at each other, across the battlefield. I see him shrug his shoulders. We don't know what is expected of us. He looks at her, he looks back at me. He looks at the bread basket with the stale bread in it right in front of him. His hand reaches out almost automatically just to take a slice. If we are sitting here anyway, at a ready-laid table? At the moment his hand touches the slice, all hell breaks loose.

She bursts out in her meaningless verbal gall and with her arm sweeps half of her still life off the table onto the carpet. She tears the piece of bread out of the hands of my astonished father. It breaks in two, he is holding only the crust. Ranting, she throws the rest of the slice onto the ground, she stamps on it and then starts going really wild. With surprising ease she knocks over a chair, and another. We sit as if rooted to the spot watching her, my father still with that crust in his hand.

Then she snatches my plate from under my nose, raises it high above her head—still spewing out her anti-language—and smashes it down on my father's empty plate. The two plates shatter, one of the crystal glasses is also broken, the milk carton falls against a couple of the bottles, milk and beer slosh around together over what remains of the still life.

While the storm rages behind us, I lead my shocked, helpless father out of the room. He lets himself be protected, as he always has.

SHE HERSELF MIGHT squabble and criticize him in the presence of all, but if anyone dared direct a nasty or harsh word at him, she would jump unreservedly into the breach for him.

During the first years of their marriage he tries still to continue his own hobby, water polo. Not an obvious choice, with two children and the business and an ear in which he gets severe inflammation. His eardrum has to be perforated to release the fluid from the inflammation. As a result he goes half deaf, and when he swims, and particularly when he dives, he feels a painful pressure on that side.

During a friendly match shortly after the operation they are taunted, outplayed and laughed at by a player from a higher division. Even the spectators become irritated at the unequal contest between two spare-time teams on a bank holiday, of which the climax is not even the match but a raffle. But the arrogant star player stays in the pool and scores goal after goal. As the best marker, my father is instructed to neutralize him. He performs his task rather too well and too enthusiastically—curiosity was not his only vice, he did not need to be taught how to taunt back and pinch.

He goes over and treads water next to the guy and does not move an inch from his side. He may play a division lower, but he still knows the tricks of obstruction through and through. Pushing a centre underwater with your elbow, just as the ball comes shooting along. Half pulling off his swimming trunks underwater. On the surface making smutty remarks about his fiancée and his mother—inventing stories supposedly dished up by gossiping types at the bar. Well, the guy did not score one more goal.

But when my father leaves the dressing room afterwards, they are waiting for him and out of nowhere he gets a punch in the face. He feels the pain moving to the ear that has been operated on. The blood spurts out of his nose and his split lip, it falls on the ribbed blue tiles of the swimming-pool floor, mixing with the chlorinated water.

Before the star player can lash out again, she comes flying at him out of nowhere. With her shoe in her hand, a mule with a pointed steel heel. She hits him bang on the head with it. Her husband will not be the only one who bleeds today. She lashes out again, at the guy's ear. If she'd had the chance to hit him again, he would have lost his eye.

The guy, two heads taller than her, starts running. They had to rescue him and restrain her or she would have beaten him to death with her one shoe.

Not long afterwards my father gave up his hobby. 'I could no longer combine it with the business. And with that pain in my ear? And the opposing teams wanted to know in advance if your mother was coming. If so, we'll wear helmets, they said.'

The ambulance crew do not ring at the door, as I asked them on the telephone. They send a warning text, and I go down and open the door for them. My mother is in the hushed living room, my father has stayed in the bedroom at my request. I want to spare him everything that is coming.

'You know the conditions?' asks one ambulance man. The other just looks around, chewing gum, peppermint by the smell of it. They are both wearing yellow fluorescent smocks. It's a private service, and on this Saturday there is only hospital-linked patient transport, not between two municipalities. They have made their profession of these kinds of trips. The three of us are standing in the passage, in front of the door that leads to the living room. We speak in muted tones.

'We take no responsibility for the behaviour of the patient, that is stipulated here and here, and here's your receipt at the same time, so would you mind signing?' The second ambulance man reads along with me, or perhaps he is checking if I am signing in the right place. 'Thank you very much. That will be two hundred and fifty euros.'

I hand the senior ambulance man the money, in cash. The notes lie openly and undeniably in the palm of his hand. I am paying to have my mother carried out of her own house. 'Nothing can happen to her, can it?' I ask. I hear myself speak and think it sounds as if I am trying to cover myself. Against shame. Against despair. 'Sir,' grins the chewer, 'we're professionals. If you knew the kind of thing we sometimes have to put up with.' 'Don't worry,' says the other man, 'it will all happen very fast. Unfortunately we can't use the stretcher, we could have tied your mother to it, but those stairs are a disaster.'

'How will it happen then?' I want to know. Though I don't want to know at all.

'We'll go in, and before she has recovered from the surprise we will have lifted her up, I by the shoulders, he by the legs, and we'll charge downstairs. The downstairs door will be open, the ambulance door too. As soon as they're sitting in it, our ambulance, they calm down. Completely different surroundings, with all that equipment and so on. Plus the awareness that it's over. It will take at most a minute. Half a minute, if there are no complications.'

'Thanks very much,' I say, as if there is something to thank them for. 'But can you wait a moment first? I'd like to support my father when it happens. I don't want him to come into the passage at that moment and see this. I don't want him to have to carry this with him as the last image of her here.'

They say that they understand, and we shake hands in farewell. Then I go into the bedroom through the passage. Just before I close the door I look at the pair again through the chink. They both give me the thumbs-up.

'What's happening?' I hear behind my back. 'Has she gone? Is there anything else we can do?'

I close the door and tell him the truth. That we must be patient for a little. That it will be over shortly. That this is better, for her, for him, for everyone. He nods and says nothing. We are silent together, sitting on the edge of their bed. It takes a while. We wait for want of anything else to do. Suddenly I hear, unexpectedly after all, a door flying open in the distance. Followed by stumbling in the living room, stumbling in the passage, then stumbling on the stairs. And then, suddenly, amplified by the echo of the stairwell, her voice rings out for a final time in her own home. She has retrieved one word wonderfully well. She screams it loud and heart-rendingly clearly. His name. She calls his name at the top of her voice.

'Can't I hear something?' asks my father, frowning, turning his half-good ear with the hearing aid slightly toward the closed door.

'That's not possible, Dad,' I say. 'They're already out of the house.'

It took until the middle of the not so wonderful 1980s before I finally arranged my coming-out and was ready for it myself. I had, with immediate and enduring homesickness, moved from Ghent to Antwerp to make the journeys for my appearances in the Netherlands less time-consuming. I had finally, after years of genuine affection and mutual self-deceit, broken with the woman for whom I had in all affection feigned love. And I had found in Antwerp—which after all turned out to offer more advantages than just a favourable position close to Roosendaal—a splendid lover with hair on his chest and hair on his chin.

My parents' period of mourning for Our Most Awkward One had elapsed, although it was far from over. 'The pain will never disappear. [she, at least once a month] You might just as well ask an ocean to disappear.' Their spiritualist zeal as converts had turned to sober withdrawal. Only if you inquired about the séances yourself were you given a summary account. Only now and then did she talk of her own accord about a new entity that had dropped in—an uncle, a teacher and once her own mother, whom she had lost so young. But her stories were no longer pleas. They were now like the meandering dream interpretations with which she used to regale us at the breakfast table and which had, moreover, not come to an end through the appearance of entities in De Graanmaat. In her sleep too half a town came to visit her.

My timing was both symbolically and practically well judged. In two weeks' time they would retire. They would have to empty their shop and hand it over to their successor, and at the same time they themselves would move to the flat one floor up. So a new phase was dawning in their lives? Then it was also time for a new look at their youngest. And with that double removal they would immediately have enough on their hands to help cope with that new look. Activity is the best therapy.

The setting was the bungalow on a sun-drenched spring day in June. The immediate pretext: a barbecue. Agent and duty process server: Winnie the Pooh, alias Winnie Mandela, Ludwina for official bodies. Over the years she had become increasingly their friend and counsellor, and less and less the intimidating medium of their first meetings. She was well enough integrated in the family to share our most intimate secrets, but still too strange and too intimidating to make scenes or trouble. My ideal referee on a bumpy pitch. Not least because I had briefed and instructed her in advance. Even if you are hatching a plot you must do it well. You've got more in you than you think! And all's allowed in family warfare.

The preparation of the barbecue proceeded as always under the command of the earth mother. Everyone helped, even the guests. Chopping onions, rinsing lettuces, cutting tomatoes, beating mayonnaise from the yolk of an egg, a dash of mustard and lots of fine oil, preparing cocktail sauce with a generous splash of flambé whisky, wrapping unpeeled potatoes in aluminium foil, skewering veal pieces and sections of paprika on wooden sticks. Lamb cutlets sprinkled with herbs on both sides, pricking holes in the pork sausages and—an exotic experiment!—wrapping the merguez, wafer-thin slices of smoked bacon around mini-portions of salmon, and meanwhile laying the table and setting the charcoal briquettes aglow, and finally prizing open a couple of kilos of mussels without letting all the liquid escape, and depositing in each remaining shell a knob of herb butter next to the mollusc, with an eye to the best aperitif snack in the open air: *moules à l'escargot*. Shortly afterwards they were the first thing on the grill, bubbling aromatically in their shells, announcing a comedy of good eating lasting hours, since for dessert there was rice pudding with brown sugar and a home-made apple cake.

This spring banquet was served at a table for at least twelve guests, set up in the middle of our at last mole-free garden. It was made up of smaller tables, in various styles and sizes and of varied origin. One was a gift on the closure of Wivina's Café, the other a bastard shunned everywhere else, from the legacy of a great-aunt, the third brought as a bonus with an umbrella stand from the auction rooms in Antwerp, all three washed up here by the unfathomable currents in the diaspora of things. During the winter they stood in a disorderly pile in the shed, but at the first ray of sunshine they were dragged outside and put next to each other in a more or less straight line, like a long and rickety altar in the grass. One side started from under our Japanese cherry, and on the other side stood our bright-red parasol on its white pole and concrete base waiting for sun-shy guests. On either side of the tabletop there was a wild array of assorted bastard chairs—wood, plastic, wicker or metal, but if you put a cushion on the seat no one felt the difference. As a whole it represented an ode to chance, displayed in the open air. A lyrically minded observer would talk of location theatre without actors, an installation without a caption.

The various tables were made into one large one by laying two or so plywood sheets on top, one as the extension of the other, where necessary supported by a pile of beer mats to compensate for the uneven height of the bastard tables. Two tablecloths were then spread out over the plywood sheets which might easily differ in colours and motifs, red and white checks alongside flowers in blue or yellow, it didn't matter what. In the middle, where they overlapped, a well-filled ice bucket was placed, while the overhanging sections were protected from gusts of wind with gleaming table clips or ingenious hanging weights—fat-bellied cockerels or tortoises that hung gently rocking to and fro from the cotton by their beaks or jaws, which incorporated a serrated clip. It just required plates, cutlery and food, and our meal could begin.

Anyone coming from abroad to these parts and having to conclude business deals, or negotiate international agreements, had better not have any illusions. Straight-talking conversations, cogent arguments, vitally important contracts, the barrage of questions and bids— they can all wait till our dessert or after it. Never let a capital crime spoil a good meal, that's our rule. The higher echelons are a perfect reflection of the situation at all lower and more intimate levels. First the food, then the news.

It is a course of events that shocks punctual peoples, because they believe in the religion of straightforwardness. But those who always sail straight ahead are more likely to hit a mine or a quay suddenly looming up out of the fog. Tacking is not always a waste of time and sometimes, oddly enough, it provides the shortest route. That is our religion and we believe in it with the fervency of zealots. Eating and drinking together creates a bond of trust and an atmosphere of reasonableness, even with increased consumption of alcohol. Once they have handed each other the pepper and salt set, or have served each other tomato soup and pureed potatoes, even sworn enemies realize their own limitations and each other's equality, if not as negotiators then at least as human beings. There is in the shared activity of chewing on fresh food something melancholy that moves one to modesty. And anyway a compromise is easier to find with a full stomach and a balloon glass of brandy in one's hand. The picture may look like a bacchanalian orgy, but at bottom dining together is a purifying exercise in thought.

And hence also the best preparation for a possibly intense confrontation.

(In the place I grew up in there was only one official gay. Not even in the circle of our hamlet within the town. He lived just outside, above the café that he ran in the Ankerstraat, Chez William. Lewdness and the French language are as inextricably bound up as provincial gay sex and dressing-up.

His cross-dressing show, on every first and last Saturday of the month, was his unique selling proposition in the whole area. He mimed in expensive dresses, on which he spent the complete proceeds of his business, on top of the fortune that he had had to borrow to fit the place out. Tinted mirrors, disco balls and gilt did not come free. Judy Garland, Barbra Streisand, Soeur Sourire and Mae West did. They passed smoothly in succession, but his greatest hits were Dalida and later Amanda Lear, two divas who he maintained through thick and thin were in true life reconstructed men. 'I have my sources,' he said, with a wink. He said everything with a wink and a downward turn of his head. And when he was silent his mouth pouted as if he were sucking on an imaginary orange. He had a big nose and a big mouth. 'And that's not the only thing about me [wink] that's big.' For years I hated him from the bottom of my heart. He roamed like a spectre through my youth. The pity I felt for him made me feel disgust. At him and at myself.

Every Saturday when he performed, his café was chock-full of portly bourgeois couples counting on a risqué evening out, at a reasonable price and closer to home than Paris. And every time there was a family man who, to the hilarity of the company, either leapt out of the toilet in women's clothes he had smuggled in, or simply as a man disturbed the performance of La William by stubbornly calling and inviting her to do a slow number, or show her breasts, or at least her woman's prick. La William went on miming. Only once did he lash out with his beringed fist. He hit the jaw of a former parachutist who asked for nothing better than to be able to vent his uneasiness, disguised as fun, on a monster.

In ordinary life La William had a poodle and a vague past. He talked nineteen to the dozen about the former, never about the latter. On his first suicide attempt he drank a bottle of ammoniac and survived. He was forced to close the café. He couldn't even mime any more. His second suicide attempt was successful. He again drank a bottle of ammoniac, this time mixed with pills and drain cleaner. At his funeral, in accordance with his will, they played arias by Maria Callas.)

(All the dead in Waasland seemed to come to a horrid end, except for my own laughing father—'Buggered. Hu-hu-hu.' Despite the gruesomeness there was a strikingly phlegmatic tone in the way their end was reported.

I was already a student, but came home faithfully on Friday evenings in order to help in the shop the following day, the busiest day of the week, which at least guaranteed us an evening meal and sometimes a quiet breakfast so the three of us could catch up. Mostly it boiled down to me listening in amazement and their reporting on the state of their town, the world. 'Do you know who's just died? [she, gnawing a chicken bone; or he, downing with relish a butter cake topped with cheese] Our poultry supplier. You know him, don't you? With his cap. You could smell him a mile off. Dirty creatures, chickens and turkeys. The bloke finally retires, hands the business over to his children, and a week later wakes up: "What on earth is that? A black edge to my toenail." A week later his whole foot is black and is spreading more of a stench than all his chickens put together. Another week later they amputate his leg, the week after his other leg and the week after that he chokes in his sleep. He got off pretty lightly. It could have taken much longer.'

Or: 'Do you know who's just died? Willy Verbreyt, that chap. He'd been confined to bed for a year in his Art Deco place on the Spoorweglaan, with bed sores and all. Half his face was paralysed and he lost a lung. Still, he lay there with that one lung, shouting at the top of his voice, day and night: "I don't want to die! I don't want to die!" The neighbours had to send their children on holiday to family in the Campine, or they would have gone mad. He tried to hit the nurses who came to change him. Oh dear, that Willy, I've never seen anyone play *The Servant of Two Masters* better than him. The professionals in the Bourla in Antwerp could learn a thing or two from him.'

Or: 'Do you know who's just died? Your uncle Herman. At the end he no longer knew what day it was. "Give me a rope," he calls to the nurse looking after him. "Give me a rope!" The woman thinks he wants to hang himself and so she gives him just a short piece, not enough for round a neck. But he throws off his sheets and—putting it crudely, I'll say it as it is—he ties off his manhood right in front of the poor woman. "It's a snake," he cries. "It's a snake, free me from it!" The next day he lies ice-cold and stiff, staring at his ceiling. With no breath, but with that piece of rope next to him on his bedside table.')

(And always, during those stories, we eat. We eat, eat, eat, eat, eat, eat, eat, eat, eat, eat, eat, eat, eat, eat, eat, eat, eat, eat, eat, eat, eat, eat, eat, eat, eat, eat, eat, eat, eat, eat. We eat. When does eating become pathological? Not personally, but in terms of mass psychology: a collective neurosis? Is it culturally determined immaturity, or repression of ordinary fear of death, converted into stuffing oneself with goodies? Or is it a matter of spiritual emptiness, which has to be fought with gluttony? Civilized barbarism, set about with unbridled bulimia? We urgently need to eat. To go on talking endlessly about it.)

The barbecue is still smouldering. Dessert has been eaten, coffee drunk, the atmosphere is languid and indolent, the sun has passed its zenith, the perfect moment has come for a coup de theâtre. I look at Winnie, she nods, and we both help to clear away the empty plates and dishes.

In the kitchen where Winnie took my mother by the chin, years ago, I now ask if she has a moment for me. Because I have something to tell her. As I make the latter announcement I see from her face that I don't have to say that it's about something important, which I'd rather the other guests don't hear. It really wasn't the intention that they should be here, she invited them at the last moment, of her own accord. That's fine by me. Now they are here, I have an extra guarantee that crying fits or outbursts will be kept to a minimum. If anything is maintained, just before a retirement, it is the appearance of perfection. A rounded whole, without snags.

In the heart of the bungalow, the small living room with its walls of wood bark and ceiling of fibreboard and cement tiles, they each sit in a bucket chair, in their summer gear, next to each other. She in her swimsuit, barefoot, arms folded. He in his wide blue shorts and his white sleeveless vest, with grey socks and brown sandals on his feet. He has put his arms on the armrests, waiting. She looks displeased in advance, he curious and fearful at the same time. I have remained standing, and Winnie stands obliquely behind me. Height offers advantage of terrain and mental superiority. I don't give Winnie the chance to say 'Say your piece'. I say it.

It is amazingly simple. And it can be said in amazingly few words. It is my father who, amazingly enough, speaks first. He says: 'Would you say that again, lad? That hearing aid, you know.' With his right forefinger he makes a turning movement in his right ear, where the knob of the hearing aid is located. It is now set to maximum, and he turns his ear toward me again too, so that I certainly do not have to speak any louder than before. And I don't. I calmly repeat my announcement. There is a very long silence, afterwards. We don't move much either. No finch sings, but there are dogs barking in the distance again.

Before Winnie can say anything, my mother stands up. She looks at me, then at Winnie and she nods. She sees the construction, she understands the checkmate, she accepts. 'Then that's how it is,' she says, whereupon she hurries out, chin held high.

I follow her with my eyes and see her go over to the

remaining guests, who are sitting talking around our long altar, an Italian mural in the colours of a late afternoon. She says something that is greeted with laughter, pours herself a stiff cognac and cadges a cigarette from someone. She lights up and inhales deeply. For the first time in five years.

(She never stopped again, until her second stroke. Her friendship with Winnie, however, diluted. Gradually but systematically. Finally they lost all contact with each other. Without argument, without regret. No new séances replaced the old. She had heard the messages of the entities often enough to trust that they would be the same for ever. She did, though, light a tea light every evening in front of the obituary card of her Most Awkward One, around which more and more new dead collected in the form of other obituary cards.)

My father sat in his bucket chair for another quarter of an hour. Then he got up with a sigh, deadly sad, visibly broken, inexpressibly troubled. He found no other words than those of his wife. 'Well then. Then that's how it is.' Everything seemed signed, sealed and delivered.

I, however, knew better when I saw her from a distance drinking her cognac far too eagerly and saw her smoking—one after another—and saw her laughing and entertaining her company. I had far from checkmated her. It was a draw at most. The real confrontation was still to come.

At a time and on a terrain of her choosing.

Without referees or witnesses.

AS SOON AS she had left the facility in Beveren, things went downhill for good with her. Not quickly, not drastically, but steadily. Each week she could do a little less, and each month that came to a lot. Less *was* less. And less became nothing.

Her speech remained unintelligible, but now also reduced in its number of syllables. Ultimately only a language skeleton would be left of only the occasional word and sound, and finally not even that any more. You could no longer even imagine whether she was being silent with you from stubbornness or despair. She was silent as a snowy landscape is silent, or a stuffed deer. Because they have no option. Likewise the gestural language and the mimicry which she had used to such good effect in Beveren, her trade tricks which in the past had stood her in such good stead on stage too—they dissolved, faded, they fell away from her little by little. You can't go on losing indefinitely. At a certain moment all has gone.

Her eyes became less clear, unfocused, without the least expectation. At the end she only seemed lucid enough by moments to recognize you, without your knowing whether she actually did recognize you. You wanted it to be true. You hoped it was. And because of that hope a raised eyebrow or a curled corner of the mouth seemed to take on the meaning that they once really had. A painting exists in the eye of the beholder, not on the canvas.

She was increasingly tied to her bed to protect her from a fall. At first not at night. For security, though, bars were fitted to either side of her mattress, an adult version of what you sometimes see with a child's bed. That was sufficient to provoke her. Her unceasing rebelliousness, her mutiny against all that she disliked, forced her to clamber over the bars at night and crash down even harder, from half a metre higher than if she had just fallen out of bed. From then on she was tied in her bed. And for extra security the bars were fitted again anyway. You never knew with her.

During the day too she was tied more and more for security, after she had fallen forward while suddenly springing up from her single armchair in a spasm of inexplicable energy. When walking had also become a big problem, she found herself in a wheelchair from morning to night in which she would eventually also be tied, so that she would no longer slide forward out of it, which had happened to her more and more in the preceding days. No one knew whether it was a new act of mutiny. Until shortly before she had still been allowed and able to use her wheelchair as a rollator walker. She had always refused a real rollator, let alone a walking frame. She preferred to shuffle about supporting herself on the handles of her empty wheelchair, which she pushed along as if she were transporting her own ghost, or rather she seemed to be in search of a fellow sufferer who was still worse off than she was and whom she welcomed for a ride, under her escort and her orders. To everyone she passed she still gave a polite, measured nod. To the last: everything to preserve the semblance of normality, everything with as much style as possible, everything not to give in to defeatism. Until she herself landed once and for all in her wheelchair and after a few rides no longer nodded to anyone.

Like the rest of my family, I tried to get her to walk occasionally. 'Good for the circulation!' That walking was a step at a time. She leant at an angle against you, hanging on your arm. The first few times that produced a triumphant walk down the corridor of yet another institution, there and back. A few weeks later she was already hanging so heavily on your arm that you had to admit that what you were doing was more you forcing her into an imitation of walking together because you craved for it, than her walking because she longed to do it again. After which you allowed her to be put back in her wheelchair. And secured for her own safety.

Only when she went into what was called a sub-coma did she no longer need to be secured for her safety. Except for her arms, that is.

Even in that period of decline there were lots of lovely moments. She recognized the banana you had brought for her and ate it with relish while you were there. Although it has to be said that she could no longer peel it so fast herself, and gradually could no longer hold it without dropping it or squashing it accidentally into a mush in her stubborn, malevolent hand. No problem. She allowed herself willingly to be fed by you. It even seemed to give her pleasure that you should take on this role.

Sometimes she took her false teeth out of her mouth, quite unembarrassed, to clean them on her handkerchief, which you then with no comment and without showing your own dismay replaced with a clean one.

Without her dentures her lips collapsed, a spider's web of creases. She looked 100 years old. In the past she would never have wanted to be seen like this, now nothing seemed to bother her. She reinserted the dentures and clawed or pointed at the remainder of the banana in your hand.

What she liked best were the wheelchair walks that you took her on in the neighbouring park which gave its name to our illustrious approach road, our Parklaan. She was born in a side street of it, the Moerland. She pointed at it vaguely, at that house where she was born, with an uncertain index finger. Eventually she pointed at the wrong house.

With the same finger she also pointed at the ducks and the spouting fountain in the pond in front of Château Walburg. But a walk like that needn't last much more than half an hour. She suddenly started yawning without putting her hand in front of her mouth and shortly afterwards fell asleep and snored. With her emaciated body hanging to one side, her head to the other. Just like the sleeping toddler in the buggy of a passing young father.

For me these were the nicest moments of the last period. She saw me come in and grabbed for her handbag. She did not take out one of her countless plastic bags, in which she kept well-thumbed pieces of chocolate or sweets or half-crumbled biscuits—no one ate any, not even her, but she made such a fuss if you threatened to throw them away or replace them that we let her keep everything. What she did fish out was her beauty case. She pressed it into my hands and pointed to her chin, top lip or eyebrow. Just as when she had dressed in full regalia for one last time, I took out the gold-coloured tweezers and gratefully fulfilled a noble task. I could after all be of some use to her. I plucked every hair that I knew she herself would have found excessive or unappetizing.

For the first few times she checked the result herself in her hand mirror, and commanded me to continue. Look, she pointed, here! Reinforcing her gesture after all with a stream of diabolic gibberish. Here another rascal was rearing its head. She pointed to her nostril, from which a hair was indeed protruding. I went to work with my tweezers, gripping the hair accurately and pulling it out with a swift motion. 'Ow,' she cried, as perfectly as she used to, grimacing and laughing at the same time, because of the typical stab of pain which is also a tickle when you pull a hair out of your nose. She even gave me a playful push, a sign that this was a good day. A beautiful day. A day when you hesitated, when you told yourself, against your better judgement, that there might perhaps one day be after all, who knows, a turn for the better on its way—she wasn't taking all that medication for nothing, was she?

A few weeks later, after I came in, I had to fish out her beauty case all by myself and myself look for the hairs that begged to be plucked. She let me get on with it. She lay slumped back staring at a point next to my face. She no longer checked anything afterwards in the mirror and she no longer gave me any playful pushes. Even the 'Ow!' had gone. At most it was replaced by a short grimace of pain with which she contorted her face. I had to be satisfied with that.

There were also enough unpleasant and unedifying moments. Sometimes she tried to go wandering off again, supporting herself against the wall, looking maniacally for an exit. During one of those attempts at escape she managed to get downstairs in the lift, as far as the entrance hall, where she fell over, spraining her wrist and almost breaking her hip. Half her face was still blue two weeks later.

When through a combination of circumstances and a misunderstanding no one had visited her for a few days in succession, she sat there looking neglected. She was half dehydrated and unwashed. My eldest brother but one found mould under the palate of her dentures. He was furious, and demanded successfully that she be transferred to another department, with intensive care.

The nursing improved. The decline continued.

There, in that other department, I once found my father hesitating at the door of her room. We had travelled here separately, without knowing that the other had come. I didn't know whether he preferred to be alone with her today or just the reverse. I decided to wait a bit before I signalled my presence.

Over his shoulder, through the half-open door, I saw his wife sitting there, his idol, his Josée. Staring straight ahead, breathing heavily, slumped back, her arms hanging ponderously against the armchair into which she was strapped. Despite the bouquet of lilies on her table and the vague whiff of her usual eau de toilette, with which he sprinkled her at each visit, the smell that reached us from her room was not pleasant. Heavy sweat and, probably, urine. He was still hesitating. I saw him close his eyes and breathe deeply as if gathering courage. At the same time I saw that her eyes were closed too. She was asleep.

He saw it too. His manliness disappeared. He looked around, still did not notice me, stood for a good few minutes indecisively with the door handle in his hand while nurses and visitors passed him talking softly without paying him any attention. Finally he let go of the handle and did not go in. He sat down on the bench next to the door, his head in his hands. I allowed him a few minutes' rest and respite and then sat down next to him. He was slightly alarmed, surprised to see me pop up.

'She's asleep,' he said. Apologetically.

'I know,' I said. Reassuringly.

(Despite their lifelong thriftiness, after they retired they allowed themselves only one indulgence. A classy extravaganza. It was her suggestion, but his gift. Her order, his *cadeau d'amour*. A brand-new mink coat, as expensive as a second-hand car. She had dreamt of it all her life, and at last she had it. It astonished her that the enthusiasm was not general. 'Well, Mum? So you've bought a new coat? Aren't minks a threatened species? Or are they only now finally extinct, thanks to this coat?'

'A coat, a coat! [she, immediately on her high horse] Are we going to call that a coat? Halfway to the knee. So with my height it's only half-length. And those animals are specially bred for it, properly and efficiently. Rodents that are unhappy get gaps in their fur, they have that in common with people. And why should I deny an honest breeder his profit. The whole world wears leather shoes, carries leather satchels and has leather straps on its wristwatches. And nowadays who doesn't lie on a leather sofa gawping at TV? We have to kill a herd of cows for that, you know. A *herd*. But a woman like me is suddenly not allowed to wear a fur jacket? Halfway to the knee? As a consolation for her old age? As her only folly? After a life of hard graft for her five children and wages that were far too low and scarcely any pension? Not that I'm complaining. But what I want to say is: shouldn't everyone first look at himself before he opens his mouth? It would be a lot quieter everywhere.')

(She wore it for two of the three small professional parts she played after her retirement. And she also turned up in it to each of my premieres and book launches. She adored summer weather and going around in her old swimsuit, but after she had got the mink winter couldn't come soon enough for her. After her death it hung unused in my father's wardrobe for two years, in his room in the care home where he died. After that we couldn't get rid of it for love or money. Furriers don't go in for second-hand, second-hand shops don't sell fur. It now belongs to the granddaughter who helped doll her up for the last time and scarcely dares wear her coat. Frightened of the reactions of friends and strangers, with her two animal-loving children at their head.)

He: [after a glance into her room] 'She's still asleep.'

I: 'We're okay here, Dad. Close to her, close to each other.'

(I committed my matricide by telephone. I had no choice, she called me herself. A week after my coming-out and a week before they retired. Timing was always one of her biggest trumps.

I had had a rough night, and I wasn't the only one. My new lover was sleeping off his hangover in bed. It was the first time she and I had had contact since the spring barbecue and my announcement in the living room with tree bark on the wall and fibreboard and cement tiles on the ceiling.

She: 'I'm calling you about what we said.'

I: 'Said what? When?'

She: 'Don't play the innocent. You know what I mean.'

I: 'Don't play green behind the ears yourself. What's eating you?'

She: 'Eating me? What are you talking about?'

I: 'Organizing my life like you taught me.'

She: 'Did I teach you dirtiness? That's new.'

I: 'Is it dirty to be what you are?'

She: 'No one is like that. You're made like that.'

I: 'Half the psychiatrists say that too.'

She: 'Voilà.'

I: 'They say it's the mother's fault.'

She: 'I knew you were going to say that.'

I: 'If you know, why do you ring?'

She: 'Because it's not true. There's such a thing as free will.'

I: 'I've never noticed much of that, around you.'

She: 'Are you going to complain about me? Are you ashamed of me?'

I: 'No more than you are ashamed of me.'

She: 'What do the other psychiatrists say?'

I: 'Sorry?'

She: 'If it's not because of the mother, what is it then?'

I: 'I was born like it.'

She: 'That's quite possible.'

I: 'Voilà!'

She: 'We should have left it at four. My body was already too old with you.'

I: 'What?'

She: 'We were so glad you were normal and not a Mongol.'

I: 'I see. And now you feel cheated after all.'

She: 'With a Mongol you get less snubs than with someone like you.'

I: [laughing, because I *can* laugh, because I won't let myself be blown away, because from now on I will go on laughing, whatever she says] 'I'll look for a Mongol as a lover. Then you'll get less snubs.'

She: 'Choose who you like. He'll never come into our place.'

I: [no longer laughing, on the contrary indignant and seething because I'm seething—now she's got me by the scruff of the neck after all] 'Who says he'll want to show up at your place? Who says that *I'll* want to?'

She: 'You must do what you have to do. Sort it out.'

I: [no longer seething, but upset and shocked] 'You're throwing me out? Do you want to break the link with me?'

She: 'You remain welcome by yourself. We won't speak about the rest again.'

I: 'Shame. We were just getting going.'

She: 'You have your life, we have ours.'

I: 'Oh yes? And why? Can you give me *one* reason?'

She: 'I think you can work that out for yourself.'

I: [knowing what she is going to say] 'No, Mum! [no, please don't let her say it] No, I don't know the reason!' [thinking: now she'll definitely say it]

She: 'You're the worst thing that can happen to a mother.'

I: [thinking: no, I don't want to answer this, no: not this!] 'Oh yes? Is this the worst thing? [thinking: I'll say it to her anyway] Perhaps I should also drive into a tree in a Honda.'

She: [after a silence] 'I think that's cruel of you.'

I: 'So do I. That's precisely why I'm saying it.'

She: 'Do you know what I'll do? That will solve everything.'

I: 'I wonder what you mean.'

She: 'I'll hang myself. Perhaps that's simplest.'

I: 'Do you know what, Mum? [laughing again, and laughing because I can laugh] That *is* simplest. Hang yourself. And Dad as well. [realizing with a jolt: my God, I think and speak exactly like her—I *am* exactly like her, I'll say anything, just to get the upper hand] But be sure to hang yourself this week, okay? Then we only need move your things once. Everything to a house clearer and the recycling centre, instead of first going to that shitty apartment of Fat Liza's.' [hanging up so hard that the receiver cracks])

I: 'If you want you can go home, Dad. I'll take over from you.'

He: 'We'll see lad. Let's wait a bit.'

(Apart from a telephone receiver nothing cracked or broke as a result of my announcement among the tree barks and under the cement-fibre sheets. A week after the turbulent phone conversation I simply went and helped with the clearing of their shop and the moving of their personal things to the first floor. I acted innocent and was treated accordingly. My then lover looked after the rest of the reconciliation.

After a theatre performance in Antwerp which we all attended unplanned, as two couples, to my horror he made a beeline for her in the bar, with a broad grin and an outstretched hand. Sometimes politeness is the key to the universe. She did not dare to refuse to shake hands with him with so many strangers around, and though my lover had not given any details apart from his name, she understood perfectly what was what, as could be seen by the poisonous look she shot me. But she was already too involved in a lively discussion with him on the performance and the acting, before she realized that she could no longer decently break off such a conversation. An hour later she was sufficiently charmed to let him kiss her on the cheek in farewell. Not that she allowed him, he just did it. The look that I got from her this time hesitated between horror and coquettishness. I never dared ask her whether it was his conversation that had charmed her or my taste in men.)

(A hostile conversation was to follow, years later. About my second male lover, heart-stealer. He and I were the first gays in Belgium to enter into a civil partnership, a shot across the bows for the later gay marriage. All very symbolic and mediagenic at the time, lots of press there, some politicians frantic while others had gone to ground, at least two policemen in a state of alarm, too much fuss and commotion to describe. And she who, believe it or not, had become increasingly charmed by my male lovers, she who 'could chat and banter' with this second one until even I couldn't get a word in edgeways, she then rang me unexpectedly. Surly, in the middle of the night, a few hours after hearing of our plan:

She: 'Do you really have to be first again? Isn't it bad enough that you are as you are, for you to want to shout it from the rooftops?'

I: 'I'm just doing what you taught me. I'm fighting for my rights.'

She: 'You're not fighting for anything, you're flaunting the way you are.'

I: 'As if I didn't learn *that* from you too.'

She: 'I think that's nasty, daring to say something like that.'

I: 'I think it's nasty that you dare deny such a thing.'

Petit-bourgeois regression on her side, petit-bourgeois

rage on mine, again almost resulting in a cracked receiver.

But by the time the happy day came round and the ceremony was concluded—'Mothers! You are not losing a son! You are getting a second one!'—she had reconciled herself with a role which, contrary to her expectations, caused such interest and social upheaval that she herself finally came to believe in its value. The fact that a cartload of photos were taken of her also made up for a lot.

By the time that the television camera was roaming around after the concluding meal and homed in on her, one of the two mothers, she behaved like a condescending Queen of Cool, disturbed by a bumblebee but still pleased that that her discomfort should be recorded for posterity: 'As long as they're happy, sir.' Words to that effect. And something about pride and motherhood. After which she waved away the lens and the crew operating it with her ring-laden, worldly-wise hand. Directing them on to other places in the world, to real hotbeds and real disaster areas, where their presence would be more valuable than here. Certainly now she had had her say.)

I HAD MANAGED to persuade my father that he no longer needed to wait outside her door on the bench in that corridor. I would look after this visit. He was ready to be relieved, ready for a break. He nodded and went.

I sat for quite a while by myself, waiting. Until behind me, from her room, I heard noises that indicated signs of life. Scarce signs. A remnant of life. A smothered cough, heavy breathing, a slight swish of an arm moving, fingernails scratching over the artificial leather cover of an armchair. I decided to go in. It was time for a final meeting. The only thing that really matters. All the rest fades away.

Come on, Johnny. Sketch this scene too.

Without lies, without embarrassment. Go ahead.

I undo her straps and help her, support her, almost carry her, with one of her arms over my shoulder, to her bathroom. There I release her from her undergarments and her thoroughly soiled nappy and start, first trying to hold her upright and then getting her to sit down on the toilet bowl, to clean her with toilet paper. It's not easy. She also tends to slump again like a lay figure. Mutiny no longer has anything to do with it. She is tired, she is defenceless. I breathe through my mouth, the smell is unbearable. I don't know how to interpret the look with which she fixes me. Does she still understand what's happening? If so, what does she think of it? She who was always keen on cleanliness, to the point of a pathological fear of infection, and on flair and elegant style. She who was sometimes too prudish for nudity and found it unnecessary, offensive even, in modern art on TV. It is the first time I have seen her without clothes. One of the most famous paintings was by Gustave Courbet and shows a recumbent naked woman with her thighs apart. Her face is not visible, her wildly hairy genitalia are the centre of attention. The title is telling: *L'Origine du monde*.

What I am washing is the end of a world. With all its irrevocable wrinkles, its sandy-ish flesh, its touchingly scanty tuft of grey and thinning hair. I rinse the flannel round and round in the bowl, in lukewarm water. Afterwards—I don't know if she realizes—I am liberal with the talc, of which she has so often sung the praises. Then I stick a new nappy round her alarmingly thin buttocks. And all that time, as one does, I drive away my fearfulness and my pity by talking to her nineteen to the dozen. What particularly cuts me to the quick about this is that there is now no answer at all. I even long for her diabolical dialect. Anything is better than this goddamn silence that is eating me up.

I: 'Voilà, there you are. I'll throw all this in the waste bin, shall I?'

She: '...'

I: 'Careful. Don't move, Mum. Come on. Watch it. Can you understand me?'

She: '...'

I: 'Come on, stand up for a bit. I'll help you. Come on.'
She: '...'

I: 'Just a bit longer. Patience, patience. We're almost there.'

She: ' ... '

I: 'No, don't touch. Wait a minute. Wait, I said.'

She: ' ... '

I: 'Lift your other leg a bit. Come on, Mum. Please.'

She: ' ... '

I: 'Right, yes. Do you see? We're there. You're there, Mum. You see.'

She: ' ... '

Shortly afterwards she fell into the sub-coma from which she would never awaken. Because she could no longer swallow she was fed via a drip through her nose. It caused pneumonia and irritated mucus membranes. Her high blood pressure was forced down with crude methods, and in her brain the predicted bombardment of tiny strokes was under way. She lay emaciated on her deathbed. With a side full of bruises, acquired in a last painful fall. Her arms were still strapped, so that she did not tear the wires and tubes out of her body. That sight, despite everything, made me grin. Her rebelliousness even in a coma. A rebel to the very end.

The next step should have been a catheter directly into her stomach. We, her descendants, her new world, resisted that. Why should we have felt obliged to force-feed her via a tube in the stomach? My mother isn't a goose and I find the practice barbarous in geese too. A catheter via the nose is bad enough. Do more surgery on a dying woman? Over *my* dead body.

With that catheter in her stomach she could have gone on for weeks, if not months. We were assured of that. I don't need those kinds of reassurances. You can say what you like about the Middle Ages, with their Black Death and defective hygiene, their wars, furies and stakes, and their corresponding life expectancy—

but when it was time to go, you were allowed to go. Death was an old friend, not a reason for hysteria. What little science there was had not yet transformed into a grotesque affliction that could maintain and increase ailments instead of combating them. And in the background that forever-gnawing distrust was not yet a factor: when on earth did our wonderful social security, comforter of the weak, change into a jackpot for the pharmaceutical industry and all its branches? The long-term sick produce more than a milch cow. Every extra day is a day of profit. That makes the praise of resignation and patience more profitable than selling short-term pain.

Not a bad word about the servants of science—doctors, therapists, and not least the nursing staff. I don't believe in heroes, unless they are called nurses. They know the other side of the belligerent braying about 'respect for every spark of life'. They know what that means in practice. They help the impotent and demented to withstand their everyday humiliations, from feeding to evacuation. These are the things people prefer to be silent about, from politician to prelate. The ridiculously spilt runny food, the stomas, the urine bags hanging on a clothes stand next to the bed that you will never leave again, the never-ending tragicomedy of evacuation. The whole bitter repertoire of sick and shit.

She had no pain, that's true. I can scarcely call it a comforting thought. She of all people had to lose her speech first. She of all people had to lose her life for want of food.

Was it two years too late? ('Let me go. Let the old woman go.') I still don't know. I would not have wanted to miss the nice moments. But I would have liked even more, retrospectively, to have erased the gruesome hours and days. In the first place for her. In my view, I never showed her more devotion and respect than when we finally allowed her to go. A person is only really indebted to one person. I wiped the slate clean. Perhaps one can only really do one thing. Kill out of love.

I

(OR: WHAT NOW)

SHE WAS LAID out at the parlour of the successor of Jef the Undertaker—by now a specialized family business, without cabinet-making or other secondary activities— and only accessible by immediate family.('I don't want any strangers around my coffin! [she, fantasizing in better days about her funeral, drying her hands on her apron] People only come and look for the frisson and to be able to tell others how rough you look. I'm not a *pièce montée*. They must remember me as I was, and not as a piece of cold meat, dressed in her Sunday best and made up by an amateur.')

I had feared the worst, given her long though peaceful battle for life, but she looked—in a coffin lined with white silk and laid out in a room with reassuringly obtrusive wallpaper—peaceful. Even emaciated and with eyes closed her waxen face radiated something of her stubborn pride. As if she wanted to impress on everyone one last time that, considering all the circumstances —'be honest!'—she hadn't done a bad job, with that life of hers.

At the head of her coffin two candles as thick as an arm were burning on brass candle holders over a metre high, relicts of a vanished age, prize items of which she would definitely have wanted to know the price, had she still been alive, plus the name of the auctioneers where one could pick up something like that. At the foot two bouquets could be admired on two wrought-iron stands, professionally illuminated. You wondered if the flowers could be real, so intense was the sheen of the green, the glow of the red and the sparkle of the yellow and light blue. The purple ribbons bore her name in gilt letters.

We stood, one after the other, in front of her coffin, pretending that we had invented a secular form of praying. Then we went and stood awkwardly beside the coffin, stroking now her hand, now her forehead, both with their chilly dew of condensation. At the last minute, just before she was to be taken away to the crematorium, my father asked if he could be alone with her for a moment. We went and waited in the corridor and for a quarter of an hour heard him murmuring uninterruptedly to her, longer that we had ever heard him speaking to a living person who was not a customer. The undertaker had to interrupt him, the hearse was ready, the oven awaited.

A mother-of-pearl rosary had been arranged between her interwoven fingers. The cross lay on her stomach. At the top, between her intertwined thumbs, protruded the funeral card of her Most Awkward One, which she had always kept in her purse. It had become matt at the edges, and even the photo was rather worn. The card seemed appropriate, the rosary folklore. I never saw her saying the rosary, if you ask me she had neither the inclination nor the patience for it. It wasn't even folklore any more, it was a kitsch accessory of the modern Flemish funeral industry. And sure enough, my father also had one arranged in his intertwined fingers, when he was laid out two years later, at the same undertaker's, in the same room, as he had explicitly asked. The obituary card between his thumbs was one of hers. He too looked at peace, touchingly happy even. It was professional excellence, in both cases. Except for one detail. With embalming it's like portrait-painting. You concentrate on the face, but the fingers are the most difficult. They could be crossed and wound with prayer ribbons as much as you like, but they lacked force and volume and to be honest looked in both cases like limp asparagus. I had to smile when I first saw the connection with her. It was the same with him.

Such a moment was to follow during the scattering of her ashes. The flash of an involuntary smile, the recognition of a coincidence dreamt up by chance. It was a windless, splendid autumn day in the new Sint-Niklaas cemetery, which with its slopes and enormous pond looked as if were competing for a part as the decor in an American film. The man who emptied her urn—a giant with a serious and fleshy face, a long black raincoat full of gold stitching, a kepi that was too big for him and leather gloves—acquitted himself meticulously of his task. He swung the strewing urn to and fro with slow movements, about twenty centimetres above the grass, with every moment as measured, as long and as slow as if he were aware that it was a perfectionist that he was consigning to the elements here. And yet when I saw that square pattern, I couldn't help thinking two things. One. It was definitely on the small side. According to me in her mind she had always filled the whole area. Two. After those present had taken turns to consign flowers from a waiting basket to the breeze that was getting up and the lush lawn, and after they had subsequently given a last nod of farewell and left, whispering to each other or crying on someone's shoulder, she probably wouldn't have liked to see how that lonely square of hers was left behind. Blowing apart, surrounded by a careless swarm of leaves. I would bet on the fact that her fingers were itching to fetch a dustpan and brush, and her vacuum cleaner. You couldn't really call it clean, all that grit and those careless leaves on that wonderfully maintained lawn, worthy of an English stately home.

(I once caught them in such an absurd cleaning frenzy, when I finally got round to organizing a barbecue for my friends at that bloody bungalow that I had let her palm off on me. The agreement was that they were not to concern themselves with anything, I would prepare and serve it all. But I turn into the drive and I see her standing there, in her swimsuit, on the formidably sloping roof made of pink corrugated sheets that she is scrubbing furiously, since there is moss growing on it here and there.

I: [shouting angrily] 'Do you really think that my friends will check whether your roof is clean enough before they start barbecuing on the ground floor?'

She: [shouting back] 'You never know, with those friends of yours. Some of them know more about scrubbing and sewing than I do.'

Meanwhile my father was—no one believes it, but it's true—vacuuming the lawn. Here and there were a few fallen blossoms of the Japanese cherry.

She: 'If I ask him to rake them up, it'll take him longer, you know him.'

As he turned his back with the vacuum cleaner hose in his hands, new blossoms from the cherry fluttered down onto the newly vacuumed grass carpet. I had to turn the electricity off or he would have been vacuuming, on her orders, while we were sitting down to eat.)

(Now I'm writing anyway and this book, novel or not, is finally coming to an end, this can be added. We, her descendants, her new world, we tried our utmost to convince them of the advantages of the new age, just as they had passed on to us the knowledge of their period. We bought them a dishwasher for their wedding anniversary. After a few weeks they hadn't used it once. [she, she, she] 'It just uses up water and electricity, and it can never be as clean as by hand.' We made her swear solemnly to try the appliance at least once. She obeyed. She first washed up everything by hand, put the whole lot in the machine and washed it up again. 'Everybody happy.'

We tried to get them to have a cleaner, who could help them with the heaviest work—scrubbing floors, cleaning display cases and windows. They scrubbed and cleaned everything before the woman arrived and then helped to clean everything a second time. 'I wouldn't like that poor soul to go trumpeting around that we're dirty.')

After both funerals there was a lavish meal for scores of guests in the establishment named after the residence of Reynard the Fox, where she, got up like the Belle of the Ball, had made her last public appearance. The remaining West Flemish relations of my father came twice faithfully to celebrate the loss, making their way from Middelkerke, Torhout and the surrounding area, for a hot meal with three courses, with a dessert, plus coffee with cognac and petits fours. Not only finding a compromise but also celebrating a rich life is easier for us with a well-filled stomach, a glass of cognac and the odd cigarillo in our hand, surrounded by friendly tongues that soon loosen and dish up the stories that are necessary on a day like this. We don't even shy away from a joke and a song, while the *garçons* are already clearing away.

Although there are traditions one can easily depart from. The flowers that after each funeral are normally taken to the cemetery, where they are left at the graveside or the edge of the strewing meadow, in both cases remained at the back of the brick Church of the Sacred Heart.

It was, by the way, the first time that she, although only as dust and ashes, had been back to the church where her Most Awkward One had been twice covered in incense, once literally and once in the words of his Dutch boss. She never listened to the tape of the speech. (One day it went wrong. It was jammed, it could no longer be prised out of the machine, and when he managed to after all, it turned out that the thin brown magnetic tape had come out of its plastic holder and had rolled into a tangle, deep in the mechanical innards of the tape recorder. She seemed relieved. Certainly that the tape could no longer be wound back into the cassette, however long her Roger sat there turning one of the spools with a pencil. Finally he threw everything away. He knew the words by heart anyway.)

Her urn stood on a pedestal in front of the altar. The spot where her son's coffin had stood twenty-five years before. The spot where two years later her husband's urn would stand. And since that last funeral, that was the point I was trying to make, there have been strikingly fewer flowers in the Church of the Sacred Heart in front of the picture of St Antony and the statue of Christ with the bleeding side and the crown of thorns. After her first stroke he had anyway adopted the habit of leaving flowers on the steps of the parsonage. He just never took them himself. They shouldn't expect the earth, those priests of the Sacred Heart with their funny Bible quotations.

The stories that I came up with at the funeral meal, sipping cognac and surrounded by other loosened tongues, are the same stories I am telling now, years later, each time in virtually the same words and with the same gestures, perfecting my little epic a bit at a time, searching for just a little more effect, without losing the glow of the previous time. As she always did, you bet.

'All my friends and acquaintances,' I begin for example, 'who ever met my mother, always checked afterwards whether she was always so loud, not to say flamboyant. I enjoyed replying with full conviction: "You met her at a weak moment. You should see her when she's in top form."'

Sometimes, admittedly, she was more in top form than I would have liked. At a birthday party of mine in the Majolica Room at the Vooruit building in Ghent, she first got into an argument with the female disc jockey because the music was too loud. 'It's bad for your ears, my girl, and I can't make myself understood.' When the girl had the nerve to turn round with a shrug of the shoulders, she turned one speaker away from the dance floor and pulled the lead out of the other. When I told her to behave herself, by way of a senior citizen's protest she stuck a filter cigarette in each ear and began parading around the whole dance floor, doing an Egyptian walk, with those two white antennae coming out of her ears, the two fuses of a permanent fragmentation bomb. Because of the huge success—a group of applauding fans formed around her, she nearly started breakdancing from acute hipness—she also walked around downstairs in the packed grand café to show me up. Posing, now with a cigarette in each nostril.

Other mini-epics are connected with a tour in South Africa, which we were able to go on together when they were still hale and hearty, but no longer fully mobile, my father certainly not, with his lazy foot. I thought it was sensible that they should use the older passenger service, which meant that they would be taken in electric vehicles or wheelchair by the airport staff from the check-in desk to the plane and later from the plane to the exit, with priority for passport and security checks.

At first she was mightily indignant. 'We're not invalids!' She changed her opinion when she saw Zsa Zsa Gabor sitting in an electric car in a documentary, driving down the corridors of Atlanta Airport, with a Yorkshire terrier and a beauty case on her lap, waving to her many fans. She did not need much more than that as a role model.

Now, on the contrary, she tried too hard, and her Roger had to join in. They really had to earn those cars and wheelchairs, she felt. So she enters the departure lounge at Zaventem, and there starts groaning and dragging her leg. He too. Half the people in the airport look pityingly at them and indignantly at me—how did I take it into my head to drive such a decrepit couple ahead of me on foot to the check-in desk? The airport staff who receive us pull up seats and provide water. She thanks everyone personally, fighting for oxygen and gasping as if ready to fake another heart attack.

Later, as they leave the aircraft, it's the same story. 'Roger!' she hisses at him, as he has forgotten his instructions and is only slightly dragging his foot. At once they both start limping and groaning as if they had been shot in both legs only yesterday. I have never got so fast from an aircraft to the exit of an airport.

In Cape Town they met our own bosom friend Marianne, our asthmatic speedy lesbo Mama Africa, fifty-eight kilos in her birthday suit, journalist and stand-up comedienne, daughter of a Portuguese mother and a Berlin father old enough to have served in the Luftwaffe. She and Marianne are intrigued by each other. They share cigarettes and chat about the war and the bombing raids in a mixture of English, Flemish, Afrikaans and even a word or two of German. Then she questions Marianne about sangomas, the black medicine men who remind her of Wardje, her herb doctor in Waasland. She then launches into a litany about the famous South African red-bush tea, which she doesn't like at all and which can never compete with her home-brewed tea of verbena and dandelion root. 'And if you're not sleeping well, add a leaf of sage.'

Marianne nods admiringly, encouragingly, egging her on. So what does my mother predict? To this feminist lesbo tiger? In a tone that she reserves for the most ordinary matters in the world?

'If I come back? In a next life or so? I will come back as a man.'

'No kidding,' laughs Marianne, between horror and amusement.

She: 'Why not? A man is strong? A man is powerful. A man is in control. Isn't that so, Roger?'

And my father, next to her, nods: 'Of course it is, Josée. Of course, Josée. The man has everything under control.'

I had already been to Krüger National Park, one of the largest nature reserves in the world. On that occasion I had got to know it as an idyllic, breathtaking spot, overpowering because of its peace and its flora and fauna. I visit the same spot with Josée the Prophetic at my side, and we drive into hell. A huge bush fire is blazing on the evening horizon.

'We're driving toward it,' she assures me.

The gates have already closed behind us. We shall

spend the night in the park. There is no way back.

'Not at all,' I say soothingly, so as not to alarm her, 'we have to go in a completely different direction.'

'Nonsense,' she states with the certainty of someone who has had personal experience of the capriciousness of fire. 'We're driving straight toward it.'

She is proved right. We are driving toward that fire. Just before we are completely encircled by the flames, we arrive in the bush camp, which thank God looks deep green from the abundant watering and is surrounded by fire trenches. The road we were hurrying along a quarter of an hour ago is now ablaze on both sides. But we are safe. We think. The fire encloses us more and more, it bellows and crackles with rage, the flames lick up metres high, trees are burning like torches, there are bangs, crowns explode, closer and closer.

Then there are completely different sorts of bangs, duller, more extended, first rumbling toward us from a distance and only then striking. The wardens, who just now had been standing hosing down the trees inside the fence with their pathetic equipment, are dancing with joy. A Biblical storm erupts. It is pouring with rain, the fire turns to steam, the sky thunders and crackles and lightens. Now we must hope that the smoke will sink to the ground or lift, or we'll die anyway of suffocation.

We crawl into bed with wet handkerchiefs over our noses and hear a strange silence falling outside. The storm is obviously saving all its force for a decisive clap. It comes a long while after midnight. Just above our chalet. A flash of lightning, immediately followed by a rattling bloody bang. Two seconds later: a horrific scream that goes right through one.

My lover sleeps through everything, but I charge out of our room, into my parents' bedroom. My father is sitting drowsily, head nodding around, on the edge of his bed, she is standing terrified in a corner, her hand protectively round her neck. 'I've been attacked! Something jumped at my neck! I smashed it against the wall!' My father and I look at each other. Our looks betray what we're thinking. 'You've had a heavy day, Mum. You've got a vivid imagination, Josée, certainly when you dream. Go back to bed, okay?'

We hadn't counted on her reaction. 'I'll prove it to you,' she chuckled, and with one tug moves her camp bed aside. And sure enough. There in the corner there is something black. It looks like a bird spider the size of a child's hand, but with limp wings. A bat. In all that gigantic national park, larger than all the Benelux countries put together, there is a bang above one chalet, a bat tumbles down from the thatched roof in the dark. Where does it land? On her neck.

Guiltily I hunt for a salad bowl and place it over the creature, which is dazed, half stunned by the blow and the scare. The next morning, when I turn over the salad bowl again, it is completely dead. Josée looks over my shoulder, undeterred—though with a scarf round her neck. 'Oh dear, poor creature. But well, it shouldn't have jumped on my neck. You see what happens.'

And so on.
And so forth.

I should really have stopped long ago. Forgive me for not having done so. My fingers go on typing, the words just keep on appearing, on my screen and on your page. Should I apologize for my gutlessness? If you'd like that: I'll do so with pleasure. Because it's all my fault. As long as I don't put down the final full stop, at the bottom of the last page, it won't be finished, and won't have fully drawn that thick bold cross. That cross over her, over him. Their neighbourhood, their period, their lives. Grant me that respite. And rest assured. It will soon be over.

I have only two things left to do.

First a question. Has this become the book with which I could best honour her? The book that she would have most liked to read, and that she wanted from me? I have my doubts. Writing is like embalming. However, you may maintain and even know that your work is only temporary, that you are counterfeiting something that is trying to vie with reality, or at least are trying to preserve her, if only for a moment. That is a contradiction, certainly with this book, which above all is a book of transience. And such a book should have been entirely different. I am not always crazy about modern visual art, but in one area writing has to concede defeat. Admitting transience, in the very choice of materials. No longer bronze, but butter. Not marble any longer, but pieces of rotting wood and slices of ham and crumbling rubber. Flotsam found on a beach or a rubbish tip. Materials that are allowed to disappear, that must decay, as a part and even the essence of the work.

That would be some book. While you were still reading it the paper could crumble and rot. Or no, the ink would disintegrate. That would be nicest of all. You get to the bottom of the page, the thumb with which you are holding the book is bottom right, just under the last word. You glance upward, at the page you have just read, and the top line has already completely disappeared, swallowed up by the whiteness of its page. In the middle the paragraphs are just visible through it, like drowning people, lying flat out on a beach—they are surrounded by rising water, only their faces and bellies and the tips of their shoes are still visible, disappearing as you look, sucked up by their paper. And at the bottom, just above your thumb, that last word is already fading. In just a little while it will have taken leave of you unanimously with its predecessors. Irrevocably, without a trace, irretrievable. Delete, delete, the emptiness.

After the questioning, the last scene. The real goodbye. The last time I saw her when she was still breathing. She is lying in a sun-drenched yet chilly room, thanks to the air conditioning. White the sheets, white the curtains, white the walls, white the hair on the white cushion. Her eyes are closed, her face is thin, her mouth without dentures ugly and sunken, her nose disfigured by that drip. She is not breathing but rattling. The doctors have assured me that such rattling is normal, not painful and even inevitable. Our lungs fill with water. In essence we are fish with pretensions. I sit down next to her, with one buttock on the bed. She doesn't notice, she goes on rattling. No one knows how long she has to go. That stubborn, angry, strong heart of hers, it won't hear of failing, it just goes on beating. Her hands are lying on top of the sheets. I slide my finger under one palm, hoping that her fingers will clench into a soft fist, if necessary just as a reflex. I tell myself I can feel a vibration, but there is no sign of that fist. Under her nose I see a brand-new hair. I can also see a new hair on her chin. Would I dare pluck it out? Where will I find a pair of tweezers here? Shall I try with my fingers? Aren't my nails too short? Then a nurse comes in. The woman does her work precisely. She checks the plastic bag of liquid, then the drip, then the pulse, then an eye—she pulls the eyelid up respectfully, and for the last time I see that iris in blue-grey. Finally the nurse, who smiles and gives me a good-natured, sympathetic nod, takes two latex gloves from the pocket of her apron. She puts them on with a routine gesture. She looks at me again for a moment, in doubt. Then she does her work anyway. She inserts two fingers of one hand carefully between the lower and upper jaws of the patient and wedges them open. With the forefinger of her other hand she frees, from the place from where the language came that I learnt, just a couple of bits of mucus and wipes them off on a tissue. And then and there I swore to myself that from now on I have one vocation, one aim, one godforsaken self-chosen duty, because I can't do much else, haven't learnt anything else and don't believe in anything else. That I, when I see the chance, will combat the silence with my voice, will try to out-argue silence with my word, will try to attack all the available paper in the world with my language. Let that be my rebellion, my revolt, against mucus, against rattling. Let me do this at least as a mutiny. Let there no longer be a second, a page, a book, that does not speak in a hundred thousand tongues, that does not testify to vocabulary. Never again silent, always writing, never again speechless.

Begin.

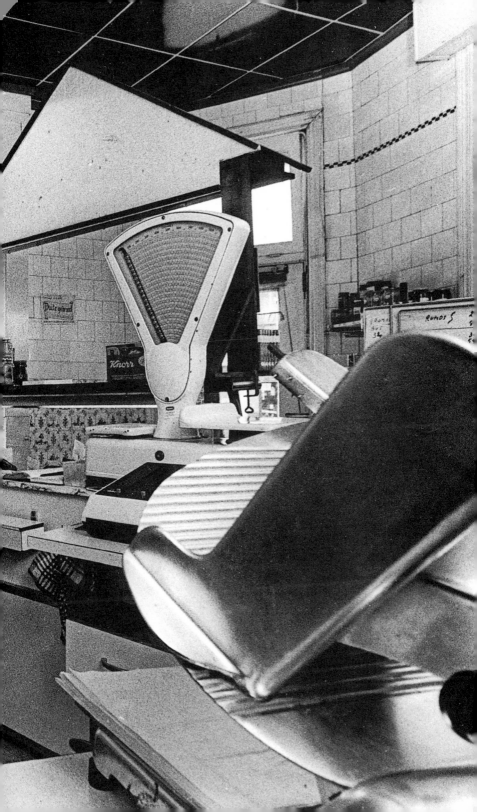

On the Design

As book design is an integral part of the reading experience, we would like to acknowledge the work of those who shaped the form in which the story is housed.

Tessa van der Waals (Netherlands) is responsible for the cover design, cover typography and art direction of all World Editions books. She works in the internationally renowned tradition of Dutch Design. Her bright and powerful visual aesthetic maintains a harmony between image and typography and captures the unique atmosphere of each book. She works closely with internationally celebrated photographers, artists, and letter designers. Her work has frequently been awarded prizes for Best Dutch Book Design.

The photograph on the cover is of Tom Lanoye's mother. In his own words, 'the photo was processed by the photographer when he printed it to make it look older. A so-called half-blurred edge, *flou artistique*. A few scratches, coincidentally right next to her face. False wear and tear: a costume drama squared.'

Suzan Beijer (Netherlands) is responsible for the typography and careful interior book design of all World Editions titles.

The text on the inside covers and the press quotes are set in Circular, designed by Laurenz Brunner (Switzerland) and published by Swiss type foundry Lineto.

All World Editions books are set in the typeface Dolly, specifically designed for book typography. Dolly creates a warm page image perfect for an enjoyable reading experience. This typeface is designed by Underware, a European collective formed by Bas Jacobs (Netherlands), Akiem Helmling (Germany), and Sami Kortemäki (Finland). Underware are also the creators of the World Editions logo, which meets the design requirement that 'a strong shape can always be drawn with a toe in the sand.'